The Mersey Monastery Murders

# The Mersey Monastery Murders

Mersey Murder Mysteries Book VII

*Brian L. Porter*

*Dedicated to the memory of Leslie and Enid Porter.*
*Sleep sound, Mum and Dad.*

# Introduction

Welcome to *The Mersey Monastery Murders*, the seventh book in my series of Mersey Mysteries. You, the readers, have taken Detective Inspector Andy Ross, Detective Sergeant Izzy Drake, and the rest of the members of The Merseyside Police Special Murder Investigation Team very much to your hearts over the time span of the first six books. I hope you will enjoy this, the latest instalment of their adventures as the team is faced with one of the strangest and most difficult cases to date.

All the usual characters are here, though the ending might be tinged with a little sadness for some readers. It's the usual roller-coaster ride, with elements of the investigation taking one of the team to Austria when the investigation expands beyond the boundaries of Liverpool.

So, without further ado, I hand you over to DI Ross and the team, and hope you enjoy the ride.

Brian L Porter

# A Short Glossary

Z Cars – A popular British TV Police Procedural series, set in the fictional town of Newtown, near Liverpool. Ran from 1962 - 1978.

La' – Lad, a common abbreviated version of the word lad, used extensively in Liverpool.

Scally – Scallywag, a local version of the word referring to a ne'er do well, a petty criminal or general workshy person.

Scottie Road – Scotland Road, now modernised, once a notorious area of the city.

# Prologue

Brother Charles, the Abbot of the abbey church of St. Basil, sat in his office, little more than a broom cupboard in size, finalising the abbey's accounts for the previous month. Once a grand series of buildings, the original abbey had been virtually destroyed in the 16$^{th}$ century during King Henry VIII's reign, under the edict that led to the dissolution of the monasteries. This was part of his revenge against the Roman Catholic Church for the Pope's refusal to allow him to divorce his queen, Catherine of Aragon, who had failed to provide him with a male heir. The *Act of Supremacy*, passed in 1534 (woe betide any English noble who voted against Henry's wishes), would lead to the Reformation and the creation of the Anglican Church, with Henry as its head.

Once a grand collection of buildings, the Benedictine monastery at one time comprised the church, a dormitory, cloister, refectory, a superb library, and even a school where the monks would provide a basic education to some of the local children, boys only of course. Girls were not considered to be in need of formal education during the Middle Ages. Any such education they did receive would be undertaken at home, and might have included instruction in reading, sewing, and for the lucky daughters of the wealthy, the ability to write. Following the dissolution, all that remained of the original buildings was the shell of the church and a few ruined walls.

It wasn't until the 19th century that the church was renovated, a new dormitory was built and a new though small community of Benedictine monks once again took up residence at St. Basil. Standing in open ground, a few miles from the modern city of Liverpool, the 'new' monastery was very different to the original, which existed when the population of Liverpool stood at only a few hundred, and the borough, (it didn't become a city until 1880), comprised mostly agricultural workers.

Now, in the early years of the 20th century, the partially rebuilt St. Basil once again provided a school for the local children and the monks whose needs were few, led a self-sufficient life funded mostly by the sale of the produce, vegetables and fruit, grown in their gardens.

The church, open to all, was generally well-attended and the monks of St. Basil had become a familiar sight around the modern suburb of the city known as Grassendale, which was gradually growing into an affluent community where the well-off members of the local population were keen to build their mansions and grand villas.

Brother Charles' eyes were growing tired. He finally decided that working on the accounts would be a task best suited to being completed in daylight, and not bent over his desk working by candlelight. At the age of seventy-five, his eyes weren't quite as good as they once were. He rose from his straight-backed, hard wood chair and stretched. The clock on the wall that faced him informed the Abbot that it was almost nine p.m. Time to put the papers and the books away and retire for the night; he took a minute to arrange the ledgers and receipts, etc., ready to continue in the morning.

Daily life began early for Charles and the small community of twelve monks who lived, worked, and shared their lives with him in their small religious community. Their day began at five a.m. each day, which explained why all the other brothers in the community were already asleep in their cells. Satisfied all was as it should be, Charles stepped towards the doorway and suddenly felt a crushing pain in his chest, accompanied by further pains, which seemed to begin in his neck and extended down his left arm.

Charles cried out, but there was no one to hear him, no one except his God, who swiftly reached out to claim the soul of his devoted follower. As Brother Charles breathed his last, and the darkness rushed out to envelop his final seconds on earth, he had no knowledge of the fact that—as he fell to the floor—his flailing arm had knocked over the candle that burned upon his desk.

The gentle flame of the candle managed to ignite the carefully placed pile of receipts on the desk. Within no more than sixty seconds, the flames had spread, consuming everything they touched, which eventually included the body of the faithful servant of God. Unfortunately, the dormitory, which was at the rear of the church, where the rest of the monastic community slept, was too far away for anyone to hear or see the conflagration—until the flames, fanned by the wind, reached in through the opened burning roof. Quickly, they spread to the adjoining buildings. Soon, they engulfed every building within close proximity.

By the time one of the brothers woke to the awful sound of the church roof collapsing in on itself, all that remained standing apart from the dormitory was the small school building. The local fire brigade, such as it was, made up mostly from volunteers from the neighbouring area, and was small and inefficient. They had no up-to-date firefighting equipment and could do more than pour water upon the ashen remains of the monastery buildings, in hopes of preventing a stray spark spreading flames to any remaining buildings.

Soon after the fire, St. Basil once again lay wrecked and disused, and would stay in its distressed state for almost a century before life returned to the abandoned monastery. In 1992, a new religious community rose, like a phoenix from the ashes as the Priory of St. Emma was established, complete with a restored rebuilt church that looked even more gothic in appearance than its predecessor, along with a small mixed-gender community of monks and nuns, unusual but not unknown among the Benedictines.

With hard work, led wonderfully by its new Prior, Father Gerontius, the priory soon flourished; the tragedies of the past that appeared to have haunted the site of St. Basil, became nothing more than distant memories. The millennium came and went, and the small community grew and quickly became fully integrated into the community of Grassendale, an enclave of wealth in the suburbs of modern Liverpool. The good works of the monks and nuns that made up the growing religious community endeared them to the local populace and to the outside world. The Priory of St. Emma, which by tradition the locals still referred to as the Monastery, gave off an aura of a community at peace with itself and with the world. All of this, therefore, made the events that would transpire in 2006, even more difficult to believe.

# Chapter 1

**The Priory of St. Emma, April 2005**

Spring had arrived early, or so it appeared to the members of the community at St. Emma. The first week of April had begun with an unseasonal warm spell, temperatures creeping above average for that time of year.

With the clocks having gone forward an hour to British summertime the previous weekend, Brother Ignatius and Sister Paulette were taking advantage of the slightly lighter evenings to plant vegetable seeds in the kitchen garden. They were surrounded by borders of daffodils, mostly yellow, but some were an unusual white, tinged with pink, at the petal edges. These borders, as well as being decorative, helped protect the young seedlings when they began to appear, affording them protection from strong winds blowing in from the coast. The daffodils would soon be replaced by tulips, the bulbs having been planted by Ignatius three years previously. They now grew each year and maintained a constant splash of colour in the kitchen garden. Every few yards, rose bushes stood, as yet bare, but with new growth buds already showing, ensuring a supply of beautiful flowers as the spring turned to summer. The floral borders, interspersed with various hues of pansies and violas, would surround the well-laid out kitchen garden with dazzling colour.

For now though, cabbages and cauliflowers were the order of the day, and the older monk and slightly younger nun, utilising a couple of kneeling pads to protect their knees, chatted amiably as they worked.

"I do so love the feeling one gets from planting these innocuous little seeds and then seeing them grow into full-grown plants in just a few short months, don't you?" Sister Paulette asked her colleague as she tamped down earth over another row of cabbage seeds.

"Yes indeed, Sister," Brother Ignatious replied. "Before I joined the order, I was a gardener by profession, and the way nature works has always fascinated me."

"I always wondered if you had special skills in the garden," the little nun, no more than five feet tall, said. "You always seem to know all there is to know about the best way to plant things and how to cultivate the growing crop."

"I'm pleased you think so," he said as he opened another packet of seeds. "Father Gerontius was quick to put me in charge of the kitchen garden once he became aware of my previous life."

"Did you tell him about being a gardener?"

"Oh no, Sister, that would not have been the correct thing to do. The Father found out from reading my personal records once they arrived, and I was pleased to accept the responsibility when he offered it to me. I can be far more productive here in the soil than I could be, for example, working as a cook in the kitchens. I'd be more likely to poison someone than give them a healthy meal."

The two laughed at Ignatius' remark.

"It's true that Father Gerontius always seems to find the right person for each job around the priory though, isn't it?" Paulette asked.

"Yes, it is," the monk replied, "but then, I suppose that's why he was placed in charge of the place, after all. What did you do before taking the veil, Sister? You're very young, if you don't mind me saying so."

Paulette smiled, and laughed softly at Ignatius' comment. "I think you'll find I'm older than you think, Brother," she grinned. "I'm actually twenty-four, but I have always been taken for being younger than my years. For what it's worth, I always wanted to be a nun but, when

I left school, they told me I had to be eighteen to begin my training to become a nun. So, wanting to make sure I could be useful when I eventually did take the veil, I went to college and studied horticulture for two years."

"Aha," said Ignatius, "so that's why you ended up out here planting seeds with me."

"I guess so. Father Gerontius told me I could be very useful helping in the gardens and, to be honest, I love it. It makes me feel close to nature and to God's creation of earth itself."

The pair continued the conversation for another ten minutes or so, until all the seeds in Ignatius' tray had been planted. Ignatius looked up and saw the last remains of sunshine slowly melting into the distant horizon. Evening had fallen and the work could wait until the next day before they moved on to the next prepared seedbed.

"Time to give up for the day, I think," the monk said, rising to his feet, placing his hands on his hips, and stretching his back to ease the stiffness that had formed in his muscles.

Sister Paulette gathered her small collection of gardening tools and placed everything in an old-fashioned wicker basket. Together, the two gardeners made their way from the kitchen garden to the refectory, where they'd partake of the evening meal ahead of taking part in evening prayers, before retiring for the night to their own rooms, or cells, where they would usually remain until morning.

The priory very much adhered to the standard layout of a typical Benedictine monastery, with most of the building situated within a cloister, or courtyard, which served as an area through which everyone passed on the way to various locations within the priory. The rebuilt church stood on the north side of the cloister, facing east, this being important in preventing the church from blotting out the sun from the courtyard. Next to the church stood the sacristy and the chapter house, where the monks and nuns held chapter meetings. In one marked difference from the traditional layout, the dormitories, one each for the monks and the nuns, stood to one side; the latrines were located close by, for obvious reasons. Apart from the church, the rest of the buildings had a more modern appearance as they'd been built with practicality in mind, not aestheticism, and the whole site had been created in an overall L-shaped formation.

The kitchen garden stood aside from the main buildings of the priory. To reach the refectory, Brother Ignatius and Sister Paulette had to exit the garden by walking to the end of the path they'd been working beside, and make a sharp left turn onto another gravel path that led through an archway of ornamental ivy to the gateway that led back into the courtyard.

As they turned, walking slowly and enjoying the sky, tinged pink by the setting sun, they could make out a shape on the path twenty or so yards ahead. As they drew closer, they could clearly see that it was the figure of a man. Worried, in case one of their brethren had fallen and been hurt, they increased their pace.

Brother Ignatious called out as they drew close. "Hello, are you alright? Is something wrong?"

They could see that it was indeed a member of their order, or at least a man dressed in the habit of the order, his back towards them, and his body curled up in a foetal position. Fearing the worst, that one of the brothers had fallen and hurt himself, or worse still, suffered a heart attack or similar, Ignatius placed a hand on Sister Paulette's shoulder, and instructed her to stay where she was while he checked it out first.

Paulette did as asked, remaining five yards back from the prone figure, and placed her hands together in prayer as her companion arrived beside the curled-up individual, and knelt on the path. Slowly, he turned the figure. One look was all he needed and Ignatius quickly laid the body back in its original position, made the sign of the cross and uttered a quick whispered prayer to God before turning to the young sister.

"Please, Sister, go and fetch Prior Gerontius. We have an emergency on our hands."

Unable to hold back, the nun made to walk closer to the body on the ground, but Brother Ignatius urged her to stay back.

"Who is it?" she asked. "Please, I must see him."

"Sister, please, no."

"I've seen death before, Brother," she said, pushing his restraining arm away and walking around to the front of the man on the ground. She wasn't quite prepared for the sight she beheld however and a gasp escaped. "Brother Bernárd," was all she could say as she recognised the man. The expression on his face spoke to her of sheer terror, frozen in the moment of death. "That look! It's as if he saw the Devil himself."

"Please Sister, there's nothing you can do for him. Please, go quickly and bring Prior Gerontius."

"Yes, yes, of course," Paulette said as she scurried away to bring the head of their community to the scene.

Five minutes later, she returned with the Prior at her side. Brother Ignatius was still kneeling, praying beside the fallen body of their fellow brother. He rose as the pair approached.

"Please, allow me to see what has happened to our brother," Gerontius spoke softly, but with authority.

Brother Ignatius gave way to the Prior, who conducted a brief examination of their fellow monk. One look at the face of Brother Bernárd was all he needed to make an important decision. The horror Brother Bernárd had suffered in his last moments as a living servant of God told Gerontius there was only one choice open to him.

"Ignatius, please be kind enough to go the office, dial 999, and summon the police. Whatever has taken place here has not, I believe, occurred through natural causes. If I'm not mistaken, the Devil has been at work here. Brother Bernárd, our simple, kind, loving Brother Bernárd has been *murdered!*"

# Chapter 2

### The Call

Andy Ross was in the middle of his usual nightly check around the house, ensuring all the windows were closed and the front and back doors were securely locked, and ready to join his wife, Maria, waiting patiently for him to join her in bed.

Wearing a slinky dark blue, knee-length satin nightdress, and nothing else, the couple had enjoyed a peaceful, romantic dinner, which Maria had prepared. They'd started with a good old-fashioned prawn cocktail, which they both loved, then enjoyed grilled pork loins with apple sauce and served with sautéed potatoes and green beans. This was followed by one of Maria's favourite desserts, a simple but delicious bowl of cherry vanilla ice-cream.

The meal over and the dishes placed in the latest addition to the kitchen, a brand-new dishwasher (which Maria had been wanting for ages), they'd spent an hour or so cuddled on the sofa. Lighting was dim as they'd listened to romantic classical CDs. Feeling suitably relaxed, and ready to fall into bed for a night of what both hoped would be unbridled passion, Maria had left Andy to see to the night security routine, while she made her way upstairs.

Done, Ross breathed a sigh of satisfaction, and was about to make his way upstairs when his mobile phone rang. Cursing, he picked it up from where it had sat silently all evening on the hallstand and looked at the screen. The ringtone was one he'd selected for work, and he was shocked to see the name and number of Detective Chief Superintendent Sarah Hollingsworth displayed before his eyes.

"Oh God, now what?" he asked out loud, wishing he'd ignored the ringing phone, but knowing he couldn't have done that in all good conscience. He pressed the green 'talk' button. "Ma'am" he said, the one word enough for now.

"Detective Inspector, I'm sorry to disturb you at home. I hope I haven't interrupted anything important?"

Thinking of Maria lying upstairs, primed and waiting for the aforementioned night of passion, what could he say except, "Oh no, nothing important, ma'am. How can I help you?"

"I've rung you myself as DCI Agostini is away on his brief holiday until tomorrow, as you know. We have a situation that could need careful handling, and one that most definitely requires the services of your team."

"Andy? Is everything alright?" Maria's voice shouted from the bedroom.

"Fine, darling, just a work matter," he called up as he returned to his phone conversation. "Sorry about that, ma'am. My wife was just wondering who's on the phone."

"That's okay, but listen. This is potentially a very sensitive and tricky case. Have you ever heard of the Priory of St. Emma?"

Wracking his brains, Ross was forced to reply, "I can't say as I have, ma'am, no."

"Well, you're about to become *extremely* familiar with it. They appear to have had a murder committed on their grounds, one of their own monks, apparently."

"Monks?" he replied, a little slow on the uptake for once.

"Yes, Detective Inspector, monks; you know, habits, tonsures, sandals and so on, that kind of thing."

"Sorry, ma'am, yes, I'm aware of what a monk is. I just didn't realise we had any around here."

"Well, now you know. The priory stands on the site of what was once St. Basil's Monastery, and two of their members discovered the body of one of their colleagues on a path in the grounds a couple of hours ago. Uniform branch responded to a 999 call and found the body exactly where it was discovered, confirmed the suspicion of foul play, and contacted CID. While all this was going on the Prior, Brother Gerontius, who's apparently a friend of the Chief Constable, made a phone call and the next thing I know, I receive a call instructing me to place my best people on the case. That means you and your team, DI Ross. Like I said, I apologise to you and your wife if you had plans, but I hope you can understand the position I was placed in."

It was as if the DCS knew exactly what Andy and Maria Ross had planned for the next hour or two, or more, but he gritted his teeth and replied politely, "Of course, ma'am. I'll call DS Drake and have her meet me there immediately. Do you know if the ME has been called yet?"

"Good man, and yes, I understand CID immediately summoned help and Doctor Nugent was on his way when I spoke with them. He'll meet you on site."

"Okay, I'll get on to Izzie Drake and get to it," Ross replied, already mentally phrasing the way to break the news to his partner, who'd be enjoying her evening with her husband Peter and would be equally irate at having her night interrupted by a call-out. "Just one question, ma'am."

"Yes?"

"Er, where is St. Emma's Priory?"

"The correct name is the Priory of St. Emma, but I suppose St. Emma's Priory will do, shorter anyway. It's at Grassendale, easy enough to find. I'm told it's signposted."

"Thanks. Right, better get going then. I expect Doc Nugent will be there already and he'll love chewing my ear out for arriving late."

The Chief Super actually chuckled slightly at Ross's remark, a first as far as he could remember.

"I'll expect an update sometime tomorrow," Hollingsworth stated. "I know you'll have plenty to do initially, so I'm not expecting a report in the morning. Call me in the afternoon and let me have a progress report, okay?"

"No problem," Ross replied and was left holding a silent phone as Hollingsworth hung up, leaving him to get on with the job. First things first, though. Andy Ross slowly climbed the stairs and sheepishly poked his head round the bedroom door, where Maria sat propped up against the pillows with a resigned look on her face.

"I take it that call means no passionate sex for us tonight, then?

"Afraid not, darling. That was DCS Hollingsworth, of all people. Oscar's on holiday and she's taken direct charge of the team. Seems the Chief Constable had friends in Godly places." He drew a deep breath and smiled regretfully. "There's been a murder at a place called St. Emma's Priory in Grassendale. Got to get there right away. The Prior, head guy, is a mate of the Chief Constable's and had asked for the best people available."

"And that's you and the team presumably?"

He nodded ruefully.

"It's a double-edged sword, being the best, eh?" Maria was grinning now. Fame at work, but a severe case of coitus interruptus at home. And by the way, it's called The Priory of St. Emma, Andy."

"Not you too," he said, and then, "never mind" as Maria was about to ask what he meant.

Ross quickly changed into suitable attire while calling his partner, Detective Sergeant Izzie Drake on his hands-free phone as he did so. Her response was predictable.

"Oh shit, boss. Just when we were about to ... "

"Don't tell me. If it's anything like what me and Maria were about to get up to, I can understand your frustration, Peter's too."

"Actually, we were about to go for a late night walk in the moonlight, as it's such a nice evening," she laughed.

"Oh, right," said Ross. "Very romantic."

"It might have been," Drake replied gruffly.

"Sorry, Izzie,"

"Don't sweat it, Boss. Tell me where to meet you."

After giving Drake directions to the priory, Ross quickly kissed Maria, gave her a loving hug, and was soon out of the door. The journey from his home in Prescot to the priory in Grassendale would take twenty minutes to cover the twelve miles or so to the destination.

Never having visited a priory before, he wasn't sure what to expect when he arrived, but as he mused on his way to Grassendale, murder is murder, wherever it happened, and his job was the same as always: to discover and apprehend a killer. The fact that this one had been committed on what was technically God's own property might add a few complications. He'd just have to wait and see.

As he drove, he placed calls to Sergeant Sofie Meyer and Detective Constables Derek McLennan and Nick Dodds. He'd leave the rest of the team to sleep. They could be brought up to speed in the morning. As he thought about it, he made one more call—he remembered that DC Sam Gable had been brought up as a Roman Catholic and her knowledge of the Catholic religion might be useful from the start. Gable was still awake and sharing the evening with her boyfriend, Ian Gilligan, a detective sergeant on the Greater Manchester Police Force. She was happy enough to be called in. It was part of the job when working for the Merseyside Police, Specialist Murder Investigation Team.

Ross smiled to himself as he realised that the only officers he hadn't dragged out of their homes were Detective Sergeant Paul Ferris, the team's computer genius, and newest member, DC Gary 'Ginger' Devenish, so-nicknamed because of his head of fiery red hair. At least they, and the team's administrative assistant Kat Bellamy, would be bright-eyed and bushy-tailed in the morning.

As the Chief Superintendent had indicated, the Priory of St. Emma was signposted as he drove through the leafy, affluent suburb of Grassendale. Ross was impressed by the number of large villas and mansions that had been built in this quiet area of Liverpool. He turned into the entrance: two two large stone pillars that held a pair of old but serviceable cast iron gates, painted forest green. Atop each pillar stood a pair of kneeling concrete angels, each with its hands joined in prayer. A wooden sign sunk into the grass verge beside the gates announced that he was about to enter The Priory of St. Emma.

In the moonlight, the outstanding feature of the priory was without doubt the tall spire of the rebuilt church, which the builders had succeeded in giving the original look of a gothic church. With moonlight now glowing almost incandescently behind the building, it seemed to Ross to take on a mean and brooding countenance. The few buildings situated around a sort of courtyard resembled a random collection of barrack blocks, such as might be found at a remote military establishment, where conformity to any form of regular military design had been thrown out with the previous week's rubbish.

Bringing the car to a halt, he stepped from the vehicle and quickly surveyed his surroundings, such as could be made out in the absence of external lighting on the site. Fortunately, every light in every building appeared to be switched on, and as the lights registered in his brain, Ross became aware of headlights following the narrow, winding asphalt drive he'd manoeuvred a few minutes earlier.

He assumed, correctly, that this would be his partner, Detective Sergeant Izzie Drake, and a minute later, she pulled up beside him in her new car. Her husband, Peter Foster, had insisted that her faithful Mini would be too small to drive comfortably as her pregnancy advanced, and this was the first time Ross had seen the couple's latest purchase.

"Very nice," Ross said, as soon as she alighted from the two-year-old, 1.6-litre. Vauxhall Astra estate car.

"Thanks. Not very sporty looking, but Peter thought it would be a more practical vehicle once the little one arrives."

"I agree. Lots of space for a pushchair, shopping, and all that kind of stuff."

"DI Ross, is it?" came the voice of an approaching uniformed police sergeant.

"That's me, Sergeant...?"

"Blake, sir. I was told to remain here, secure the crime scene, and await your arrival. Nobody's been near the site since we cordoned it off. I've got two lads keeping watch there."

"Good man," Ross said with a quick nod. "We'll take it from here now. Your boys can go as soon as the SOCOs (Scenes of Crime Officers) arrive. But please arrange to have a constable stationed on site overnight to ensure the scene remains undisturbed until my people can give it a thorough going over in daylight. Please let Sergeant Drake here have a copy of your report as soon as you can, okay?

"Okay, sir. It's all yours."

"Now then, about this baby of yours," Ross turned back to Drake, a warm smile on his face.

"Don't remind me what's to come in a few months." She dismissed the subject with a wave of her right hand, while her left arm made a sweeping gesture to take in their new surroundings. "Bit different for us, isn't it?"

"Definitely, Izzie, and we'd better be on the ball with this one as the Chief Constable is a mate of the guy in charge."

"That would be me, Inspector Ross" a deep, resonating voice spoke from behind the two detectives, almost making them jump out of their skins. Turning, Ross and Drake found themselves confronted by the Prior of St. Emma, Brother Gerontius. In the dark, in his sandaled feet, he'd approached in virtual silence.

Quickly regaining his composure, Ross held a hand out to the tall monk who, despite the reason for their visit, had an amiable smile on his face as he spoke.

"Sorry if I made you jump," he apologised. "I always forget these sandals make it almost impossible to be heard by anyone if they don't see you coming."

"No problem, er, Father, is it? I'm not sure what we should call you, sorry."

"That's okay, Inspector. I'm the Prior here and my name is Brother Gerontius. You can call me Brother Gerontius, or if there are no fellow monks with us at the time, Brother for short."

"Thanks, right," Ross smiled at the monk and introduced Drake. "This is my partner, Detective Sergeant Clarissa Drake … Izzie for short."

"Please to meet you, Sergeant. I just wish you could both have been here under happier circumstances," the Prior said, in a first reference to their reason for being at the priory in the middle of the night.

"Yes indeed," Ross replied. "Please accept our condolences on the death of your colleague, Brother …?"

"Brother Bernárd," Gerontius responded. "A kinder, gentler man you couldn't hope to meet, Inspector. I simply have no idea why anyone would wish to commit such a vile act against him."

"The information my Chief gave me said you called your friend the Chief Constable soon after the officers from the uniform branch responded to your 999 call … that you yourself had informed him that a murder had been committed. How were you so certain that Brother Bernárd had been murdered, as opposed to him having died from natural causes?"

"First of all, please don't think I was 'pulling rank' or anything in regards me phoning the Chief Constable. It wasn't meant like that at all, but he *is* an old friend who was very helpful to us when were first embarking on this venture at St. Emma, and he told me to call if ever we needed support. Owing to the nature of Brother Bernárd's death, I wanted to be sure the local police sent someone suitably qualified to handle a case that appears—to me—to be a little unusual, which leads me to answer your question about how I knew Brother Bernárd was murdered. I wasn't always a monk, Inspector Ross. In my previous, secular life I was a chemist, a pharmacist, and I'm well aware of the effects of certain poisons on the human body. When I arrived after being summoned by Sister Paulette, the first thing I did was see if I could do anything to help Brother Bernárd, but when I got close to him, I could catch the scent of bitter almonds from his mouth, a sure sign of poisoning. Your Medical Examiner is with Brother Bernárd now and I'm sure he'll confirm that my friend and colleague was killed by the use of cyanide poison."

"Cyanide?" Ross was aghast. "I haven't heard of a case of cyanide poisoning for years."

"Nonetheless, I'm convinced you'll find it to be the cause of Brother Bernárd's death. Now, I suppose I should take you to the body and your Medical Examiner. You'll want to speak to Brother Ignatius and Sister Paulette in due course, and they'll be waiting for you in the refectory."

Brother Gerontius said no more for the time being, merely turned and led the way to the kitchen garden. There, as soon as they turned the corner from the main path onto the narrower path to the vegetable path, Ross and Drake could see Doctor William Nugent and his assistant, Francis Lees, already at work. They could just make out the body of Brother Bernárd, on the ground, partially hidden by the bulk of the brilliant but grossly overweight pathologist. Two constables stood guard nearby, as promised by Sergeant Blake.

"I'll leave you to confer with the doctor now," said the Prior matter-of-factly. "If you need me, please send for me. I'll leave one of the brothers at the gate to the garden, in case you need anything. He will not interfere in any way with you or your people."

Ross thanked the Prior and informed him that a forensic team would also be arriving shortly, and he'd appreciate someone being available to escort Miles Booker and his team to their location. Brother Gerontius agreed to leave on watch to guide the SOCOs to Ross' location upon arrival.

"Well, fancy meeting you here?" Ross said, not too loudly, being mindful of where they were, as he and Drake strode across to where William Nugent and Francis Lees where hard at work.

"Ah, decided to join us have you, Detective Inspector Ross, Sergeant Drake?" Nugent stood up to his full height, almost six feet, but it was his bulk that people tended to remember. Known behind his back by most of those in the police force who had cause to deal with him as 'Fat Willie,' the doctor had originated from Glasgow. Given he'd lived and worked in Liverpool for over twenty years, most of the Glaswegian accent had disappeared from his everyday speech. Ross knew only too well, however, that at times of stress or excitement, William Nugent slipped effortlessly into a broad Glaswegian accent that could have come straight from the Gorbals, a once notorious suburb of the largest city in Scotland.

"The Prior tells me we're looking at a case of murder by cyanide poisoning." Ross said the words as a statement, not a question. As he spoke, the flash of Francis Lees' camera continued to snap photo after photo of the crime scene, using special lenses that Ross assumed took good images in the dark.

"Well, does he now?" Nugent looked aggrieved. "If yon monk chappie is so certain of the cause of this poor chap's demise, I'm surprised you're needing my presence at all."

"Oh, you know me, Doc. I always like a second opinion," Ross grinned.

"You're a bloody cheeky young bugger, that's what you are. A second opinion? Ah'll give ye a second opinion in a minute."

"Calm down Doc, just pulling your leg."

"Aye, well, as it so happens, yon Brother Gerontius chappie appears to be spot on with his speculation. Cyanide looks highly likely." Nugent beckoned Ross and Drake close enough they could see what he indicated, though not too close as to contaminate the crime scene, in case there was trace evidence or footprints in the immediate vicinity. As he rolled the body slightly, so they could see the face of the dead man.

Izzie Drake gasped. "My God! He looks as if he was in terror just before he died. His face … is so contorted."

"Aye, Sergeant Drake, right enough. One of the symptoms of cyanide poisoning is seizure, and it does appear that this poor man suffered just such a thing prior to his demise. Don't be fooled by old war or spy movies that show a spy biting into a cyanide capsule and instantly dropping dead. In reality, it can take up to three minutes of pure agony for the victim to succumb."

"You'll be able to confirm this at autopsy, I presume, Doc?" Ross posed.

"Aye, but I'll need to get him back to the lab sharpish. If it *is* cyanide, I'm afraid it only has a sort half-life in the human body—and apart from a few tell-take signs, it will have disappeared from his system completely in twenty-four to fort-eight hours."

"So, let's hope Miles and his SOCOs get here fast so you can get the body removed quickly."

As if on cue, the approaching sound of a siren cut through the night air like the howl of a banshee. Escorted by Brother Simon, who'd been allocated the duty by Gerontius, Miles Booker, the Crime Scene Manager as he was now referred to, and his team of technicians were soon on scene and busily checking the immediate area around the body. Before long, William Nugent authorised the removal of the body to the city morgue and a pair of waiting paramedics quickly and carefully placed the remains in a black body bag; the body of Brother Bernárd began its journey towards its appointment with autopsy scalpels, saws, and other paraphernalia.

Ross and Drake left the scene on the garden path. It was time they spoke to the unfortunate pair who'd discovered the body. Ross summoned Brother Simon from where he stood, looking decidedly uncomfortable some twenty yards away, and asked the monk to lead them to the refectory where they'd apparently find Brother Ignatius and Sister Paulette. As they followed, Ross made good use of their time with him.

"Did you know Brother Bernárd well, Brother Simon?" he asked as the monk led them along the dark pathway, helped slightly by a battery-operated torch that did little to penetrate the sense of doom and gloom that Drake was increasingly experiencing,

"No, not well at all," Brother Simon replied quietly. "I don't know anyone very well yet. I've only been here a short time. Only about three months, you see."

Ross felt a slight sense of exasperation at the monk's reply. Three months and he *hardly* knew anyone? "Don't these people talk to each other?" he whispered to Drake as they walked,

"Three bloody months and he hardly knows a soul? Unbelievable in any other environment, but here, I suppose that's pretty normal—you know, all that praying and time spent in doing whatever it is monks and nuns do. Little time for social intercourse."

"Bloody hell, Izzie, that's pretty deep stuff," Ross smiled, but before they could say anything else, Brother Simon stopped and they had to be careful not to walk into his back.

"Here we are," he said, gesturing. "I'll leave you to it. Everyone else has been asked to stay in their own rooms, or cells we call them. Brother Ignatius and Sister Paulette are waiting for you."

Ross thanked the monk who, he noticed for the first time, had a nasty looking scar on the left side of his face. He wondered what Simon had done in his previous life; that scar was a bad one. An industrial accident perhaps? For now though, he had other things on his mind. Out of politeness, he knocked once on the refectory door, and he and Drake entered. It was time to begin the investigation.

# Chapter 3

### When the Birds Stopped Singing

As Ross and Drake entered the refectory, the first thing that came to Ross's mind was that the place resembled a school dining room. Metal-framed chairs with plastic seats were situated at a series of similarly framed tables with wipe-clean pale grey surfaces, made of indeterminate laminate. At one end of the room stood a small servery, presently empty, beside which stood two large urns, presumably for tea and coffee, and a large water cooler.

Brother Ignatius and Sister Paulette sat opposite each other at the table nearest the urns, for ease of obtaining refills Ross assumed. As he and Drake approached them, the monk and the nun rose to greet them.

"Please, sit down," Ross said and the pair resumed their seats. "I'm sorry we're forced to meet under such sad circumstances," he said by way of greeting and then introduced himself and Drake. He could see that the young nun had been crying, evidenced by the redness around her eyes and the tear streaks on her flushed cheeks. The monk also looked upset and a look of something else, fear perhaps, seemed to lurk behind his eyes. "I'm sure you understand that it's important we speak to you both as you were the first people to encounter the body of Brother Bernárd."

"Yes, of course," Brother Ignatius said, apparently speaking for them both. "It was a heck of a shock, Inspector, I can tell you."

"Of course, I'm sure it was," Ross replied smoothly. "Please, can you tell us what you were both doing immediately prior to finding the body?"

"We were planting seeds—cabbages and cauliflowers. We grow fresh produce all year round if we can. It helps feed us. And we also sell our produce at local markets when we have enough."

Before Ignatius could go on, Sister Paulette surprised Ross by interjecting, "It was horrible, just horrible. I've seen bodies before, but the look on poor Brother Bernárd's face. ...It was as if he'd come face to face with Satan himself."

Ross could tell that the young woman was clearly on the verge of hysteria. The glance at Drake was acknowledged and she sat beside the nun, taking hold of one hand and squeezing it, offering the poor woman a modicum of support.

"It must have been terrible for you," Drake said quietly and calmly, trying to induce similar feelings in the nun who'd begun sniffling again,

"You say you've seen death before, Sister. You seem rather young to be saying such things. Where did you encounter the bodies you speak of?" Ross enquired.

"I spent two years as a volunteer for the order in South America, helping with our relief operation in Venezuela. There'd been a lot of internal strife in the country and there were, and still are, a large number of displaced persons there who need our help, Inspector. Sadly, there were many deaths, from wounds, starvation, natural causes, all sorts of reasons, but none of those poor people looked the way poor Brother Bernárd did."

The conversation carried on for five minutes, with Ross and Drake alternately taking over the questioning as they sought anything of importance the pair might reveal. It soon became apparent that, apart from quite literally stumbling over the body, there was little the two could add that might be helpful.

Nevertheless, Ross made one more attempt to elicit something from the pair. "Please, think very carefully." He could see that Ignatius and

Paulette were doing their best to focus on his words, though he was certain their minds were still on the path at the moment they'd found the body, a fact that might prove helpful with the next question. "While you were both busy planting your seeds and then clearing everything, ready to finish work, did either of you see or hear anything—no matter how inconsequential it may have seemed at the time—coming from the direction of Brother Bernárd's body?"

"It's Bernárd, as in the French *Bernaaard*, Inspector, not as in the English, Bernard," Ignatious said, correcting Ross's faulty pronunciation.

"I'm sorry, I stand corrected," he responded. "But did you hear anything, either of you?"

Sister Paulette looked quizzical. Drake could tell she was hesitating about something. "Please Sister, if you've thought of something, no matter how small, tell us. It could be important."

The nun wavered as she decided whether to speak. Finally, she made her decision. "You see, it's not so much a case of what I heard as more what I didn't hear," she said cryptically.

"Please tell us, Sister," Ross urged.

"Brother Ignatius had just told me it was about time we were calling it a day, and I looked up and thought what a beautiful evening it was. The sun was setting ever so slowly, casting a lovely pinkness on the clouds. There was a blackbird singing in a nearby tree and the little birds, sparrows and so on, were tweeting all around us, making it all seem even more perfect, a *real* gift from God I thought. I'd just placed my pack of seeds in the basket used for carrying them when all of a sudden, the birds weren't there any more … or at least, they weren't singing any more. Everything was silent, for about maybe twenty or thirty seconds, I'm not sure, and then gradually they started singing and tweeting again. I thought perhaps they'd been disturbed by a fox or something. Now, I'm thinking it might have been, you know, when poor Bernard was being …"

"Yes, thanks Sister. We get the idea. Do you have any idea what time that was?"

"I'm sorry, but neither of us was wearing a watch," came the reply from Brother Ignatius.

"The 999 call was made at 6.44," Ross advised, "and the uniform division arrived here just after seven p.m. It would seem if that was indeed the time Brother Bernárd was killed, it must have been between 6.30 and 6.40 p.m. which means you probably came along literally minutes after he died."

"Oh my," Paulette said in a voice that gave Ross the impression that the phrase was as close to swearing as the young nun would ever come to. "But no one came past us, did they Brother? So that means … "

"That means the killer left in the opposite direction, which leads where, exactly?"

"That's the route we'd have taken to get to the refectory," Brother Ignatius provided. "In fact, that's where we did walk after putting our tools and seeds in the little shed on the corner of the garden plot. But the path opens out on to the cloister—what you'd call the courtyard—and allows access to most of the other buildings on the site, Inspector."

"And how many people know the precise layout of the priory?" Drake asked.

"Everyone who lives here of course, plus any regular visitors, the doctor, the bishop and any of the various ecclesiastical people who have regular contact with us for a variety of reasons."

"Did either of you know Brother Bernard well?" Ross asked.

"I hardly knew him," Sister Paulette quickly replied. "I only spoke to him a few times, usually to pass the time of day, to be truthful."

"I spoke to him quite a bit when he first arrived," Brother Ignatius stated. "He was Swiss by birth apparently and I was interested in finding out about his homeland. We don't get much opportunity to talk about foreign lands and so forth, living our fairly cloistered existence, but Bernard really wasn't very forthcoming. Said it was a long time ago and he could barely remember his childhood years, he told me, so I didn't press the matter."

"I see," said Ross. "So he wasn't very talkative?"

"No, I'd agree with that," said Ignatius, and Paulette nodded.

"So the killer would have had to walk across the cloister in full view of everyone?" Izzie Drake quickly caught on.

"Well, yes, I suppose they would have done," the monk said, looking thoughtful.

"We're going to have to speak to everyone who was present in the priory during the early part of this evening," Ross was thinking as he spoke. "How many people are here, Brother?

"In addition to myself and Sister Paulette here, and Brother Gerontius who you've already met, we have six other monks, one less without poor Brother Bernárd, and four more nuns. We're not a large community, Inspector."

"Right, Brother, Sister. I think that's all for now, thank you. We'll probably need to talk with you again some time tomorrow, unless either of you saw anyone suspicious hanging around before or after Brother Bernárd's death?"

With both monk and nun shaking their heads, Ross and Drake left them to get whatever sleep they could manage and walked towards the site where Miles Booker and his team were hard at work. Before leaving for the night, they'd need to have words again with Brother Gerontius but, for now, Ross was anxious to learn if the forensic technicians had discovered anything helpful.

The last remnants of daylight had given way to the night, and Ross knew there was little hope of Booker's people turning up anything they hadn't already located, at least until daylight returned to the Priory of St. Emma.

# Chapter 4

## Priory vs Monastery

Miles Booker gave every sign of being a frustrated man when Ross and Drake finally managed to pull him away from the murder scene.

"Not a lot to go on Andy," he said immediately. "A few fibres where the body was found. If there's anything present on the actual victim, I'm sure Doc Nugent will find it, but I strongly suspect the fibres will prove to be from the monk's habit. As for the killer, if he attacked the victim, there's no sign of a struggle, so it would have had to be a lightning fast attack that immobilised the poor bugger immediately. Of course, as there's no wound involved, there's no blood we can work with, and it doesn't appear as if the man or woman involved dropped anything at the scene or left anything behind. It's like we're looking at a blank canvas. We'll go over everything again in broad daylight of course, but don't go building your hopes up mate, sorry."

"That's all we need." Ross looked frustrated. "Not your fault, Miles. You can only work with what you're presented. Bloody typical, the Chief Constable's watching over the case, Oscar Agostini's on holiday, and I've got the bloody DCS directly overseeing the investigation!"

"Sarah Hollingsworth, the Queen Bee herself?"

"Yep, and here I am, on the grounds of a monastery in the middle of the night without a friggin' clue to go on."

"Er, it's a priory, sir," Drake corrected.

"Oh right, priory. I stand corrected. What's the difference between a monastery and a priory, anyway?"

"Maybe we should ask the Prior when we talk to him again," she suggested.

"Good idea. Right, Miles, if there's nothing you can give me here and now, we'd better go and have that word with Brother Gerontius. Izzie?"

Walking towards the administration building, where Brother Gerontius would be patiently waiting for them, Ross and Drake took a moment to exchange a few words.

"That was clever of Sister Paulette to put the silence of the birds together with the time of the Brother's death, don't you think?"

"Yes, she's quite an astute young lady. Observant, too. Not everyone would have thought of that and associated the two events."

"Comes from her having a close connection with nature, I suppose. She's probably very attuned to the sounds of wildlife and so on," Ross agreed.

"You got any thoughts yet?" Drake asked.

"Not any worth sharing," Ross shook his head. "From the sounds of it, almost anyone could have wandered onto the property and killed the monk, but one thing is really baffling me at present. Why *poison*?"

"It might help us formulate a theory when we get the results of the autopsy, always assuming Fat Willie can come up with a definitive cause of death and give us some idea how the poison, *if* that's indeed what killed Brother Bernárd, was administered."

Ross could say no more for the time being, as they were entering the building where they would find Brother Gerontius, who they located easily in his office at the end of a long corridor; it was the only one with lights streaming through the open doorway. All the other doors were open, but led only to darkness.

\* \* \*

"To answer your question, Sergeant," the Prior began in response to Drake's query about the difference between a priory and a monastery, "it's a little complicated,"

*Somehow, I knew it would be,* Ross thought, but said nothing.

"To put it in the most simple terms, I can tell you that a monastery, in most cases, is larger than a priory, and houses more monks and/or nuns, usually a minimum of twelve. Ecclesiastically speaking, a monastery is senior in rank to a priory and is under the control of an Abbott. A Prior, such as myself, is of a lower rank in the order than an Abbott. The word 'prior' is actually derived from the Medieval Latin word *prioria*, which simply means a monastery governed by a Prior. The nuns are usually governed by a Prioress, and though we have five nuns in this community, someone has to take responsibility for them, so Sister Ariadne is our Prioress. I have overall responsibility for the day-to-day running of the priory, with Sister Ariadne in charge of all things pertaining to the nuns. I can have her summoned here if you wish to speak with her."

"No, Brother, that won't be necessary tonight," Ross replied, "though we will need to talk to her, and everyone else in your community, tomorrow."

"That won't be a problem, Inspector. We're at your disposal, if it helps to find whoever perpetrated this heinous act. I hope I've managed to answer your question also, Sergeant Drake?"

"Yes, I think so, as much as I need to know in relation to the case, thank you," Drake replied as Ross cleared his throat, ready to begin his questioning of the Prior once more.

"Tell me, please," he began, "just how much you know about the people who make up your religious community, and whether you also employ any people here who aren't actually members of your religious order."

Ross noticed that the Prior had a large, old-fashioned dappled-grey box file on his desk, annotated on the spine with the words 'Personal Files'. At this point, though, he made no move to open it.

"When it comes to our fellow monks and the nuns who make up our community, Inspector, we know as much about them as they share with us when they enter the order."

"That sounds a little vague, if you don't mind me saying so," Ross said with a hint of frustration.

"It's not intended to be. You must understand however, that we are not the army or the security services. In order to become a monk or a nun, one only has to demonstrate one's fealty to God, and to the aims and beliefs of our order. What a person was, or was not before coming to us, is of no real importance, apart from it being useful to know if a monk has, for example, a specific skill which could be of use or significance in maintaining our community. You've already met Brother Ignatius of course, who's blessed with the skills of a gardener, what is known in everyday parlance as having 'green fingers'. What better person could we wish for when it comes to maintaining the kitchen garden? Likewise, Sister Paulette also has some expertise in that area."

"I think I see what you mean," said Ross nonchalantly. "So if one of your monks, hypothetically speaking, had a criminal record, you might have no knowledge of it, am I correct?"

"Inspector, God sent his son Jesus Christ to earth to take upon himself the sins of mankind. If a new recruit to our order chooses to inform us of a criminal act perpetrated in the past, it wouldn't necessarily preclude that person from becoming part of the order. Christianity is based on love and forgiveness, as I'm sure you know."

"Yes, of course, but …"

"I think I've explained it as much as necessary, Inspector." Brother Gerontius appeared firm in his resolve to reveal nothing else about the members of his community.

Ross decided to leave things at that, at least until the morning. He was tired, it was getting late, and they weren't about to solve this case in the next few minutes. A good night's sleep had become a priority in his mind. "I think we've done all we can for tonight," he announced, much to the Prior's surprise. "We'll wish you goodnight, but we'll be returning in the morning with the rest of my investigative team. I hope your people will cooperate fully with our investigation, as I'm sure you'll want the killer of your fellow Brother apprehended as soon as possible."

"Yes, yes, of course," the Prior agreed quickly. "You can count on our full cooperation."

Ross and Drake rose and, before leaving, took a brisk walk around the grounds, ensuring they knew the lay of the land, but also making sure there were no unauthorised persons lurking where they shouldn't be. Lastly, they checked in with one of two uniformed constables who'd been assigned to keep watch over the murder scene until morning.

"Keep your eyes peeled, Constable. I don't want the scene disturbed," Ross advised the young man.

"No problem, sir," the constable acknowledged.

"There's supposed to be two of you. Where's your oppo?" Drake wanted to know.

"Constable Shepherd's gone to take a turn round the premises Sarge. He thought we could do alternate patrols around the place through the night to deter any intruders or maybe your killer who might be hiding somewhere, waiting for a chance to sneak away."

"That's good thinking." Drake was impressed.

"Very good thinking indeed," Ross agreed. "Okay lad, have a good night. Stay alert, Constable …?"

"Pearson, sir."

"Just fancy that, someone showing a bit of initiative," said Drake as she and Ross stood by their cars.

"I'm impressed with Constables Shepherd and Pearson," Ross concurred. "Let's hope those lads don't meet up with the killer in the night, though. One victim is enough for me."

Both detectives climbed into their cars and, as their taillights receded from view, a pair of eyes, well hidden from the sight of either Constable Pearson or Constable Shepherd, breathed a sigh of relief. A smile of grim satisfaction spread across a face twisted with hatred. So much for number one, the killer reasoned. With one gone, the next one would seem so much easier.

# Chapter 5

### A Turbulent Past

"A monastery?" Detective Constable Lenny 'Tony' Curtis exclaimed at the morning briefing, after Ross informed the rest of the team where he and Drake had spent most of their night. The pair had finally managed to grab about three hours sleep before rising and quickly showering, dressing and heading back to headquarters, both arriving almost simultaneously.

"That's what I said," Ross replied flatly and, seeing the fixed look from Drake, corrected himself. "Actually, it's a priory, not a monastery?"

"What's the difference, Boss?" Curtis smiled.

"Later. For now, just be aware that it's home to a small community of monks and nuns … where last night a monk was murdered in a particularly horrific way. The Prior just happens to be a friend of the Chief Constable. Not only that, but while DCI Agostini's on holiday, DCS Hollingsworth has taken overall command of the investigation."

"Oh no, the Ice Queen cometh," Curtis quipped.

"That's enough of that, thanks Tony. A little respect please and, anyway, The Chief Super's not that bad when you get to know her."

"Okay, Boss, if you say so," Curtis grinned.

"Come on, sir, what's the case?" Sam Gable asked, getting things back on track. She looked good, Ross thought. His detective was obviously blooming as a result of her new relationship with a Greater Manchester detective sergeant, who'd been helpful in their previous case.

"Right Sam, everyone, listen carefully. Last night, Izzie and I attended an incident at the Priory of St. Emma, at Grassendale. The place used to be St. Basil's Monastery, years ago, but the place burned down and was left derelict until it was partially rebuilt and reopened as St. Emma. When we arrived, we discovered that one of the monks, Brother Bernárd," Ross ensured he used the correct pronunciation for the benefit of the team, "had been found lying dead on a pathway close to the priory's kitchen garden. He was found by a young nun and monk; they'd been taking advantage of the lighter evenings to work later than usual and were planting seeds. After finishing, they were walking back to the main buildings when they virtually stumbled over the body." He gazed solemnly from face to face. "It appears that Brother Bernárd may have been the victim of murder by cyanide poisoning. We should know for certain this morning. Doc Nugent was on the scene when we arrived and, with the Chief Constable's interest in the case, he's assured me the autopsy would receive top priority; hence, I expect a call from him sooner than later."

Drake responded to a nod from Ross and took over the briefing, as pre-arranged. "We interviewed the pair who found the body, as well as the Prior, Brother Gerontius, who first suspected cyanide poisoning. It seems he was a pharmacist before finding religion. Thanks to the fact that Sister Paulette had her wits about her, we were able to pin down an approximate time of death, as she noticed a sudden silence when the birds all fell quiet and then began again a couple of minutes later. What we don't know, and need to find out is who, apart from the monks and nuns, might have been on the grounds of the priory around that time. The killer could be one of their own, or have come in from outside. The priory is pretty much open house for anyone wandering in from outside."

"So we have an intimate suspect pool, but the possibility of a wider ranging one too," Nick Dodds commented.

"Looks like it, but my betting is on an insider being responsible," Ross replied evenly. "It's time to get on with the job." He turned to the team's computer expert, Sergeant Paul Ferris. "While we're out there, Paul, I want you and Kat to find out all you can about St. Emma's Priory."

"Got it," he acknowledged.

In minutes, the squad room was deserted except for Ferris and the team's admin assistant Kat Bellamy, who were already at work on the computers, digging into the history, short as it was, of St. Emma's. If there was anything there that could throw light on why anybody might want to murder one of their number, the pair was confident they could find it.

* * *

The space available for car parking at St. Emma's had probably never looked so full. As well as two vehicles from Miles Booker's forensic team, there were four unmarked police cars and two regular police vehicles, which had brought half a dozen uniformed officers along as backup to Ross's team. DCS Hollingsworth was making sure that Ross had every resource possible available. With the Chief Constable watching over her every move, she couldn't afford to appear as if she were being anything other than 100% diligent in terms of the investigation.

While Ross' detectives waited by the vehicles and received a quick briefing from Izzie Drake, he made arrangements with Brother Gerontius to interview the monks and nuns that made up the permanent priory population.

"I've made the refectory available for you to speak to the monks, Inspector, and our small library is free for you to converse with our small group of nuns. I take it you have female detectives with you? The nuns would, I think, feel more comfortable speaking with women."

"That sounds fine, thank you, Brother. And yes, I have three women detectives here, including DS Drake, whom you met last night."

"Of course. I don't wish to impede your investigation of the murder of dear Bernárd, Inspector, so I'll allow you to get on with your job. I must inform Bernárd's next of kin of the tragedy that has befallen him."

"I don't envy you that task, Brother." Ross was sympathetic to the Prior's responsibility, having had to inform relatives of the violent deaths of loved ones many times during his career.

"Indeed, Inspector. I also expect you'll be receiving news of the autopsy soon?"

"Later today, I hope. I know you'll want to be able to give the Brother's family as much information as you can, but I must stress that this is now an active murder investigation. Certain facts can't be made public at this time. Do you understand?"

The Prior nodded. "I'll do and say nothing to compromise your investigation. On that, you have my solemn oath." Brother Gerontius handed Ross two sheets of A4 paper. "Here are the names of the community members. I've spilt them into two lists, one of the monks and one of the nuns. I anticipated you might find them useful to carry out your interviews."

"Thanks. They'll come in useful, I'm sure." He looked at the two lists, wondering which one of them, if any, was the name of Brother Bernárd's cold-blooded killer. With that, he left the Prior to his own devices, and began arranging the interviews with the various members.

He looked down the list of monks' names. Brother Ignatius they'd already spoken to last night but would speak to him again to see if he remembered anything else. He'd briefly met Brother Simon, and he now saw that they would need to speak to Brothers Gareth, Antonio and Geoffrey and the nuns, Sisters Ariadne, Rebecca, Letitia and Sarah.

\* \* \*

Ferris and Bellamy worked well together. When the admin assistant had first been assigned to the team, some of the detectives had been unsure whether the appointment of a civilian to a group of highly trained, expert investigators would be an asset or a detriment. Katrina Bellamy, known to all as Kat, had soon proved invaluable however; together with Sergeant Paul Ferris, she'd been instrumental in uncovering information that had assisted in solving many cases. This was courtesy of her quick mind and superlative abilities with the computer, which Ferris readily admitted were almost on a par with his own.

The pair of them were busy conducting what nowadays appeared to be referred to as 'data mining', but which they simply saw as normal research into the history of the Priory of St. Emma.

"Interesting, isn't it?" Bellamy said as she finished a broad-based look into the past use of the site where the priory stood. "It was a monastery for years and was virtually destroyed during the Reformation, rebuilt hundreds of years later, only to be destroyed a second time in the fire of 1912. It's almost as if St. Basil's carried a curse upon it, if you believe in that sort of thing."

"Which neither of us believes, of course … do we?" Ferris turned and met her gaze.

"Of course not, but it is strange, isn't it? A bit like lightning striking twice in the same place."

"I'll grant you that, but here, I just came up with a little gem from the days of St. Basil's. Just before Henry VIII ordered the dissolution of the monasteries, it was rumoured that St. Basil's held a 'great treasure', as referred to in a vague historical document written by a man called Bishop Simon de Carborough. Unfortunately, I can find no other references to this so-called treasure or to the mysterious Bishop. It's as if he never existed … and if he did, he simply vanished off the face of the earth."

"That *is* a mystery," Bellamy concurred. "Where did you dig this up from?"

Ferris turned his computer screen so she could read the page he was referring to. It was from a website that listed 'facts and legends' of pre-Reformation monasteries of the North of England, and only indirectly referred to St. Basil.

"What made you look in this site?" she asked, curious to discover how Ferris' mind worked. She'd always been proficient in her use of computers, but since joining Ross' team, she'd come to view Ferris as something of a mentor. Her skills had grown greatly as she'd watched, listened, and learned from the sergeant.

"No great credit on my part," Ferris smiled cheerily. "I was simply looking at the history of St. Basil and this came up in the web listings for similar sites. I can't take credit for it, Kat."

"At least you're honest," she smiled in return. "That's what I like about you, and why it's good to learn from you."

"Thanks, but please, where the others are concerned ..."

"I know, you're a genius," she giggled. "Don't worry, your secret's safe with me."

"Good girl. Now, what do you think about this so-called treasure?"

"We've not got a thing to corroborate its existence so far, so do we give it any credence, or devote more time to it? You're the boss; you decide."

Ferris scratched his head as he thought it over. "We've just had a murder committed on a site where we now have a vague refer-ence to something of value having been present there, shortly before King Henry's troops moved in and vandalised the original monastery. That's the only word for what they did back in those days: sheer bloody *vandalism*. For whatever reason, the Benedictines left the ruins lying derelict for nearly three hundred years and then, for reasons only they knew, rebuilt the place. Why? How many monasteries, destroyed at the time of the Reformation, did they subsequently rebuild—which, let's face it, must have cost the order a bloody great wad of cash."

"I can see where your thoughts are taking you," Bellamy nodded sagely, as if every word Ferris had said made perfect sense. "You think there was something there, even after all those years ... something the Benedictines knew about and which they wanted to protect, right?"

"I think there's a possibility, if the so far unsubstantiated story about the treasure is true. What I'm also thinking is that the monks, who then lived in the rebuilt monastery, could have been sent there as some sort of 'guardians' of this unknown treasure—which, for all we know, if it did exist, might *not* have been gold-and-jewels treasure, but a religious relic, valuable only to the monks, or to religious believers."

"Of course," said Bellamy with a nod. "From what I've been reading about the Reformation, Henry VIII's troops looted and damaged much of what they found in the great monasteries of England. If the St. Basil's monks did possess something very valuable, they'd have done all they could to protect it from Henry's troops, and hidden it so well that it was never found."

"Yes, but that leaves me with one burning question," said Ferris with a pensive frown.

"Go on. What is it?"

"Why wait nearly three *centuries* to rebuild the monastery?"

"They couldn't do it during the years of the religious persecution of Catholics, could they?" she replied. "If the Benedictines were aware that the ruined monastery held a great religious relic, or gold or silver or whatever, they couldn't have retrieved it while Catholics were being persecuted throughout England, could they?"

"Good point," Ferris nodded in agreement. He opened another historical website. "Look here, we had a turbulent period where we had Protestant Kings and Queens, but then there were attempts by other rulers to reintroduce Catholicism to England. The Pope even declared Queen Elizabeth I a heretic and ordered her subjects to rise up against her in an attempt to restore the Catholic faith. There was a lot of bloodshed, Kat, and it wasn't until the early nineteenth century that Catholicism was declared legal again in England, though there was still great hostility towards them in some areas. Even so, the law of England states that a Catholic can't become King or Queen of England."

"I never knew all this stuff." Bellamy was intrigued by the brief look into England's past. "The gunpowder plot by Guy Fawkes and his friends was an attempt to kill the King and destroy Parliament, and reinstate a Catholic on the throne. Lots of people blamed the Great Fire of London on the Catholics. Terrible, wasn't it?"

Suddenly, Ferris pointed to the screen. "Look!" She fell silent as he read from the page. "Following *The Roman Catholic Relief Act 1829*, Catholics were allowed to sit in Parliament. The re-establishment of the Roman Catholic ecclesiastical hierarchy by Pope Pius IX took place in 1850." He stopped reading aloud as he waited to see if his colleague was catching on.

"You think that's significant?" she asked, bemused.

"Think about it," he said. "The Roman Catholic Church in England was re-created in 1850 and just a few years later, the Church began the restoration of St. Basil's and quickly installed a group of monks in the place. They lived in relative peace and harmony until suddenly in 1912, a devastating fire sweeps through the place—and I don't yet know if any of the monks survived. If they did, they might have taken the treasure with them, or ..."

"Or it might still be there, buried under the new St. Emma's Priory," she stated softly, as if afraid someone might overhear.

"Exactly," nodded Ferris, "and wouldn't that provide someone who knows about—and wants to get their hands on—the treasure with a perfect motive for murder if they thought someone else might know about it and, as such, be in their way."

"Good God, Paul. What are you going to do now?"

"We still need to look at the history of St. Emma from when it was opened on the site of the ruined St. Basil, but for now I think it's worth a quick phone call to the boss. I think he might like to hear what we've found so far."

# Chapter 6

## Brothers and Sisters

Sister Ariadne, technically the Prioress at St. Emma's, looked to Izzie Drake to be well suited for the role. Despite her diminutive size, Drake guessed she wasn't much more than five-feet tall. Something about the nun's demeanour and the way she carried herself gave her an air of authority that sat perfectly well with the middle-aged woman as she sat opposite Drake, waiting for the questions to begin.

"Thank you for talking with me this morning, Sister," Drake began, trying to put the nun at ease, but realising this was totally unnecessary.

"I didn't really have a choice, Sergeant Drake, did I?" The nun smiled warmly as she spoke. There was no malice in her words.

"You're right, of course, Sister, but thank you anyway."

"Please do call me Ariadne, or you'll wear out your voice calling me Sister Ariadne … if you call me Sister, before you know it, you'll forget which one of us you're talking to."

Drake liked this woman and she relaxed into the interview. "How well did you know Brother Bernárd?"

"Not well, I'm sorry to say. Apart from occasions when we have cause to work with the monks, or at certain services in church and at mealtimes, we don't engage in a great deal of social discourse with them. As for Brother Bernárd, I perhaps spoke with him on about half a dozen occasions, usually to pass the time of day."

"That's a shame." Drake thought that the leader of the priory's nuns might have had more contact than most with the monks. Obviously not.

"I do know he wasn't English," Ariadne said.

"We understand he was from Switzerland."

"Ah," was the nun's quiet reply.

"Apart from being the ... the Prioress? Is that right?

"Yes, that's my official title."

"Good, so what else does your role entail?"

"Apart from overseeing the spiritual needs and welfare of our small community of nuns, I take care of the administrative side of the nunnery within the priory. There isn't a lot of work involved to be truthful, Sergeant, so I use much of my time helping out with various community projects. We try our best to assist the homeless, the poor—believe me there are still a lot of people living below the breadline in the city—and, naturally, we try to spread the word of God wherever and whenever the opportunity presents itself."

Drake thought some of the Prioress's duties were rather vague-sounding, but then, with such a small group of Sisters, she guessed there wasn't an awful lot of work to do.

"I see, and do you do anything within the priory, like Sister Paulette working in the garden?"

"Ah, you think being the Prioress is a nice easy task, eh, Sergeant? No, please," she smiled genially as she held up a slim hand. "I'm only joking in my own way. Yes, I am also in charge of the refectory. I'm quite a passable cook and together with Sister Rebecca and Brother Geoffrey, we provide the meals for our fellow Brothers and Sisters, and for any visitors who we may entertain."

"And do you have many visitors here?"

"We do, yes. Quite often, there's Bishop Charles, who is usually accompanied by his assistant, Father Michael. We also have occasional visits from our Brothers and Sisters from other areas who sometimes spend a few days, enjoying something of a retreat, a little peace and quiet."

"I see. And, if I may, can I ask a more personal question?"

"Of course you can. We have no secrets here, Sergeant Drake."

Drake looked a little embarrassed to be asking what followed, but she really wanted to know more about the Sisterhood. "Well, in the movie, *Sister Act,* for example, the nuns all had names that began with Mary, followed by another name. Why don't you do that here?"

Sister Ariadne laughed. "Is that all? I thought you were going to ask some deep religious question about our order, or me in particular. I've seen that film; it made me laugh. We do have a small television set here, with which we're able to keep up with international news and so on, and sometimes we do use it for entertainment. Once, it was common practice for nuns to be given a new name when they took their vows, and depending on the convent, or the order, they belonged to, this could be the name Mary, as an example, followed by a saint's name or other religious figure. In these modern, enlightened times, however, it is now much more common for nuns to retain their baptismal or birth name, though if they wish, they can take a new name, but the choice is theirs. It's not something we impose on new sisters here."

"Thank you, Sister. So, is Ariadne …?"

"My real name? Yes, it is. I was born Ariadne Schofield in Perth, Western Australia, forty-seven years ago. My parents were originally from Lancaster and when my grandmother on my father's side was struck by a terminal illness, they decided to move back to the 'old country', as they referred to England. I was eighteen and had always wanted to become a nun, so my career path would have been the same wherever in the world I'd ended up."

"Thank you for that information." Drake felt she'd learned all she could from the Prioress for the moment and saw no reason to question her further as her contact with the dead monk had appeared to have been minimal. She allowed the Prioress to leave and go about her duties, which she'd said would include making preparations for the midday meal.

\* \* \*

Sam Gable was talking with Sister Rebecca, and Sofie Meyer was engaged in a deep conversation with Sister Letitia, who, they'd discovered, was like Sofie, German by birth. Their shared language gave them a good platform for open communication.

Ross, meanwhile was already nearing the end of his interview with Brother Gareth, who, as his name suggested, hailed from Wales, a small village on the West Coast, named Aberporth, located on the beautiful coastal area of Cardigan Bay. He excused himself when his phone rang and he found himself being informed by Ferris of the rumours of some long-lost treasure relating to the original monastery of St. Basil.

Pressing the 'end call' button, he turned to Brother Gareth, thinking there was no time like the present to try out Ferris' theory of the treasure. "Tell me Gareth, if you've ever heard of a mystery treasure being located here."

"Treasure … here … at St. Emma?" The monk looked more amused than surprised.

"At St. Basil actually, when the monastery first stood here, back in the days of good old Henry VIII."

"You're pulling my leg, boyo," said Gareth in his sing-song Welsh lilt.

Ross had got used to being addressed as 'boyo'. Gareth seemed to have no intention of addressing him as 'inspector' or anything else denoting his status as a police officer. "It's a serious question."

"I can only say no, I've never heard of such a thing. Then again, I've not done what you'd call a lot of research into the history of St. Basil while I've been here, see."

"And your main job, apart from your time spent in prayers and contemplation, is driving the priory's minibus, as you mentioned earlier?"

"That's it. You've got me in a nutshell. I used to be a taxi driver once, look you, so they trust me to ferry the others around when they're doing fundraisers or attending bazaars, and so forth. We have a nice, second-hand bright-blue Mercedes Sprinter, 17-seat minibus that was donated to the priory by a well-wisher. I love driving it. Although I haven't done much research into the priory, I've been doing a whole load of research into the history of the Benedictines since my arrival." He met Ross' intense gaze with a fleeting smile. "You'd be amazed at how interesting it is, boyo. Some really exciting stuff happened during the Middle Ages, I can tell you, but no mention of treasure, look you. Sister Ariadne has been here the longest. If anyone has heard rumours of a long-lost treasure associated with the old monastery, she's the one to ask. As for Bernárd, God Bless his soul, I spoke to him maybe half a dozen times. He was a very private sort of person, perfectly suited to monastic life."

"Thank you, Gareth," Ross said to the amiable, somewhat eccentric fellow, and he shook his head as the monk shuffled away, humming a hymn, one that Ross had recollections of from his time in grammar school, but couldn't put a title to.

Ross rose and took himself off to talk with Brother Gerontius about the treasure rumour, knowing that Drake was already talking to Sister Ariadne. The treasure question could wait where she was concerned.

Brother Gerontius was as much in the dark about the supposed treasure as Brother Gareth, though the thought did come to Ross that, if for any reason there was some important religious relic associated with the old monastery site, and the monks knew about it, they could easily hide such knowledge from the police and anyone else. That, however, would mean the monks and sisters were collectively lying to the police. Would they do that, Ross wondered?

As he was leaving Brother Gerontius' priory office, his phone rang once again. "Doc," he said as he recognised the pathologist's number. He'd given it a specific ringtone and the sounds of Darth Vader's theme from *Star Wars* could belong to no other caller. "I wasn't expecting you to call so soon."

"Aye, well, with the Chief Constable and the Chief Super hovering in the background, I thought you might need all the help you can get. I've been working on your victim since seven a.m., ably assisted by young Francis, to come up with the preliminary results of the autopsy for you."

Ross silently blessed the rotund medic, who he'd worked with for many years. Their relationship was one of friendly but witty repartee, with irony and sarcasm thrown in to the mix. In short, they worked bloody well together. He also knew that Nugent rarely began work before eight a.m. so he doubly appreciated the early start he'd made to help Ross with his case. "You're a saint, Doc. So come on, tell me what you've got."

"Ah think yon place ye're at now is more likely to produce a saint or two, Inspector." The fact his Glaswegian accent was evident meant the pathologist was excited about something. Ross knew better than to push him too hard however, or he'd drag things out just for devilment's sake.

"Okay, I'm listening."

"Rightio, here we go. Your victim was most definitely murdered. Now, here's the thing. I found a small pinprick on the inside of his right arm. Whoever killed your monk made sure he died quickly by injecting him with a massive dose of sodium cyanide, enough to have killed at least four, maybe five people."

"Bloody hell, Doc. So surely Brother Bernárd must have been incapacitated before being injected. I can't believe he'd have simply stood there and allowed someone to inject him with a lethal dose of cyanide poison."

"Aye, and ye'd be quite correct in your assumption. Brother Bernárd was struck over the head with a heavy, blunt object prior to him receiving the injection. There's a large indentation in the rear of his skull, indicating he was hit with something heavy and fairly flat, like maybe a flat iron or something like that."

Ross had a thought, based on where the body was found. "Or how about with a garden spade?"

"Aye, that could account for the indentation in the skull. If ye can come up with a potential weapon I can soon determine if it was used to strike the blow. Oh, one more point of interest for you. There's every chance the blow to the head might have been enough to kill Brother Bernárd *without* the need for the poison. The damage to the skull was extensive. As I say, it might have been enough to cause his death, but would certainly have led, at the very least, to extensive brain damage."

"So, it looks like whoever did it wanted to be sure the poor bugger was dead. A definite case of overkill."

"Aye, I was thinking the same thing myself. One last thing. At some time in the past, your victim has undergone some kind of reconstructive surgery, maybe to correct some facial deformity or for cosmetic reasons. I cannae say for sure. So, if I find anything else, I'll be in touch."

"Thanks, Doc. I really appreciate you moving Bernárd to the top of your list for me."

"Nae problem, Inspector. Ah hope it helps. Get back to me if ye find yon shovel, spade or whatever."

"I will. See you." Ross hung up, grateful to Nugent, who could be a grumpy old sod sometimes, was one of the best in the business; he fully appreciated having him available to cover most, if not all of his cases. When the Specialist Murder Investigation Team had been established, it had been agreed that, whenever possible, the area's chief pathologist, William Nugent, would handle their cases if available. Over time, Nugent and his cadaver-like assistant, Francis Lees, armed with his trusty camera, had become synonymous with the investigations carried out by Ross and his team. Ross found himself smiling at the thought that over the years, he and Nugent had always maintained a certain reserve in their relationship, never having progressed any further than 'Doc' and 'Inspector' in their conversations. First-name terms? God forbid, he chuckled.

Ross needed to talk to his partner and as luck would have it, when he approached the library building where the nuns were being interviewed, he saw Drake coming out of the building. He waved and called to her.

Drake waved back and walked briskly towards him. His body language was enough to tell her he had something important to share. "At least there's no doubt about it being murder," she said, after being informed of Nugent's findings.

"And now, we need to search for the weapon that laid him out," Ross responded grimly.

"The body was found right next to the kitchen garden, too," she commented. "If I remember rightly, didn't we see a small tool shed near the end of that path?"

"We did," Ross agreed. "Let's go take a look while you tell me what you've learned from Sister Ariadne. Any of the others finished their interviews yet."

"No," she replied with a quick shake of the head, "and what I learned from Ariadne wasn't enough to fill the back of a postage stamp."

"Ah, we might have to speak with her again later. For now, let's go take a look at that tool shed." Ross led the way towards the kitchen garden, striding in front like a bloodhound on a scent.

"Hey, not so fast!" Drake jogged along in his wake.

Ross felt determined. If the weapon used to strike down Brother Bernárd was located quickly, they stood a chance of achieving an early resolution to the case, thereby placating both the Chief Constable and DCS Hollingsworth.

"There it is." He pointed as they turned the corner onto the path at right angles to the one where the body was found. He slowed down, allowing Drake to catch up with him a few yards from the shed. Even before they reached it however, they could clearly see that the door was firmly held shut by a large padlock.

Ross took hold of the padlock and found it locked, barring entry. "Damn," he cursed as frustration got the better of him.

"I suppose we'd better go and ask the Prior for the key." Drake stood beside him, almost breathless.

"I suppose you're right." He sighed. "The fact that a garden spade might have been used to batter the poor monk about the head, might lead us to suspect the two people who were actually working out here in the garden at the time—who then conveniently found the body and raised the alarm, don't you think?"

"Or is that just the way someone wants us to think?"

"Standing here staring at a locked padlock isn't going to answer any of our questions is it? Let's go see the Prior."

# Chapter 7

## A Solitary Man?

Detective Constable Sam Gable was growing increasingly frustrated. She'd been tasked with interviewing Sister Rebecca, who was proving exceedingly difficult to talk to. She had no problem accepting that they were working within the cloistered confines of a religious community, but something about the tall, middle-aged nun was irritating the hell out of the detective. Gable asked the same basic questions as the rest of the team, and hoped the others were meeting with greater cooperation than she was.

Sister Rebecca had what seemed an annoying habit to Gable of wanting to talk about nothing but religion, and God in particular. When Gable had innocently asked Rebecca how well she'd known the murdered monk, instead of providing a straight answer, the nun had replied, "Ah, the dear brother, called by our Lord before his time, you may think. But our Lord doesn't make mistakes, Detective Gable, and therefore we must assume that God himself had a plan for Brother Bernárd that required his presence in the company of our Lord and his angels."

"Yes, perhaps you're right, Sister," she responded casually, "but how well did you know him on a personal level?"

"The Lord calls us to do his bidding and we must follow the path he lays out. Brother Bernárd, though no longer with us, is, undoubtedly continuing God's work as he walks the paths of Heaven above."

"Sister Rebecca, did you know Brother Bernárd *personally*?" Gable was becoming exasperated.

"As two souls passing on their way through life, we communicated on matters pertaining to the Lord and his Word as written in the Holy Scriptures. If that constitutes knowing someone, then you may infer that, yes, I did know the dear brother."

Gable felt as if she were banging her head against a brick wall. If it was going to take this long to elicit a reply to a simple question, she'd be here all day.

\* \* \*

Sofie Meyer was having better luck. When it was mentioned that Sister Letitia was of German origin, it was natural for the team's German officer to handle her interview. If nothing else, it would ensure there were no language difficulties between them. They could converse in either English or German, whatever they preferred; they might like to revert to their native tongue, as they spent most of their time presently speaking English. As it turned out, they stuck to English. The nun, who told Meyer she was twenty-eight, was pleasantly surprised to find a fellow countrywoman serving with the British police. Sofie spent the first five minutes of the interview explaining the logistics of her loan attachment to the Merseyside Police Force, which Letitia found fascinating.

"So, we're similar, are we not?" she asked. "I am, I hope, here at the Priory of St. Emma for two more years, having spent almost three years here already, which have passed pleasantly until now … after which I shall return to my convent in the Danube Valley."

"That sounds a very pretty location," Meyer said, making small talk to help put the nun at ease.

"It is very close to a lovely small stream that runs through the pretty valley. The location is sheltered and makes for a most pleasant climate."

Meyer moved to the matter at hand. "What can you tell me about Brother Bernárd?"

"Very little, I'm afraid," Letitia replied quietly.

"When I arrived, someone mentioned we had a monk here from Switzerland. I tried to seek him out and perhaps find out if he was Swiss German perhaps, that maybe we had something in common as foreigners in a strange land, but ... "

"But what, Sister?" Meyer prodded gently as Letitia appeared unsure what to say next.

"Brother Bernárd was what I would describe as a very anti-social person. He didn't really engage in any meaningful conversations with anyone, Solitary is the word I would use to describe him."

"But, Sister," Meyer pointed out, "Is that not the way of many who choose the monastic life?"

"Of course," Letitia agreed. "And yet, even those who choose the life of a monk or a nun, and spend most of their lives in solitude and prayer, are able to integrate themselves into the life of the community in which they live. We all have our daily tasks here at the priory, and during them we often find ourselves interacting with our colleagues, or even at times with the public, who are free to attend the services at our church or just to visit the priory and spend time in quiet contemplation. Brother Bernárd, placed in charge of our library, was able to immerse himself in his studies and would spend many hours closeted away, out of contact with the rest of us, except for times of services and collective prayer. He would speak a few words after services perhaps, and then return to his cell or to the library."

"What about mealtimes?" Meyer inquired.

"You must understand," the nun responded, "that I am not in the habit, excuse the pun, of people-watching as I sit down to eat. Plus, we nuns sit together, while the monks sit on two separate tables as a rule. You would be better asking that question to the other monks rather than me or the other nuns. But to ensure you receive an answer to your question, no I didn't speak to Brother Bernárd at mealtimes. You might think we could have occasionally swapped pleasantries as we entered or exited the refectory, but I honestly can't remember that happening. I did have cause to speak with him on a couple of occasions, in the library, I remember. I asked where it was possible to find certain books that might be of use to me in my own studies. He was helpful, I must admit, though he kept words to a minimum, almost as though he didn't enjoy talking."

"Do you know anything about his background, before he came to St. Emma's?" Meyer asked but, again, Sister Felicia answered in the negative. Meyer expected little else, based on the nun's previous replies.

Sofie Meyer and Sam Gable, having completed fruitless interviews of Sisters Rebecca and Felicia, met up outside the refectory, where it had been arranged for them to eat lunch with the rest of the team and the monks and nuns of the priory. With Sister Ariadne having been interviewed by Izzie Drake, and Sister Paulette having given her statement after the discovery of the body, it left Sister Sarah as the only nun still to be interviewed. Gable agreed to handle that interview after lunch.

* * *

An hour earlier, Detective Constable Derek McLennan had been rather enjoying his interview with the elderly white-haired Brother Geoffrey, who was the eldest inhabitant of the priory, though his brain was no less sharp and active despite his 75 years. He had moved to St. Emma to be nearer to his only surviving relative, a brother who lived in Bootle and who was infirm and suffering from a whole raft of infirmities. Geoffrey had left his previous place at a monastery near Bude in Cornwall to be close to his sibling, in case his help might be needed in caring for the octogenarian. However, when asked about Brother Bernárd, he was less than charitable in his words relating to the dead monk.

"He was definitely not my favourite person on the planet, though that sounds rather unkind and uncharitable, doesn't it, Derek?" Brother Geoffrey had started using McLennan's Christian name within minutes of meeting the detective. McLennan was quite comfortable with this, in deference to the monk's age and life experience.

"Not at all, Brother Geoffrey. Just because you're a monk and a man of God, it surely doesn't necessarily follow that you have to like everyone you meet as you go through life. Surely, if God gave us the gift of free will, He also gave us the power to choose those we like and dislike."

The Brother smiled. "Wise words, young Derek. Have you ever considered joining the church?"

"You told me you came here seven years ago. You must have seen a few other monks come and go in that time. Are you telling me Bernárd was the only one you didn't like much?"

"To be totally truthful, young Derek, I didn't actively dislike our dear departed brother; it was more a case of not really *knowing* him, I suppose. Until he arrived, I was in charge of the library, but my eyesight has been failing for years, and even with these," he tapped the spectacles he was wearing, "I still struggled to see some things clearly, not very helpful when cataloguing or categorising books or papers of antiquity, you follow?"

"So far, yes, but there's more, isn't there?"

"Hmm, perceptive too. I shall have to watch you, young Derek." Brother Geoffrey laughed wickedly. "But yes, of course, there's more. When Bernárd arrived, Brother Gerontius informed me that he would be taking over the role of librarian, purely due to my sight difficulties. I accepted this of course, and it became my responsibility to explain how our library system worked. Well, what a palaver!" He paused for effect.

"Come on, out with it." Derek grinned, having forged a firm, quick friendship with the old monk.

"Well, young Derek, the man just didn't want to know anything. He told me in that guttural and annoying accent of his that he'd find out what he needed to know all by himself and would be effecting his own system of categorising and cataloguing our library, which to be honest, is not very large or particularly impressive. Far be it from me to tell him how to do what was now, after all, his job, I merely showed him where everything was and left him to get on with it. Was he devout? Probably. Was he a good librarian? Not as far as I was concerned. Did he mess up my system after he took over? Most definitely. Did he deserve to die for the crime of messing up the library? Not at all. Do I know who might have wished him harm? No. Anything else I can tell you, young Derek?" Smiling enigmatically, he leaned back in his chair and crossed his arms under the pouch of his habit, hiding them from view.

McLennan couldn't help smiling himself. "I think you've told me all you can for the moment, thank you. You *will* tell me if you think of anything that might help us, won't you?" He handed over one of his cards, which Brother Geoffrey took before he returned his hand under his habit.

"But of course. Now, I believe it must be nearly time for lunch. I've heard a strong rumour that we're having steak and kidney pie today, my favourite. Are you staying for lunch?"

"Yes, we are, so I hear."

"Splendid." Brother Geoffrey rose and, taking McLennan by the arm, led him to the promised land of steak and kidney pie, mashed potatoes and fresh carrots from the priory's own kitchen garden.

\* \* \*

Having been brought up as a strict Catholic, now relapsed, DC Nick Dodds couldn't help feeling a little in awe of Brother Simon, who as far as Nick was concerned, stood only one place removed from God himself. He therefore treated the monk, who looked to be in his early thirties, with a deference born of his upbringing. There was, however, one question that he needed to ask, having been primed by Ross. After a few minutes of being told that Brother Simon was originally from the country town of Great Malvern in Worcestershire, and had been a monk since he was twenty-two, Dodds decided to slip in the question.

"Brother Simon, it may seem a very personal matter, but please, can you tell me how you received that fierce looking scar on your face? It must have been a painful injury."

He smiled and nodded before replying. "I don't mind you asking at all, DC Dodds. It looks like a duelling scar, doesn't it?"

It was Dodds' turn to nod.

"Well, that's exactly what it is: a duelling scar!"

"You're kidding?" Dodds appeared surprised. "How …?"

"It's not what you think." The monk was still smiling as he spoke. "Believe it or not, long before I became Brother Simon, I was a movie stuntman, and I got this when a stunt went wrong."

Dodds gasped in amazement. "But I thought those things were all strictly choreographed for safety?"

"Ah, you're a knowledgeable man, Detective, and yes, you're quite right. But now and then the unexpected happens, and that's what happened in my case. I was a pirate in a sword fight with the film's hero and he had me backed up against the side of the ship. He was supposed to slash at me with his sword and as I leaned back, an automatic charge should have gone off, blowing out the side of the ship; I'd fall through the gap into the sea. The damn charge failed to go off and, instead of falling back and out of the way of his sword, I was left standing as his blade slashed down the side of my face. I was lucky it didn't go any deeper or it could have taken half my face off."

"Bloody hell—oops, sorry about that." Dodds apologised for his swearing, but Simon waved his apology away. "I hope you received a good compensation pay-out for negligence or something."

"I did as a matter of fact, and feeling lucky to have come out of it so lightly, I donated it to a children's charity and gave up film work. Not long afterwards I found my true calling, and within a couple of years, Simon Denbigh, stunt man extraordinaire became Brother Simon, the simple monk you see before you today."

"Thank you for telling me. Now, what can you tell me about Brother Bernárd? Where were you around the time of his death?"

"It's odd, you know? I don't think any of us ever got to know much about him. He kept very much to himself. I did try to talk to him one day, as we sat at our evening meal. I can recall the conversation very well." Brother Simon proceeded to retell it word for word.

"Welcome to St. Emma's. I'm Brother Simon. I'm told you are from Switzerland, is that right?"

"*Ja*, that is correct."

"I've visited Switzerland a few times in my younger days. What part of the country do you come from, Brother Bernárd? I may know it."

"I am from Lausanne."

Brother Simon advised Dodds that he'd been to Lausanne on a filming job, thinking it might give the two men common ground. "All he said was that he'd not been there for many years and simply turned to his meal, and never said another word, despite me trying to engage him in friendly conversation. I assumed he was reluctant to talk about his past or maybe he wasn't confident in his ability to converse in English. I did try to talk to him on other occasions, but just met with the same brick wall of silence. In the end, I gave up."

"Sounds like a pretty unsavoury character, if you ask me," Dodds stated.

"You have to realise that many people who enter a monastic existence don't feel the same need for day-to-day human interaction as people such as yourself and the majority of the population. We are on the whole solitary individuals who are happy to spend our lives in communion with God. Most of us do, however, maintain regular contact with our fellow human beings, just that we don't necessarily require it on a regular basis as you or your fellow detectives do, for example. I will say, however, that there was one thing about Brother Bernárd that bugged me a little."

"And what was that?"

"You probably know that Switzerland is made of various cantons, and the people of the country can be either Swiss German, French or Italian, or Romansh, though the Romansh language is only spoken in the canton of Graubünden. Anyway, when Brother Bernárd said he was from Lausanne, I thought it a bit odd as Lausanne is located in the French-speaking area of Switzerland … though I suppose it's possible his parents moved there before he was born. It wasn't important I suppose, but at the time I just thought it was odd, as when I asked if he spoke French and he said he only spoke it a little."

"I see, I think." Dodds was a little confused. He hadn't come for a geography lesson such as he'd just received from Brother Simon, though later he would realise he'd missed an important point. "So, you were a little suspicious of his background?"

"Not necessarily. I just thought it was a little out of the ordinary."

"Okay, and when he was killed—again, where were you?"

"I've been told he died between 6.30 and 7.00 that evening. If that's true, then I was in the monks' dormitory on housekeeping chores. We take turns to keep the place habitable, and this week is my turn. I started at around, oh, about 5.30, and I vacuumed, dusted, cleaned the windows and so on … and also took dirty washing out of the washing basket, and put it in the washing machine in the utility room. We have a washing machine, a tumble dryer, spin dryer for things that can't go into the tumble dryer, and an indoor drying area with retractable clothes lines to hang the washing on if the weather is unsuitable for outdoor drying. All mod cons here Detective." He smiled cheerfully. "I bet you thought we did everything the old-fashioned way, by hand, eh?"

"Well, no, though I hadn't even thought of things like that," Dodds replied with a shrug. "So when did you finish cleaning in the dormitory?"

"I think it was around about 6.30 when I left the dormitory and made my way to the utility room with the dirty washing. That's where I was when I heard the screams, which must have been those of Sister Paulette." He considered it. "I'd just started the washing machine and it took me a minute to work out what was going on outside. By the time I found myself heading for the kitchen garden, everyone else had gathered close by, and Brother Gerontius had taken charge. So, you see, I don't have what you'd call a cast-iron alibi, though I assure you I didn't kill Brother Bernárd, for all that's worth."

Dodds regarded Brother Simon's statement as being pretty much irrelevant. He left the monk and went to find his way to the refectory where Dodds and the rest of the investigators would meet up with DI Ross and the team for lunch, the time for which was fast approaching.

"We don't seem to have made much headway do we, people?" Ross asked as the team gathered around him outside the refectory.

"From what we've heard ourselves, and from what everyone appears to be telling us, it sounds like: a) we're dealing with the most boring group of potential suspects imaginable, and, b) Brother Bernárd sounds as if he wasn't very sociable or well-liked by his fellow monks," advised Drake after they'd heard the reports from those who'd so far spoken to monks and nuns.

* * *

Once the lunch break was over, they still had Brother Antonio to speak to. He'd been assigned to DC Curtis and Sister Sarah had been earmarked for interview by Sam Gable, her second interview of the day. Brother Antonio had been left until the afternoon as he was attending a hospital appointment that morning.

"One thing is coming across to me though," Ross said thoughtfully. "Our victim seems to have been reluctant to talk about his home country. Brother Simon and Sister Letitia, a German speaker, both sound as if they had reservations about the man."

DC Curtis, who together with DC Devenish had spent the morning speaking with the priory's nearest neighbours, spoke up. "You know, Boss, I haven't been here while you've all been talking to everyone, but all the things you've summarised regarding the interviews makes me think of one thing."

"And what might that be, Tony?"

"Well, I've read stories and seen movies in the past."

Nick Dodds groaned; everyone knew Curtis's taste in movies.

"Shut up, Nick. I'm serious."

"Sorry mate, go on," Dodds apologised, realising his friend was serious.

Nodding curtly, Curtis continued. "Right, so as I was saying before I was so rudely interrupted, I've seen films and read books with storylines about blokes running away from bad things in their pasts … and hiding in *plain sight* in a monastery."

"That's not such a wild theory," Derek McLennan agreed with Curtis. "I've heard of such things, too."

"Well," Ross said, pleased that his team was trying to make sense of what had occurred at the priory, "Brother Gerontius is making contact with Brother Bernárd's next of kin, so we'll maybe know more about him in a little while. For now, let's go eat! I'm bloody starving."

Sure enough, the steak and kidney pie mentioned by Brother Geoffrey earlier, and prepared by Sister Sarah, assisted by Sister Rebeca, was superb, served with creamy buttered mashed potatoes and fresh carrots and garden peas, all grown in the kitchen garden. It was so good that, when given the opportunity, both Curtis and Dodds gratefully accepted second helpings.

The detectives were then surprised when the two sisters summoned everyone for dessert, another home-made production of apple crumble served with piping hot custard. Sister Sarah informed them that St. Emma's had its own small orchard behind the church, some distance from the kitchen garden.

"This is *so* tasty," Drake said enthusiastically, and her compliment was echoed by Sam Gable and Sofie Meyer.

Curtis and Dodds, already replete with their double helpings of steak and kidney pie, struggled with the dessert, but manfully struggled through it. Finally, they leaned back in their chairs and rubbing their tummies after finishing their rather heavy lunchtime meal.

"Right everyone, let's get back to work." Ross decided they needed to push forward with their investigation. "Tony and Sam, you'd better get on with your interviews. Izzie, you come with me and we'll see what Brother Gerontius is up to. Ginger, bring the others up to date with anything you've heard on your travels. While you're at it, give

Paul Ferris a call and find out if he's learned anything more about St. Emma's that might be of help to the investigation."

"Right sir, will do," Devenish replied, after which Ross brought everyone up to date on what Sergeant Ferris had unearthed relating to the rumours of some kind of treasure or at least, buried items of high value, somewhere in or under the grounds of the priory.

"Does this mean we're involved in a treasure hunt as well as a murder inquiry?" Curtis asked, with his usual mischievous grin plastered all over his face.

"My God, sir, if Tony ever grows up we'll all have to spend a month in counselling to get over the shock," Sam Gable joked.

"You could be right, Sam." Ross smiled genially. "Anyway, Tony, to answer your question: no, we are not involved in a treasure hunt. But if such a treasure does exist, it may have provided someone with a motive for murder, *if* we assume that Brother Bernárd had some knowledge of it. Shutting him up might have been the killer's only way to keep the secret known only to his or herself."

"You think the murderer could be a woman, sir?" Devenish asked.

"I'm ruling nothing out at present, Ginger. As things stand, we have a fairly limited suspect pool and we're going to have to dig deep into the personal history of every monk and nun to find out if they might have a previous connection with the murdered man. It's not going to be easy, as the order doesn't appear to be too accurate in its keeping of records concerning its members previous lives before they joined, either as monks or nuns."

"Sounds like we're going to be doing some very deep fishing into the individuals at the priory," Dodds commented quietly, appearing serious for once.

"That's right, Nick. We are, and I only hope the Prior and the Prioress will cooperate fully to enable us to do so."

* * *

"Oh, I'm so glad you're here." Bother Gerontius smiled as Ross and Drake entered his small office a little while later, having seen the rest of the team set off on their own assignments.

The smile on the Prior's face did little to hide the worried look that sat behind it. Ross noticed an open file lying on the Prior's desk, which he correctly assumed was Brother Bernárd's personal file. He was aware that Bother Gerontius had planned to notify the monk's family of his death that morning, while he and his team were busy conducting their interviews with the inhabitants of the priory.

"You look troubled, Brother," Ross said as he and Drake sat down, having been ushered to two chairs placed opposite the Prior's desk by a wave of the hand.

"I am, Inspector Ross. Deeply troubled, to tell you the truth."

"Tell me how we can help," Ross spoke sincerely, seeing the perplexed, worried look on the monk's face.

"Well, as you know, I'd planned to notify Brother Bernárd's family of his tragic death. I set about doing just that after breakfast. As you can see, I have his personal file here." He gestured and eyed the file for a few seconds. "I was about to call the telephone number listed for his parents in Switzerland, when something struck me as odd."

Ross and Drake looked at each other, their interest piqued. The pair waited patiently for the Prior to continue.

"Please tell me I'm not going mad, but look closely at the photograph contained in Bernárd's file. Then look at the one in his passport, which we have here for safe keeping."

Gerontius passed both to Ross, who scanned them with a professional eye before passing them to Drake, who did the same and then passed them back to Ross.

"What do you think, Izzie?" Ross looked for confirmation of what he thought he'd seen.

"At a glance, they look the same, but when you look more closely, the photos appear to be of two *different* people."

Before Ross could say anything, the Prior said, "I thought so, too. I wasn't sure whether to believe my eyes, but that's exactly what I thought. The man in the passport photo is definitely *not* the man in the personal file."

"Which of these is most recent?" Ross asked.

"The passport," Brother Gerontius replied. "The photo in the personal file was updated the year before he came to us. There are older ones in the back of the file from when Brother Bernárd joined the order and others every few years. I've looked at them and you can notice a difference between them and the passport photo."

"We have a real mystery on our hands." Rubbing his forehead, Ross appeared thoughtful. "Brother Bernárd has been here for three years you say. Yet we have photographs that show the man who arrived on that passport—while looking very much like him—isn't the real Brother. That leads to more questions. First, why would someone want to take the place of a monk at a small Liverpool priory and second, having decided to do so, what happened to the *real* Brother Bernárd? I think there's little doubt what the second answer is." He drew a deep breath and nodded. "What Doctor Nugent said is beginning to make sense. I hadn't thought about it much until now."

"Can I ask what you're referring to?" the Prior asked, curious.

"Our Medical Examiner found evidence that the victim had undergone facial surgery at some time. I'd bet anything you like, that the man who died looked similar to Brother Bernárd, had surgery to make him appear identical. He then disposed of the real Bernárd and took his place before moving to England; hence, the passport photo."

"This is insane," the Prior exclaimed, stunned. "You're saying that the real Brother Bernárd was killed, presumably murdered, and the man we knew as Bernárd was surgically altered to look identical to him ... and then took his place, came here, and lived a peaceful life as a monk, and was then also murdered?"

"That's exactly what I'm saying," Ross declared. "It's the only thing that makes sense. Or, the real Brother arrived here, and at some time soon afterwards, he was killed and the impostor took his place."

"But you only saw him in death. Yet you were able to see the difference between the real Bernárd and the impostor. So whoever did the surgery, didn't exactly do a perfect job, did they?"

"No, but they didn't need to, did they? Under normal circumstances, who'd suspect your Brother Bernárd of being an impostor?"

"Nobody of course, because there'd be no reason to think such a thing had taken place."

"Exactly," Drake stated, entering the conversation. "What it means is that whoever the impostor was, he'd had to have a vital reason for changing his identity—someone with a serious criminal record, perhaps a major criminal who felt he was close to being caught and locked away for a long time."

"Or a high-profile fugitive. Maybe a murderer or someone who'd double-crossed an organised crime syndicate, and who needed to bury himself in a place he'd never be suspected, like a monastery," Ross added solemnly, agreeing with Nick Dodds's point.

"What will you do, Inspector Ross?" the Prior asked, eyeing him closely.

"I'm going to need that file," he replied, "and we're going to have to make contact with your diocesan authorities. By the way, where was Brother Bernárd before he came to St. Emma's?"

"Yes, of course, whatever you need. The real Brother Bernárd was sent here from a small monastery in Austria. He was interested in researching the history of the Benedictines in England. We needed a new librarian at the time and he was thought to be ideal for us. I can assure you we'll do whatever is needed to solve this terrible crime. Now, is there anything else I can do for you right now?"

"Just one thing," Ross replied.

The Prior appeared bemused. "Of course, just name it."

"Can we borrow the key to the tool shed padlock?"

# Chapter 8

### 'In Österreich'

"This case is looking a lot more complicated than we first envisaged," Detective Chief Superintendent Sarah Hollingsworth said as Ross stood before her desk, having just given her a briefing on what they'd discovered so far. As promised, she'd patiently waited for his initial report and was now quite horrified at the potential implications presented by his findings on the first day of the investigation.

"It is, Ma'am," Ross agreed. "We're going to have to cast our net much further afield than we first expected."

"Do you feel you have sufficient resources at your disposal to carry out an efficient and thorough investigation?"

"As you know, we've been drawn into a number of cases with international connections in the past, Ma'am. I see no reason why this one should be any different."

"I know that, DI Ross, and I'm proud of what you and your team have accomplished in recent years, but my worry is that in cases such as this, you may need *more* pairs of hands than you currently have at your disposal." She scanned his stoic face. "In fact, even before this case came along, I'd had a conversation about this very subject during my last meeting with the Chief Constable. He actually agreed with my suggestion to increase the number of personnel in the Specialist Murder Investigation Team by two additional detectives. The relevant paperwork is already sitting on DCI Agostinis's desk; he should find it a pleasant surprise upon his return from holiday."

Ross was flabbergasted. While other police forces around the country were shedding personnel—even in Merseyside numbers had dwindled in recent years—here was the Chief Constable authorising additional people for his team, without the persuasion of lengthy discussions and arguments.

"I see, Ma'am. Thank you. I'm not sure what else to say. It will definitely help. There are times when my people have had to work eighteen-hour days on some cases; additional personnel would have allowed them adequate rest periods, which would have increased their sharpness at crucial moments."

"Precisely. Now, about this priory murder, what are your immediate plans?"

Ross thought about the question for a few seconds, wanting to give the Chief Super a viable plan for tackling the next stage of the investigation.

"We need to speak to the Bishop, or his assistant, at the Diocesan office. I believe that's the best place to initiate inquiries into the background of Brother Bernárd. Hopefully, they can tell us who we need to contact at his old monastery in Austria for further information. Someone over there had to have targeted him somehow."

"Explain that, please."

"Look, Ma'am, somebody obviously wanted to get out of Austria fast. It had to have been a criminal, or someone with a past that was about to catch up with him. But then, why this particular monk?" he asked, looking grave. "He, or someone connected with him, must have met Brother Bernárd and noticed a resemblance to our man. The imposter thought it possible to take over his identity and escape whoever was after him. When they heard the real Bernárd was scheduled to be transferred to St. Emma's in England, it undoubtedly sounded perfect for their purposes. I'm speaking in plural terms because there's no way one man could have organised all this, I'm sure. There has to be methodical organisation behind it."

"A conspiracy of evil, in other words," the chief superintendent defined Ross's theory with a grim smile.

"Nicely put, Ma'am. Anyway, my people are concluding the interviews at the priory as we speak, and others are canvassing local residents, but I don't expect that to produce anything helpful."

"Sounds as if you have things in hand. Not bad for the first few hours of the investigation. Well done, Ross. If you need anything else, be sure to let me know. It won't be long before DCI Agostini will be back and you won't have me on your back so much."

"Right, Ma'am. Yes, it will be good to have him back, not that there's a problem working with you directly, of course," Ross felt like he was grovelling a little.

"Bugger off, Ross. You know perfectly well what I mean. You'd be happy if you never saw me from one month to the next."

"Oh, you're not that bad," Ross smiled disarmingly.

"Oh, really? That's kind of you to say so, Detective Inspector Ross. Now go and catch this bastard and make me look good for the press conference." Hollingsworth smiled cordially.

His impassive expression suggested he wasn't sure how to reply to her last comment.

She decided to put him out of his misery.

"I'm joking, pulling your leg, you plonker. I do have a sense of humour you know. Contrary to popular belief, Ross, it wasn't surgically amputated at birth."

He laughed at her last remark, realising that even the great Detective Chief Superintendent Sarah Hollingsworth was human, after all.

"I heard you found something in the priory's tool shed that might be of significance too."

He wondered just how the DCS gleaned all these pieces of information that he hadn't so far mentioned, but he was too polite to push for an explanation.

"That's right. We found a garden spade that might well be the instrument used to incapacitate our victim before he was injected with a lethal dose of poison. I'm sorry, I know we usually refer to victims by name, but I'm finding it increasingly difficult to think of the man at the Priory as Brother Bernárd ... now that we're almost sure he's an impostor."

"I can understand that, and appreciate how you feel," Hollingsworth replied with a curt nod.

"Thanks, Ma'am. We sent the spade to Doctor Nugent and we're waiting for him to get back to us with the results of his examination."

"Wouldn't it have been easier to send it to Miles Booker's people?"

"Possibly, but I know Doctor Nugent was ready and waiting to carry out any tests for us at a moment's notice. He's very sensitive to the fact that the Chief Constable is watching the case closely."

"Of course," said Hollingsworth. "The good doctor and the Chief Constable are occasional golfing buddies I believe," providing Ross with a piece of hitherto unknown information about the pathologist's private life. Now he thought about it, he realised that despite all the years they'd worked in tandem on various murder inquiries, he actually knew very little about the life of William Nugent outside the confines of the sterile and antiseptic world of the mortuary.

"Will you be talking to the Austrian police soon?"

"We'll have to, if we're to find out who's lying on the slab in the mortuary. I'm arranging to have the fake Brother Bernárd's fingerprints taken today and then I'll be speaking with the police over there. The monastery where the real Bernárd lived at was near the town of Feldkirch, near the Swiss border, so maybe that links up in some way with the impostor claiming to be from Switzerland."

"Have we had any contact with the Austrian police in recent times?"

"Not to my knowledge, Ma'am. I had Sergeant Ferris look up the local force over there and he said things should be simple enough. Apparently, the Austrians had about six different forces in operation until last year, when in July of 2005 they amalgamated them all into a single Federal Police Force, the *Bundespolizei*. Ferris has got the name of the local *Oberstleutnant*—that's their equivalent of a Superintendent— and has sent an email, explaining our case and the need to liaise with them. Hopefully, we'll get a response from them today and we can move things forward."

"It sounds as if you have everything in hand, D.I. Ross. Is there anything else you need to help at this stage?"

"No, Ma'am. I don't think so, but if I think of anything …"

"Don't hesitate. Call me, okay?"

"Okay, and thank you Ma'am."

Hollingsworth rose and came round to the front of her desk, holding out a hand, which Ross accepted. He'd never shaken hands with the Chief Superintendent before and he was surprised at how firm her handshake was. Despite being no more than five-foot-five and of small build, Sarah Hollingsworth was definitely no weakling, he decided.

"Oh, one last thing, Ross," she said as he made to take his leave.

"Yes, Ma'am?"

"As long as I'm in direct control of the team until DCI Agostini returns, please cut out the 'ma'am' okay. Boss or Guv is quite sufficient. You make me sound like the bloody queen or something. I've been fully expecting you to curtsy."

She smiled, and for a couple of seconds, Andy Ross felt he was seeing the woman behind the rank for the first time.

"And we must think about cover for DS Drake when she goes on maternity leave, too."

"Got it," he smiled back at her. "*Boss*, I've had some thoughts about cover for Izzie when she's away, by the way."

"We'll talk more about that and those new additions to the team when Oscar Agostini returns. Now, you'd better go and get the team moving on this rather strange case."

"Sure thing." He smiled and nodded. "Boss."

\* \* \*

"She told you to call her what?" Drake was incredulous when Ross told her what Hollingsworth had said to him.

"It's true, Izzie. As long as she's standing in for Oscar, we're to refer to her as 'Guv' or 'Boss'.

"Bloody hell. And which term of endearment did you decide on, DI Ross, *sir*?"

"Boss," he replied. 'Guv' wouldn't have sounded right when applied to the Chief Super. "Anyway, what do you think about the extra personnel we've been promised?"

"Great. It's about time we were afforded extra manpower. Maybe, in future, we won't have to rely on calling in extra help from the uniform division quite so often."

"We'll be talking about it when Oscar's back. Meanwhile, let's see if Paul's come up with anything yet."

The pair left Ross's office and headed over to where Sergeant Paul Ferris and Admin Assistant Kat Bellamy were busily working on their computer terminals.

"Hey, Paul, anything back from Austria yet?" Ross asked the team's resident computer specialist.

"Good timing, Boss," Ferris replied cheerily. "Just had a reply from the *Bundespolizei* in Feldkirch!"

"And?"

"See for yourself." Ferris rose from his seat so Ross might sit and read the email on the screen.

To save time, he read it aloud so Drake could hear it first-hand.

"From *Kontrollinspektor*—Divisional Inspector—Klaus Richter. Dear Sergeant Ferris, I am pleased to contact you on the orders of *Oberstleutnant* Wilhelm Gruber, in connection with your inquiry relating to your case in connection with the death of a man in Liverpool who you believe to have been impersonating a Brother Bernárd, formerly of the Benadictine Monastery of St. Thomas, near Feldkirch. Because I speak and write in passable English, I have been selected to assist you in this matter. If you or your superior wish to speak directly with me, I can be contacted on the telephone number below. I assure you of our best assistance in this matter.

Klaus Richter,

*Kontrollinspektor*,

*Bundepolizei,*
Feldkirch Division.
0043 5522 6789."

"He sounds rather helpful," Drake said casually.

"He does indeed," Ross agreed. "Let's hope the Austrian connection can be more productive than our interviews at St. Emma's."

The final interviews at the priory had proved as fruitless at those that had gone before. Sam Gable had spoken to Sister Sarah who, like the other residents of St. Emma's could tell her little about their Brother Bernárd. Like the others, she'd had little contact with the monk and had described him as being rather unsociable, a common description of the man, and very reluctant to engage in conversation; this she, quite charitably, assumed might be because of his lack of skill with the English language. Her alibi at the time of his death: she was in the infirmary, completing a stock-take of medical supplies, as she was a trained nurse and in daily charge of the infirmary. A doctor would only be called, if required, for more serious matters, she advised Gable.

D.C. Tony Curtis had completed the interviews of the monks by talking with Brother Antonio, who was, as his name implied, of Italian descent. He was born in England, though, in the northern industrial town of Doncaster. His parents ran a restaurant in the town centre, but Antonio had never felt the need, or any ambition, to follow in his father's footsteps. He did however, speak fluent Italian and surprised Curtis by informing him that he'd once engaged in a conversation with the dead man in Italian. In the library, they'd discussed the merits of a particular religious tome, written in 18$^{th}$-century Brindisi by an Italian monk.

Thankfully, Brother Antonio go into the didn't boring details of what the book was about, but he did state he'd spent almost an hour in discussion with the dead monk—who he felt didn't possess a particularly great grasp of the book's subject matter. He told Curtis he felt the monk had been using him to practice his Italian rather than engage in a serious book discussion. As Brother Antonio had said, "It was as if he was bluffing his way through the conversation and afterwards. I felt as if I was the one doing most of the talking, and that Brother Bernárd was using me to test his linguistic skills."

None of this helped with the investigation, so Ross had thought at the time. Up to now, the more they tried to delve into Brother Bernárd's life, the more brick walls and blind alleys they found themselves running into.

His first phone conversation with *Kontrolinspektor* Klaus Richter was short but amiable.

"I am pleased to speak with you, Inspector Ross. I wish to do all I can to assist you in this case."

"Thank you. Please, let's not be too formal. Call me Andy. It's shorter and less time consuming than Inspector Ross."

He sensed a smile on the Austrian's face as he replied,

"And you must call me Klaus. Now, please tell me what I can do to assist you."

Ross spent the following ten minutes outlining the case, who was busily taking notes as he listened to the report of the facts so far known.

When Ross finally fell silent, Richter spoke, sounding decisive and enthusiastic.

"It is indeed a strange case, as you say. Obviously, between us, we must first try to find out what has happened to the real Brother Bernárd. Then, we must try and discover who the impostor was. There is little I can do to help you with the murder in your city, but perhaps it will help your investigation if we can find out who your victim actually was."

"You've got it in a nutshell, Klaus." Ross was impressed with the Austrian's quick grasp of the case.

Richter went on.

"First of all, I will go to the monastery. It does not matter what time I go there. The brothers are not exactly going to be going anywhere, are they?" He laughed softly. "They will probably be busy making wine."

"Wine?"

"Yes, Andy. The Monks at St. Thomas's are famed for their wine-making prowess."

"Sounds like a useful side-line for them," Ross commented.

"Indeed yes. They sell their wines in many markets and are quite well known, which may be what drew your impostor to them in the first place maybe?"

"I admit I really don't know. Anything you can discover for us will be greatly appreciated."

"I am assuming you are thinking the impostor may have been a fugitive, either from justice, or from some criminal organisation, yes?"

"That's exactly what I'm thinking, yes," Ross replied solemnly. "But, what's really bugging me is the coincidence of him finding an almost perfect lookalike in a monastery in Austria."

"Perhaps he had help? Maybe whatever organisation he worked for has a network set up to assist their people in finding new identities and evading capture by the authorities. It is something I have heard of in connection with fleeing Nazis at the end of World War Two."

"Good point," Ross concurred. "Something like in the movie *The Odessa File*, but this man was too young to have been involved in the war."

"But maybe he was involved in something, some conflict, of more modern times."

The Austrian detective was kicking ideas around already, impressing Ross, who knew this man wasn't one who'd just go through the motions, but would do all he could to help with the case.

"But we must not indulge in conjecture, right, my friend? I must first go to the monastery and speak to the Abbot, and learn what I can about the real Brother Bernárd, yes? Then I will report my findings to you."

Impressed with the level of cooperation and professionalism displayed by the Austrian policeman, Ross agreed to wait for more information. He knew he had no other options if he was to move his case forward. He hated the inactivity of waiting and before he knew it, he was tapping his fingers on his desk, frustration casting him into a dark mood for the rest of the day.

# Chapter 9

### Agostini's Return

"Can't a man go away for a few days without returning to a bloody complicated mess like this?" Detective Chief Inspector Oscar Agostini was grinning as he spoke.

Ross had just provided a briefing on matters relating to the squad on Agostini's first day back at work. Together with Izzie Drake, Ross sat in Agostini's office, admiring his old friend's tan. The pair had worked together in their early careers, when they'd formed a formidable detective partnership. Agostini had taken over the day-to-day overall control of the squad when Ross had turned down a promotion in order to remain at the sharp end of operational matters. He refused to take a job that would see him stuck behind a desk for the majority of his working days.

"Well, we had to have something lined up for when you came back," Ross joked with his old friend. "With you being a Catholic and all that, I can't think of anything more appropriate than a murder in a monastery." Ross grinned.

"It's a priory, not a monastery, remember?" Drake butted in.

"I know, I know, but monastery sounds better." Ross was thoroughly enjoying himself.

"Andy, for fuck's sake, do you know the last time I was in a Roman Catholic church?"

"Knowing you, probably your wedding day," Ross quipped.

"Not far off," said Agostini. "You should know I'm about as religious as a house fly. Now come on, man, tell me about this case and where we stand on the investigation."

Ross and Drake jointly spent the next ten minutes bringing Agostini up to date with the case, including the most recent developments of the contact with the Austrian *Bundespolizei*.

"Sounds like we have a real mystery on our hands," Agostini affirmed after sitting silently and listening intently to the ghastly goings-on at St. Emma's. "Without a doubt, we need to know what happened to the real Brother Bernárd, so we can only hope your new friend, Klaus Richter, gets back to you soon. Then we need to discover the motive behind the impersonation. Whatever it was, it had to be aimed at getting the victim out of Austria, but whoever organised it didn't cover their tracks enough because someone got to the guy, didn't they?"

"You know, Oscar. You just gave me an idea. What if they've also infiltrated the priory? Maybe one of the monks or nuns is our killer and was sent there with the precise purpose of killing the fake Brother."

"A *second* impostor?" Drake looked horrified at the thought.

"Anything is possible," Agostini agreed with Ross. "From what you've told me, it definitely looks like an inside job—unless an unknown assailant sneaked onto the grounds of St. Emma's, killed the monk, and then crept out without anyone noticing a stranger wandering freely around the place."

"Extrapolating on that theory," Ross said, thinking aloud. "If the killer came from within and was there specifically to murder the impostor, whoever it is must have arrived at St. Emma's *after* the fake Brother Bernárd. If we concentrate on those who arrived at the priory since his arrival, it should reduce our suspect pool significantly."

"But wouldn't the killer want to get out of there as soon as possible?" Drake asked with a frown. "After all, they must know we'll soon work that bit out and then expect us to close in on them in no time."

Ross murmured agreement. "It all sounds a bit too easy. Maybe there's something else going on that we haven't seen yet."

"Like a gang of shadowy treasure hunters who come and go like ghosts in the night?" Agostini smiled as he brought up the theory of the mysterious treasure mentioned in Paul Ferris's detailed report on the priory's history as a monastery.

"As you said, anything's possible," said Ross with a wink.

Before sending Ross and Drake on their way, Agostini posed a question he was dying to ask. "Tell me how you got on with the DCS in charge while I was away in sunny Spain."

"Oh, fantastic, Oscar. Me and Sarah, we're bezzies now you know." Ross grinned. "Even told me to call her Guv."

"You're having me on, surely?"

"Nope, almost on first-name terms, we are," he replied nonchalantly, continuing to grin.

"Next thing you'll be telling me is she invited you to one of the black-mass Satanic rituals she regularly participates in," Agostini said with a totally straight face.

"What?" Ross looked shocked. "She's a bloody Satanist?"

"Ha-ha." Agostini burst into hearty laughter. "Got you there! Don't try and kid me, mate. First name terms with the dragon lady? Yeah, sure you were."

Ross joined in the laughter as Izzie Drake added her voice to the merriment.

"Okay, well, it wasn't quite like that, but she did prove she was human, much to my surprise, and she couldn't have given us more support if she'd tried."

"Good. I had visions of coming back to find you lying in a pool of blood, destroyed in a mad fit of anger by the Chief Super after she got fed up with your terrible sense of humour."

Oscar Agostini got on well with the Detective Chief Superintendent and knew she was well aware of her fearsome reputation among the rank and file, a reputation she did nothing to quell; she felt it gave extra oomph when communicating her orders and ensured her policies were strictly adhered to. In fact, Sarah Hollingsworth was a damn good, old-fashioned copper. She'd worked her way up the promotion ladder through sheer hard work and tenacity, during the days when women weren't universally accepted in positions of authority within the police force, not just on Merseyside, but generally throughout the UK. Thankfully, such sexist prejudices had gradually died out and women were now regarded with equal respect when it came to rising to positions of higher rank in the police. Sarah Hollingsworth had become an example of just how well women could do the job when promoted to higher rank within the command structure.

"Okay, joking aside, Andy, let's get on with the job. What do you know about Austria?"

"Not a lot Boss," Ross replied with a shrug. "A country in Europe, next door to Germany, once annexed by the Nazis during Hitler's days, a popular tourist destination for skiers … and the delights of Vienna, home of Johann Strauss and the world-famous Spanish Riding School."

"You got me there. How do you know all that?"

Ross grinned again. "I looked it up on *Wikipedia*."

"Genius," Agostini smiled back at him. "So your knowledge of Austria is on a par with mine, then. In other words, virtually non-existent."

"Afraid so," Ross agreed. "But, never fear, Paul Ferris is putting together as much information as he can glean about the place where the real Brother Bernárd was located and is liaising with Klaus Richter's people too, so both sides will be keeping each other updated."

"When do you expect to hear from Richter?"

"As soon as he knows something, I suppose."

"Okay, well, don't let me hold you up. Off you go, the pair of you, and keep me posted."

Ross and Drake returned to the squad room, where an aura of despondency seemed to hang heavily. Despite all their initial inquiries, the team of detectives, some of the best on the force, had been unable to unearth anything that might lead to the identity of the killer. Paul Ferris and Kat Bellamy were hard at work, delving into the past of St. Emma's and its predecessor, St. Basil's Monastery. More specifically, they were keen to try and unearth any information relating to the rumoured treasure mentioned in early to late Middle-Age manuscripts.

"Any progress, you two?" Drake asked as Ross made his way to his office, where he'd review what had been learned so far.

"Not really," a depressed-looking Paul Ferris admitted. "As far as we can determine, St. Emma's has had a totally unimpressive history from its first opening back in '92. Nothing has happened to attract attention. They've had a couple of mentions in the *Echo* and in the local Grassendale free ads paper, when they've held summer fêtes, but never for anything to do with treasure. I'd have thought that if there had been even a hint of some historical reference to a treasure of some sort even if it might just be some religious artefact, it would have found a place in the history or folklore of the old monastery. That being the case, it would have then been associated with the new priory when it was built on the site."

He stopped talking to draw breath and Drake smiled. He regarded her intently, as if waiting for her to say something in response to his rather long-winded explanation.

"Okay, Paul, I think I get the picture. What about the Church authorities? Do you think they might have any obscure records that someone may have found, that could have set some kind of search in progress?" She eyed him questioningly. "It would have to be something pretty important though, for it to be considered worthy of committing murder to get their hands on it."

"Oh, Izzie, I agree, but we haven't given up by a long chalk. I'll let Kat fill you in on that side of our inquiries," Ferris said and let Kat Bellamy take over.

The diminutive admin assistant took a moment to stretch her arms high above her head, easing the stiffness in her muscles from sitting at the terminal almost non-stop for the last hour and a half. She shook her head, her blond tresses swishing from side to side, and took a quick swig of spring water from a large bottle on the desk; then, she began.

"Paul was so kind to give me the task of contacting the Church authorities," Kat said sarcastically, but grinning at the same time. "Thanks." Playfully, she swiped Ferris across the back of the head with a sheet of paper, causing him to smile sheepishly.

"I didn't know it would be so difficult, did I?" He fell silent and allowed Kat to tell her tale.

"Anyway, the first thing I did was contact the Prior at St. Emma's, Brother Gerontius. He was okay and gave me the telephone numbers of the Bishop's office and Diocesan office, which administers the Priory on behalf of the Church, and is the custodian of the official records of all the Church properties in their Diocese. So far, so good. But, honestly, Izzie, trying to get anything out of that place was like trying to get blood from a stone. Anyone would think I was trying to get them to commit a breach of the Official Secrets Act, not simply tell me something about their history." She rolled her eyes and smiled fleetingly. "First of all, the Bishop's office was helpful enough and I even got to talk to the Bishop himself, Monseigneur Frederick. He sounded very jolly, and even though he wants to help us in any way he can to solve the murder of Brother Bernárd—or whoever he really is—he was totally in the dark when I asked him if he knew anything about a rumoured treasure being associated with the priory or the original monastery. So I forgot about him and contacted the Diocesan office, and that's when I seemed to hit a brick wall."

"That sounds strange, Kat. Why would they be so secretive about the history of the place?"

"That's what I thought. At first, the official historian, a priest, not a monk by the way, called Father Matthew O'Riordan, was helpful enough when we were talking about St. Emma's. He was very forthcoming about the history of the priory, which to be fair, hasn't been in existence very long, in the greater scale of things, only just over twenty years. As he told me, St Emma's hasn't really been around long enough to accumulate a detailed history. He did fill me in on how the priory came about. Nothing sinister there. It was simply Church land that was lying deserted without any useful purpose, so a decision was taken to bring the old site back to life by allowing it to be used as something akin to its original purpose. So, again, nothing underhanded or sinister there. Then I got to the bit where I wanted to know about the detailed history of the old monastery, St. Basil's." She fell silent and pulled a face.

"Go on, Kat, what happened?" Drake urged.

"Up till that point he'd sounded quite open and chatty, but then he began to sound more like he was just reading from a prepared document, if you know what I mean."

Drake nodded her understanding.

"It was obvious they have a standard blurb when it comes to the history of St. Basil's. As he was taking to me, I pulled up the information about St. Basil's on the net and—surprise, surprise—it was virtually word for word what the priest was telling me. So, I had to come to one of two conclusions. One, everything that's known about the monastery is contained on that webpage and the little leaflets that they pass out at St. Emma's to visitors who might be interested in the site's history or, two, the Church authorities know much more than they make available to the public, and *don't* want us to know about it."

"Come on, Kat, really? What could be so important about St. Basil's monastery that the Roman Catholic Church would treat it like a great state secret?"

Smiling, both Kat Bellamy and Paul Ferris chorused together, "Treasure!"

# Chapter 10

*Kontrollinspektor* Klaus Richter, sitting opposite his superior officer, *Oberstleutnant* Wilhelm Gruber, wasn't sure where to begin. Having been given the responsibility of liaising with the police in Liverpool over the strange case of the murder of the fake Brother Bernárd, he'd begun to realise the case might be much more complex than at first thought. Richter was an experienced officer with over ten years on the force to his name, and he instinctively knew when a case held more intrigue than appeared at first sight.

The superintendent, to give him his equivalent rank in English, had asked Richter for an update on his return from St. Thomas 's Monastery, where the real Brother Bernárd had lived until his supposed departure for the UK. Taking a deep breath, the inspector said,

"As per your orders, sir, I paid a visit to the monastery and took *Gruppeninspektor* (Sergeant) Wägner with me. As you know, he's a good man and can think for himself, so I thought he might pick up on anything I might miss."

Gruber nodded and waved a fleshy hand, urging Richter to continue with his report.

"The Abbot, Brother Michael was surprised to see us, but made us very welcome. Of course, he had no idea what we were doing at his monastery, and expressed great shock on hearing what I had to relate to him. Let me say, sir, that Brother Michael instantly offered his unequivocal help in this matter. His priority, obviously, was Brother Bernárd. He instantly looked up their records and gave us the date when the Brother departed the monastery for his time in England. He also showed me a letter he'd received from Bernárd soon after his arrival at the Priory of St. Emma near Liverpool."

Gruber took the proffered folder from Richter and quickly read the contents. Sure enough, Brother Bernárd had—so it appeared—arrived safely in England. The letter he'd written to the Abbot was, according to Brother Michael, definitely in his own hand, as Bernárd had a very distinctive writing style; it also mentioned matters which only the real Bernárd had discussed with Brother Michael prior to leaving for England.

Richter went on when Gruber looked up.

"It's my supposition, therefore, that whoever wished harm on Brother Bernárd, must have followed him to England and murdered him there, after making sure he'd first confirmed his safe arrival at the Priory of St. Emma."

"What about his family?" Gruber asked. The superintendent was a sharp investigator; he'd never allow a simple avenue of investigation to lie unchecked.

"Yes, indeed, sir. I asked that question and Brother Michael informed me their records had shown that Brother Bernárd has one brother, Gustav, living in Lausanne, Switzerland. I asked if Gustav had ever tried to contact his brother whilst he was at St. Thomas's, and the Abbot told me that Brother Bernárd once confided in him that he and Gustav had fallen out many years ago ... when Gustav expressed his opposition to Bernárd's decision to become a monk."

"No parents?" Gruber probed further.

"No, sir. Both parents were killed in a road traffic accident when the boys were young. They'd been raised by their maternal grandparents, both now deceased also, and they had no other family."

"Very convenient for whoever wanted to steal Bernárd's identity," Gruber concluded. "All he had to do was learn as much as possible about the real Bernárd, follow him until he reached England, give him time to establish his bona fides with the English monks, then murder him and take his place. It wouldn't have been hard to do if the monk was a foreigner who wasn't particularly well known by the residents of the community in England."

"And, of course, he'd been surgically enhanced to look like the real monk, so once he replaced the original, the impostor simply needed to maintain a standoffish attitude towards his companion monks, not be very friendly for example, and he'd have had no problem fitting in. I say this because Sergeant Ferris has advised this is precisely how the man they thought of as Brother Bernárd behaved," Richter communicated, completing the theory for his boss.

Gruber leaned back in his chair, his thick arms folded across his chest for a few seconds, his usual position when thinking deeply. A couple of minutes later, the superintendent spoke.

"It would seem to me, Richter, as if our friends in England therefore have not one, but two murders to solve on their territory. For whatever reason, some organisation wanted the impostor to leave Austria … and possibly spent considerable time looking for a suitable person they could use in order to change their man's identity. They found him in the real Brother Bernárd and set in motion the actions that led to their man replacing the real Brother. Then, after their man had been accepted at the priory and had lived there for a few years, it's possible that someone found out about the deception and made a plan to dispose of the impostor, thus leaving our English colleagues with two separate murderers to find."

"My God, sir! That's a nightmare scenario because, unless the police in Liverpool can discover the imposter's real identity, finding out who killed him would be next to impossible."

"Those are my thoughts, also, Richter. Maybe you should call your contact, this Sergeant Ferris, and fill him in with what we've learned."

Richter nodded and made to leave Gruber's office, but the superintendent had one last instruction for his inspector; as Richter grabbed the door handle, Gruber said,

"Ask if they can send us their victim's fingerprints. If they thought they were simply dealing with the murder of a genuine monk, they might not have taken prints—and we may be too late, if they've already allowed the victim to be buried or cremated. It's still worth a try, because if the impostor has a record here, he'll surely show up on our database."

Richter had already thought of the fingerprints, but had said nothing, allowing Gruber to believe he'd thought of it first.

* * *

"Shit," Ross shouted with frustration after Paul Ferris gave him the latest update from Klaus Richter in Austria. "So now we have *two* murderers to find? I was hoping the identity switch had taken place in Austria and poor Brother Bernárd's body was disposed of before the impostor arrived here." He drew a deep breath and straightened. "We need to find out who that body is in the morgue, and fast." He turned to Meyer. "Sofie, give Fat Willie a call and see if he can get us a good set of prints from the body. The Austrians appear to be treating this case seriously, I'm pleased to say. Let's hope the victim's in their records."

"I'll get on to it right away," Meyer replied. "If we can identify our corpse, it would give us a starting point in working out why he needed to flee from Austria."

"It's becoming like a jigsaw puzzle," Izzie Drake observed. "In this case though, most of the pieces are missing and we have to find them one a time. Then, with luck, we can begin to piece it all together."

"Nothing's ever simple, is it?" Paul Ferris asked from his seat at his computer terminal.

"That's why we were set up, Paul," Ross answered. "But that doesn't mean we have to like it, I agree."

Turning to the rest of his team, who were all gathered, awaiting instructions on the next steps in their investigation, Ross called for the results of the house calls they'd made since the discovery of the body of the man who they'd continue to refer to as *Brother Bernárd* until his real identity could be revealed.

"Sir, Ginge and myself visited the nearest house to the priory. As you already know, Grassendale is a pretty upscale area, none of your regular modern detached homes here, thank you very much. Most of the houses in the area can only be described as villas or, in some cases, full-blown mansions."

"Okay, Samantha." Ross offered an impatient smile. "We don't need the full estate agent's report on the area. Just get on with it."

"Right sir, sorry. Just setting the scene a bit. Our first call was to a home called Lyon's Mount. Two bloody great concrete lions were mounted on two pillars that supported a pair of wrought-iron gates that must be at least ten feet high. The gates were locked and we had to request entry by means of an intercom positioned on a stone gatepost. While we waited for someone to answer our ringing of the buzzer, we could see the walls surrounding the property were the same height as the gates."

"Yeah, talk about bloody Fort Knox," DC Devenish added.

"It really was," Gable agreed with Ginger's comment. "When we finally got in and drove up to the house, along a winding driveway, a real grand affair it was too, it turned out that the house, if you can call it a house, is the home of Sir Richard and Lady Catharine Lyons."

"And he is?" Ross had never heard of the man.

"He was actually a very nice man," Sam replied. "Sir Richard Lyons is the owner of a rather large fleet of super tankers that carries oil over the world and was granted his knighthood for services to industry five years ago. He didn't tell us that himself, by the way. His wife told us. I doubt he'd have bothered if she hadn't said anything."

"Definitely not a boastful type," Devenish agreed.

"Exactly," Gable continued. "As you can imagine, the pair of them knew absolutely nothing about what had taken place at St. Emma's. Sir Richard was in London at the time of the murder and Lady Catharine was attending a fundraising event for a charity supported by Everton Football Club, a cause close to your heart, Boss."

Sam Gable was referring to the fact that Andy Ross was a lifetime supporter of Everton Football Club, often a cause of friendly banter between the Inspector and DC Derek McLennan who, in Ross's opinion, had been born with one serious character defect—that of being a supporter of Everton's fierce rivals, Liverpool F.C.

"Ah, well, she can't be all bad then," Ross grinned. "Tony, anything from you?

"Not much different to Sam and Ginge, Boss," he replied.

"The residents of Greenacres, which adjoins the priory on the other side in relation to the Lyons' home, are a Mr and Mrs Sean Cabot who were both at home at the time of the murder. Their property, like the Lyons' is separated from the priory ground by a high wall, one too high to see over. In any case, their grounds are on the far side of the priory in relation to where the murder took place. The Cabots are both in their seventies and were apparently watching golf on satellite TV at the time of the murder. Even if the murder had taken place in the next room, I doubt they'd have heard anything. The old dears are both as deaf as posts. I had to shout to make myself heard, and that was with them both turning their hearing aids up to full volume."

Curtis's words were followed by ripples of laughter from the others.

"Anyone got anything useful from talking to the well-heeled folks of Grassendale?" Ross knew what to expect, as Nick Dodds told a similar tale to the others after visiting the nearest property on the opposite side of the road to St. Emma's.

"Terry and Pauline Farrow live in a place called Tallow House, which apparently was named almost seventy years ago by the original owner, who happened to own a candle-making factory; hence the name, as was explained by Terry 'Call me Tel'. He's a retired market trader, believe it or not, who made a small fortune by running stalls all over the northwest for over thirty years. He bought Tallow House ten years ago and has never set foot in the priory, being as religious as a fart in a bakery, to use his own words. Honest, Boss, we're flogging a dead horse, expecting any help from the locals round there. They all keep themselves to themselves and I doubt they even know the names of their own neighbours, never mind what goes on behind the walls of the priory."

"Right, it's looking more and more as if our killer is someone who lives within the walls of the priory, and, unless the murder was of a personal nature, which I somehow doubt, I'm laying odds the killing was somehow connected to the impostor's past." He glanced around solemnly. "Someone in that place knows *exactly* who the impostor was and where he'd come from, and what he'd done to be marked for death. From now on, we concentrate our efforts into looking closely at every member of St. Emma's who arrived *after* Brother Bernárd. I think we have a cold-blooded assassin masquerading as a monk, or a nun, in that priory and we just need to unmask him or her. Considering we're supposed to be the best friggin' team of detectives this city can produce, that's surely not beyond our capabilities, now, is it?"

# Chapter 11

## INTERPOL

Paul Ferris and Kat Bellamy were tired. Together, the Detective
Sergeant and the team's admin assistant had been working for almost
twelve hours non-stop, ignoring warnings about spending too much
time staring at their computer screens.

The pair were still investigating the past history of St. Emma's
and its predecessor, St. Basil's monastery, hoping they might unearth
something, anything, that might serve as a motive for murder. Once
it had been established that the murder victim had been an impostor,
Ross and Ferris had put their heads together and determined to seek a
reason for the impostor to have infiltrated the priory. Ferris and Bellamy kept returning to the obscure and unsubstantiated story of there
being some kind of treasure located within the grounds of the original monastery. If such a thing existed, it would surely prove to be a
perfect stimulus for murder.

"Go home, Kat," He suddenly touched Bellamy's arm and she
jumped, startled to wakefulness.

Her head had dropped when she'd literally nodded off before the
screen.

"Oh God, sorry Paul." She smiled ruefully and rubbed her eyes. "I
s'pose I'm more tired than I thought I was. What time is it?"

"It's eight o'clock. We've been at it since eight this morning," Ferris said, looking at the clock. "The others knocked off over an hour ago. The boss said we shouldn't overdo it. It's not as if we've discovered anything of significance after all, have we?"

"What? Apart from the fact that the Benedictines seem to have been tied into the history of Liverpool since the time of King John, and that it was Benedictine monks who provided the first Mersey Ferry and that they used to prepare food and deliver it to the original fishing community of about fifty souls who lived on the banks of the Mersey?" She stifled a yawn. "Apparently the population then grew to about 750 by the middle of the 13$^{th}$ century, and the monks were still hard at it."

"Yes, I know, but what relevance does it have to our case, Kat? Admit it. We've found nothing so far and we've been digging into the history of the place for three days now."

"Maybe the case has got nothing to do with the history of the priory or monastery," Kat said with a hint of disappointment in her voice.

"I know. We can't keep flogging a dead horse, so to speak, by following vague references to a legendary treasure that might or might not exist. I'll tell the boss we don't think the history of the place has any bearing on the murder. At least, it'll eliminate one avenue of inquiry."

"Right. So, what do we do now?"

"I need to get the victim's fingerprints sent to Klaus Richter in Austria. I've just received them from Doc Nugent. Maybe we can make some progress if he appears in the *Bundespolizei* fingerprint archive."

Within minutes, the fingerprints of the man who was originally thought to be Brother Bernárd were being transmitted by email to the Austrian police. Ferris hoped that Klaus Richter would come up trumps and produce the true identity of the man stored 'on ice' in the city mortuary.

* * *

"Nothing?" Klaus Richter exclaimed, to Sergeant Emil Wägner with disbelief. "The damn fingerprints failed to produce a single match anywhere in our system?"

"Did you also run them through the database of ex-government employees, sir? You know, former soldiers, public-service employees, and so forth?" Wägner asked, trying to be helpful.

"Yes, I did, Emil, and still nothing. It's as if the man never existed. My new friend, Sergeant Ferris in Liverpool, will *not* be a happy man I think."

"Hang on, sir. You just said it was as if the man never existed, but maybe he just never existed here in Austria?"

"You're suggesting he might have been a foreigner, is that it?"

"Why not, sir? We have many foreign nationals living here in Austria. He could have been German, Polish, Italian, French, anything I suppose," Wägner offered with a shrug.

"That's true, of course, but foreigners with a criminal past should be contained within our system, unless … damn it. If he didn't have a criminal record here, but had one in say Germany, he wouldn't be in our system, would he?"

Wägner nodded in agreement and waited, knowing his inspector would know what to do next.

"But he might be on INTERPOL's radar," Richter stated, looking thoughtful.

"That's what I was thinking, sir."

"But is it for us to contact INTERPOL, or should it be done by the English? It is their case, after all. I think I must speak with *Oberstleutnant* Gruber."

A short time later, after consulting with his superintendent, Klaus Richter picked up the telephone and held a ten-minute conversation with Paul Ferris in Liverpool. Though Richter's English was good, there were a couple of times when his language skills failed him and he was surprised to hear the voice of Sofie Meyer on the line, who came to his rescue and ensured his conversation with Paul Ferris concluded accurately, without any linguistic errors in translation.

They agreed that Ferris would consult with D.I. Ross, who, as senior investigating officer, should be the one to decide on the correct protocol to follow. Again, a ten-minute wait ensued as Ferris talked to

Ross, who in turn phoned Oscar Agostini and after a brief discussion, a decision was made.

"Okay Paul, DCI Agostini agrees with me. It's our case, so first contact with INTERPOL should be made by us. I'd like you to pass that on to our Austrian colleagues, but once we receive any intel from INTERPOL, we'll share it with them, so that any action they feel able to take to assist us can be initiated without delay."

"Right you are, Boss," Ferris agreed, having expected just such a decision before he'd entered Ross's office. The team's computer expert, however, had another thought that he wanted to put to Ross, however.

"This is just an idea, but with us bringing INTERPOL onto the scene, I was thinking it might be a good idea to bring Sofie in as a liaison between us, the Austrians, and INTERPOL. God knows who we might have to deal with at INTERPOL, and Sofie has the multiple language skills that might make for swifter communication without the chance of cock-ups with faulty translations and so on."

"I like that idea," Izzie Drake said from her seat in Ross's visitor's chair. She and Ross had been going through the statements from St. Emma's monks and nuns when Ferris had walked in. "If INTERPOL does have any information on file about our impostor, it's possible that it might be in German or French perhaps, and Sofie is fluent in six languages, after all. Obviously, I've never dealt with INTERPOL, so it's possible they automatically translate everything into English anyway, but it wouldn't hurt to be prepared, just in case they don't."

"Agreed," Ross nodded, convinced. "Let Sofie know she's working with you on this now, Paul. Agostini is on the phone to INTERPOL as we speak. It could be an interesting experience for us all, working with them."

"Okay," said Ferris. "Just let me know what the form is when the Chief's spoken with them, and I can update Klaus Richter, Meanwhile, I'll let him know we're contacting INTERPOL from our end and will continue to keep him in the loop." He left Ross's office and quickly brought Kat Bellamy up to date before making a quick phone call to

Klaus Richter, who sounded relieved that Merseyside Police would be leading the contact with INTERPOL.

It wouldn't be long before he'd be back in touch again.

\* \* \*

Contrary to popular belief, the International Criminal Police Organisation, commonly known as, is not some kind of supranational law enforcement agency, and has no agents of its own who are allowed to make arrests. An international organisation, it operates as a network of criminal law-enforcement agencies from different countries. From its central headquarters in Lyon, France, it therefore functions as an administrative liaison between the law-enforcement agencies of its member countries, which number almost two hundred, by providing communications, administrative and database assistance. Using its unique, encrypted database, the INTERPOL network allows member countries to contact each other at any time, and enables cross-border cooperation and sharing of information. Thus, if a crime takes place in the USA and it's thought the perpetrators are active in Italy, as an example, it is possible for law-enforcement agencies in the USA to gain access to information about similar criminal activities in Italy where their own jurisdiction doesn't apply, and where they wouldn't normally have access to information contained in the files of the Italian law- enforcement agency.

So it was that Detective Chief Inspector Oscar Agostini spent ten minutes in conversation with Serge Bleriot, an INTERPOL analyst in Lyon, with whom he discussed the strange case of the fake monk and the disappearance of the real Brother Bernárd. Despite the fact that both murders had taken place in the UK, Agostini was seeking help from INTERPOL on two fronts. First of all, they had the fingerprints of the dead man in the morgue and, secondly, Agostini was looking for any cases bearing similarities to their own that might reside within INTERPOL's database.

Bleriot promised he'd get on to the case immediately and was optimistic that, if nothing else, the fingerprints would lead to a positive identification *if* the dead man had a criminal record in any INTERPOL affiliated nation. As for cases bearing similarities to the St. Emma's murder, he was less optimistic. There were few real facts to go on and, up to now, little evidence or motive readily available with which to compare the case to others; still, he promised to do his best.

Bleriot's information was then passed from Agostini to Ross, and then on to Ferris and Meyer, and eventually from Ferris to Richter. At the latest team briefing, Ross faced his team with a sour look on his face. He wasn't used to their cases being so bereft of facts to base their investigation on. Whoever had set this chain of events in motion had been nothing if not thoroughly professional in their implementation of the imposter's murder. As for the murder of the real Brother Bernárd, his frustration was reaching boiling point. Without a body, or even a time and place of the murder, he and his team were impotent in terms of dealing with the case.

Ultra-helpful, Serge Bleriot had also suggested to Agostini that he may wish to submit a request for information to The European Union Agency for Law Enforcement Cooperation, better known as Europol. Formed in 1998, Europol operated in a similar way to INTERPOL, being the European Union's own law-enforcement agency, set up to handle criminal intelligence, and to combat organised crime and terrorism. If the man Ross's team were seeking had been connected to an organised crime syndicate within the European Union, there was a good chance that his details may well be stored on their records. Not wanting Ferris and Meyer working two separate inquiries into the dead man's possible identity, Ross now placed the onus of contacting Europol on the capable shoulders of Derek McLennan. It shouldn't take long, Ross hoped, for one of the two international agencies to produce a result.

"Meanwhile," he concluded firmly. "I want the rest of us to probe deeper into the people at the priory. From what I can ascertain after the first round of interviews, it looks like the only people who arrived there after Brother Bernárd, were Brother Simon and Sisters Rebecca, Paulette and Sarah. On the basis that the killer had to have followed or been sent to deal with the impostor after he'd arrived at St. Emma's those four have to be considered our chief suspects. Any questions?"

"One point springs to mind now we've narrowed things down a bit." Izzie Drake had been giving serious thought to this theory since she and Ross had discussed it earlier.

"Go ahead, Izzie. Have I missed something out?"

"Not at all," she replied, "but, if one of those four is the killer, it means we have a murdering nun or monk on our hands—or, God forbid, one of them is also a fake, an impostor. We also still need to discover what happened to the real Brother Bernárd."

"You're right, of course," Ross agreed, taking a sharp breath. "And that's why we are going to begin a *new* inquiry. Our contact in Austria, Klaus Richter, has provided Paul with the real Bernárd's travel itinerary, from when he left his Austrian monastery to when he supposedly arrived in England, on a ferry at Hull. We're pretty certain he arrived safely and made his way to St. Emma's and was murdered and replaced by the impostor very soon after his arrival, once he'd established himself at the priory. If what we suspect is true, then the real Bernárd was killed and his body disposed of very soon after taking up residence at St. Emma's. So, people, that means there's a body somewhere and we need to find it, and *soon*."

He gazed around the room, his expression resolute. "Sam, I want you, Nick and Ginger to start delving into the backgrounds of the main suspects. Be discreet, talk with Brother Gerontius first, and try not to alarm him by accusing one of his people. It's not going to be easy, I know. Tell him we need to look at everyone's background and we're starting with the four most recent arrivals. That shouldn't sound too sinister. "Tony," he said to D.C. Curtis, "I want you to pay a visit to the Diocesan office and do your best to follow the records of our suspects from the time before they came to St. Emma's. It's possible that when you compare what, if anything, you discover, with what exists, records-wise at St. Emma's, we might identify a discrepancy that opens a window of inquiry for us."

It wasn't long before most of the team had left the squad room, apart from those working on their computers, and Ross and Drake made their way up to the office of DCI Agostini, where they soon brought him up to date with the latest, not very promising, developments. Ross knew they needed a break, something, no matter how small, to give them an inroad into the immense veil of mystery that appeared to enshroud the Priory of St. Emma. Something, they both agreed, was seriously amiss at the outwardly innocent religious community.

# Chapter 12

### Suspicions

Sam Gable suggested to her colleagues that they begin their task at the priory with another interview with the Prior, Brother Gerontius. As they drove into the grounds of the priory, they observed a man sitting astride a large motorised lawnmower, busily cutting the grass. Dodds wondered who the man was and if he might be worth investigating, but he snapped back to the present when Sam referred to Brother Gerontius.

"He might not be so interested in our looking into our suspects if we begin by making him believe we need to talk to him as well," she said.

Dodds and Devenish agreed.

Upon arrival at St. Emma's they were met by Brother Simon, who escorted them to the office where Brother Gerontius was working on a theological text. He was pleased, however, to greet his guests when Simon showed them in.

"How can I help you today, officers?" he asked.

Gable explained, using their pre-arranged excuse for the interviews they needed to carry out.

"Of course, I understand. I'm well aware that people often recall things later when questioned a second time about a given event."

When Gable looked quizzically at him, he smiled and said, *"Inspector Morse,"* D.C. Gable. I'm a big fan of the TV series and try to watch it, if

I can, whenever it's on. It's something I learned from an episode that was shown recently."

Sam Gable smiled in return. The TV series starring John Thaw as the irascible Morse clearly had fans in the most unlikely places.

Before beginning the interviews, Nick Dodds had a question for the Prior.

"Brother, on our way in, we saw a man on a motorised lawn mower attending to the grass along the driveway. From his clothes, I assumed he wasn't one of your monks. I was wondering who he is." "Ah, yes, that's Mr Parker, Daniel Parker. He's a very kind gentleman who helps us out whenever he can. He lives about a mile away and has his own business as a gardener. When he has time to spare, he comes along and cuts the grass for us. It saves us having to pay to hire someone to do it. I'm afraid the grounds are, as you've no doubt observed, quite large and there's no way we could keep them under control with the tools at our disposal. Oh, and before you ask, the answer is no, "Mr Parker wasn't here on the day of the murder. If you check with him, I'm sure he can provide you with a satisfactory alibi. If we're lucky, he stops by once a month to trim the grounds for us. We previously paid a company called Green Fingers to keep our lawns and grassed areas cut, but when Mr. Parker came along and offered his services for free about five months ago, we couldn't very well look a gift horse in the mouth."

Talk soon moved on to the reason for their visit and the Prior proved his usual, cooperative self.

"You already know that we'll do all we can to help you in your in-vestigation. Even, as it now seems, Brother Bernárd was not all he appeared to be, I did come to know him during his time here, and I'm sure he didn't deserve to die in the manner he did. What worries and upsets me is that your Inspector Ross seems to think the man we're mourning could also have murdered the real Brother Bernárd almost as soon as he arrived, disposed of his body, and blatantly assumed his place, and has lived among us ever since, never once showing any signs of being an impostor. We, and by that I really mean me, never suspected or saw through his disguise, and his knowledge of our ways and our religious rituals etc."

"He wasn't disguised, Brother," Sam corrected him quietly, "He'd been surgically enhanced to look like the real Bernárd; as you were never likely to look that intimately at him, it's unlikely you'd ever have noticed the difference, especially as you hadn't known him long. It's only when you compared his face with the one on his original file that you suspected something and informed DI Ross, so please, don't reproach yourself."

Brother Gerontius nodded, but didn't really seem mollified by Gable's words. She guessed this mild-mannered, deeply religious man would probably carry a heavy burden of guilt on his shoulders for years to come once this case was over. Perhaps, for the Prior of St. Emma's, it would never truly be over, no matter what the outcome. Taking a deep breath, Gerontius spoke again.

"Please tell me, do you have any idea what happened to the real Brother Bernárd? I have nightmarish visions of his body lying somewhere, exposed to the elements, gradually decomposing, never having received the last rites or a proper Christian burial."

"One thing's certain," Gary Devenish interjected, "his remains, assuming he's dead of course, won't be exposed to the elements, or he'd have been found long before now."

"That's true," Nick Dodds agreed. "It's obviously well hidden—and we may never find the body, something we have to consider."

Looking sad and dejected, the Prior was forced to agree.

"What you say makes sense of course, Detective Constable, but it's still a sobering thought that in this day and age, someone could disappear off the face of the earth and not leave a single trace of where they might be."

"Whoever the impostor was, he was clearly a professional," Devenish added. "He knew exactly what he was doing. The poor bloke's body could even have been dumped in the Mersey and been carried out to sea."

"It doesn't bear thinking about." Brother Gerontius appeared on the verge of breaking down in tears.

Sam Gable quickly brought the conversation back on track and it was agreed with the Prior that, to save time, each detective would speak to a different person. She'd stay and speak to Gerontius while Dodds spoke with Brother Simon, and Devenish with Sister Paulette. Sisters Rebecca and Sarah would be the last to be interviewed that day.

Two hours later, the three detectives met to compare notes after completing their interviews. As each one of them related the results of their conversations with the monks and nuns, it was painfully evident that little progress had been made.

"All I'm picking up from Brother Gerontius is feelings of guilt over the fact that the real Brother Bernárd is probably lying out there somewhere in an unmarked and unsanctified grave," Sam reported to the others. "I don't think he knows the faintest thing about the murder."

Ginger Devenish had something similar to say about Sister Paulette. "As far as I can make out, she's still pretty much in a state of shock from having found the body. Unless she and Brother Ignacius were working together, there's just no way she could have been involved in the murder."

"What about you, Nick?" Sam asked Dodds, whose interview with Brother Simon had been his second with the former stuntman-turned-monk.

"It's funny," Dodds advised, "But I'd swear Brother Simon seemed a little edgy this time when I spoke with him."

"How come?" Sam was intrigued by Dodd's feelings.

"Okay, it's nothing I can quite put my finger on, but, the first time I met him he was pretty open and chatty, you know? Seemed to enjoy telling me how he got that scar when he worked as a film and TV stuntman. He smiled a lot and nothing seemed to be too much trouble … being helpful and so on."

"And what's changed, Nick?" Devenish asked.

"This time, it felt like I was trying to get blood from a stone. When I went through some of the stuff we talked about last time, it was almost as if he was having trouble recalling what we actually spoke about before. Even the story of the accident leading to him getting the scar seemed a bit different, not much, but enough to set my alarm bells ringing. There's something about our friend Brother Simon that isn't quite as simple as we first thought. I'd recommend we pull his file from the Prior's office, and get as much as we can from the Diocesan office on this guy. Then, let's find out just how genuine his story about being a stunt man really is. There's just something that *doesn't* stack up where he's concerned."

"I think the boss will be pleased to hear you might have a suspect, Nick," Sam Gable said. "Maybe it means this visit hasn't been a total waste of time."

"What about the others?" Devenish asked.

"What, Sisters Rebecca and Sarah? Come on, Ginge, tell us what you thought of Sister Rebecca," Sam urged, prompting Devenish to groan.

"My God, that woman!" Devenish exclaimed. "Talk about single-minded. Almost every sentence that comes out of her mouth is like a bloody sermon. I know monks and nuns are supposed to be totally dedicated to God and their religious beliefs, but all the others I've spoken to have been, well, pretty much normal people with a strong religious belief and motivation in their lives. Sister bleedin' Rebecca is like a fucking one-woman rabble-rousing Evangelical mission. She's totally obsessed with God and the Bible and how we should relate everything in our lives to the Word of God. I reckon, if she'd discovered the guy impersonating Brother Bernárd was involved in any kind of non-Christian activity, she'd be perfectly capable of coming up with a motive to want to send him to Hell. Whether she'd have the nerve to actually commit murder, I wouldn't like to say."

Devenish fell silent and the others just sat and stared at him for a few seconds. Gradually, a grin appeared on the face of Sam Gable, who'd been the first of the team to have interviewed Sister Rebecca. She felt sorry for Gary Devenish; she knew just how he must be feeling after spending time with the nun who she herself thought was rather 'over the top' in terms of her religious fervour.

"I'm sorry, Ginge," she said at last. "I could have warned you, but I wanted to let you make up your own mind about the woman. Personally, I think she's possibly one lightbulb short of a candelabra, but whether she's capable of murder, I'm not certain I can go along with that. It's a big step from being a committed Christian to being a cold-blooded murderer."

"Yeah, well, what about the Templars?" Devenish countered.

Gable looked mystified. "Eh? What have they got to do with anything?"

"I saw a documentary about the Knights Templar on Sky TV," said the red-haired detective. "It was dead interesting. The Templars were all totally committed Christians and they originally went out to the Holy Land to protect Pilgrims heading for Jerusalem. They were all knights, of course, well trained in the fighting skills of their day. They grew to be the finest group of fighting men of their time, to the extent that they grew so powerful, the Pope and the King of France at that time decided they were too damn powerful and made the decision to eliminate them. They were virtually wiped out by a carefully co-ordinated attack on Friday the 13th, I can't remember the year, but apparently, that's why Friday the 13th has always been considered unlucky ever since. Anyway, my point is that the Templars, like Sister Rebecca, were totally committed to their religious beliefs and as they were fully prepared to kill in defence of Christianity—so why couldn't she be?"

It was Devenish's turn to grin as he concluded the history lesson.

"Bloody hell, Ginge," Dodds responded before Sam Gable could say a word. "I never knew you were such a scholar, mate. I always just thought the Templars were the good guys and helped start that organisation that was in that film, *The Da Vinci Code*, you know, the—fuck me, I can't remember their name."

"You mean the Illuminati," Gable said. "That was just a movie, Nick, based on a fictional novel. I don't think the Illuminati even existed, and if they did, I doubt they had anything to do with the Templars.

Anyway, I do see your point, Ginge, but I still think it's stretching things a bit to compare Sister Rebecca with the Knights Templar."

"Maybe it is, but I always think people like her are as bad as those hard-line fundamentalists in the Middle East, you know? They won't listen to anyone else's opinions or beliefs. Either you agree with them, or you're a heretic, that kind of thing."

Sam Gable couldn't stop herself from laughing, albeit quietly, at Devenish's latest pronouncement. "Sorry, Ginge, I know I shouldn't laugh, but she was just as bad when I talked to her the other day. It's like you say something to her and she shoots off on a tangent, lecturing you on some aspect of the Bible or religion in general, her version of it at any rate."

"Yeah, that's it exactly," Devenish nodded.

"And you think she could be our killer?" Dodds asked, curious.

"I think she's fanatical enough to be part of it, depending on the motive," Devenish confirmed his belief.

"So, we've gone from zero suspects to two potentials," Sam said. "Nick, what about Sister Sarah?"

"No chance," said Dodds. "I don't think she's got the intelligence to be a killer. She came across as being a bit naïve, not too brainy, if you catch my drift. Not like Sister Rebecca, but totally committed to her life as a nun, in my opinion, anyway."

"So, nothing certain and no hard evidence, but a couple of what we might call gut feelings to report, looks about it for today. We'll have to see what the boss thinks about looking deeper into Sister Rebecca and Brother Simon." Sam summed up their time at the priory.

"I don't think I can remember a case so damned infuriating," Dodds said as they made their way back to the car. "You'd think with such a small group of suspects, we'd have cracked it in no time."

"I agree, Nick," Devenish concurred. "Somehow, I get the feeling we're as far from solving the murder as were on day one … and this just isn't normal for God's sake."

Sam Gable wished she could say something to contradict the men's view that the inquiry was going nowhere but found herself as mystified as Dodds and Devenish. It was a disconsolate trio of detectives that made their way back to headquarters—with two tenuous links to two of their suspects with which to try and build their case.

As they were soon to learn to their cost however, rather than getting better, things were about to get a whole lot worse.

# Chapter 13

**Result!**

The call from Serge Bleriot came at just the right time as far as Andy Ross was concerned. He'd just returned to his office after being called to a meeting with DCI Oscar Agostini and DCS Sarah Hollingsworth. Although everyone was fully aware that Ross and his team were doing all they could, the fact that the Chief Constable was regularly asking Hollingsworth for updates meant the murder at St. Emma's was attracting more attention than usual from on high, and Hollingsworth had made it clear that progress was expected sooner rather than later. Ross agreed that results so far were disappointing but stressed that until they had the victim's true identity, it would be almost impossible to even determine who could have had a motive to murder him. Now came the call he'd been hoping for.

"I have news for you. DI Ross," Bleriot announced, betraying almost no trace of his French accent.

"Please tell me you have a name for our victim," Ross almost pleaded.

"I do indeed, and it may surprise you when I reveal to you his true identity."

"Don't keep me guessing, Serge, *please*. I need some good news to-day."

"Very well." Bleriot sensed the urgency in Ross's tone of voice. "I shall keep you waiting no longer. The body in your mortuary would appear to be that of a man named Paul Schneider, a native of the old German Democratic Republic, or East Germany as it is better known in the west. That is the first piece of news. Secondly, Herr Schneider was a member of The *Ministerium für Staatssicherheitsdienst*, or The State Security Service."

Bleriot paused to allow Ross to assimilate this information.

"I have a feeling I should know more than I do about what you've just told me, but I'm sorry, my brain's just not working today. Please tell me the significance of this information."

"Ah, my friend, you are about to kick yourself as you English say. The East German State Security Service, as you will know, I'm sure, is—or rather was—better known as the Stasi."

"Shit, of course," Ross exclaimed as the name struck home like an arrow from a bow. "Now I can maybe understand why someone wanted him dead. Am I correct in assuming that Herr Schneider was wanted for crimes of some kind?"

"Oh yes, Inspector Ross, perhaps crimes of the worst kind. Up until the collapse of communism in the east, and the coming down of the Berlin Wall, Paul Schneider was a *Hauptman*, that's a captain to you, stationed in East Berlin. When Germany was reunified, and the Stasi Records Agency was formed to investigate the thousands of files they had failed to destroy in their panic as the East German state fell, many of their most terrible crimes against their own people came to light. To the outside world Paul Schneider had appeared to be nothing more than an administrative officer, but was eventually identified as one of the Stasi's most feared torturers, and as far as investigators could tell, he'd been personally responsible for the deaths of hundreds of citizens of the so-called German Democratic Republic. Before he could be arrested and brought to trial however, he disappeared and all attempts to trace him sadly failed.

"It was believed he was smuggled out of the country by a rather shady organisation known as *Der Freiheitszug*, which ironically translates into English as The Freedom Train. This organisation was set up in secret almost as soon as communism fell and it became obvious that certain members of the Stasi would soon be arrested and brought to justice. They made it their mission to help former Stasi officials to flee the country and set up new lives and identities in other countries. Your man, Paul Schneider, was thought to have been aided by this organisation. After he disappeared in 1991, he was never heard of again. I can't imagine where he has been in hiding for fifteen years, or why he suddenly resurfaced in England with this new face and false identity, but perhaps his location had been discovered and the organisation decided to move him to keep him safe from prosecution."

Ross was stunned by Bleriot's revelation regarding their murder victim. This was a much darker and murkier case than he or anyone else, the Chief Constable included, could possibly have imagined. Before concluding his conversation with Serge Bleriot, he had a couple of questions relating to the underground escape organisation he felt he needed clarification on.

"Serge, I'm grateful to you for your great work in tracing Schneider, but please tell me: are there any details of who might be in charge of this escape organisation or, indeed, if there are any *other* groups who might be trying to uncover these former Stasi officers?"

"I'm sorry, my friend, but we do not have any information on the things you ask, but I would suggest you contact the Stasi Records Agency in Berlin, who I'm sure will be more than interested in your information about Schneider's death, and may be able to assist you further in your inquiries."

"That's just what we'll do. Thank you again, Serge. Your help has been invaluable to us."

"We live to serve," said Bleriot. "I am glad we were able to assist you and hope your case reaches a successful conclusion, though I doubt there will be many people left who will mourn the passing of Paul Schneider. *Bon chance, mon ami.*"

Ross lost no time in calling Izzie Drake into his office, together with Sofie Meyer, who he was sure would know far more about the Stasi than anyone else on his team.

"Ach, *Der Stasi*," Meyer virtually spat the name out. "Those people did so many bad things in Germany. When our country was reunified after communism fell, only then did the truth begin to emerge about those evil monsters."

"You know something about it, then, Sofie?" Izzie Drake asked her.

"I saw much of what happened on the news at the time. When the Communists were forced from power, the people saw smoke rising from the Stasi headquarters building one day. Of course, the people knew that the building was heated by gas, and that the smoke produced by the heating system was clean white smoke. This was *black*, foul-smelling smoke and could only be caused by burning paper. The people forced their way into the building and found Stasi officers trying to burn all the records … to prevent their crimes against the people being discovered. As I'm sure you know," Meyer stated with a wry smile, "we Germans are well known for our efficiency in the keeping of records. Even the Nazis during the war kept meticulous records of their evil crimes against humanity, right down to the last gold filling or lock of hair taken from the unfortunate victims of the concentration camps. So too with the Stasi. After news spread about the people storming the Stasi headquarters, people in other towns in the East stormed similar Stasi buildings and prevented records from being destroyed. The people in the East lived in fear of the Stasi, and they wanted the truth about them to be revealed to the world."

"East Germany must have been a terrible pace to live," Ross added after hearing Sofie's descriptions.

"It truly was," Sofie agreed with a soft sigh. "Even the famous Nazi Hunter, Simon Wiesenthal, spoke of them when he described the Stasi as being more oppressive than Hitler's Gestapo."

"Good God." Drake was shocked. "So, what happened to them after reunification?"

"Well, the head of the Stasi, Erich Mielke, and other senior figures were prosecuted for their crimes against the people, as were certain others who were proved to have committed such crimes. It was not deemed to have been a crime just to have been a member of the Stasi. Proof of wrongdoing was required."

"Sounds fair enough to me," Ross said.

"Yeah, but I bet a lot of ordinary people wanted revenge on the whole organisation, eh, Sofie?" Drake made an obvious point.

"Quite so, Izzie, but it would have been piling injustice upon injustice to have followed such a path, and there have been plenty of prosecutions since reunification, so there was clearly no attempt to cover up the crimes committed by the Stasi."

It was generally agreed that, in all likelihood, Paul Schneider aka Brother Bernárd, had been tracked down by members of one of the many groups set up to bring former members of the Stasi to justice. Not all, it appeared, were interested in bringing those people to trial and, in this case, there remained the possibility that the killer held a personal grudge against Schneider.

There remained of course, the fact that somewhere, quite probably in the area surrounding the city of Liverpool, the undetected remains of the real Brother Bernárd were hidden and would have to be found in order to truly solve the mystery of what had happened to the monk.

Andy Ross was quick to update Oscar Agostini with the news about their murder victim's true identity, and the DCI pledged to inform Detective Chief Superintendent Hollingsworth who, in turn, would update the Chief Constable of this highly significant piece of information.

Turning to Drake and Meyer, Ross announced their next course of action.

"Time to call a special briefing, I think. As difficult as it's going to be, we need to look at the case from a new angle. First of all, we need to continue investigating the murder of the man we now know as Paul SchneiderI think you're going to become a pivotal member of the team as far as contact with the German police is concerned, Sofie. Possibly the Austrians too."

Meyer nodded her understanding. As a member of the *Bundeskriminalamt* she could probably open doors that might otherwise be closed to the Merseyside force.

Ross nodded in return and continued. "Next, I want to set up a second team within the team to investigate the disappearance and subsequent murder of the real Brother Bernárd. I presume you both agree there's little chance that he *wasn't* murdered soon after arriving in England?"

Both sergeants nodded their agreement with his thoughts.

"We'll treat it as we would any cold case inquiry and start by assembling every scrap of information we can relating to the initial arrival of Brother Bernárd at St. Emma's. At some point, probably within days of his arrival, he must have been lured to his death. He was killed either by Schneider, or some other member, or members, of this shadowy organisation, established to look after on-the-run wanted former members of the Stasi. Any questions?"

"Not from me," replied Drake. "Now that we know the truth about the dead man, I could almost say I'd like to shake the hand of whoever put an end to the evil he represented ... but let's concentrate on finding his killer. Hopefully that might lead us to the killer of the real Brother Bernárd, the real and innocent victim in all this."

"I agree, also," Meyer added gravely. "Let us get the team together and the briefing underway. If there are other members of the Stasi living here in England, under the protection of some shadow organisation, this might help us to expose them."

"Right then," Ross said, seemingly galvanised as he almost leapt up from behind his desk. "Come on! Let's get this show on the road, ladies."

# Chapter 14

### Spooks

At the impromptu briefing called by Ross, the whole team appeared galvanised by having something they could at last get their teeth into.

Ross had invited both DCI Agostini and, to the surprise of some of the team, DCS Hollingsworth to be present. As she'd been in charge of the initial stages of the investigation while Agostini was away on holiday, Ross felt it politic to include an invitation for her to be there, but, privately, he was somewhat surprised by the fact that she'd actually turned up with little more than half an hour's notice.

Once again, he found himself reappraising his opinion of the Detective Chief Superintendent who, he now realised, felt herself to be more than just an office-bound figurehead. Underneath her hard exterior as a tough administrator and organiser, he could tell she was still a 'real copper' beneath the bluff exterior she usually portrayed.

Ross politely thanked her for taking the time from her busy schedule to attend the briefing at short notice and she responded by congratulating him on his team's efforts so far, in particular his productive cooperation with the continental forces of law and order.

Nodding his thanks to her, he continued the briefing. "Okay people, now we have something to get our teeth into, so here's how we're going to proceed. What was originally, as we believed, the single murder of a monk, has now become a case of the murders at the monastery and..."

"Sir, it's a priory," Drake interrupted.

"I know, I know," Ross responded with a dry smile. "I just keep thinking of a priory as a small monastery; it's got stuck in my mind. Anyway, you all know what I mean, and Mersey Monastery Murders sounds better than Mersey Priory Murders."

A ripple of laughter rang round the briefing room.

"As I was saying before Sergeant Drake corrected me," he grinned at Izzie, "we're going to try and work this as two separate but interlinked cases. If we tried to do it all at the same time, we'd get bogged down and start tripping over ourselves by trying to come at it from two different directions. Everyone agree with that?"

Heads nodded and there was a chorus of quiet affirmatives around the room.

"So, based on the fact that our primary murder victim was a German national, I'm putting Sergeant Meyer in charge of the investigation into the murder of Paul Schneider." He turned to her and leaned forward, his gaze intent. "Sofie, you will have DCs Curtis, Dodds, and Gable working with you. Sergeant Ferris and Kat will be available with the computer resources to provide anything you need. You can contact Klaus Richter in Austria for all the info relating to the real Brother Bernárd. Try to discover how this Stasi escape group latched on to him and selected him as their choice for Schneider's double or substitute, or whatever you want to call it. You have personal knowledge of the Stasi from your work at home in Germany, so use your contacts back home. Try and put together a trail to see if we can find out how the escape route works. Second, you need to be looking into any organised groups that might be seeking to bring these ex-Stasi criminals to justice, or whether this was a personal vendetta that resulted in the murder."

Sofie Meyer, replied, earnestly.

"You can count on us, sir."

"Sergeant Drake will lead DCs McLennan and Devenish in the search for the body of the real Brother Bernárd. Whoever murdered him disposed of the body *somewhere*. This is going to be like looking for a needle in a haystack." He gazed from face to face, his expression stern. "Contact every mortuary, every police force in the area. We're searching for an unidentified corpse somewhere, possibly with mutilated features. They may have tried to make sure that if the body was found, it would be impossible for a positive I.D. to be made. At this point, we're assuming Schneider was the murderer, but he may have had help from this Stasi escape group, or they may have killed the monk without Schneider being present, so he could seamlessly step into his new role." He drew a deep breath and straightened. "One thing's for sure. If we can locate the body, it could hold precious clues to the killer. I'll be here to co-ordinate the two arms of the inquiry and will lend my input to whichever case needs me at the time. Sergeant Drake and I will push ahead with the inquiry into the death at the Priory of St. Emma, though I think your inquiries will, at some point, gel together and also help us in that inquiry. I think that's all for now."

Ross paused and regarded the faces of his assembled team; he saw determination etched into each and every one.

"Any questions?"

Before anyone could speak, DCI Agostini jumped in.

"I just want you to know that the Chief Constable has let it be known that this killer *has* to be found. The fact that the genuine monk appears to have been an innocent victim in all this means he's authorised whatever resources you feel you may need to solve this one, Andy."

Ross nodded determinedly. He knew that meant the Chief Constable was going to be watching developments very closely. He just hoped he and his team could produce a positive result—two in fact, as it now seemed certain they were searching for two entirely separate murderers.

Detective Chief Superintendent Hollingsworth was quick to reinforce Agostini's words. "Whatever you want, DI Ross, you only have to say the word to DCI Agostini, and I will authorise it within minutes; clear?"

"Clear, Ma'am."

"Then, if there are no pertinent questions, I suggest calling this briefing closed and we all get back to doing our jobs," Hollingsworth said crisply and exited.

\* \* \*

Sofie Meyer lost no time in getting on the phone and establishing contact with Klaus Richter in Feldkirch, in Austria. Richter was pleasantly surprised to hear Sofie speaking to him in German, and was extremely interested to hear about her time working on loan with the British Police in Liverpool.

She spent a few minutes answering his questions, being as polite as possible, whilst wanting to push ahead with the task in hand. Eventually managing to bring the conversation back to the point, she lost no time in bringing Richter fully up to date with the latest developments in Liverpool, thanks to some help from INTERPOL.

Richter was impressed and felt good at being involved in a case involving INTERPOL, his own day-to-day work having been, up to that point, relatively mundane. Feldkirch was hardly a hotbed of crime and exciting cases for an ambitious young policeman were few and far between.

Meyer quickly explained her plan.

"It's quite clear that Paul Schneider was assisted by others, quite possibly an organisation known as *Der Freiheitszug*, the Freedom Train—"

"Please, what is this Freedom Train?" he interrupted politely.

"It is an organisation that exists in the shadows, Klaus, and works to help former members of the Stasi, who may be wanted for crimes, of varying degrees, to escape and evade capture. Schneider is wanted for multiple murder and torture offences, and would have been a prime candidate for their services, What's clear is that their influence extends well beyond the borders of Germany; he must have received help from agents of the organisation in Austria and in England, if not elsewhere too."

"This is not good, Sofie," Richter said. "I must report the existence of this Freedom Train group to my superior, *Oberstleutnant* Gruber. He has asked to be kept informed of the progress of the case."

"Of course," Sofie agreed. "But please, Klaus, stress to him that we don't want these people to know we're aware of their activities. If they realise we are after them, they could quickly disappear back under the rock they crawled out from. I also suspect they may have friends in high places in Germany, so we must tread carefully."

"I understand," Richter replied, as he began to understand what she was saying—that investigating this shadowy organisation could be hazardous to those poking their noses into the Freedom Train's affairs.

Meyer explained that DCs Dodds, Curtis and Gable would be working with her, and any or all of them could be in contact with him during the course of their investigation. Richter explained that their police force in Feldkirch had neither the manpower nor the resources of the Liverpool force, but he was sure that *Oberstleutnant* Gruber would allow him to use *Gruppeninspektor* Emil Wägner on the case. The sergeant was experienced and resourceful and would relish the opportunity to be involved in what, for the force in Feldkirch, would be a major investigation.

"What do you want me to do to assist you, Sofie?" Richter asked, and she outlined what she wanted, which was to discover who was working for the ex-Stasi people in Austria and how they targeted Brother Bernárd as the man whose identity was chosen for their impostor, Paul Schneider, to replace.

"I see," Richter replied. "My superior *Oberstleutnant* Gruber has just entered the office. Please allow me to tell him what you have told me and he will I'm sure, have something to say."

Meyer waited for Richter to very quickly inform Wilhelm Gruber of what she'd informed him and a baritone voice then said,

"This is *Oberstleutnant* Gruber, I have asked Klaus to put this call on speaker phone, if you're agreeable with that."

"Of course sir," Sofie replied, and waited for Gruber to continue.

"Good. Sergeant Meyer, I had a call from Detective Chief Inspector Agostini requesting that we cooperate with your investigation. I am happy to allow Richter and Wägner to work with you on this case, especially as it involves our friends at St. Thomas's Monastery. Your Chief tells me you are actually a *Kriminalkommisar* in the *Bundeskriminalamt* back home in Germany. Why would an inspector in the BKA take the rank of sergeant in England? I'm interested to know, before we go on."

"That's easy, sir. When I was assigned to the exchange programme, I hardly expected to be then assigned to an elite unit such as I now work with. I felt it inappropriate to walk into such a post and immediately outrank most of the experienced detectives already working for Detective Inspector Ross, the man in operational charge of the team. Therefore, I asked to be granted the honorary rank of sergeant during my time with the Specialist Murder Investigation Team. Anything else would have made me feel uncomfortable, as these are some of the best detectives in the country, and I couldn't see myself giving orders to them when I was initially, *quite* frankly, at first, unable to travel from one side of the city to the other without help, never mind understand the local dialect."

Wilhelm Gruber laughed as he responded to Sofie's explanation. "Well done, Sofie—I hope I may call you that," he said cordially. "I'm impressed with your professionalism and it was indeed an honourable thing to do. You might wonder why I laughed, but it is not directed at you. No, it is just that I visited Liverpool myself a couple of years ago. I was in England on holiday and wished to see the sights of the city where the Beatles came from. I'm a big fan, and I did the tour of the city and all the places associated with them. I enjoyed myself immensely, but, *Mein Gott,* as you say, the dialect of the local people was almost unrecognisable as English at first. I'm sorry, I'm digressing. I understand and respect what you did in taking the lower rank, and Herr Agostini tells me you have made yourself an invaluable member of the team during your time there. He'll be sorry to see you return to Germany later this year."

"I'll be sorry to leave when my two-year attachment is over. I've made some very good friends."

"Still, we must get back to work," said Gruber, his voice turning professional again. "My people and I will do all we can to find the people who so callously murdered an innocent monk from our local monastery. I know the Stasi committed some dreadful crimes against the people of your country, Sofie and it is vital, for the sake of justice, that the worst of the criminals who worked for them are apprehended and tried."

"Thank you, sir," Meyer replied, impressed with Gruber's sincerity. "So, what do you plan to do next?"

"I would appreciate it if Herr Richter and his sergeant could begin by trying to track down any known former Stasi officers who might be living and working in your area. If there are none that are known, it may be necessary to expand the search to cover a greater area and, if so, you may have to call in help from your superiors."

"That will not be a problem. I have friends in many places, Sofie. I can call on help from Federal Police Headquarters in Vienna, if need be. German nationals registered as living here in Austria can be traced and their backgrounds looked into. It may take time, but I have a friend who might be able to help speed things up a little."

\* \* \*

Meanwhile, back in Liverpool, Sam Gable had spent most of the morning on the telephone to various people and organisations in London. She felt sure that the UK authorities, somewhere in the chain of official command, must have some knowledge of the secretive organisation responsible for assisting wanted former Stasi officers in their bid to escape from justice. On advice from DS Paul Ferris, her first port of call was Scotland Yard. Ferris had provided the name of a useful contact of his in London and she was duly put through to Detective Inspector Dave Hollis of the Metropolitan Police's External Investigations Unit, set up to investigate and combat crimes originating outside the UK. This placed the Stasi organisation firmly within their purview.

"Good to talk to you, Samantha," Hollis said after she'd identified herself and her reason for calling." Any friend of Paul's is a friend of mine."

"Thank you, sir, and please call me Sam. Nobody uses my full name nowadays."

"Sure thing and you can call me Dave. Forget the 'sir' while we're working together, okay?"

She immediately warmed to the man. "Okay, sir—er, Dave."

"So, tell me what I can do for you, Sam, in as much detail as you can, please."

Sam spent the next ten minutes giving Hollis an overview of the case, after which he left her holding on for a few seconds before replying.

"Sorry to keep you hanging on, but I wanted to talk to a friend of mine in another organisation before replying to you."

"That's okay," Sam wondered what was coming next.

"As it happens, this Freedom Train mob you talked about are known to the Metropolitan Police. We've had certain dealings with them in recent years, but I'm not permitted to discuss details with you. The friend I just mentioned isn't, strictly speaking, a police officer, but he's willing to talk with you."

Sam was experienced enough to have a damn good idea who Hollis's friend worked for.

"You mean this guy works for MI6, right, Dave?" she asked, referring to the everyday name of the SIS, (Secret Intelligence Service).

"I'm not naming names, but, if you give me a direct number there in Liverpool, he told me he'll call you right away and speak to you. If you think I can be of any further help, call me, okay?"

"Okay, Dave, and thanks."

Ten minutes later, the phone on Sam's desk rang, and she picked up immediately.

"Gable." She attempted to sound as official as she possibly could.

"Is that Samantha?" a voice with a distinct Irish lilt asked.

"It is. How can I help you?"

"I think, 'tis more a case of how I can help you, *Sam*," the deep voice said.

Meyer sensed the man on the other end was smiling as he spoke.

"You're Dave Hollis's friend, right?"

"I sure am, and you can call me Vince, but let's keep that to ourselves for now, okay? Now listen, Dave tells me you have a case up there that might involve our old friends, the ex-Stasi officers Freedom Train, right?"

"That's right. Do you want me to give you a run-through on what we have so far?"

"No need. Dave Hollis recorded your call and he played the important bits back to me. Sounds like the kind of nasty business our old East German friends would be involved in. Let me tell you now, Paul Schneider was a *seriously* wanted man. I have photographs of some of that bastard's victims, after he'd finished with them. Schneider had one objective, Sam, and that was to obtain a confession or, alternatively, whatever information the Stasi believed that particular individual might have been withholding from them."

Meyer felt a grim shudder run through her bones as she attempted to imagine what those photos might reveal. Almost subconsciously, she found herself asking,

"Vince, do you think you could send me examples of some of those victims, including names, please?"

"I don't think seeing the photos is going to help your case, Sam, really. They're not the sort of things a well brought-up young lady such as yourself should be seeing, I promise you."

"Forget the well brought-up young lady crap. I'm an experienced police officer and I've seen sights to make your hair curl so, please, send me the fucking photos, okay? Unless they're classified of course?"

"I'll send you some examples, Sam," Vince said in an apologetic tone. "If I can, I'll select some that might have connections with either Austria, the UK, or both. They *might* be helpful, maybe not. But that's not what you really want to talk to me about, is it?"

Vince knew Sam needed to know more about the Freedom Train, and its workings, and so proceeded to give her a brief rundown on the way the organisation worked. There was something else he needed her to know, however.

"Listen, Sam, I'm not saying this to scare you, but these people can be dangerous. They're very protective of their people and have been known to resort to extreme violence to safeguard those they protect."

This was hardly surprising news to Sam, who'd half-expected such news. It was obvious from what they'd already learned that those connected with the so-called Freedom Train could be utterly ruthless.

"I expected nothing less, Vince," she replied. "Don't worry. We have some pretty ruthless people on our team, too. If those bastards want to cut up rough, we'll meet fire with fire."

Meyer's bravado was well-placed. Most of the members of the Specialist Murder Investigation Team were not only firearms trained, but also possessed martial arts skills that could, if necessary, be brought into play when dealing with violent criminals.

"Would you be an angel and send copies of those photos and any files you send me to my boss, Detective Inspector Andy Ross? I want to make certain he knows exactly what we're dealing with here. Oh yes, another thing. Do you have any names for me? Surely, if your people know about this organisation, you must have some idea who's running it?"

"I knew you'd ask that. I'll copy DI Ross on everything I send you. As for names, we've been consulting with our German counterparts ever since we learned of this mob's existence. They know more about them than we do, as it's an internal, domestic thing for them; most of what we know comes from them. We've managed to identify a couple of wealthy German citizens living here, who we suspect could be the paymasters for the British end of their operation. I'll include what we have on them but, Sam, please be very careful with these people. Let me know if you learn anything, okay?"

He provided a number, which she noted, and as she prepared to thank him for his time and his help, Vince added one more thing.

"We know very little about these people and, although we know of their existence, we can only keep a watching brief on them. For all intents and purposes, they haven't committed any crimes in the UK. You might be in a position to change that, which could make you and your team targets for them. Do you understand what I'm saying?"

"Got it, Vince, and thanks again, Never thought I'd be receiving help on a case from MI6, I must admit."

"Who said I was from MI6?" he chuckled softly.

"Alright, have it your way. I don't mind playing Secret Squirrel with you, but thanks again. I appreciate your help and advice."

The phone line went dead when he terminated the call without saying anything else. Sam Gable looked at the notes she'd made during her calls to Vince and Hollis, turned off the recorder attached to her phone, and smiled to herself as she rose from her desk and headed for Ross's office, intending to bring him up to date with her morning's work.

"Bloody spooks," she said to no one in particular as she strode across the busy squad room, causing Paul Ferris and Kat Bellamy to turn from their computer screens and smile back at her as she passed them.

"Everything alright, Sam?" Ferris asked.

"Never better, Sarge," she replied with a wink. "Never better."

# Chapter 15

### Affairs of the Heart

While Sofie Meyer was busy following the trail with the Austrians and Sam Gable was making her inquiries with Scotland Yard, DCs Tony Curtis and Nick Dodds had drawn what they considered to be the short straw in the search for connections to the imposter's life. Meyer had instructed them to look into the deaths or disappearances of any German or Austrian citizens within the UK during the preceding five years. She'd included Austrians as it would have been simple for a German to have passed themselves off as an Austrian if they'd been a member of the Stasi. She surmised that Schneider may not have been the first victim of the group responsible for his death.

Meyer herself would look into the possibility that a vigilante-type group might exist, dedicated to bringing former Stasi officers to justice. She'd mentioned this to Dodds and Curtis, and told them to keep their eyes and ears open in case they came across a suggestion of the existence of such a group as their own inquiry progressed.

"This could take forever, Nick," Curtis said to his friend as the pair sat in the canteen at headquarters, doing their best to enjoy the simple lunchtime fare.

"I think we got the shitty end of the stick for sure, mate," Curtis replied as he speared a fat greasy chip, smothered in salt and vinegar, into his mouth, as he also passed comment on the food. "My God, Nick, I swear this fish was dead before they pulled it out of the sea."

"Why d'you think I had the cottage pie? I hate the fish they serve up in here. Cheapskates don't serve cod or haddock you know. Betty, one of the cooks, told me they use a fish called pollock nowadays, 'cause it's cheaper."

"Pollock? You're fuckin' kidding me." Curtis was astonished at this revelation. "There's no such fish."

"God's honest truth, Tony. It's a fish, really. They catch them up around Canada or somewhere like that. Betty says they're even serving it in lots of fish and chip shops too."

"Fuck me," said Curtis with a grimace. "Pollock, eh? Well, I don't know about pollock, but it tastes like a load of old bollocks." He laughed and pushed his half-full plate to one side.

Dodds laughed with him and pulled a side plate holding a thick slice of black forest gâteau towards him. "Anyway, as we were saying. It could take ages to find out how many Germans and Austrians died in the UK in the last five bloody years."

"We ought to see what the PNC and HOLMES can come up with," Curtis suggested. He was referring to the Police National Computer System and then to the Home Office Large Major Enquiry System, both databases being available to assist the police nationwide in their need for information; the second acronym was, amusingly, based on the name of Sherlock Holmes.

"Right," said Dodds. "Are we okay doing it ourselves … or should we go through Paul Ferris, do you think?"

"We can do it," Curtis replied, "but let's keep Sergeant Ferris in the loop. He might be able to suggest some short cuts we can use to circumvent some of the bullshit we'll find on the systems."

"Circumvent? Bloody hell, Tony, you been eating a dictionary or something?" Dodds joked.

"Cheeky sod, Dodds. I'm not some Scottie Road Scally, I'll have you know, la'." Curtis laughed. "I did go to bloody school once, you know."

"Does that mean once, as in one day?" Dodds was enjoying himself at his friend's expense.

"Shut it pal, or I'll tell that new girlfriend of yours you're recovering from an STD."

"You wouldn't dare, you fucking toe-rag." Dodds looked horrified, but he knew that Curtis's wicked sense of humour meant he just might.

"Try me." Curtis knew he had the upper hand, now.

"Okay, peace." Dodds pleaded.

The two friends bumped knuckles in a friendly truce and returned to thoughts about the investigation.

"Let's start closer to home," Dodds said, after a few seconds of private thought. "Fat Willy at the morgue will be able to tell us if he's had any Germans or Austrians pass through his hands during that time."

"True," Curtis agreed. "You never know, we might even be helping the other half of the investigation if we manage to unearth any unknowns that could identify the body of the real Brother Bernárd, too."

"Okay, so, let's go see Doc Nugent."

"Sure, but let me phone ahead and make sure he's free to talk to us. I don't fancy turning up to find him up to his elbows in some poor bastard's blood and guts."

"You go and make the call, la'. I'll let know Sofie know what we're doing."

Lunch over, the two detectives rose from the table and made their way back to the squad room, where Derek McLennan was just hanging up his phone as they passed his desk.

"What you up to, Derek?" Curtis asked as Derek waved a hand in greeting.

"Just been talking to Doctor Nugent. We're checking on any unidentified bodies found in his area since the time of Brother Bernárd's arrival in the country."

Curtis groaned.

"What's up, Tony?"

"Only that me and Nick aren't going to be too popular. We're about to ask Doc Nugent if he's had any German or Austrian victims on his slab in the last few years."

"Right, I see. Yes, he's definitely not going to be best pleased getting two different requests from us in the space of a few minutes."

"Was he able to give you any help?" Curtis asked.

"He's promised to look into it for us. He reckons that he's had around a dozen unidentified bodies during the timeframe we're interested in. Thing is, the boss is sure that if the killers wanted to make sure the fake Brother Bernárd was accepted, no questions asked at the priory, they'd have to have made damn sure the body of the real monk was unidentifiable, so that should make Doctor Nugent's task easier. I doubt he'd have more than a couple of corpses in that category in that time," McLennan replied.

"So what you gonna do if he can't help you?" Curtis asked.

"To be honest, Tony, it's a long shot, asking him if he can help us out. I have a feeling the killers would want to make sure there was zero chance of the body ever being identified. My theory is that they either transported the mutilated remains to another area and hid them well or—and this is more likely—they had a boat ready and carried the body downriver and out to sea, where they probably weighted it well and tossed the poor bugger in to the Irish Sea."

"Okay. I can see why that would be the best option, if it was me that was the killer," Curtis agreed. "So, as Doc Nugent won't have a lot to do for you, he might not be too averse to helping with our inquiry."

"You know he'll help if he can, Tony. He'll huff and he'll puff and make out he's doing you the biggest favour in the world, while complaining about the workload he's suffering under, but then he'll tell you he'll get back to you in a day or two. Grumpy old sod," Derek McLennan grinned at his colleague.

"Aye, right enough; his bark's worse than his bite and he definitely knows his stuff," Curtis agreed. "Catch you later, Derek, I'd better go and call our Fat Willy."

* * *

Sure enough, William Nugent did indeed 'huff and puff' as Derek McLennan had put it, but in the end he agreed to look into Curtis's request, making no promises he'd be successful in a search with such broad parameters. As he said, "DC Curtis, I hope you and your boss realise the enormity of the task you've just dropped in my lap?"

"In what way, Doctor?" Curtis asked.

"Do you have any idea how many bodies come through the mortuary in just one year, never mind five?"

"Erm, well, no, I don't."

"Aye, indeed, young man. Ye've nae idea," the Glaswegian accent was now to the fore, indicating Nugent was irritated. "God, man, not every corpse we see is a victim of suspicious circumstances, and in the case of unidentified bodies, it's not always possible to establish nationality. Do ye ken what I'm saying?"

"Yes, I think I do, Doctor. But whatever you can do, you can be sure we'll appreciate it."

"Aye, well, just you be telling that inspector of yours he's going to owe me a couple of nice, large malt whiskies when I've done half the work for you laddies, and possibly solved your case for you."

Tony Curtis smiled to himself as William Nugent proceeded to acquiesce to his request, much as Derek McLennan had predicted.

"Don't you worry, Doctor Nugent. I'll be sure to give DI Ross your message, and thanks for helping us out."

"I've nae done anything yet, laddie. Save your thanks until I've actually done something. Believe me, I know what you're working on and I will do ma best, as usual, all joking aside. I'll call ye back in a day or two, okay?"

"Thanks again." He was pleased to have secured the pathologist's assistance. "I'll wait to hear from you."

"Aye, you do that. I'll be in touch," Nugent said, hanging up before Curtis could say anything else, leaving the detective staring at the silent telephone for a few seconds, before he replaced it on its cradle, a smile tugging at his lips.

* * *

Izzie Drake and Gary, (Ginger) Devenish were once again paying a visit to St. Emma's, where, after being received by the Prior, Brother Gerontius, Drake stayed to question him, while Devenish went in search of Brother Simon. It was time to follow up on the meagre suspicion that existed where the former stuntman-turned-monk was concerned.

"Brother," Drake started as she took a seat across from the Prior. "When Brother Bernárd first arrived here, I presume he knew none of the existing monks and nuns in advance?"

"That's correct, Sergeant. He was what I call a studious type of man, not one given to talking overly much. His English was fairly good and he could have held more than passable conversations with any of us, but he was, perhaps, a little reticent, possibly nervous of his new surroundings. Some might have called him anti-social. I simply saw him as being a little introverted and even socially awkward."

"And did there ever come a point where his attitude or his personality appeared to undergo a change, no matter how slight or subtle?"

The Prior didn't reply immediately, and Drake could tell the man was giving it deep thought.

"I honestly can't say for sure. You see, we had so little direct contact or interaction. Of course, I welcomed him upon his arrival and showed him round the library, where he would take up his duties. Brother Geoffrey has had problems with his eyes for some time and it seemed logical for a scholar like Brother Bernárd to take over the duties as librarian."

"And did Brother Geoffrey show any resentment at losing the post of librarian?"

"Oh no, not at all. He'd be the first to admit to his failing eyesight and I'm sure that in the long run, he saw the change as a blessing. I did notice, just once, that Brother Bernárd seemed to have a little difficulty in recalling the names of a couple of us. This was about six weeks after his arrival. I can't be certain of exact dates. I just put it down to a spot of absent-mindedness."

This information gave Drake cause to believe that the disappearance of the real Brother and the insertion of the impostor must have taken place around that time, which led her to her next question.

"When he first arrived, did Brother Bernárd have reason to leave the priory for any reason?"

"Well, yes. We encourage all our new arrivals to get out and about during their early weeks with us to explore the place in which they are living, perhaps visit some of the local churches—basically, just explore their new environment. He told me he'd done as I suggested and made a few trips into town ... and he did tell me he'd enjoyed walking along the waterfront at the pier head. It had made him think of the thousands of souls who'd left from Liverpool to begin a new life in the New World, just as he was beginning a new stage of his own life here in Liverpool."

"Then anyone could have seen him and followed him, and planned to waylay him?"

"Theoretically, yes, but it's not like he would announce his next trip to town in advance."

"You're right, of course," Drake conceded the point. Thinking aloud, she said, "We need to try and work out when and how Brother Bernárd was taken."

"I feel awful, Sergeant Drake," the Prior admitted, his expression woeful. "At some point, the newest member of our community left the priory on some innocent premise and was abducted, and probably murdered, and I never even noticed that his place had been taken by an impostor, a doppelganger. What kind of a leader does that make me?"

"A human one," Drake insisted. "Listen, Brother Gerontius. I've been thinking about this and the reason for them choosing a monk to provide a hiding place for Paul Schneider. This was the perfect place, and they must have already had Brother Bernárd targeted in Austria, where they realised they'd found a fitting victim for the identity

swap. The Brother looked enough like Schneider for them to be able
to cosmetically change Schneider's appearance and it must have been
like manna from Heaven for them when they learned he was coming
to England. Here he was, in a location where nobody knew him and
where daily contact with you and the others would be so minimal, that
you wouldn't even notice the substitution."

"I think I understand what you're getting at," Brother Gerontius
said, feeling a little less guilty, and slightly reassured by Drake's sum-
mation of the situation. "So, whether Bernárd had come here or stayed
in the monastery in Austria, he's likely have suffered the same fate?"

"Not likely, Brother Gerontius: *definitely,*" Drake emphasised the final word. "Once they'd earmarked him as the perfect candidate for the
substitution, I'm afraid his fate was sealed."

The Prior looked incredibly sad and Drake knew that he'd probably
still feel some sense of guilt, no matter how much she or her colleagues
might try to reassure him otherwise. Returning to her inquiry regarding the real monk's activities in his time at St. Emma's, she asked,

"Okay, you couldn't have known his exact itinerary, but do you
know of any places he regularly visited on his trips into the city?"

"Yes, I can at least help you there. He told me he used to spend time
in the Central Library, on William Brown Street. He'd made friends
with one of the librarians there who was helping him to locate information on the history of the Benedictines in the North of England.
I'm sure you'll be able to find out who it was at the library. He also
found a bookshop where they sell antiquarian books, and he brought
one home one day. I was amazed, because I imagined such books must
cost a fortune. He stunned me by saying the owner of the shop had
loaned it to him. I do know the name of the shopkeeper because it was
so relevant."

"What was the name?" Drake asked quickly, hopeful that she'd have
at least one outside contact that might help them find out what happened to the missing monk.

"His name was Benedict, Sergeant Drake," the Prior chuckled. "I think his parents must have had a sense of humour, because they gave him the Christian name of Arnold."

"Arnold Benedict?" Drake considered it and then, she remembered her lessons in American history at school. "Of course! Benedict Arnold! Wasn't he a traitor to the Americans or something?"

"Indeed he was, Sergeant. He was an American general during the War of Independence against the British, and he changed sides to fight for the British. He's buried here in England, I believe."

"Well, I see what you mean about the shopkeeper's parents … or maybe they just thought the two names went together well."

"Maybe so. Anyway, that's why I remembered him. I asked why he had loaned such a valuable book to Brother Bernárd, who'd smiled at me and said it wasn't a personal loan, that the book was officially loaned to the Priory of St. Emma. I laughed at the time and congratulated him on his resourcefulness." He smiled as he stared into the distance, recalling that day. "He said God guided him in his negotiations and I couldn't really argue with him. So, the book stayed with us and I received a call from Mr Benedict a few months later asking if we'd finished with it. Of course!" Realisation dawned on the Prior and his eyes widened. "The impostor would have been unaware of the loan. That's why he looked oddly at me when I reminded him he needed to return the book to the owner. He blustered a bit about having forgotten about it and promised to return it. The book had been kept in a bag with the shop's name and address on it, or I bet he wouldn't have known where to take it back to."

"Thank you, Brother. You've given me something to go on, at least. It's not much, but it's a start."

"I just want to help, Sergeant Drake. This is a nightmare for all of us, as I'm sure you realise."

Drake did indeed realise how this must be affecting the Prior and all those in his care at St. Emma's, and she was able to reassure him that they were doing all they could to resolve both murders, as it was 99% certain that this was the fate that had befallen the real Brother Bernárd.

\* \* \*

Brother Simon was growing agitated as DC Devenish tried to get him to admit to knowing more than he'd disclosed about the murder of the man he'd known as Brother Bernárd.

"Look, Constable—"

"That's Detective Constable," Devenish asserted, cutting him off.

Brother Simon grew more frustrated.

"Sorry, Detective Constable. I know you seem to think I had something to do with the death of Brother Bernárd, or whatever his real name was, but you're wrong, *very* wrong. I don't know how else to convince you. I never knew him before coming here. I hardly spoke to him while he was here and I am, after all, a man of God."

"You wouldn't be the first man of God in history to have committed an act of murder, Brother," Devenish said curtly.

Gary, (Ginger) Devenish often surprised people who found themselves in his presence. The young detective, at twenty-five years old, had a look that belied the steely interior behind surface appearances. With his red hair, 'Ginger' Devenish (hence the nickname), and a face that would have looked at home on an eighteen-year old teenager, slim, but standing almost six feet tall, he'd undergone a great apprenticeship before being invited to join Ross's team. He'd previously served with Liverpool's Port Police, and had faced many a tough adversary in some of his dealings with the criminal elements that almost inevitably populated the dockside area of the city. He was not a man to underestimate, as Brother Simon was now realising.

"Why is it you believe I'm involved in the murder? Can you at least tell me that?"

"You were a stuntman in the film industry. You're physically fit and definitely have the strength to have overcome Brother Bernárd, as he was known, who was no weakling, by all accounts. You have no solid alibi for the half hour or so immediately before his death, and to top it all, you were quite evasive while being questioned on our last visit.

Nothing solid there, I admit, but you were holding something back, my colleague was sure of it."

The monk hesitated before replying.

It appeared to Devenish that the man was fighting against some inner turmoil. His body language was that of a man with something to hide, but *what* exactly could it be?

Finally, Brother Simon appeared to reconcile his inner torment and with a shrug of his shoulders, he revealed all.

"What I'm about to tell you could get me thrown out of the order and stripped of my status, so please, if it's possible, I'd be grateful if you could keep this information confidential."

"That will depend on whether what you tell me has any bearing on the murder," Devenish stated firmly.

"I told your colleague I was in the utility room when the murder occurred, and that was true, but what I didn't reveal was that I was in there with someone else."

"Tell me," Devenish said.

"There's a lady who occasionally comes to visit the priory and does a few odd jobs for us. She's a single mother and the few pounds she earns helps her keep her two kids fed and clothed. She wasn't supposed to be here that day, and she'd entered the grounds through the gate in the rear wall and had met me in the utility room."

Now that Devenish had squeezed the truth from the former stunt man, he soon managed to unravel the rest of his sordid story.

"Her name's Eileen Burke. She lives in a two-bedroomed semi in Norris Green. We just got talking one day and then as time passed, we grew closer … until one day, I couldn't stop myself and I pulled her to me and kissed her. I knew it was wrong, but I truly couldn't help myself, and one day, we … we…"

"You had sex with her," Devenish didn't mince his words.

Brother Simon's face turned a bright crimson as he did his best to avoid making direct eye contact with the detective.

"Yes," he replied, appearing crestfallen, his voice barely above a whisper.

"Was it just the once, or was this a serious relationship?" Devenish pushed for a full explanation from the crestfallen monk.

"We've done it three times, so I suppose you could say it's a bit more than a casual fling."

"And at the time of the murder, were you indulging in intimate relations with the lady while the man you knew as Brother Bernard was being murdered?"

Eyes downcast, Brother Simon nodded his head; the shame he felt at his admission weighed heavily upon him. He recalled the few minutes while he and Eileen made love, with her sat on top of one of the utility room's four washing machines as he stood, positioned between her legs, his passion overflowing.

"I'll need Eileen's address," Devenish said, bringing the monk back to reality. Then he asked the most delicate question so far. "Does the lady have an ex-husband, or maybe a partner in the picture?"

"No, thank God," the monk replied without hesitation. "I'd never have allowed the situation to develop if she was a married woman. I'm not totally without scruples, Detective Constable."

Devenish could see that the admission had taken a toll on Brother Simon, but he was quick to reassure him.

"I'm here to ascertain the facts, Brother, not to judge you on your actions with the lady in question. If she corroborates your version of events, it'll put you in the clear as far as the murder is concerned. You should feel relieved at that."

"I suppose so, but what if Brother Gerontius and the others find out about me and Eileen, I'll probably be asked to leave the order."

"As far as I'm concerned, and I'm sure my boss will agree with me, if your alibi holds up, there's no reason why we should inform the Prior of your little," Devenish hesitated as he thought of the right word, "indiscretion." With a quick smile, he instructed the recalcitrant monk to wait a moment. He guessed the man of God would soon be deep in prayer, begging for forgiveness, as he walked into the fresh air to make a call to Ross.

"Well done, Ginger," Ross said when Devenish provided the details of his interview with Brother Simon. "Leave him to stew for a while and get yourself over to Norris Green and speak to this Eileen Burke. If she confirms his story, we can pretty much eliminate Brother Simon as a suspect, unless you think she's giving him a false alibi after speaking to her."

Devenish next called Izzie Drake, who was still in the Prior's office. She was happy for him to take the car, as she estimated she'd be some time with Brother Gerontius, and to call back for her when he'd seen the lady, if she happened to be at home.

After next informing Brother Simon of his intentions, Devenish set off for the home of Eileen Burke, arriving just as she pulled up outside her home in a red ten-year-old Nissan Micra. He realised she was the woman he needed to speak to as she exited the car, removed two bulging shopping bags from the boot, and walked up to the front door of the house, using her key to gain entry.

Devenish quickly got out of his unmarked police Peugeot and followed her up the garden path. He called her name. She stopped, just as she was about to enter her home and turned to see who was trying to speak to her. Devenish identified himself and Eileen Burke instantly blushed, as though she knew precisely why a policeman was now standing in her doorway, requesting to speak with her.

"Please come in," she said nervously. "I just need to put these things away. I don't want the frozen stuff to start defrosting and going off."

"Let me help," he said, picking up the two shopping bags and following her through to the kitchen, where she quickly unpacked her shopping and installed the items in the relevant locations, mostly in the freezer, but with some fresh cabbage, carrots and onions being placed in the fridge. A number of cans of soup, baked beans and tinned spaghetti hoops, presumably for her children, went into a small pantry, along with two loaves of sliced white bread. Finally, she turned to him, thanked him for his help, and put the kettle on to boil.

"Tea or coffee?" she asked, by way of an invitation.

"Coffee, please," he replied. "Milk and one sugar for me."

She pointed to the dining table and he took the hint and seated himself on one of the four chairs positioned around it. She busied herself making the drinks and he took a good look at the woman who appeared to have tempted an otherwise pious monk away from the straight and narrow.

Eileen Burke stood around five-feet-two-inches tall, had wavy blonde hair that he guessed was dyed, given the dark roots in her scalp. Her hair fell just above collar length, in a sort of modern bobstyle. She wore a navy-blue long-sleeved dress with a narrow black belt that accentuated a narrow waist; the hem falling just above the knee, showing her legs to good effect in a pair of low-heeled black shoes. She possessed an attractive face and wore a minimum of make-up that still managed to enhance pretty blue eyes. Pale pink lipstick added fullness to her lips, and Ginger Devenish could definitely see how a normally celibate monk might be attracted to the woman who stood before him.

She placed a large mug of coffee on the table in front of him. Eileen chose not to sit, and instead stood, leaning back against the kitchen unit that held the draining board containing clean dishes and cutlery from the day's breakfast.

"I suppose you're here about Brother Simon," she said before Devenish could speak. "He said it might all come out in the course of your investigation."

"That's right, Ms Burke," he replied matter-of-factly. "I need to ask you a few questions of a very personal nature, I'm afraid."

"You want to know if he was shagging me while that poor man was being murdered, is that right?"

Taken aback by her openness, Ginger Devenish took a second or two to compose himself before responding.

"Well, yes, though I wouldn't have put it so bluntly, Ms Burke."

"Oh, for God's sake, call me Eileen. I can't be doing with all this Ms Burke rubbish, and anyway, it's Miss Burke, not Ms. I hate all that modern crap. Either I'm a Miss or a Mrs, as far as I'm concerned. I never married my children's father. We lived together for nearly eight years, and then he went and got himself killed in an accident on the oil rig in the North Sea, where he worked."

"I'm sorry for your loss," Devenish said, but she waved him to continue with his questions. "Please, can you tell me exactly what happened during the time you were with Brother Simon on the day of the murder?"

An almost playful, devilish grin crossed her face as she spoke.

"*Exactly* what happened was that I went into the Priory's utility room to put a couple of loads into the washing machines. Pauline Tennant, who does some part-time hours earlier in the day, usually sorts any washing out into the various colours and fabrics, so it's easy for me when I arrive in the evening. I usually do three days a week, from four-thirty to seven p.m. My mum looks after the kids for me. She picks them up from school, gives them their teas, and then either takes them to the nearby park or lets them watch the telly, or play games on the Nintendo game thingy she bought them for Christmas and keeps at her house for when they spend time with her. Anyway, you don't want to know all that really, do you?"

Before Devenish could reply, she continued. "I'd just loaded up one of the two machines with whites, and was bending down as I loaded the next machine with colours, when the door opened, and Simon stood in the doorway smiling at me, as I must have presented quite an inviting view. To cut a long story short, he came to me, and though I probably looked a right mess, he kissed me … and then one thing led to another. He lifted me up and sat me on top of the washing machine, Then, I just sort of hiked my skirt up and, well, we did it; you know what I mean?"

"You had sex with him, right?"

"That's what I just said, wasn't it?"

"Yes, of course you did. How long has your relationship been going on with Brother Simon?"

"About three months, I suppose … at least since we first did it, that is. It's not like we've been bonking like rabbits, or anything like that. The other day was the fourth time, I think. We never meant for it to happen in the first place. He used to talk to me when I was working and he told me about his previous life as a stunt man, and I just loved to hear him telling me about the places he'd been and some of the stars he'd worked with, and one day something just sort of clicked between us, and the next thing I knew he was on top of me, and we were making love. He was mortified afterwards, saying he'd betrayed his calling and would be thrown out of the priory if the Prior found out. I kept apologising, but he said it was his fault, he should have known better, but he found me irresistible, so he said. Since then, we've tried to contain things, but we just seem to end up like we were the day that poor man was killed." She finally stopped to catch a breath.

"I see. Thank you for being open and honest with me, Eileen."

"That's okay. You didn't think Simon killed that other monk, did you?"

"We have to look into everyone's alibi, their whereabouts, and so on," Devenish replied casually. "If what you've told me is the truth, then Brother Simon couldn't have killed the man, could he?"

"It is the truth, I'd swear on the Bible, if I had one."

"You're not a Catholic then, Eileen?"

"Me? No. I was never brought up to be religious and, to be honest, it's never interested me, either way. I suppose I'm what you'd call an agnostic."

Devenish left Eileen Burke's home soon afterwards and phoned Ross with the results of his interview with Brother Simon's lover.

"Okay, well done, Ginger. If she's being truthful with you, it clears Brother Simon of the murder."

"I got the strong impression she was telling the truth, sir," Devenish said. "Her body language and constant eye contact with me gave me no hint that she was lying or being evasive."

"Okay, for now, we'll cross him off our list, but keep his name in reserve in case something happens to discredit his and this woman's story. Better get back here, after picking Sergeant Drake up of course. We need to dig deep if we're to find this damned killer, Ginger."

"On my way," Devenish acknowledged as he set off on his return to the priory where, after picking up Drake, he'd head back to headquarters.

He couldn't help thinking that, so far, all they were succeeding in doing was eliminating suspects without having any real leads to go on. Drake agreed with him as they travelled in virtual silence on the journey. He knew Ross wasn't happy, nor were any of the team for that matter. He hoped Sofie Meyer was having better luck with her side of the investigation in Austria. Little did he know, however, that his colleague DC Samantha Gable was about to make a significant discovery.

# Chapter 16

## Another Day, Another Death

Andy Ross cut a frustrated figure after receiving Drake and Devenish's latest reports. He knew they were no further forward than they'd been a day earlier, and pressure was mounting to achieve a degree of progress with the investigation.

"We need something, Izzie," Ross said solemnly. "I've just been informed by Oscar Agostini that the brass are putting pressure on DCS Hollingsworth and, as supportive as she may be, she needs to be able to show we're not just chasing our arses up here. This bloody case has grown wings of its own and it seems certain political elements are expressing an interest in our investigation."

"Why would politicians get involved in a local murder case in Liverpool?" Drake wondered aloud.

"Maybe because one of them is somehow connected to this bloody Freedom Train for former Stasi members," Ross conjectured. "Sam has a list of names and she's doing her best to discover if any of them are connected to the old East German secret police."

"I hope she's being careful. She could be stirring up a real hornet's nest." Drake looked worried.

"I think she knows what she's doing, and she's had a similar warning from some spook in London who Scotland Yard put her on to."

"Okay, but what do we do in the meantime?"

"There's one area we've neglected so far, Izzie, and it's my fault for not realising it sooner."

"I'm all ears," Drake replied with a wry smile.

"We've looked at all the legitimate people who live at the priory, right?"

She nodded, but remained silent.

"Wrong," Ross said. "We haven't looked into the *other* people who work there—volunteers who mostly only work a few hours a week out of the kindness of their hearts. It was realising that Brother Simon has been having an affair with one of them that set me thinking on that track. We know there's a gardener who cuts the grass … and maybe three or four more who have free access to the place. I want them all checked out."

"Oh shit. I've only just got back from the place." Drake looked and felt as if she should have known to check out the ancillary volunteers while she was at the Priory.

Ross realised what she might be thinking and didn't give her a chance to feel guilty about the oversight.

"Like I said, it's my fault for not pushing for a fuller investigation in the first place. I must be getting senile in my old age."

"It's still early." Drake ignored his self-deprecating remark. "I'll grab Ginger and head back out there."

"Yes, please do it now, Izzie. I don't want this case to get away from us because we missed something obvious, that was sticking out under our noses to begin with."

Drake placed a hand on his broad shoulder as she rose, ready to leave the office. It was a mark of the familiarity that existed between the pair after so many years of working together and was simply a gesture of reassurance. She knew just how Ross's mind worked. He'd be beating himself up internally, even though there was no need to. She felt the chances of one of the voluntary workers being involved in either of the murders that centred on the priory were slim, though she mentally agreed to reserve judgement on that score.

\* \* \*

Sam Gable, meanwhile, almost stumbled on their first real clue. Working with the list of names provided by the man known only as Vince, who she was correctly convinced worked for MI6, she searched through what was known of the six men he suspected might have a connection to the old Stasi's escape organisation.

Four of the six were businessmen based in Germany; logical, she thought. Two of the names, however, raised little red flags in her mind. German citizens Joachim Weber and Jürgen Ackermann lived and worked in Austria, and the two men were apparently reasonably wealthy. By itself, of course, she realised this wasn't enough to raise suspicions, but, then her research threw up the fact that Ackermann lived in a large country house only ten miles from Feldkirch, in close proximity to the area where the monastery from which the real Brother Bernárd departed on his fateful journey to England. Gable believed she might be on to something, especially when she failed to find any information that identified the source of Ackermann's wealth. Weber lived in Vienna and was the son of a wealthy banker, and seemed less likely to be involved in the so-called Freedom Train organisation; she wouldn't rule him out yet, though.

Her next stop was the desk of Sergeant Paul Ferris, the team's computer and information specialist. If anyone could help her at that moment, Ferris was the man. As she stood just behind his chair, he turned, smiled, and said,

"Sam, I can tell by the way you're standing there that you want my help, so come on, out with it. What can I do to help?"

"You read minds very well," she smiled back at him. "I need your help to try and find out some personal information about a German national living in Austria, who seems to be independently wealthy, with no visible means of support … and who just happens to live within ten miles of the monastery at Feldkirch."

"Ah, a little mystery for us to solve, Kat," he replied, turning to bring the team's administrative assistant, Kat Bellamy into the conversation.

The attractive, blond-haired woman was experienced at working with Ferris, her computer skills being only a couple of steps below his own. "Better pull your chair over here."

Kat quickly used her feet to propel her wheeled chair across to join Ferris at his desk. His computer cursor blinked in readiness for whatever questions Sam was about to throw at him.

Working with Ferris and Bellamy, Sam was perpetually astounded at the proficiency of the Sergeant and his assistant; as always, with consummate ease, they quickly ascertained the information she needed.

"Right Sam, here's what we have," Ferris began to summarize. "Jürgen Ackermann, age fifty, was born in the Soviet sector of Berlin, making him originally a citizen of the German Democratic Republic—or as we knew it better, East Germany. Parents, Hans and Magda Ackermann. His father was a minor functionary in the local Communist party, so it's highly likely that Jürgen was brought up with strict Communist ideals. He attended the local state school and it appears he later studied mechanical engineering at college … but there's no record of him ever having earned a living from any form of occupation related to his studies. He did work in an aircraft factory however, and rose to a position of some authority, presumably aided by his political activities."

"Look, I'm sorry, but how does this explain his apparent wealth?" Sam interrupted, as she was becoming frustrated.

"I'm coming to it, Sam, patience, please."

"Sorry, Sarge, go on."

With a dry smile, Ferris did just that.

"After the fall of communism, and once reunification had taken place, Ackermann appears to have disappeared for a while, resurfacing as part of a criminal gang who it was believed were responsible for a number of bank raids, and of carrying on a large protection racket. It seems, along with democracy, free enterprise reached the criminal element pretty fast in the old East German state."

"So, crime paid for Herr Ackermann?"

"Look like it, Sam, but here's where things get interesting. Ackermann rose quickly in the criminal ranks until, he was suspected of belonging to a death squad that was systematically eliminating rival gang leaders. When the opposition gangs put out a contract on dear Jürgen, he fled the country."

"And settled in Austria, right?"

"*Wrong*, Samantha."

Sam looked baffled by this revelation.

Ferris didn't keep her waiting for the explanation.

"He next surfaced in Trieste, Italy, where he lived in relative luxury in a villa overlooking the sea. He never thought about changing his name and stayed put until a mysterious fire burned his villa to the ground. The local fire brigade suspected, but couldn't prove, arson; soon afterwards, Ackermann left Trieste, eventually showing up in Austria at his current home near Feldkirch. As far as an occupation is concerned, Ackermann has no discernible business interests, but in addition to his home, he has a small fleet of luxury cars, likes to visit casinos, where he's known as a big spender, and always has a couple of pretty girls on his arms."

"You make him sound like a villain from a Bond movie," Sam commented.

Ferris was forced to concur.

"You're right, and because I thought exactly the same, I sent an email to our friends in Feldkirch, and I just received a reply from Klaus Richter five minutes before you arrived."

"And did our Austrian friend enlighten you at all?"

"He did. He already has Herr Ackermann on a watch list and will be communicating his suspicions about the man to Sofie. Ackermann actively discourages visitors to his property and Richter believes he's involved in the illicit drugs trade, although he's not been able to prove it so far. He's never had the resources to put a full-time watch on Ackermann and his people, who has at least four heavies on his staff, according to Richter. With the current investigation now underway, however, he hopes he might have an opportunity to look *very* closely at Ackermann's activities."

"So Ackermann could just as easily be involved in the Stasi's Freedom Train. I'm sure they must have funds set aside to help their people, and that could account for his unexplained wealth," Gable offered quietly.

"Too right," Ferris agreed, "and Kat's research into the Stasi has found that when the Communists fell from power, the old ruling power, the SED, changed its name in late 1989 to the Party of Democratic Socialism, the PDS, and by some clever political chicanery, they were able to hang on to a great big chunk of the old SED's finances after reunification, so if they are funding the escape organisation, they definitely have the funds to do it and could easily be behind Ackermann's mysterious wealth."

"And you can't rule out this Weber character either, Sam," Kat Bellamy added. "I did a little digging and though he comes from a wealthy banking family, Joachim Weber doesn't actually work in the family business. In fact, he doesn't seem to work at all. He spends a lot of time travelling around Europe and makes the occasional trip to Berlin, where the family business is based ... all well and good if he worked in the business, which he doesn't, but it's also the suspected headquarters of the Freedom Train."

\* \* \*

Gable's diligence might have opened a potential door into the investigation. Andy Ross was pleased with her findings. For the first time, he felt they might have a positive lead, but he needed to explore it in more detail. After an in-depth discussion with DCI Agostini, he got what he wanted.

When Sofie Meyer entered the office, Ross quickly laid out his plan.

"Sofie, how do you fancy a trip to Austria?"

She looked stunned. "Really?"

"Really. I think if we're going to get anywhere, we need someone out there who can speak the language, and you're that person. Also, you might need to visit your colleagues in Germany, and it would put you in an ideal position to do that at short notice if needs be."

"It would certainly allow me to work closely with Officer Richter in Feldkirch, and we might learn more from me being on the spot, instead of having to ask Richter for information or relying on second-hand information from him."

"Okay," said Ross, "it's settled then. You'll leave the day after tomorrow. That gives you time to brief your team before you leave. I suggest you leave Sam to lead the investigation at this end while you're out there."

\* \* \*

Meanwhile Izzie Drake was also making progress of a different kind, having returned to the priory to speak with Brother Gerontius—though not, perhaps, as Ross would have wanted.

"Back so soon, Sergeant Drake?" The Prior was surprised by Izzie's rapid return, given she'd only left an hour previously. Ginger Devenish stood close behind her.

"I apologise for intruding upon your time again, Brother Gerontius," she replied, "but I need to ask you about your volunteer or ancillary workers. I understand you have a few unpaid workers who help out occasionally."

"Well, yes, we do, and it's odd you should mention it, but..."

He hesitated and chewed his bottom lip.

Drake encouraged him to continue.

"We only have six in total, and none of them are here more than a few hours a week, but they are usually very reliable people." Concern crossed his face. "The thing is, Daniel Parker who comes to cut the grass, seems to have disappeared. It's most unusual."

Drake was instantly alert. She recalled Nick Dodds having wondered if the man on the motorised mower was worth looking into. A look at Devenish brought a confirmatory nod. He was clearly sharing her thoughts.

"But he was here when we called a few days ago, and you told us at the time that he wasn't here on the day of the murder, right?"

"That's correct, but he should have been here today, and he hasn't showed up. He's never let us down before. I tried ringing him, but there's no reply."

Drake had a thought. "Where do you store your motorised mower and any other heavy gardening equipment?"

"In the barn. It's not really a barn of course, we just call it that. It's on the far side of the grounds, just a large shed really."

"And is it kept locked up?"

"Why, yes, of course. We trust people, but you never know if someone from outside might try and steal the mower, which is worth a few hundred pounds."

Drake had a bad feeling. "I need to see inside that barn, Brother."

Without asking any questions, the Prior took the necessary key from a drawer in his desk and led the way to the building he and the priory residents referred to as 'the barn.'

Situated about twenty yards from the walled kitchen garden, the building did indeed resemble a barn. No actual farming had ever actually taken place on the Priory grounds, so it had never been used as such, although it contained a few stalls where it was possible to keep sheep and goats if needed. The padlock that secured the double wooden doors was locked and as the Prior moved to open the doors using his key, Drake placed a hand lightly on his arm.

"Let me," she said.

"What are you expecting to find?" the Prior asked, bemused.

"I'm hoping, nothing," Drake replied quietly. "But it helps to be safe rather than sorry."

Brother Gerontius stepped back and handed the key to Drake. The well-oiled padlock opened easily when she turned the key. Slowly, she pushed open the door, and she and Devenish stepped into the barn.

Immediately, the two detectives' nostrils were assailed by the unmistakable scent of death—the metallic, coppery smell of blood. Without seeing anything, they knew they were about to find something neither of them wanted to.

"Please, stay back," Drake instructed the Prior.

Brother Gerontius wasn't immune to the wretched smell and though he wasn't quite sure what it signified, he realised it was nothing good. He did as he was asked.

"We'll check the stalls first, Ginge," she said, as she and Devenish cautiously began their examination of the barn. Drake began at one end of the row of six stalls, Devenish at the other. A sudden cry from Devenish made Drake stop in her tracks.

"Sorry, Sarge," he exclaimed. "Stubbed my toe on an old rake on the ground. Didn't see it there."

"Bloody fool, you nearly gave me a heart attack," she laughed nervously.

Mere seconds passed before Devenish spoke again. "Er, Sarge."

"Judging by the smell, you've got something."

Drake walked over and joined him by the second furthest stall from the rear.

Grimacing, Devenish retreated a few steps.

"And flies. I hate fucking flies. Why does there always have to be flies?"

"Where there's death, there's flies, Ginge. You know that."

Drake reached the stall and peered inside. Despite her years of experience, she had to fight her gag reflex. The flies were well occupied on and around the corpse. It lay on its back with blood pooled under the body; fa two-pronged hay fork had not only penetrated the upper chest, but had speared the body right through to the ground.

"Bloody hell," she spoke, just as Brother Gerontius tentatively stepped up behind her.

Peering over her shoulder, the Prior took one look at the corpse and immediately retched. Trying hard to hold on to the contents of his stomach, he turned and ran out of the barn, finally releasing it as he reached the open air. He'd had the presence of mind to know he was liable to contaminate the crime scene, as he later explained to Drake, for which she was truly grateful.

"Better call it in, Ginger," she instructed Devenish. "I need to speak to the Prior and make sure it's the lawnmower man."

While Devenish called headquarters, Drake went outside to where the Prior stood, looking ashen-faced and thoroughly shaken.

"*Why?*" he kept repeating, "Why would anyone do such a thing to the poor man?"

Drake had a good idea of the why, but she needed to confirm the victim's identity first of all.

"I'm sorry Brother, but I must ask you to take a look at the body and confirm that it's indeed the man you knew as Daniel Parker."

Slowly, almost robotically, the Prior followed her back into the barn, his footsteps leaden.

He stood beside her at the entrance to the stall containing the body.

"Yes," he nodded, wincing. "That's Daniel. How long has the poor man been lying there?"

"From the look of the body, I'd guess between one or two days," said Drake. "I think the killer paid Daniel a sum of money for the use of his key. He then used the barn from which to carry out his attack on Brother Bernárd."

"But then why kill him?"

"Possibly for one of two reasons. He either killed him because he could identify him or Daniel tried to extract more money from him to buy his silence … and this was his payoff."

The Prior was stunned at Drake's theories and could hardly believe that Parker would have done such a thing.

Andy Ross, however, was more than capable of believing it. He was fully aware of the whole gamut of human weaknesses. When he received the call from Ginger Devenish, he took the news in his stride, although he couldn't help feeling he should have investigated the volunteer workers sooner.

"I presume you've called Sergeant Ferris and got forensics organised."

"Yes, sir. Doctor Nugent is on his way, apparently."

"Right, Ginge. You can consider me on my way, too."

As soon as he hung up the phone, Ross left his office, picking up Sam Gable on the way. "We've got another body. You're with me, Sam."

"Another monk, sir?"

"No, the bloody gardener, or whatever he is."

As the pair drove towards the Priory of St. Emma, Ross couldn't escape the feeling that, somewhere along the course of this investigation, he'd made a mistake, one that could have been responsible for the death of Daniel Parker.

# Chapter 17

### Drake's Theory

On arrival at St. Emma's, Ross and Gable were surprised to find DC Derek McLennan waiting to greet them.

"Derek," Ross said with a quick smile, "What are you doing here?"

McLennan smiled in return.

"I was at the morgue when the call came through and I thought I might be useful here."

As usual, Ross was impressed by McLennan's commitment and professionalism. He had a question though.

"What were you doing at the morgue, Derek?"

"Well, sir, I'd have been giving you a call soon enough. Doctor Nugent had been looking into unidentified remains discovered from the time of the original Brother Bernárd's disappearance. He called me an hour ago to say he'd found a couple of prospects that might fit the bill. I was just getting the information from him when Sergeant Drake's call was redirected to the him and so, here I am."

"As soon as we see what's what here, you can tell me what the doc's found. Now, I take it he's with Sergeant Drake?"

"And Ginger Devenish sir, yes. Follow me."

McLennan led the way and a couple of minutes later they arrived at the barn, where the voice of William Nugent, pathologist extraordinaire, could be heard before they entered the murder site.

"No, no, Francis! I want close-ups from every angle. For God's sake man, have you no' worked with me long enough to know that?"

The strong Glaswegian accent was the clue that told Ross Nugent was in a bad mood. He'd lived in Liverpool long enough to have lost most of his accent but it had a habit of making itself known whenever he was angry or worked up about something. Ross had never previously heard him angry with Francis Lees, his cadaverous assistant, however, however.

"Best tread carefully, people," Ross ordered Sam and Derek. "Sounds like the beast has a thorn in his paw."

"Nice analogy, sir," McLennan commented and then fell silent as he and Sam Gable walked two steps behind Ross into the barn.

"That's grotesque," Sam Gable exclaimed as she took in the scene before them.

"Ah, here at last, are you?" Nugent said, and Ross, deciding that discretion was the better part of valour, simply replied, "Hello Doc."

"Aye, well, as you see, we've already started work here."

"And what can you tell us?" Ross risked a simple question as he joined Gable and McLennan in gazing at the body.

"A simple but bloody case, Inspector," Nugent was decisive. "Yon laddie was stabbed twice with the hay fork."

He indicated what he knew to be the first stab wound.

"The killer attacked from the front, stabbing the victim in the lower abdomen, hence the amount of blood you see that's pooled under the body. The second, immediately fatal wound was directed as you see, into the upper chest cavity and, either by luck or design, penetrated the heart, ending the man's life and stopping further blood flow."

"Because the heart stops pumping at the moment of death, right Doctor?"

"Exactly, DC Gable," he responded. "I can tell you something else. Your victim fell to the ground after the first stab, and then the killer followed up by pulling the hay fork from the wound and applying great force to inflict the second, fatal wound."

"How can you tell the exact sequence of events?" Ross asked and then wished he'd stayed silent.

"If you'd let me finish DI Ross, I'll explain."

"Sorry, Doc, please go on."

"You can tell the killer used extreme force to deliver the killer blow, because the hay fork has penetrated the body and *actually pinned* it to the ground below."

"The killer wanted to make sure Parker wasn't going to get up again," Derek McLennan interjected.

"Aye, you could say that," Nugent replied.

"And look at his face," Izzie Drake gestured. She'd been looking on silently, so far to give Ross a chance to form his own initial opinion.

Indeed, a look at the expression on Daniel Parker's face told them all they needed to know about the man's final seconds of life. His eyes were almost bulging with fear and his mouth was open, seemingly frozen in a grim rictus of death, as though his dying scream had frozen in time and place, a testament to the killer's savagery.

"The man knew he was going to die, and he knew how he was going to die. It's as if the killer was taunting him in those last few seconds … pulling the fork from his stomach and holding it poised, ready to strike … long enough for Parker to experience the fear of his impending demise."

"Bloody hell, Izzie, that's almost poetic," said Ross with a rueful smile. "You've painted a very vivid picture of the poor bugger's final seconds."

"Sorry. It's just the way I saw it when I first looked at him. I sensed his fear, sir, almost as if he was pleading with someone, anyone, to help him, yet at the same time knowing that nobody was coming to his aid."

"I think your sergeant has summed up your victim's last moments quite succinctly," Nugent spoke almost with reverence in his voice, perhaps affected by the holy location of the man's demise.

"She has indeed," Ross agreed, "and I suppose there's no doubt that it's Daniel Parker, Izzie?"

"No doubt at all sir," Drake replied, indicating the far side of the barn, where Brother Gerontius stood, visibly shaken, physically supported by DC Devenish, who stood beside him with a firm hand on his arm. "Brother Gerontius identified him immediately he saw him, before almost passing out from the shock."

"And your theory?" Ross invited her opinion.

"I'd say the killer somehow convinced Parker to provide him with the key to the barn. It would have been the perfect place for him to lie in wait for Brother Bernárd on the day of the murder. He comes out, does the deed, and then disappears in the initial aftermath. He could have got away by taking the path out behind the barn and exiting the grounds somewhere along the rear boundary."

"Good so far," Ross agreed. "But then why murder Parker?"

"Presuming he paid Parker for providing the key, either Parker came back asking for more money to pay for his silence, or the killer simply couldn't risk Parker identifying him and had always intended to do away with him. He could have arranged to meet him here on some pretext, perhaps to return the key, and then …"

"Sounds plausible," Ross murmured, scanning the interior. "That would also indicate that the killer came from outside the priory. An insider wouldn't need to bribe Daniel Parker with money in order to obtain the key."

"I agree, up to a point. But not all the priory's people had reason to use the barn, so maybe it was someone who needed to coerce Parker into handing over the key," she suggested. "But whoever it was must have known the layout of the place and was aware that the barn would serve well as a place of concealment."

"Good point, Izzie. It seems every time we come up with any sort of theory on this bloody case, it throws up more damn questions then we can answer, at least for the moment."

The sound of vehicles pulling up coincided with Ross's statement. Miles Booker and his forensic team had arrived.

Swiftly, they had the barn sealed off as they began their painstaking search for clues and evidence that might help identify the killer. Finally, the murder weapon was withdrawn from Daniel Parker's body, and Nugent and Lees followed it to the mortuary in the waiting ambulance. Though there was little doubt as to the cause of death, Nugent would begin the autopsy. Perhaps he'd prove lucky and would find some trace evidence that could lead Ross and his team to the killer.

Ross's team meanwhile, were put to work questioning the monks, nuns, and the two ancillary workers present at the priory. If the killer wasn't one of them, and Ross was becoming increasingly certain that it wasn't, one of them might have seen or heard something that would help the investigation.

At least, that was his hope.

# Chapter 18

### Bodies and Bones

With Izzie Drake left in charge at the priory, together with Sam Gable and Ginger Devenish, Ross made his way back to headquarters with Derek McLennan.

He needed to know what McLennan had discovered from Doctor Nugent in his search for the remains of the real Brother Bernárd. If they could find the body, or what was left of it after such a long time, it might provide evidence that could help discover those who'd helped the impostor who had spent the last three years masquerading as the monk. If the organisation known as the Freedom Train were openly operating in the UK, Ross was determined to close it down.

He and McLennan were closeted in Ross's office, together with Paul Ferris, whose presence he'd requested. Ferris's computer skills would prove vital to this side of the investigation.

"Well, Derek, I'm all ears. What did the Doc come up with?"

"We have two possibles," replied McLennan. "We owe most of the credit to Francis Lees. Doc Nugent set him to work on the search, and he came up with an initial list of five bodies found in the Mersey-side area within the timeframe, and the Doc narrowed it down to two. We've got two unidentified corpses that fit the bill. Number one was a male, a floater found in the Mersey off Seaforth, though there wasn't much left of the body when it was pulled out. Doc Nugent said it had been well got at by marine life and it was possible that it had been struck by a ship's propeller. It was actually one of Doctor Stanton's cases," he said, referring to one of the other pathologists who worked alongside Nugent.

"And number two?" Ross asked with a frown.

"That's one that was handled by Doc Nugent," said McLennan, "but as there was no suggestion of foul play at the time, it never crossed our bows or any of the other CID teams. Uniform branch handled the case."

"Derek, get on with it, please."

"Yes, sir. Sorry. Exactly two years ago, a male of approximately forty-five years was found in the undergrowth beside the Alt River, close to where it passes under Altcross Road in Croxteth. Doc Nugent felt that the body had been in the water at some time and had undergone extensive decomposition by the time it was found. There were a couple of whisky bottles found nearby, and he thought the man could have been a tramp or wino who'd drunk too much and fell in the river, half-in, half-out, and drowned as a result. Again, there was little left to examine by the time the body was found. We're fortunate that this one was passed to the cold case unit, and it's still an active case, if that's not a contradiction in terms for a cold case. Anyway, I spoke to DI Fry at the unit and he's sending his DS, a Detective Sergeant Church up to us with the file. I spoke to her when we got back and she should be here anytime now."

As McLennan finished speaking, right on cue, a slim-built woman in her mid-thirties strolled into the squad room, her appearance startling one or two of those present. She spoke briefly with Sam Gable and proceeded to Ross's office, where she paused and knocked on the door before responding to Ross's "Come in."

Dressed in a navy skirt and white blouse, the first thing Ross and the others noticed, apart from the woman's luxuriant head of hair, styled to fall over one eye in the style of 40s movie star, Veronica Lake, was the presence of significant scarring down the left side of her face. It didn't take an expert to realise that Fenella Church had been badly burned, and that her hairstyle was an attempt to cover up some of the disfigurement. From one side, she was an incredibly beautiful woman and Ross felt an immediate empathy for her.

"DS Church, I presume," he said, standing and offering his hand, which the she took, returning his hand shake.

"Yes, sir, Fenella Church. How can we help you, sir? It's not often the CCU gets a chance to assist in a live investigation."

"I'm hoping that file in your hand might lead to us identifying the victim in a three-year old murder, which in itself is linked to a series of current-day killings."

" "Wow...that's heavy stuff," she exclaimed. "This one has bugged Alan—sorry, DI Fry and I ever since it landed on his desk."

Ross knew the Cold Case Unit tended to be more informal than most units on the force and wasn't surprised to hear Fry referred to by his first name by his sergeant."

"And when was that?" he asked.

"About two years ago, just after I joined the unit ... after the fire that did this." She indicated her face, and paused for a moment."

With a heavy dose of sympathy in his voice, Ross asked, "What happened Fenella, if you don't mind me asking?"

Fenella Church hesitated and, deciding that Ross was genuinely interested and not seeking the gruesome details, replied.

"Short version, sir. I was driving through Fazakerley when I saw flames coming from a house, and the Fire Brigade weren't on site yet. I didn't even know if they'd been alerted, so I pulled over and called it in. Good job I did, because nobody had noticed the fire and called 999. It was a quiet street and there were few people about. Anyway, I stood looking at the flames, which seemed to be mostly contained in the upper floor. I saw a face at one of the bedroom windows. It was a girl, maybe eight or nine, it was hard to tell, but I could see the terror in her face, and I slipped into auto-pilot mode." She drew a slow breath as she peered across the room, revisiting that moment. "I had to try and save her ... so I ran to the front door, which was locked, damn it, so I kicked it in. I don't know where I found the strength to do that, but

I was in. There were no flames on the ground floor, but the upstairs was clearly ablaze.

"I heard the girl screaming and I didn't think about it, I just ran up the stairs. The landing was burning, but I had to get through those flames, I pulled my jacket off and put it over my head, and ran to the door where the screams were coming from. I got in and grabbed the girl, the fire was spreading fast. I picked her up, and tried to make run for it, but the landing was an inferno by then. I took my jacket and wrapped her in it and tried to make a run for it. Suddenly the ceiling above us gave way and collapsed on us." She shivered visibly. "I could feel the flames licking at my head, my hair … and the pain was indescribable. I staggered down the stairs and just about made it to the door when I collapsed. I suppose shock must have set in … because the next thing I remember, I felt hands were lifting me and then it all went black again."

She smiled woefully. "Later, I learned the Fire Brigade had arrived and someone had seen me enter the house. They got me and the girl out, and even managed to save the mother, who'd lost consciousness in the kitchen. A faulty plug had caused the fire and I spent two months in the Burns Unit. I underwent two skin-graft operations. When I was well enough, they offered me this job and I accepted it, along with the QPM, (Queen's Police Medal) for my so-called gallantry in saving the girl. That's about all there is to tell …, sir, oh, apart from the fact that the hair's a wig. Most of my own was burned to the roots and anyway it's not so bad. I can change my hairstyle without having to spend a fortune at the hairdressers."

The office fell silent as she ended her story, so silent it was possible to hear the proverbial pin drop. All three men were extremely moved by her bravery, first of all in what she'd done to save the child and secondly in having the strength to bounce back and to have the guts to relate it to them.

Andy Ross broke the silence by standing up, reaching across the desk and offering her his hand for the second time in a few minutes. She took it and accepted a second hand shake as he said, "That was a bloody brave thing you did Fenella, and you paid a high price for it. You're in good company. Derek also received the QPM a couple of years ago, different circumstances but equally brave. I'm proud to know you."

Fenella Church blushed as Paul Ferris and Derek McLennan joined Ross in shaking her hand and adding their own compliments. McLennan had received his bravery medal for tackling a gang of armed robbers while off-duty, getting shot in the process. Ross felt he was in good company and now returned to the case in question.

"So, tell us what you have, please."

"Okay, D.C. McLennan said it was urgent, so I only have our case file with me. I'll get the relevant information to you later, if you need it. The body, or what was left of it, was found by a pair of teenagers who were part of a youth project aimed at reclaiming the banks along a section of the Alt where it runs through Croxteth." She opened the folder. "You can see from the photos how overgrown it was before they started work. The body was half in-half out of the water. As these pictures reveal, there truly wasn't much left that could be described as human. The local wildlife had feasted well. Doctor Nugent explained that a body in water decomposes twice as fast in water, so the head and shoulders, which were face down in the river, were well gone by the time it was discovered, and with the other half of it in the open; well, the maggots and animals had seen to the rest."

"So was the Doctor able to find anything useful?" Ross asked, looking forlorn.

"No, not really," Church said apologetically, "but as a result of DC McLennan's inquiry the other day, he recalled the case and came to us, as it fits with your timeline."

"But what specifically made him think of *this* case? It's surely just another unidentified corpse with no means of identification." Ross was losing interest.

"Please tell him about the clothes, Sarge," McLennan pleaded.

"Please do," said Ross. "I need *something* to help me out with this case."

"Okay. I hope this is going to help." Fenella Church turned a page in the file. "As I'm sure you know, sir, natural fabrics, like cotton for example, degrade pretty quickly, while plastics and synthetics can last for hundreds of years. This guy, despite being exposed to the ravages of weather, predators and insects of all types, was found partially clothed. His shoes, made of synthetic leather, were discovered nearby. Not much of a clue, I'll grant you, but when Derek told Doctor Nugent what he was looking for, it pricked a memory in the doctor's brain. The shoes had a label inside that indicated they were *Hergestellt in Österreich*, which translates to, 'Made in Austria'." Church paused for a reaction and she certainly got one.

"It's him!" Ferris was the first to react. "It's *got* to be."

"I agree Paul," Ross concurred.

"I think it must be your man, sir," Church agreed. "Most shoes sold in the UK of foreign manufacture tend to be made in Taiwan, China, Indonesia or other Asian countries. I've never seen shoes made in Austria before, and neither has Doctor Nugent."

Ross suddenly felt a sense of optimism.

"Okay, Fenella, what else can you tell us about the body? Cause of death, for example?"

"Sorry, no luck there, I'm afraid. There were a couple of empty vodka bottles found near the body, which led the pathologist to speculate that the man might have been a down-and-out, a drunk, who imbibed a little too much, and fell. If his head dropped into the water, he could have drowned where he fell, and with the amount of alcohol likely to have been in his system, he wouldn't have known a thing about it."

"Or if he'd been murdered, the killer had bought himself some time by finding a seriously secluded body dump site. It's a perfect way to commit murder, if you think about it. The killer could have abducted Brother Bernárd, forced the alcohol down his throat, and then drowned the poor bugger in the shallows, always assuming there was no evidence to show any signs of violence on the body."

"The body had decomposed too much for Doctor Nugent to establish a definite cause of death, so he listed it as 'Cause of Death Unknown' and the coroner returned an 'Open Verdict'."

"Where are the remains now? Please don't tell me they were cremated."

"No, way sir. He was buried in Anfield Cemetery."

Anticipating what Ross was about to say next, DS Church added, "The burial plot number's in the file."

Before saying anything else, Ross picked up the phone, called DCI Agostini and Doctor Nugent, and told them he wanted the body exhumed. In addition, he asked Nugent to contact his friend, Doctor/Professor Christine Bland. Bland was a top-class forensic anthropologist, who'd helped in the past with the identification of long buried remains. Ross knew that if anyone could help in solving the puzzle of the unknown man, she could.

Oscar Agostini agreed to set the exhumation process in motion and Nugent agreed to contact Bland, and Ross finally felt they were actually getting somewhere.

# Chapter 19

### Feldkirch

Sofie Meyer had arrived in Austria, landing right on time at Friedrichshafen Airport, twenty-nine miles from Feldkirch. She was met at the airport by Klaus Richter, with whom she felt an instant rapport. She decided the Austrian detective would be easy to get along with and as they drove towards Feldkirch, he filled her in with as much information as he'd managed to gather since their last conversation.

Then, on more mundane matters, he said,

"I have booked you in to the Hotel Bären on Bahnhofstrasse, just a two-minute walk from the centre of town. It has wi-fi if you need to do any work from your room, and is well rated on the internet. I hope you will be comfortable there."

"I'm sure it will be fine thank you, Klaus. You have a nice car, by the way," Sofie replied, referring to his classic, silver 1971 Mercedes 280SE, 3.5 litre Coupe.

"Thank you. It is my pride and joy to own such a beautiful car."

"You remind me of one of my colleagues back in England, Detective Constable Derek McLennan, also a classic car fan. He drives a black 1960s Ford Zephyr 6."

"Oh, how appropriate," Richter beamed. "As used in *Z Cars*, am I right?"

Meyer was surprised. "You know of *Z Cars*?"

"Oh yes. I have seen many of the old British Police TV shows on the internet. That one was set in Newtown, a fictional suburb of Liverpool, if I'm correct."

"Yes, that's right. Derek told me all about it when he received the car as a wedding present from his father-in-law and brother-in-law. His brother-in-law restores and sells classic cars."

"I think I would like to meet your Derek McLennan," he grinned, as they pulled up at the Hotel Bären.

After checking in, and depositing her cases in her room, Meyer rejoined Richter, who had waited for her in reception, Sofie refusing his offer to call back in an hour, after giving her time to shower and change. She was keen to start work and would have time to relax and freshen up later.

"I'd rather we get moving on our investigation. DI Ross is placing his faith in me to find a link to this *Freiheitszug* group."

"*Ja*, the so-called Freedom Train. Very well, Sofie. Let us go to work. My sergeant, Emil Wägner, is waiting at the police station. He also is keen to get started."

"And your boss, *Oberstleutnant* Gruber? Will he be there, also?"

"Not at present, no. He received an invitation last night to travel to Vienna. He is meeting with *Oberst* Josef Graff, who is in charge of the Federal Police Bureau for the Investigation of War Crimes and Crimes Against Humanity."

"A very grand title," Sofie replied. "Are the crimes of the Stasi regarded as important here in Austria?"

"You must understand, Sofie. The Stasi are not so important here, but we have a very good liaison with your police in Germany, and any cross-border activity involving wanted Stasi officers is handled by *Oberst* Graff's people. When *Oberstleutnant* Gruber contacted Vienna about your visit, he was directed to the Bureau. Graff, who knows as much as anyone in Austria about the Stasi, invited him to visit his office. When he returns tomorrow we should know much more about their escape organisation."

Sofie Meyer was impressed that her Austrian counterparts were taking the matter so seriously, even more so when she met Sergeant Emil Wägner. The man looked like a slightly smaller version of the Incredible Hulk. Standing at six-feet-four inches, with close-cropped blonde hair, and shoes she guessed must be at least size 12, Wägner was not a man she could imagine anyone winning a fight with. And yet the man, she soon discovered, was an intelligent, affable, gentle giant, dedicated to the principles of law and order.

"Emil will not stand for any nonsense from anyone," Richter informed her. "Though he would prefer to reason with a suspect, he will not hesitate to break bones if he has to."

Meyer smiled at the description, as Emil Wägner sat opposite her, licking an iced-lollipop with gusto, like an excited ten year-old.

"Oh yes, Sofie," the hulk of a man said, between licks of the orange lolly, "as a famous man once said, *'It is better to jaw jaw, than war war,'*" but if I have to, I will put my size to good use."

Wägner said this as he held up his left fist.

She noticed the man's fists could indeed be prodigious weapons.

"Well, let's hope you don't have to break any bones on this case, eh, Emil?"

"Yes, I hope so too," the big sergeant said as he carefully deposited his lollipop stick in the waste bin beside his desk.

The next hour was spent with Richter and Wägner being brought up to date with developments in Liverpool. Meyer left nothing out, including the news from Ross relating to the body found in the River Alt. They then did the same for Sofie. At the end of that time all three detectives were fully conversant with the case as seen from both sides.

"Brother Michael at St. Thomas's Monastery will be most disturbed by your news, Sofie," said Richter with a frown. "Though our inquiries have, I'm sure, prepared him for just such an outcome, it will send a shockwave through the fraternity at the monastery."

"When can we go and see him?" Sofie asked.

"I suggest we wait until *Oberstleutnant* Grüber's return tomorrow. Once we know what he has learned, we can move forward with our inquiries."

Though frustrated at the delay, Sofie agreed to wait, out of courtesy to Richter's superior officer. Meanwhile, Richter and Wägner then set about enlightening her on what they'd gleaned so far about the murky figures behind the Freedom Train. As they knew little more than the Sofie, that disclosure didn't take long. Klaus Richter, however, then made a suggestion that Sofie was keen to take him up on.

"Joachim Weber lives in Vienna of course, but Jürgen Ackermann lives just a few kilometres from here. Would you like to take a look at his home? Oh, I forgot! I have had Emil keeping a watch on Herr Ackerman and guess who visited his home two days ago?"

"Joachim Weber?

"Correct, Sofie. So something definitely connects the two men."

"Now I'm even *more* interested to see where Ackermann lives," Sofie declared.

Twenty minutes later, the three detectives pulled up beside a narrow country lane a few kilometres from Feldkirch. They'd taken Wägner's own car, a six-year-old Volkswagen Passat, thinking it would be less conspicuous if they were seen by anyone from the house. From their vantage point beside a farm gate they had a good view, across a field of Friesian cows, of the home of Jurgen Ackermann. Sofie was impressed. The house resembled a scaled-down German *Schloss*, complete with tall towers at both ends of the building. Using Wägner's binoculars, she viewed three fairly brand-new cars parked in front of the building: two Porsches and a Mercedes.

"Nice motors," she commented.

"The Mercedes is the car Weber arrived in," Wägner said, as they watched two men in dark suits, and wearing sunglasses appear from the side of the building.

They stopped near the cars and appeared to scan the surroundings.

"That's the Schmidt brothers, Gustav and Helmut. Local muscle employed by Ackermann. Any chance of him being an innocent businessman can be discounted by virtue of the fact that he hired those two to guard him and/or his property," Wägner added.

"They're well known to us," Richter said. "Both have done time for various offences, usually associated with violence."

"I think that makes it certain that we need to keep an eye on Herr Ackermann," Sofie concluded.

"Agreed," said Richter.

As he spoke, the doors to the dwelling opened and two men stepped out.

"That's Ackermann on the left, Weber on the right," Wägner pointed out, for Sofie's benefit. "Looks like they're going somewhere."

"That's why the brothers are there," Richter observed, as the duo held the doors to the Mercedes open, and the two men stepped into the rear of the vehicle.

The Schmidt brothers took the front seats, and Gustav sat behind the wheel.

"Perhaps I should mention that Gustav was once jailed for his part in a bank robbery. He was the getaway driver," Emil Wägner said, grinning. "I was the arresting officer. It gave me great pleasure to put that thug away for a few years."

"The trouble is, he only got four years and was out in less than two—time off for good behaviour," Richter frowned. "He was allowed back on the streets far too soon, eh, Emil?"

"Definitely," muttered his sergeant, "but he's kept his nose clean since then."

"Maybe because he's been working for Ackermann?" Sofie suggested.

"I think you're right," said Richter as the Mercedes pulled away from the house and proceeded down the long driveway to the main road, where the car turned left and headed towards the town.

"Do we follow them?" asked Wägner.

"What do *you* think?" said Sofie as she climbed into the car. "Let's go, Emil. I want to know where those guys are going."

# Chapter 20

### Doctor Bland

The exhumation of the remains of the unknown man, now suspected of being Brother Bernárd, took place the following morning, at 6 am to be precise. DCI Agostini had obtained the necessary licence for exhumation. He, Ross and Drake, accompanied by DCs Curtis and Dodds, were present to witness the procedure, along with the deputy manager of Anfield Cemetery and the obligatory Environmental Health Officer.

An ambulance stood by to transport the remains to the morgue and a temporary casket waited, with the lid open, to receive the remains. Ross instructed his detectives to stand well back as the coffin lid was raised. He'd done this before and knew the putrid smell that would emanate from the coffin when the lid was lifted to reveal the corpse within was distinctly unpleasant,

Silently, two gravediggers dug down to the coffin and then prised open the lid to reveal what remained of the unknown occupant of grave number 1026. Everyone worked efficiently and the remains were quickly transferred to the temporary casket, loaded into the ambulance, and driven away. The gravediggers remained behind the screens erected around the gravesite to back-fill the grave. Under existing legislation, Christine Bland had forty-eight hours to examine the remains, after which they would be reinterred.

* * *

An hour later, Andy Ross stood looking out of his office window. He couldn't fail to recognise the distinctive shape and colour of Christine Bland's classic Vauxhall Carlton as it pulled into the car park. The gleaming burgundy paint job sparkled in the morning sunlight. The car, which had belonged to the forensic anthropologist's late father, had been his pride and joy. When she'd inherited it, she kept it as pristine as he'd done when he was alive. After parking in a visitor's space, she extricated her briefcase from the back seat, locked the car, and turned to walk towards the headquarters building. Suddenly, Bland stopped in her tracks and paused to admire the Ford Zephyr 6 owned by D.C. Derek MacLennan. Ross smiled.

Five minutes later, Bland was shown into the squad room by a young uniformed officer, where Ross and Drake were waiting to meet her.

"Christine," he said amiably. "Good to see you again."

"Same here," she replied cordially, "and before we get down to business, who owns that gorgeous Zephyr down there in the car park? Hello, Izzie."

"Doctor Bland," was all Drake had time to say by way of a greeting.

"Ah, I saw you admiring it from my office window," Ross chuckled. "It's Derek McLennan's, as a matter of fact."

"Really?" Bland said, a note of surprise in her voice.

"It was a wedding present," Drake added. "His new brother-in-law restores and sells classic cars."

"It's beautiful … a real-life *Z Car* on your team, in genuine police black, eh?"

"Yes, that old TV show has a lot to answer for," Ross said wryly.

"Well, good for him." Bland instantly 'changed gears', switching to her all business mode in a second. "Now, about this body."

"How much did Doc Nugent tell you?"

"Only enough to have me cancel the rest of my lectures for the week, and have me hot-footing it up to darkest Liverpool ASAP," she said dryly.

"Oh, good," Ross smiled again. The diminutive Christine Bland had that effect on him. Though in her late thirties, she could have passed for ten years younger; she always made him feel fatherly and protective towards her. Moreover, her enthusiasm for her work never ceased to amaze him; Christine Bland was the only woman he knew who could display such enthusiasm over the minutiae of death and its causes. On three previous occasions, she'd been called in to assist the Specialist Murder Investigation Team. As well as being a good friend of the pathologist, Doctor William Nugent, Bland was on the Home Office approved list of Forensic Anthropologists, and thus able to assist in an official capacity when required, (*and* get paid for doing so).

Readers may recall her having appeared previously in *A Mersey Killing, All Saints,* and *A Very Mersey Murder.* As such, she was well acquainted with Ross and his team and got on well with them all.

"How much has Doctor Nugent told you so far?" Izzie Drake asked.

"To be honest, he didn't tell me an awful lot and that was what intrigued me. He's usually full of facts and theories, and yet this time, he could only tell me that this was one of his old cases, which ended up in the cold case files. No sign of foul play. Body left in the open, partially immersed in water. No discernible cause of death. You seem to think it could be the body of a monk who disappeared and was replaced by a doppelganger. He mentioned it had something to do with a recent murder—well, two actually—and that it had links to a wanted former Stasi officer. How am I doing so far?"

"Pretty much bang on," Ross replied, impressed. "We haven't as yet managed to positively identify the remains as the real Brother Bernárd, and I don't suppose we ever will know with a hundred-percent certainty. But, I remember you once told me that you can often tell where a person comes from by trace evidence contained in the body, or something like that."

"That's right," Bland replied. "Our bodies absorb various nutrients and proteins throughout our lives, many of which are specific to the area where we were brought up or lived in. By testing for these in the remains, we can say with a high degree of certainty, and within a few miles, just where that particular person lived while they were alive."

"And you can still do that, even though the body is three years old?" Drake asked.

"Yes, even though some indicators will have degraded, there should be enough left to give you a pretty good indication of where the person spent the majority of their developing years. I'll send samples to my own lab, where we can isolate what we call stable isotopes, using a stable isotope ratio-mass spectrometer."

"You've lost me already," Ross admitted, his brow furrowed.

"Basically, we can find out where someone grew up by evidence found in the teeth and bones. The type of water we drink as a child, the food we eat, all leave traces of Carbon-13; this helps to isolate where someone lived and can often be specific to a very small area. It's a bit more complicated than that but, put simply, you have the basic idea."

"It's amazing what science can do," Ross stated. "How soon can you start, Christine?"

"Whenever you like. I'd have gone straight to the morgue on arrival, but I phoned ahead and William told me he was tied up doing a post-mortem and I'd be better to get the facts of the case from you first. So, anyway, so, here I am."

"Doctor Bland," Sam Gable had walked into the room. "How are you? It's good to see you again."

"I'm good, Sam, thank you. And you? How are you?"

"I'm well, thank you. I like your hair." Sam was the first to comment on Bland's new hairstyle.

She laughed. "Thank you. I don't think anyone else noticed." She'd shortened her hair from its usual shoulder length style to a new page-boy bob, with a fringe almost touching her eyebrows. It was more prac-tical for work, being less likely to fall forward and get in the way of an examination.

"Guilty as charged," Ross looked suitably shamefaced.

"I'd noticed," Izzie Drake said, "but hadn't had a chance to mention it. I like it, too."

Bland winked. "Thanks ladies, but I think DI Ross has other priorities than discussing my latest hairstyle."

"Don't mind me," Andy Ross smiled. "Far be it from me to stop you ladies comparing notes on Christine's hair. I know how important these things are to you girls. I once failed to notice when Maria had changed her hairstyle and I swear she had me on bread and water for a week. Well, near enough," he laughed.

"I think it's time I headed for the morgue," said Bland. "Let's see if we can find out where your mystery body originated."

"And here's just the man to escort you there," Ross said as Derek McLennan walked into the room. "Derek, I have a feeling that Professor/Doctor Bland here would appreciate a ride in your Zephyr, if you'd be kind enough to accompany her to the morgue."

"Hello Doctor Bland. It'd be a pleasure."

"If you don't mind, Derek. I'd love to say I've been in a real *Z Car*," she said enthusiastically.

"Right," said Derek. "Give me a minute, and we'll get going."

"I'll phone Doctor Nugent and let him know you're on your way," Drake advised.

"Thanks Izzie," Christine Bland responded, picking up her briefcase and following Derek out of the office.

After they'd gone, Ross and Drake met with the rest of the team in the squad room. Ross was hoping that Bland would be able to provide them with enough evidence to clarify whether the body that had been on ice in the morgue for so long was, in all probability, that of the real Brother Bernárd. That, at least, would help towards putting together a time frame for when the case really began.

"Even if it is," DC Dodds commented, "I don't see how it helps us find the killer at the priory, if you don't mind me saying so, Boss."

"Right now, Nick, we really don't know where to look for the killer of the real Brother Bernárd, because we don't know for sure when he was killed. We're pretty certain he was murdered by this Freedom Train organisation, to allow them to insert the impostor in his place." Ross peered from around the room, his expression set. "If we can put a rough time to his death, we can search for organisation members active in the UK at that time. If we find the person or persons involved in the murder, it will go towards shutting them down here. They can't be a big group. I don't think the Stasi were as big as the Nazis after World War Two, and Sam's contact at MI6 gave her the impression there are a limited number of former Stasi officers on the Germans' wanted list. So, the number of those helping them to evade justice has to be relatively small."

"So if we can find out who was active in this country around the time the Brother was murdered, we narrow the suspect pool accordingly, right?" Dodds thought aloud, comprehending what Ross was getting at.

"That's it, Nick. More importantly, I suspect the killer will have arrived here soon after Brother Bernárd. So, if we can pinpoint when the original murder took place, we can go back to MI6 and ask them if they have any intel on the comings and goings of the group around that time."

"Got it," I think," Dodds replied with a quick nod.

"I want the bastard who murdered that poor monk," Ross said adamantly, thumping the desk. "Let's hope Doctor Bland comes up trumps for us!"

\* \* \*

Gary (Ginger) Devenish had been handed the task of looking into the background of the murdered gardener, Daniel Parker. He stood outside the front door to the house Parker rented in Walton. The Prior had informed Devenish that, as far as he knew, Parker was divorced and lived in a house he shared with a friend. Although the Prior didn't have an address, which Devenish thought incredibly lax of him, he'd traced Parker's home with the help of DS Ferris, who'd located it through the man's driving licence.

He knocked loudly and was just about to repeat the procedure, his hand poised to knock, when the door opened. Devenish found himself face-to-face not with a man, as he expected, but a good-looking woman of about fortyish. She wore a white blouse with a pale blue silk scarf and a dark blue skirt, which Devenish correctly assumed was some kind of work uniform.

"Yes, can I help you?" she asked, scanning the smartly dressed young man standing on her front doorstep.

Devenish, caught unawares by the presence of the woman, hesitated, then pulled himself together and introduced himself.

"Erm, yes, I'm Detective Constable Devenish, from Merseyside Police. Is this the home of Daniel Parker?"

"Yes it is. Why do you want to know? Has something happened to Daniel?"

"Can I just ask who you are, Miss …?"

He paused, awaiting her reply.

"It's Mrs," she finally said. "Mrs Lynn Major. If you must know, I'm Daniel's cousin. He's been letting me stay here since I split up with my husband. If you're wanting to speak to him, he's not here. Hasn't been for a couple of days, as a matter of fact."

"Weren't you worried when he didn't come home, Mrs Major?"

"I'm his cousin, not his keeper. He comes and goes as he pleases. He often stays away for a few days. If you must know, he has a lady friend, somewhere in Kirkby. All I know is her name's Janet."

"No surname?" Devenish asked. He was finding this interview harder than he expected.

"No idea," Lynn Major shrugged. "Look here, I don't know what this is all about, but you'd better come in. I don't want half the street knowing my business."

Devenish followed her through to a neat and tidy lounge, furnished with an oatmeal coloured carpet, a dark brown three-piece-suite, glass coffee table, and a large-screen TV in a corner. She invited him to sit and he seated himself in one of the two armchairs. Lynn took a place on the sofa. Her skirt rode up as she sat, revealing her shapely thighs, and she quickly pulled the hem down.

He caught the action and realised this was a very nice lady, hating the news he was about to impart.

"Now, will you please tell me what this is all about? It can't be something trivial, or they wouldn't send a detective, would they? Has Daniel been in an accident, or got himself into trouble?"

"I'm sorry, Mrs Major," he said at last. "There's no easy way to tell you this, but Mr Parker was murdered two days ago at the Priory of St. Emma, where he did volunteer work."

"What? This is a joke, right? Sure, Daniel cut the grass there, occasionally, but who at the priory would want to kill him? They're all religious people, monks and nuns, for God's sake."

"I'm sorry. It's true. We believe he was killed by the same person who murdered one of the monks recently."

"He told me about that. Who'd want to kill a monk?" She looked flabbergasted. "Who'd want to kill my cousin?"

Devenish didn't want to go into the details of the monk being an impostor, or the complicity of her cousin in the murder, no matter how unwittingly. He realised she was probably in a state of shock and such information could wait … for now at least.

"That's what we're trying to discover," he replied. "Did your cousin mention whether he had any money problems recently?"

"I don't know why you want to know that, but as it happens, Daniel was *always* in financial trouble. He was a gambler, you see. He'd bet on almost anything: dogs, horses, two flies crawling up a window. Then a couple of weeks ago, he told me he'd met someone who was going to pay him a sizable sum for doing them a favour."

If Devenish had possessed a set of antennae, they'd have kicked in at that moment. This could be important information.

"Did he tell you the person's name, and whether it was a man or a woman who'd made him this offer?"

"Well, yes and no."

He waited for her to elaborate. After a pause she continued.

She released a slow breath as she scanned his face. "He said the person was German and called him Fritz. When I asked him if that was the man's real name, he told me he didn't know, that the man told him he didn't need to know his name … but when my cousin told him he needed a name to call him by, he'd said to call him Fritz. He told me he didn't think it was his real name, and I was suspicious of this job he was going to do for the man, but he reassured me by saying it was just a simple job, nothing of great consequence, and it was easy money."

Devenish realised his next question could open a door to solving the murder of Daniel Parker.

"Did he tell you where he met this man?"

"No, but he usually drank in The Lion or The Mariners Arms. They're both within walking distance. Daniel was there virtually every day, so I'd bet that's where they met. Can I ask you ... well ... that is... how did my cousin die?"

Devenish felt bad about his next reply, but he hadn't been given the authority to reveal that information.

"I'm sorry, but I'm not at liberty to reveal that information at this time. Once I relay what you've told me, a more senior officer will doubtless pay you a visit."

Lynn Major called her boss at the insurance company office where she worked to say she'd be absent from work for a couple of days. A few minutes later, after arranging for a Police Family Liaison Officer to visit her, Gary Devenish sat in his car and called Ross with the results of his interview.

"Bloody good work, Ginger," Ross commended him, after hearing his news. "This could be significant. I want you back here as soon as possible, and then you and I are going to the pub."

"Really, sir?" said the surprised Detective Constable, who then understood what Ross meant when Ross added,

"Yes, you and I are going to pay a visit to The Lion and The Mariners Arms. Someone in one of those pubs just might know this German friend of Parker's. With luck, something we've been sadly lacking in this case so far, you might just have discovered a lead to the killer of Daniel Parker and Paul Schneider. We're going to find this Fritz character, Ginger!"

"Right, sir," Devenish replied, as he started the car. He was pleased to have stumbled on the information regarding 'the man known as

Fritz' but, more importantly, he was going to accompany DI Ross in trying to track him down. As the newest member of the squad, he felt as if he'd finally been fully accepted by the boss.

The journey to headquarters passed in a blur and, before he knew it, he was leaving the building again, this time with Ross in the driving seat. He also knew that, even if they found the killer of Parker and Schneider, they still had to learn who murdered the real Brother Bernárd. They assumed he'd been murdered by Freedom Train members to allow their impostor to take his place at the priory; this meant their murderer in this case was opposed to the Freedom Train, having just killed their man and an innocent member of the priory staff, Daniel Parker. *Not so innocent* Devenish thought; he'd been complicit in the murder of Paul Schneider. The Detective Constable was convinced he'd made the right choice in accepting the invitation to join the Specialist Murder Investigation Team. It definitely beat his time spent with the Liverpool Port Police!

# Chapter 21

### Surveillance

Although she was from the town of Regensburg, Sofie Meyer, before her transfer to Liverpool, worked in Munich. As she and the two Austrian detectives followed the car containing their suspects, she explained that she intended to contact her boss there, later that day, to elicit his help in gaining more information about the Stasi's escape organisation.

Richter and Wägner both agreed that was a good idea, and together with the information *Obersleutnant* Gruber was likely to bring back from Vienna, they felt they should have a sound knowledge of what they were up against. Meanwhile, the car containing Weber, Ackermann and the Schmidt brothers finally halted on the street outside a large, long building that looked as if it predated World War Two.

"This is very much what you might call the 'old town'," Richter explained. "As you can see, most of the buildings here have great character, more so than some of today's modern monstrosities."

"I can see that," Meyer replied, then gestured. "Look, they're getting out."

The Schmidt brothers exited the Mercedes, followed by Weber and Ackermann, who quickly walked into the building, while the two minders waited outside. Helmut took up a position just outside the door to the building while Gustav lit a cigarette and leaned laconically against a lamppost a couple of yards away.

"Pull up a respectable distance away, Emil," Richter instructed. "You'll have to stay in the car while Sofie and I go and see what that place is. They know you, so best not take a chance on them making us as cops."

Wägner did as instructed and parked the car sixty metres along the street, out of the Schmidt brothers' line of sight. Richter and Meyer exited the car and walked towards the building, walking arm-in-arm like a pair of lovers out for a stroll. As they neared the building, Meyer deliberately looked Gustav Schmidt in the eye and flashed him a dazzling smile. Unable to resist her charms, he returned the smile and touched a hand to his forehead in a surprising act of old-world courtesy.

By contrast, his brother gave the two an unfriendly scowl as they passed. She smiled at him, regardless. By catching their attention, however fleetingly, she'd given Richter the chance to get a good look at the brass nameplate affixed to the wall of the building beside the main entrance door. As soon as they were out of earshot, she asked, "Well, could you read the plaque?"

"Yes," Richter nodded. "Conrad Ritter, Financial Consultant, and some letters that I assume are his professional qualifications."

"So, a money man," Meyer commented. "That could fit if this Ritter is part of the Freedom Train. Is there any way to find out if he's a German citizen?"

"If his business is legally registered, his nationality will be recorded. We can check it out when we get back to the station. Have you seen enough, or do you want to see where they go next?"

"Let's get back," said Sofie. "I want to find out who Ritter is."

The couple walked around the block so they wouldn't have to pass the brothers again, possibly alerting them to the fact they were being tailed by the local police. Emil Wagner drove back to the station, taking a different route so they didn't have to drive past the suspects who were standing by their car, engaged in conversation.

In less than thirty minutes, Klaus Richter had discovered all they needed to know about Conrad Ritter. It transpired that Ritter was a German citizen born in Leipzig fifty years earlier, which was at that time part of the German Democratic Republic [East Germany] at that time.

Richter explained: "He showed great intelligence at school and was invited to attend university in Berlin after he completed his compulsory period of National Service in the NVA, *National Volksarmee*, known as The National People's Army," he explained. "There he studied information technology and accountancy. He was soon 'spotted' by the Communist Party and recruited by them and became a loyal party member. He worked as an accountant for a company that manufactured cameras and high-quality optical equipment, until the fall of Communism. As he was working in Berlin when the wall came down, it was easy for him to integrate himself into western culture when Germany was reunified. He soon set himself up as a financial consultant, appeared to make a good living, and then, five years ago, he relocated to Austria, and settled here in Feldkirch. That's about all our records show."

"Interesting," Meyer mused, scratching her head. "But why Feldkirch? With all due respect, Klaus, it's not as if it's a major financial centre, or even a sizeable city, where he could attract moneyed clients."

"Could it have anything to do with our close proximity to the border with Switzerland and Liechtenstein?" Wägner posed the question.

"You could be on to something there, Emil," Richter agreed with his sergeant.

"Yes," she concurred. "It would be interesting to know if Herr Ritter visits Switzerland on a regular basis."

"Do you have a specific thought in mind, Sofie?" Richter asked, noting the concentrated expression on her face.

"Just the germ of an idea," she said thoughtfully. "We know the Stasi was allowed to retain a large proportion of their funds when the DDR broke up. If they're using that money, or some of it at least, to fund their escape organisation for those wanted for crimes against the people, they need a way to transfer those funds without drawing attention to themselves."

"But can't they use electronic bank transfers for that?" Wägner asked.

"Yes, Emil. They could, but using the banking system leaves a paper trail that could eventually be traced, no matter how clever they might be in disguising the transactions. But let's suppose for a minute that they have a network of people, involved in the financial sector, in Germany and around Europe, perhaps even internationally. Ritter, for example, has access to the finances of his clients. Suppose again that they need to transfer large amounts of cash to their people, if they have any, in Switzerland and beyond. He withdraws the funds, probably in small instalments, from various accounts and then drives across the open border into Switzerland or Lichtenstein, passes the money to a middleman, who then transfers it to its intended destination."

"And there's no trail, paper or otherwise, to trip them up." Wägner was impressed with her deductive reasoning.

"Weber and Ackermann could have been passing on instructions to Ritter, related to just such a transfer," Richter agreed. "We didn't see them leaving Ritter's building with a briefcase or anything that could have held cash, so I'd say they were there for a planning meeting."

"Yes," Meyer agreed with a quick smile, "and the clever thing about it, if that's what they were doing, is that there's nothing to connect them to the transfer of potentially large sums of money across European borders."

"Do you really think we can bring this Freedom Train down?" Wägner sounded as if he'd really got the bit between his teeth.

"We can certainly try, Emil. But now, I think I need some rest. I'll retire to my hotel and we'll resume in the morning. By that time, I'll have spoken to my boss and your superior, Herr Gruber, will have returned … and there'll be more relevant information to help our investigation."

She allowed Richter to drive her the short distance to the Hotel Bären, where she showered and changed. This was followed with a pleasant meal of *spaetzle, (a popular pasta dish in Austria)* and a call to her boss in Germany to pick his brains for assistance in dealing with the Freedom Train.

It would prove to be a long evening.

# Chapter 22

**Bedtime in Prescot**

Andy Ross was doing his best to relax in the company of his wife, Maria. It had been another long and frustrating day, with little to show for the team's efforts.

Paul Ferris and Kat Bellamy had been hard at work, digging deeper into the backgrounds of the monks and nuns currently resident at the Priory of St. Emma. Father O'Riordan at the diocesan office was proving much more helpful than previously, when Kat Bellamy had tried to extract information from him. This time, Paul Ferris spoke to the priest in charge of the diocesan records, and when he made it clear that he wasn't interested in anything to do with the previous monastery that stood on the site, Father O'Riordan underwent a transformation. Apparently, the Bishop had spoken with him and as it was obvious, due to the nature of the case, that an impostor had been murdered while posing as one of their monks, who'd also been murdered, the Church's whole attitude had changed.

"Why did they have to be so secretive in the first place?" Maria asked as the pair sat together on the sofa, in their lounge in the comfortable home they shared in Prescot, on the outskirts of the city, sipping wine and listening to the music of Johann Strauss, played by the London Philharmonic Orchestra. Ross had thought it appropriate, considering the case they were working on.

"There was a hint of treasure at St. Basil's Monastery, which once stood on the site of St. Emma's. Whether there's any truth in the rumour, I don't know, but obviously there's a secret connected with the place that the Church guard religiously, pardon the pun. Now they know we're not going to be poking around in the wrong places, I suppose the Bishop doesn't mind cooperating with us."

"But that's ridiculous," Maria replied, frowning. "You'd think the murder of one of their own people would be enough to guarantee cooperation."

"Bit of a grey area there. The first man killed at the priory has been shown to be an impostor, and the second victim is a volunteer gardener."

"I know, but seriously, Andy, the real Brother was murdered as well, and nobody at St. Emma's noticed another man had taken his place? They should be ashamed of themselves."

Maria, a local GP, could be quite forthright and often gave Ross helpful insights into his cases when he chose to discuss aspects of an investigation with her.

"Don't forget, Paul Schneider underwent extensive plastic surgery in order for him to resemble the real Brother Bernárd. Because of the monastic way of life at the priory, nobody really got close to him or developed a close relationship with him, so it's understandable."

"Even so, I'd have thought someone would have noticed something *different* about the impostor," she pressed the point.

"Bloody hell, you've got a point … in a way."

"I have?" Maria was surprised her husband had conceded the point.

"Not exactly as you suggest, my darling girl, but the impostor must have spent some time with the real Bernárd, in order to pick up his voice, mannerisms, and body language. Otherwise, just looking like him wouldn't have been enough to fool even casual acquaintances. Either back in Austria or here, Schneider must have struck up a friendship or some kind of relationship with the man, so he could learn those things. My money would be someone over here, or they'd have made the switch sooner."

"Not necessarily," his wife responded. "Remember Andy, reconstructive surgery is no minor thing. The operation and recovery would have taken quite some time. He could have met Brother Bernárd and got to know him in Austria and then, once he left for England, undergone the operation and whatever other preparations his bosses decided were necessary, before coming over here, when they thought him ready."

"Yes, of course, trust a doctor to put me straight on that." He smiled wryly. "He'd have had a lot to learn about the life of the man he was replacing. That would have taken some time, and from what we've learned of this Freedom Train, they're nothing if not meticulous."

"But not as clever as they like to think, eh?"

"You're right, or how did the killer know where to find him? I wouldn't be surprised if the group responsible for Schneider's murder had a mole within the Freedom Train, who was able to identify him to the killer. Shit, this gets more complicated by the day. I'll need to tell Sofie in the morning. She needs to look into it from the Austrian end, while we investigate further at this end. Bloody hell, Maria, I think I'm getting too old for this lark."

"Nonsense, you're just tired and overthinking things. You'll get there, I'm sure. Don't forget, you've got some of the best detectives on the force working for you."

Maria removed her head from where it rested on her husband's shoulder, put her glass down on the coffee table in front of them, rose and walked around the back of the sofa. There, she proceeded to give her husband a relaxing neck massage, always guaranteed to soothe away his tension after a long and taxing day.

"Ah, that's good," he said, as her fingers played a symphony of relaxation on his muscles. Within minutes, he began to feel sleepy, as the tension in those muscles gradually gave way to a feeling of soporific well-being.

He allowed his eyes to close and when Maria softly asked him if he was ready for bed, she received no reply. Under the tender ministrations of his wife's talented fingers, Andy had fallen fast asleep.

Maria didn't want to disturb him, but she knew she couldn't leave him on the sofa all night, so she tucked a cushion behind his head, lifted his feet so he was lying down on the sofa, and cuddled up beside him. She'd always found it impossible to sleep on the sofa, but she had no worries about him waking up in the morning with a stiff neck. Instead, she dozed contentedly for an hour beside him, then quietly and gently, she kissed her husband, shook him until he woke, and while he was still half asleep, led him up the stairs. She laid him on the bed, pulled his trousers and shirt off and having undressed herself, she covered them both with the duvet.

Ross had enough wakefulness in him to turn towards her and kiss her.

"Mmm," he said, yawning. "Is it time for bed?"

"Shush," she whispered, as she lay beside her husband, who was on his back. "I love you." Maria turned on her side, draped an arm across his chest and the pair were asleep in seconds.

# Chapter 23

### *Die Strafe* (Retribution)

Sofie Meyer's evening had extended well into the night. After the meal in the hotel's excellent restaurant, she closeted herself in her room and waited for the expected call from her boss in Munich.

The call came through at 8.30 pm, and she found herself speaking with *Hauptman,* (Chief Inspector) Boris Witt. His full title was *Polizeihauptkommisar,* but *Hauptman* was a lot easier on the tongue. Sofie was, in fact, an *Oberleutnant,* (Inspector) in Germany's Federal Police Service, the BKA or *Bundeskriminalamt,* but when she'd accepted the attachment to the UK police, and was assigned to the Merseyside Police's Specialist Murder Investigation Team, she'd asked to be given the temporary rank of Detective Sergeant. It was a gesture greatly appreciated by the team, as Sofie hadn't felt good about being placed on a par with the team leader, DI Ross and above his existing Detective Sergeants, all who had more experience working in the city than herself.

Witt was an experienced officer, 45 years of age, but Sofie was yet to meet him in person. He'd replaced her previous boss a year ago, and she'd spoken with him often.

"Sofie, hello," he said as she answered her phone.

"Sir, it's good to hear from you," she said cheerfully when he greeted her.

"Are you still enjoying working in Liverpool?"

"Very much, sir, thank you."

"And now you have a case which brings you closer to home, *ja*?"

"Yes, sir. I presume you know all the details?"

"Yes indeed. I have some interesting information for you. When I received your inquiry, I spoke with *Hauptman* Erich Broch at BKA Headquarters."

An image of the BKA headquarters, located in the city of Wiesbaden, in the state of Hesse, flashed before her. "Erich Broch?"

"He is a member of the task force investigating wanted members of the Stasi."

"I didn't know the task force still existed."

"It's much scaled down, compared to the early years, but it still exists and continues to actively seek those who have so far escaped justice."

"And was *Hauptman* Broch able to be much help?" she asked, absently crossing her fingers.

"He was, Sofie. I hope you're sitting down. This could take a while, but don't worry about remembering it all, as I'll email you the information when we end this call. Tell me, how much do you know about the Stasi?"

"Well sir, I know they were the State Security Service, the SSD, of the DDR, until the fall of communism and reunification. They were an effective and repressive intelligence and secret police agency, with headquarters in East Berlin. They had various facilities around the city, and offices all over the East German state. I know it was headed in its later years by Erich Mielke, and he ended up in prison after reunification. They were responsible for spying on their own people and internationally, and perpetrated many crimes against their own people."

"Good," Witt interrupted. "You know something of their activities, but there is much you don't know. Torture was rife for many of those who fell into their hands. People were encouraged to spy on their own families, and many died in their cellars and prisons. It was Mielke, by the way, who oversaw the building of the Berlin Wall and he was the man who co-signed the order to shoot all East Germans trying to defect to the west. He also held the rank of General in the *National Volsarmee*, (The National People's Army). You might be surprised to learn that after reunification, he wasn't imprisoned for his Stasi activities but for the murders of two police captains, Anlauf and Lenck in 1931. He was released early due to ill-health and died in a Berlin nursing home in 2000."

"I knew he was bad, but not how bad." Sofie managed to interject. It seemed Witt was in full flow, and he went on,

"He certainly was. You might wonder why I'm giving you all this background information … what relevance it could possibly have to your current case. It's important you realise just what you are dealing with, Sofie. I presume you've heard of Simon Wiesenthal?"

"Of course," she replied. "The famous Jewish Holocaust survivor and Nazi Hunter."

"That's right. That man spent time in five concentration camps himself and was witness to many of the atrocities perpetrated by the Nazis during the Second World War. Well, Wiesenthal himself stated that the Stasi, regarding the internal repression of its own people, were far worse than the Nazis."

"My God," Sofie exclaimed. "For such a man to say such a thing, they must have been far worse than I could have imagined."

"They were, believe me. My own Uncle Wolfgang, aged twenty-eight at the time, was murdered by the Stasi, shot while trying to cross to the West."

"I didn't know that, sir. I'm so sorry."

"You couldn't be expected to know, but now you see why I'm keen to help you in your investigation."

"Yes, sir, I do."

"Now, let me tell you some of what *Hauptman* Broch told me. Paul Schneider was close to Mielke, one of his privileged interrogators and, I'm afraid, a skilled torturer. He was an accomplished exponent of both psychological and physical torture. He held the rank of Colonel in the *NVA* and, at one time he was the head of the Secret Police in Dresden. He was later recalled to Stasi headquarters in East Berlin, after Mielke studied his record and realised the man was without mercy in his interrogation techniques, many of which he'd devised himself." He inhaled sharply. "He was particularly adept in extricating information and 'confessions' from female prisoners. Schneider was a handsome man and he used his good looks and fake charm to lull women into a false sense of security before hitting them with his psychological and/or physical torture methods. Imagine being threatened by this ostensibly charming but ultimately cold and unfeeling man, with some of the worst things that could happen to a woman. Did I mention his eyes? No, I didn't, did I? Paul Schneider, despite his good looks, blonde hair and winning smile, had eyes that appeared as black as coals. It's believed he really had blue eyes, but he had special contact lenses made to make them look black. Anyway, a woman looking into those eyes would feel as if she were looking into an emotionless pit, cold and unfeeling.

"One of his favourite methods of dealing with female 'suspects' was to subject them to a lengthy interrogation, denying them food and water … and if they didn't tell him what he wanted to hear, he'd threaten them with gang rape. If the woman still didn't crack, she would receive a visit some hours later in her cell, from Schneider himself. He'd ask her once again if she was ready to talk and if she said no, he wouldn't say a word, but would turn and quietly leave her cell. A minute later, he'd would be followed by three or four guards, who'd brutally strip and rape the poor woman, repeatedly, until she was virtually begging to talk to Schneider. When she finally cracked, she'd be given food, water, and clothing, and if she was lucky, she'd face a sham trial and receive a lengthy prison sentence."

"And what if she wasn't lucky?" Sofie was almost afraid to ask.

"Oh, then she she'd likely be murdered in the bowels of the Stasi's own dungeons, and her family would be told some lie about 'committing suicide to avoid interrogation' or some such concoction. For his excellent service to the State, Schneider was decorated and awarded, among others, the Karl Marx Order—for exceptional merit in relation to ideology, culture, economy and other designations—the country's highest order. He also received the Patriotic Order of Merit, which was awarded for special services to the state and to society, and the Medal for Exemplary Border Service, which was given for exemplary performance and personal commitment in securing the state border of the DDR," he explained with a hint of distaste. "It's said that as a young officer on border duties, he personally shot and killed over a dozen attempted escapees to the West. All of this brought him to the attention of Mielke, who appointed him to his personal staff. He transferred to Berlin and carried on with his 'excellent' work on behalf of the State. Schneider then grew more sophisticated in his methods, gravitating to the use of electricity in his interrogations. Both men and women suffered under this form of brutality, with electric shocks to their genitals being his favourite interrogation strategy."

"*Mein Gott.*" Sofie was appalled. "The man was truly a monster."

"He was indeed and he wasn't the worst of the Stasi's so-called interrogators. There were others who were far worse than him. When the Communists were driven out, he and several others, knowing they would probably be singled out for prosecution under a unified Germany, quickly went into hiding. That was when *Der Freiheitszug,* the Freedom Train came into being. Erich Broch thinks that the mechanics of the Freedom Train had been in place for some time before the end of the DDR, and the organisation was set in motion as soon as the Berlin Wall came down."

"So those bastards were ready to make a run for it long before reunification."

"Yes, it wasn't a sudden decision," he concurred. "A lot of minor Stasi officials were quickly arrested when the Stasi files were seized and made public, but by then, some of the vilest members of this evil organisation had already made a bolt for freedom. Some left Germany and headed for countries without extradition agreements with the Federal Republic, but then, they became aware that there was another group, known simply as *Die Strafe,* (Retribution), had been formed with the stated aim of seeking vengeance against the Stasi killers. These people aren't particularly interested in seeing the former Stasi officers brought to trial. They're purely concerned with seeking vengeance."

"But why did we not know of this group of vigilantes before now, sir?"

"You mentioned to me that your colleagues in Liverpool had been in touch with MI6, yes?"

"Yes, that's right. They provided us with some information about the Stasi, and it was they who gave us the name of The Freedom Train, I believe."

"Ah yes, they would know of that group, of course, but now that I think on it, it would be unlikely they'd know anything about *Die Strafe*; as it's unlikely to have come up if they'd never operated in England before now. Broch was surprised to hear they had struck in England, if indeed they are behind Schneider's killing. They're thought to have been responsible for the deaths of two former Stasi officers in Argentina and one in Brazil, and they may have been responsible for the murder of a female ex-Stasi officer in Serbia … but this is the first time they've struck in England." He paused to consider it. "Perhaps Schneider was the first to be infiltrated into the UK, so the authorities there wouldn't have any great knowledge of them. Broch will now, I think, be informing them of the existence of *Die Strafe*, as they've struck on UK soil. I'll contact him in the morning and also ask him to inform the Merseyside Police of their existence. Is there anyone he should specifically direct the information to in Liverpool?"

"Yes, sir. Please ask him to notify Detective Chief Inspector Oscar Agostini, the head of the Specialist Murder Investigation Team. Thank you for asking him to do that. It will, I'm sure, greatly assist them in the investigation."

"Let's hope so, Sofie. Yes, let's hope so," Witt said quietly.

A few minutes of general conversation followed as the two officers exchanged some general information and discussed her role on his team when she returned to Germany in the autumn, after completing her attachment to the Merseyside force. After ending the call with Boris Witt, Sofie lay back on her bed, exhausted. It had been a very long and exhausting day, and the next one held no promises of being any less strenuous.

She finally found the energy to lift herself from the bed and made her way to the bathroom. Rather than take another shower, she decided to fill the bath, complete with bubbles, and luxuriated in the hot, relaxing scented water for half an hour, almost falling asleep three times. After climbing out of the bath, towelling herself dry and applying body lotion all over, she felt wonderfully relaxed.

Pulling back the soft quilt, Sofie Meyer let the giant-sized bath sheet fall to the floor and climbed into bed naked; she fell asleep almost as soon as her head touched the pillow.

# Chapter 24

## Chief's Orders

Christine Bland had news for Ross. After conducting her examination of the exhumed remains of the body interred in Anfield Cemetery, she was ready to deliver her verdict.

At a hastily convened meeting in the office of Doctor William Nugent, the forensic anthropologist and medical examiner, Ross, Izzie Drake, and Derek McLennan waited as she entered the room along with Nugent. They'd been directed to the office by the mortuary's chief administrator, Peter Foster, who also happened to be the husband of Izzie Drake. Izzie had kept her maiden name for work purposes, but out of hours, she was pleased to be known as Mrs. Foster.

Ross had included DC McLennan in the meeting, as he wanted the detective constable who was one of his most experienced officers, to have a greater knowledge of forensics.

"Well," the forensic anthropologist began, "You were quite correct in your assumptions, Andy. You're aware that I'm also trained in forensic archaeology, so my findings are, I believe, as accurate as they possibly could be. The remains that were exhumed and presented to me for analysis, although degraded by time in the grave, belonged to a man aged between twenty-five and forty."

"Brother Bernárd was thirty-nine," Izzie interjected.

"So he fits, age-wise," said Ross.

"Do you know if your victim suffered any broken bones during his lifetime?" Bland asked.

"We obtained Brother Bernárd's medical records from the Prior. From those we know he suffered a broken arm in a fall from a library ladder," Ross replied.

"The man in the grave sustained a broken ulna of the right arm at some time in the past," Bland announced. "This much was evident at the time of the original post-mortem examination, carried out by Doctor Nugent."

"I was as thorough as I could possibly be, given the circumstances at the time," Nugent spoke up, almost sounding defensive.

"Nobody is suggesting otherwise, William."

"As for cause of death, as you found at the time of your original post-mortem, there were no markers present after this length of time that would help in determining what killed him. I'm not one to speculate, but I can say there were no apparent marks of violence on what was left of the man, but drowning can't be discounted. There was also evidence of a blunt force trauma to the head, though this could have been an older injury."

"Could that have occurred at the time of the fall that led to the broken arm?" Derek McLennan spoke up for the first time in the meeting.

"It's a possibility," Bland agreed. "Perhaps the most important thing, in respect of your investigation, is that this person grew up in Western Europe, more specifically in Switzerland, no more than forty kilometres from the city of Basel."

"That's it. It's Brother Bernárd," Izzie Drake said excitedly, astounded. "You can really be that specific?"

"Yes. I can give you the technical data now, if you like, or include it all in my official report."

"We'll take your word for it, Christine," Ross had heard enough to allow him to decide that the remains pulled from the River Alt were those of the real Brother Bernárd. All they had to do now was find his killer. "I'll read the report in full later. Thank you so much for coming up here to help us again, at short notice too."

"I'm glad I was able to help. And it got me a ride in Derek's Zephyr as well, so it was worth the journey," Bland couldn't help a smile and a wink, directed towards Derek McLennan, who beamed proudly.

"Now come on," he said, grinning. "I let you have a go behind the wheel, as well."

"Yes, you did, for which I'm really grateful, even though it took me a few minutes to get used to the column change," Bland replied, referring to the old style gear change, which was column mounted, as opposed to the floor change almost universally adopted by modern car makers.

"I'm surprised he let you have a go in his pride and joy," Drake commented, slightly surprised.

"Ah well, I told him he can have a drive in my Carlton before I leave," Bland retorted with a smile.

"And when will that be?" Ross asked, getting the conversation back on track.

"That depends on you, Andy," she answered. "It depends on whether you think I might be able to help in your more up-to-date murders."

"Oh yes? Do you think that's a possibility?" Ross was intrigued.

"William suggested I might want to take a look at the latest victim. He knows he did a thorough job, but he's always open to a second opinion. I said I'd be happy to, if you were agreeable."

"You bet I'm agreeable," Ross replied enthusiastically. "You seem to be able to find things ordinary pathologists don't."

"That's because I'm trained to look for the unusual," she responded. "If you want me to take a look, just call William and I'm yours. Perhaps Derek could drive us there in my Carlton."

"I'll make the call," Ross said. "Maybe you can find something that will lead us to the killer."

"No promises, but I'll do my best … but don't forget that William is one of the best. It's not often he misses something important."

"I know, but the great thing about Doctor Nugent is that he's not afraid to ask for help."

"That's why he's one of the best men in the country," Bland declared.

"I thank you both for the compliments, but I am still here ye know," Nugent smiled as he soaked up the praise. "I can arrange to fit you in tomorrow, it is suits you both. No need for you to go away and think about it."

"That's settled then, assuming DI Ross can spare DC McLennan from the investigation for a couple of hours. Is ten in the morning acceptable to everyone?"

"It's okay with me, barring emergencies of course," said the pathologist.

"I'm happy for Derek to attend with you. He'll be on the spot if you find anything we need to know," Ross agreed to the arrangement.

"Tomorrow it is, then," a smiling DC McLennan added. "I promise to drive your Carlton very carefully, Doctor Bland."

\* \* \*

Ross wasn't surprised when, an hour later, he received a call for himself and Izzie Drake to report to the office of Detective Chief Inspector Oscar Agostini, for a hastily convened case conference. What did surprise him, however, as he and Drake entered Agostini's office, was the presence of Detective Chief Superintendent Sarah Hollingsworth.

Having been involved at the outset of the case, the DCS had been responsible for assigning Ross's team to the investigation, at the same time making him aware of the Chief Constable's interest in the murder at the Priory of St. Emma. The Prior, Brother Gerontius was apparently a friend of the Chief Constable, Sir Anthony Sinclair, who was also, it transpired, a supporter of the Priory. Sinclair had close ties to the church in general, and at the time the Priory came into being, he'd personally donated to the funds of the fledgling priory. At that time, he'd held the rank of Assistant Chief Constable, before he eventually rose to Deputy Chief and finally attained his current position at the head of the force.

A man of great personal presence, Sir Anthony wasn't a man to be trifled with, and when he spoke, people listened; nobody would dream of not giving one of his orders their full attention. Ross had been made aware that this case was important, though what the Chief's thoughts on it now that it had escalated into something more than first envisaged, he had no idea whatsoever.

That was about to change, as Sarah Hollingsworth quickly took control of the meeting.

"Gentleman, Sergeant Drake, you're all aware that the Chief Constable has taken an avid interest in this case from the beginning."

Murmurs of agreement and nodding heads replied to the comment as she continued.

"Things have taken many a turn since you and I spoke in the beginning, DI Ross."

"They have, Ma'am."

"DCI Agostini has been keeping me appraised of your progress or, where appropriate, *lack* of progress. Before you protest, let me say you are not to blame for any failures in the case so far." She offered a fleeting smile. "At first, we thought this was a straightforward murder of an innocent monk at the priory. We now know it's something far more sinister than that, and after bringing the Chief Constable up to date, he's prepared to grant you additional resources to help your investigation. Not that he feels your team is inadequate to the task, but with the scale of potential international involvement, he believes you may benefit from a couple of pairs of additional hands."

"Ma'am," Ross spoke up immediately. "It's not numbers we need. I think we have enough hands on the job. It's more and better intel that we require. With Sergeant Meyer working on the case with our Austrian colleagues, we're only one pair of hands down. My people are good enough to crack this case, but it might take longer than expected."

"Your point is taken," Hollingsworth responded with a warm smile.

That in itself was enough to give Ross chills. That smile hid something, he was sure.

"But, the chief has made the decision and it's my job to see it's implemented. But I'm sure you'll be pleased to know that he's so impressed with the work of the Specialist Murder Investigation Team that he has authorised two additional permanent team members. The choice of those personnel, as always, is yours DI Ross—in consultation with DCI Agostini and subject to my approval. The extra personnel will enable the team to tackle more cases going forward and increase overall efficiency."

Ross was stunned. The force was used to cutbacks in an effort to save money and resources, and here was his team being granted two more officers on a permanent basis.

"I see, Ma'am. Thank you."

"DCI Agostini and I have discussed this already, and he feels that one pair of hands is an imperative for the moment. You can take a little longer to recruit the second of your new officers. Now, the initial question, DI Ross, is this: do you have anyone in mind who could meet the needs of your team at short notice, with a view to becoming a full-time member of your squad?"

Andy Ross didn't hesitate in providing the DCS with an answer.

"As a matter of fact, Ma'am, I most certainly do."

# Chapter 25

### Developments

Shafts of weak sunlight intruded through the slight crack in the curtains of Sofie Meyer's hotel room. She'd quickly fallen asleep the previous night and now found herself being woken up by the annoying sound of the telephone ringing. The alien sound of the Austrian ringtone differed greatly from the sound of the British one she'd grown accustomed to over the last three years. She'd hardly noticed it the night before, but now, as it disturbed her sleep, it made her wonder for a moment where she was. Realisation dawned and she reached across to the bedside table and lifted the annoying device from its cradle.

"*Ja*, Meyer," she croaked, her throat dry and her voice hoarse from sleep.

"Sofie, is that you?" Andy Ross's voice broke through the fog of her half-sleep state.

"Sir?" Sofie recognised Ross's voice and was instantly alert and fully awake. If her boss from the Murder Investigation Team in Liverpool was calling her at—a glance at her watch told her it was 6.30 a.m. it must be important.

"I hope I didn't wake you?"

"Of course not, sir," she lied. "I was just getting up."

"Good, well, I'm sorry to call so early, but I wanted to make sure we spoke before you got on with your side of the investigation over there."

"Have there been developments?" Meyer asked, now fully alert and focussed.

"You could say that," he replied. "Doctor Bland has confirmed that the body found in the River Alt was brought up in Switzerland and is likely to be the real Brother Bernárd."

"So, we have a better timeframe to work with," she declared, catching the significance of Bland's conclusion.

"So, Schneider must have made first contact with him while he was at the monastery here." She realised this immediately, as Ross and the team back in Liverpool had done. "He needed time to learn his voice, mannerisms, and personal history in order to effect the impersonation."

"You're right, Sofie. We've come to the same conclusion. I think the killer must have met him and maybe gained his trust, so he could get close to him once he arrived in England."

"I hate to contradict you, sir, but wouldn't it have made more sense if Schneider himself carried out the murder and then simply disposed of the body and returned to the priory?"

"I hate to differ, but don't you think Brother Bernárd might have found it odd for his new friend from Austria to suddenly turn up not long after he arrived in Liverpool?"

Considering it, Sofie was forced to agree.

"Yes, I see, sir. I wasn't thinking clearly. It is very early, after all."

"Whoa! I'm not saying it couldn't have happened as you said, just that I think it's unlikely. We need more information on this damned Freedom Train."

"I'm working on it, sir, and I may have a lead to the group that murdered Schneider."

"I'm all ears," Ross waited for her to continue. He needed some good news.

"There's a group in Germany known as *Die Strafe*, which means Retribution in English. As far as my boss, *Hauptman* Witt over here knows, it's a loose collection of individuals dedicated to bringing former Stasi criminals to justice, particularly those wanted for particularly heinous crimes against the people."

"People like Schneider, in other words."

"That's right, sir. Usually, they're concerned with identifying these fugitives and notifying the relevant authorities, but recently they've begun taking matters into their own hands."

"Any idea why?" he asked, curious.

"Yes," she replied firmly. "Word is they are angry that some of their recent, apparent successes have not led to arrests or prosecutions. The former Stasi officers have either been warned of impending arrest and disappeared or the authorities, in whatever country they tracked them to, refused to take action. These countries usually had no extradition treaties with Germany and the criminals went free."

"So, they've turned into vigilantes, then."

"*Hauptman* Witt believes so, sir."

"Do the German authorities have any idea of the people involved in this Retribution group?"

"That's the problem, sir. Most of them are thought to be ordinary citizens living ordinary lives; they might be recruited for just one specific task and then left to lie in the background until they may be helpful again."

"Good Lord, Sofie. It sounds like a terrorist sleeper cell."

"That's what I thought, too."

Ross knew that if such an organisation was behind the murder of Paul Schneider, the chances of tracking the killer to justice was going to be very slim. Meyer knew it too. They realised that they had an almost impossible task ahead of them but resolved to do everything they could to find the killers of Brother Bernárd and Paul Schneider.

"Look Sofie, for now, concentrate on the Freedom Train. Someone in that group organised the insertion of Schneider into the priory and is therefore involved in organising the murder of the monk. With luck, if we get a break, this case could come together all at once … with one solution leading us to both killers."

"I see what you mean," Sofie replied. "I'm going to meet with Klaus Richter's boss today and then we'll be heading to the local monastery, where I hope we'll learn more about Brother Bernárd's life before he left for England."

"Just be careful out there. These are dangerous people."

"I will be, sir. Don't worry."

After ending the call with Ross, Meyer quickly showered and dressed, selecting a dark grey trouser suit from her wardrobe. She stopped off in the hotel dining room for a quick breakfast of black bread with cheese and ham, washed down with good strong coffee, and then made her way to the police station. Klaus Richter and Emil Wägner were already in the office, ready for the arrival of *Oberstleutnant* Gruber.

She only had time to say a brief 'good morning' to the two men before the door to the Detective Division swung open and who could only be Wilhelm Gruber swept into the room, a broad smile on his round face.

Gruber looked exactly what he was: an overworked but dedicated fifty-ish police officer. He stood six feet tall and was slightly overweight and going bald. He clearly loved his work and revelled in being back in his own domain. His plain ash-grey suit was neatly pressed, his black leather shoes shone bright enough to reflect the rays of the early morning sun, and his white shirt was topped off with a blue-and-black diagonally striped tie.

Meyer sensed the man was married and that his wife cared enough to see that he left home dressed in a manner that reflected his position in the town. Obviously, she took pride in her husband's post as chief of detectives.

Under his arm, he carried a battered and worn brown briefcase. It looked old and didn't really match the rest of the man's attire. She guessed, quite rightly as she later learned, that the briefcase held a sentimental value for Gruber, and that it would take more than his wife's sartorial skills to prise it away from him.

He dropped the briefcase on the nearest desk and held both arms out in a gesture of bonhomie as he smiled at his men. "Klaus, Emil, it is good to be back my friends ... and you must be our honoured guest, Sofie Meyer?"

Sofie nodded and before she could say a word, Gruber wrapped his arms around her in a welcoming bear hug, releasing her mere seconds later. Rather than take exception to this unexpected show of intimacy, she took it in the spirit it was given and smiled back at Gruber, taking a step backwards as she did so.

"Herr *Oberst*, it's good to meet you, sir. I hope your trip to Vienna was a profitable one, as far as the case is concerned."

"*Ja ja*, Sofie, it is good to meet you too. Welcome to our town. To answer your question, yes it was a good meeting in Vienna. Now, perhaps Emil will get coffee for us all and I will explain."

Wägner did as requested. Gruber opened his briefcase and removed a pale green folder from within. Coffees served, he gestured for everyone to be seated, and once Richter, Wagner and Meyer complied he perched on the corner of his desk and proceeded to relate the results of his trip to the capital.

"Like most of you, I was in ignorance of this Freedom Train organisation. The Stasi, being very much an East German State Police Force, is little known in Austria, particularly regarding its various machinations, legal or covert. However, I learned a lot in a short time from Assistant State Commissioner Felix Wolf. Apparently, we do keep in contact with our colleagues across the border and we have a list of all former Stasi operatives wanted for serious crimes against the people of the old DDR. We know this organisation helps them evade capture and eventual justice, and we do have our own people who have investigated their activities on Austrian soil. This folder is classified 'Confidential' and must not leave this building."

"Did you learn anything about this strange group, *Die Strafe* as well, sir?" Richter asked.

"Patience, Klaus, patience," Gruber replied, smiling. "I learned a little, but not much, and I'll come to that later, if you'll permit."

"Of course, sir. I didn't mean to rush you."

"Don't be silly. I'm pleased that you're thinking about this case and what we must do to assist our colleague here and the Liverpool police."

With that, Gruber began his confidential report on his visit to Vienna and the Federal Police Headquarters. In truth, he hadn't discovered much that Meyer was unaware of; and she was anxious to hit the road and pay a visit to St. Thomas's Monastery.

\* \* \*

In contrast to the bright warming sunshine enjoyed by Sofie Meyer and the residents of Feldkirch, in Austria, Andy Ross and the rest of Merseyside were being treated to a downpour of almost Biblical proportions. From early that morning, a deluge had engulfed the city, casting an air of gloom and depression on most of its citizens.

Ross stood looking out of his office window at an almost solid sheet of rain as it swept across the city, driven by a powerful westerly wind relentlessly sweeping in from the Irish Sea. As he tried to daydream himself into a bright, warm and sunny environment, he turned at a knock on his door, calling "Come in," and knowing exactly who was there before the door opened. He was about to welcome the latest member of the team.

The door opened and Izzie Drake entered first, saying, "You ready for us, sir?"

"I am, Izzie. Don't stand on ceremony, for God's sake."

Drake stood to one side as she entered the small office and was immediately followed by a smartly-dressed Detective Sergeant Fenella Church.

Ross came around his desk and held out a hand in greeting. Church took it and he was rewarded with a reassuringly firm handshake.

"Fenella," he said as he released her hand, "Welcome to the team."

"I'm happy to be here, sir. Happy but shocked, to be honest."

Church smiled but looked rather stunned. In truth, she'd hardly believed it when her boss, Detective Inspector Alan Fry, had called her into his office at the Cold Case Unit to inform her that he'd received a request for her transfer to the Specialist Murder Investigation Team. It had taken him at least five minutes to convince her that the transfer was real and not some kind of wind-up. Now, she was really here, in DI Ross's office, and she knew it was official.

"Why shocked?" Ross smiled.

"Well sir, it's not as if you know me that well, and I've been out of mainstream investigation since returning to duty after the fire."

"Sit down, please." Ross indicated the visitor chair and as she took her seat, with Drake standing by the door, Ross seated himself behind his desk and explained to his new DS just why he'd requested her as his newest team member.

"You're here, Fenella, because I *want* you here. After I met you a few days ago, I did a little investigation into your background. Before the fire that led to your injuries, you were a first-class investigator. Your previous DI, Bob Hollis is an old mate of mine, and he gave me a glowing report of your abilities. DI Fry reckoned you're wasted in the Cold Case Unit, so I decided to keep your name on file in case we had a future vacancy. When the Chief Constable surprised us by authorising not one but two new team members, you were right there, at the top of my list. A few phone calls, and … here you are. Now, any questions?"

Church was truly impressed that Ross had seen something in her that even she thought might have been lost following her appalling near-death experience in a burning house … and here she was, the latest recruit to the city's elite murder investigation team.

"Why me, sir? Surely there are plenty of other detectives on the force equally as capable as me? Don't get me wrong, I'm glad you picked me. I'm just curious. I mean, it's not as if you know me well, or anything."

"Listen, Fenella, it's not often we have a vacancy on this unit, so when we do, I want that person to be right for the team. You proved your bravery during your actions in the fire, and you had a great track record even before then. You were quite modest when we first met and played down your actions during that fire. I read your bravery citation, and you went a lot further than you told me. We need that level of commitment here and DI Fry was correct in saying you're wasted in the Cold Case Unit. Now, I'll only ask this once: are you in or are you out?"

"In, oh yes, I'm in, sir," Church almost jumped out of her seat and stood to attention. She managed to restrain herself, however. "Just tell me what you want from me, and I'm your woman, if you see what I mean."

"Indeed I do, DS Church. Now, Izzie here will take you to meet DS Ferris, and our Administrative Assistant, Kat Bellamy. Between them, they'll bring you up to speed with our current investigation. Once you've got a handle on what we're involved in, I'll get you going, working with DC Sam Gable."

"Come on, Fenella. Let's get you introduced to our computer genius. You'll like Paul Ferris." Izzie Drake spoke from her place by the door and Fenella Church rose from her seat, turned and followed Izzie from the office back into the squad room.

She was immediately ensconced with Ferris and Bellamy on a crash course on working with the Specialist Murder Investigation Team.

Drake returned to Ross's office and closed the door behind her.

"She seemed a little nervous, don't you think?" she asked as soon as they were alone.

"I'd rather have a little nervousness than overconfidence on her first day in the job. Don't forget, Izzie, she's been stuck in the Cold Case Unit and away from live investigations. She's bound to be a little anxious in the beginning."

"I didn't mean it as a criticism, just an observation. I think she'll be a great asset to the team." Drake smiled. "You gave me her folder, remember?"

"Yes, and you helped me choose her. She should fit in nicely. Now we can take our time searching for our second new recruit but DCI Agostini has started the hunt for us."

"Right, so it's back to the case," said Drake, taking a seat. "How's Sofie getting on in Austria?" she asked.

"Making progress, according to her latest report," Ross said, quickly filling her in on the results of his early morning conversation with Sofie Meyer. "I have a feeling that if we're going to make a breakthrough in this bloody awful case, it may well come from Sofie's investigations in Austria."

"Let's hope so." Drake tried putting a positive spin on her words. "What do you want the rest of the team to do next?"

Ross seemed pensive for a few seconds. He stood and turned to look out of his window, as if seeking inspiration from the drumming of the torrential rain on the glass.

"Something Maria said to me has been simmering in my brain, Izzie. Maybe we should look at things from a slightly different perspective. So far, we've concentrated on trying to go back in time, looking for the killer of the real Brother Bernárd, thinking that if we can solve that part of the puzzle, it would help with part two: the murder of the impostor. But there probably isn't any direct connection between the two, so, I want to go back to St. Emma's." He gazed at her intently. "We've almost rejected the idea of the killer being one of the monks or nuns up to now, but what if we're wrong?"

"You seriously think we might have overlooked something, or someone, at the priory?"

"I think we'd be fools not to go back and double, maybe even triple check the people there. Are we maybe giving them too much respect, too much leeway, because of the fact they are monks or nuns … and therefore we assume their 'goodness'?" He made the sign for parenthesis with his fingers.

"It can't do any harm, that's for sure. How about we send Fenella and Sam over there?"

"Great minds think alike. I'd already decided to do just that," Ross confirmed. The old almost psychic connection between the pair of them was working overtime, as Drake then said,

"Let the girls talk to the nuns and put Tony and Nick to work on the monks. Tell them to exert some pressure on them."

"You reading my mind this morning?" Ross laughed.

"Yeah, go on, you'd already decided on that course of action too?" she smirked.

"You've got it, Izzie my girl."

"And what are we going to be doing while all this questioning is going on?"

"Well, funny you should ask that, Sergeant Drake. I spoke to Oscar Agostini straight after I spoke with Sofie this morning, and he agrees with what I suggested to him."

"Come on, boss man, spit it out. You know I hate secrets."

Ross produced a smile that Drake recognised only too well—the one that said he had a plan, and the plan was beginning to come together.

"You and I are going to London. We have an appointment with the Secret Intelligence Service."

"The spooks have agreed to talk to us?" Drake's surprise was evident.

"Yep. Oscar put it to DCS Hollingsworth straight away, and she called the Chief Constable, who made a phone call, and the bloke Sam spoke to originally—"

"*Secret Squirrel* Simon?" Drake interrupted with a chuckle.

"That's him. Apparently he's been instructed to be a bit more open with us, but as he can't be spared from the office and the information we want can't be discussed over the phone ... well, you know that old saying about the mountain and Mahomet?"

Drake pulled her shoulders back and appeared determined.

"When do we leave?"

"As soon as we get out there, detail the troops, and leave Paul in charge till we get back. Oh yes, and Derek's coming with us too."

"Ah, do I suspect a promotion in the air for our DC McLennan?"

"Someone has to fill your shoes when you go on Maternity Leave, and I can't think of anyone better than Derek, can you?"

"I have to agree with you. He'd be a good choice. Will it be a full promotion or Acting Sergeant?"

"That'll be up to the boss. Derek passed his sergeant's exams nearly a year ago, so he's qualified for substantive rank if Oscar wants another full-time sergeant on the team."

"Well, I'd better go and get him and tell him he's going for a day out to the Smoke."

"Do that, will you? Then I want to get everything sorted out so we can leave in an hour or so."

Drake gave a smart salute, smiled, and walked out of the office, shouting, "Derek, get your arse over here!"

# Chapter 26

**St. Thomas's Monastery, near Feldkirch, Austria**

Sofie Meyer, sitting in the passenger seat of Richter's classic 1971 Mercedes, was entranced by her first view of the Monastery of St. Thomas. Richter had phoned ahead and Brother Michael, the Abbot, had agreed to meet them at eleven that morning.

Now, they approached their destination, and Emil Wägner, seated in the back, asked,

"Impressive, is it not, Sofie?"

"It is," she replied. "It reminds me of something out of a Disney fairy tale."

The monastery had come into view as they rounded a bend in the road about a kilometre from their destination. Set in rolling countryside, surrounded by lush green fields, some filled with grazing cows and others with newly sheared sheep, the grand monastery stood on a hill that rose gently from ground level until it reached perhaps half a kilometre in height. The thing that made it stand out from a distance was the spire of the monastery's Church of St. Thomas, which stood some 30 metres, almost 100 feet, in height. Gothic in appearance, Meyer could imagine many scenarios being attached to that building, and a mental picture of the church in the dead of night, being illuminated by lightning amidst a raging thunderstorm, came into her mind, unbidden and somehow refused to budge.

The rest of the monastery buildings were set around the hilltop in the standard ecclesiastical layout, yet all of them looked as if they'd been built by a Hollywood set designer intent on producing a spooky horror film setting. In fact, Richter explained that St. Thomas's had stood in this picturesque hilltop location for over two hundred years. Meyer's quick calculation put the building of the monastery somewhere in the early nineteenth century, definitely making it suitable for a Gothic horror film.

Set apart from the Monastery complex was a second series of buildings, which Richter explained, was the famed St. Thomas's Winery.

"You must try their wine while you are here, Sofie. It might not be the most expensive red wine in the world, but I can guarantee that it is of fine quality."

"I'll make sure I do," she replied as Emil Wägner negotiated the twisting, gravelled drive that led to the monastery.

"I once called here to buy wine for a family event, as it's less expensive to buy directly from the monks than it is in the shops, and I asked the monk who served me why the drive was built like a switchback railroad. He told me that it had been deliberately laid out like this to prevent accidents—by forcing traffic to move slowly. In years past, people have been known to drive too fast, in cars and horse-drawn carriages, and were often hurt. Things came to a head when the local mayor, after imbibing too much wine in the company of the Abbott at the time, lost control of his car, which went off the road, hit a tree, and he was killed."

"The dangers of the demon drink, eh?" Meyer couldn't stop herself from smiling at the thought of a drunken Abbott waving off an equally drunken mayor, and soon afterwards hearing of his unfortunate demise. Did the Abbott perform penance for a month or two? she wondered. Her reverie was broken when Wägner announced their arrival, and the car slowly pulled up, the tyres crunching on the gravel as the engine fell silent.

She realised that they'd actually passed the main monastery buildings and the church with the tall spire, and had driven to what she guessed was the office or reception building of St. Thomas's Winery.

"The Abbott said he would meet us here," Richter announced as he led Meyer and Wägner into what Sofie could see was a far more modern building than those of the original monastery.

They entered through a set of heavy double doors and were almost immediately met by a tall middle-aged man dressed in full monk's habit. Meyer was impressed by the Abbott's appearance. Standing at around six-feet-three, Brother Michael had an air of authority about him, from his upright bearing to a face that suggested this was a man in charge.

When he spoke, his voice did nothing to dispel her first impression, being deep and resonant, yet exuding warmth at the same time.

"Herr Richter, Herr Wägner, it is good to see you. And this must be *Fräulein* Meyer, who you have told me about."

"Thank you, Brother Michael," Richter replied, shaking hands with the Abbott, who proceeded to do the same with Wägner. Then, with an old-world gesture, he took hold of Meyer's right hand and raised it to his lips, kissing it very gently.

"You are welcome of course." He offered a benevolent smile. "Though I am so very sorry that the matter we must discuss is one of loss and tragedy."

Sofie thought that even his manner of speaking would have put the Abbott perfectly at home in the nineteenth or early twentieth century. There was a touch of the old aristocracy about the man, and she found herself wondering about his antecedents. Was he descended from an old, moneyed family? She also realised just how Anglicised her speech had become during her time in Liverpool. She now spoke English almost as a native, whereas her new friends spoke the language as they would have learned it in school, correctly without contractions such as 'it's' or 'won't'. They would rightly say 'it is' or 'will not' etc.

"Please, *Fräulein* Meyer, let me show you our winery before we speak of the grave matter that has brought you to our humble monastery all the way from England."

"I would be honoured if you would show me where you make your famous wines," she replied genially, as she and the two Austrian detectives followed the Abbott through another door that led to main wine-making facility.

Over the next twenty minutes, with great pride, Brother Michael explained that although the majority of Austrian wines were of the sweet or dry white varieties, St. Thomas's specialised in red wine. It was made from the *Blaufränkisch* grape, widely grown across Central Europe and known in Hungary as *Kékfrancos* which, he explained, was used in the famed Hungarian red known as Bull's Blood, and which she may have heard of.

"I have drunk Bull's Blood of Eger," Meyer confirmed. "If your wine is anything like it, it will be a real treat to taste it."

"Of course, many vintners use the same grape, and it is in the making of the wine that the process differs and allows for variations in flavour, body and texture."

"I wouldn't ask you to divulge any secrets, Brother Michael," she assured him.

"I know that, *Fräulein*," said the Abbott as he led the way through to an enormous vaulted room that could have served as a large chapel, but was, in fact, the wine store. Sofie Meyer estimated that there must have been at least a thousand bottles of wine stored in the massive floor-to-ceiling racks.

"Wow!" she exclaimed.

"Impressive, *ja*?" the Abbott asked proudly. "At any given time, we have fourteen-hundred bottles of *Engelsflügel*, (Angel's Wings), stored here."

"An appropriate name, Brother Michael," Klaus Richter commented. "My wife and I usually enjoy a bottle on special occasions."

"I'm pleased to hear it," said the Abbott. "Now, please, come. I would like for our special visitor to taste our humble wine."

With that, he led his guests to a table that stood ready near one corner of the wine cellar. On it stood a bottle of *Engelsflügen* and four glasses. Brother Michael picked up the bottle and, using an old-fashioned corkscrew, pulled the cork like an expert wine waiter, and proceeded to pour four glasses, one for each of his guests and one for himself.

"Please, drink," he ordered and they each sipped from their glasses. "Let us drink to the success of your investigations into the callous and brutal murder of our friend and brother, Bernárd Rochat."

They joined the Abbott in his toast, after which Meyer said, "That's the first time I've heard Brother Bernárd referred to by his full name, Brother Michael. I think somewhere along the line we forget he was a normal human being under that monk's habit."

"Most people only see the habit, and not the man," the Abbott said, and continued, "They forget we too have dreams, hopes and aspirations. Just because they are different to those of you who live in the secular world, doesn't mean they are any less real and meaningful. For example, I know that Brother Bernárd hoped one day to become a Prior or an Abbott in his own right. Whether he would have achieved that goal, we cannot say, but it was wrong, very wrong of the person who deprived him of that opportunity."

As he finished, Brother Michael bowed his head in a silent prayer for his departed friend and fellow monk. The detectives dutifully bowed their heads also, until he spoke again.

"Now my friends, let us go to my humble office. There we can sit comfortably, and you can ask me anything you want. I am ready to answer your questions and if I can help you to apprehend this murderer of innocent monks, I will do so. The same goes for everyone else at St. Thomas's"

The welcome was over and now the serious business was about to begin. Sofie Meyer liked the Abbott. She felt that if anyone could help them unravel part of the mystery surrounding the disappearance and eventual murder of Brother Bernárd, this was the man to do so.

# Chapter 27

### The Mysterious Mr Schmidt

Brother Michael led the trio at a brisk pace across the perfectly mani-cured grass that separated the winery from the main complex, which comprised the traditional monastery buildings. As they entered the main complex, he led them around the cloister and through the monk's dormitory; exiting through a door, they entered a small garden in which stood the Abbot's house. This was a purpose-built dwelling whose title required no explanation.

Not large or ostentatious, the Abbott's house was built in the style of the 18th-century monastery and was in keeping with its surround-ings. Brother Michael explained that is was built over a hundred years ago when the Abbotts of St. Thomas's entertained church dignitaries on a regular basis. He didn't bother to explain what those meetings involved and Meyer and the men weren't really interested.

They were soon seated in his office, a medium-sized room that was plain and simply decorated; walls were painted a pale cream colour, the floor was of polished wood, and simple blackout drapes adorned a single window. The Abbott's desk was situated in front of the window. Meyer felt that once the Abbott sat in his functional office chair, he'd be cutting off much of the light that the window afforded to the user.

The only furniture in the office was an L-shaped desk set against one wall that held a modern laptop computer and a wireless printer.

Beside the desk, an equally modern filing cabinet stood and the detectives guessed that much of the monastery's wine-producing business was administered from the room. A second office chair was currently pushed up against the computer desk. Three wooden chairs, completely out of keeping with the décor, had been brought in from the refectory to provide seating for the detectives.

When everyone was suitably seated the Abbott spoke first, his hand resting on a pale blue folder that lay on his desk.

"Before you say anything, let me tell you about this folder." He tapped an index finger against the file. "It contains everything the order knows about Brother Bernárd, from the time he joined us until his disappearance after he went to England. I've read it through three times, since I knew you were coming here today, and though I admit I am not a policeman, I can find nothing in it that might give any clues as to who might have killed him. You are welcome to take the file with you when you leave. All I ask is that it be returned to me when you conclude your investigation. On a personal level, I considered Bernárd to be a friend … and I wish to do whatever I can to assist you in finding the man who murdered that gentle, peaceable man."

As the senior officer present, Klaus Richter began the interview.

"Brother Michael, the most important thing we need to know—the thing that will help us the most, here and in England—is if you're aware of anyone who might have spent considerable time with Brother Bernárd in the weeks or even months before he left for England."

"Well, there was a man with whom he became friendly, as a result of his work here at St. Thomas's."

"What exactly did the brother do here?" Sofie Meyer quickly asked.

"His main interest, outside of his theological studies, was books, particularly antiquarian books. He was interested specifically in the history of the various monastic orders from the Middle Ages to the present time. He was also interested in the wine-making process, and he spent two days a week assisting Brother Ignatius in the winery. It was through the winery that he met his new friend."

The detectives ears pricked up at that piece of information.

"Do you know this man's name?" Richter asked, leaning forward, his expression intent.

"You will think me extremely remiss, but I only met the man once. Bernárd may have mentioned his name, but I honestly don't recall it. Brother Ignatius will know, though, I'm sure. Would you like me to ask him to come and see you?"

"Yes, please," Richter replied and then turning to Wägner…

"Emil, the photograph if you please."

The sergeant reached into his briefcase and removed a blown-up copy of a photo of Paul Schneider, taken some years earlier. He passed it to Richter, who in turn offered it to the Abbott, who took it and stared hard at it.

"Was this the man?" Richter asked.

"I'm sorry. As I said, I only met the man once. It *may* have been this man, but I can't be certain. Wait a moment, please."

The Abbott picked up the telephone and quickly dialled what was clearly an internal number. An audible click could be clearly heard as someone picked up at the other end.

"Ah, yes, Brother Garth, would you please ask Brother Ignatius to come see me in the Abbott's house. Tell him it's a matter of great importance and that the police wish to speak with him. It's in relation to Brother Bernárd's disappearance and murder in England."

Hanging up the phone he turned to the detectives and smiled wryly.

"That should get him here in a hurry. It would usually take nothing less than an earthquake or an explosion to drag Brother Ignatius away from the winery. I swear that our Lord blessed that man with the God-given ability to produce superb wine. The only trouble is, he virtually lives in the winery. It's not unknown for one of the brothers to find him fast asleep there in the early morning, because he forgot the time and found it too late to be bothered walking back to the dormitory, so he slept where he was."

Meyer wondered if the real reason for Brother Ignatius sleeping in the winery was that the man had tasted too much *Engelsflügel* during the day but kept that thought to herself.

A few minutes later, the Monastery's chief winemaker entered the room and Meyer found herself looking up at a man even taller and more imposing in stature than the Abbott. Brother Ignatius stood at least six-feet six-inches tall, and was built like a rugby prop forward. She could quite imagine this behemoth of a man single-handedly picking up and carrying one of the vast wine vats she'd seen in the Monastery's wine cellar.

"You wished to see me?" he asked as he strolled into the office, and the office felt smaller once he closed the door behind him.

"*Ja*, Brother Ignatius. These are the police officers investigating the murder of our old friend, Brother Bernárd," the Abbott said by way of an introduction and Ignatius bowed his head in greeting.

"They wish to know if you recognise this man," the Abbott continued, and passed the photograph of Schneider to Ignatius.

"*Ja, ja*." The large man nodded his head profusely, his German accent very pronounced. "Zis is Paul Schmidt, the wine buyer. He knew Bernárd very well."

"Yes!" Meyer couldn't help herself. They had their connection between Schneider and the real Brother Bernárd.

"Allow me to explain." Richter took over, going on to explain to Brother Ignatius that the man he'd known as Paul Schmidt was really Paul Schneider, a former Stasi officer wanted for various crimes, including torture and murder.

"*Nein*, is this possible?" asked the monk, perturbed. "Herr Schmidt seemed such a nice man, a kind man. When Brother Bernárd told him he was interested in learning more about the making of fine wines; he would spend much time with him in the winery, and often walking and talking in the grounds. Schmidt was very knowledgeable about the history of wine making, which was natural, as we thought he was a wine merchant. But a member of the Stasi? If I was not a man of

God, I would be sorely tempted to spit. They were truly murderous, and nothing but a gang of thugs, believe me, this I know."

"You sound as if you have some personal knowledge of the Stasi," said Meyer, having noticed the vehemence in the monk's voice at the mention of the Stasi.

Brother Ignacious nodded, and a combination of sadness and anger flitted across his face.

"Fräulein, I am German by birth … born and raised in Magdeburg, in the east. My family had first-hand experience of the Stasi at work. One day, my brother was arrested because one of our neighbours, a so-called loyal party member, denounced him for spreading Western propaganda. We never saw him again and were later told he died when he was attacked by a fellow prisoner. We did not believe a word of it but could not disprove the official version. Soon after his death, I took Holy Orders and still had to wait for reunification before I could leave the DDR."

"I'm sorry," said Meyer. "So how much can you tell us about this man you knew as Schmidt?"

"I have all the details of the company he represented in the winery. I can get them for you. They were a legitimate German importer of wines and spirits, but now I am thinking that perhaps the company could be what you would call a 'front' for other activities."

"We need those details please, Brother." Richter had the bit between his teeth now. Inwardly, he was furious at these criminals operating within his country.

"I will get them for you," Ignatious replied, and he rose and left the office without further ado, returning ten minutes later with copies of all the purchase invoices and other correspondence from 'Schmidt'.

"Did you ever hear any of their conversations?" Wägner asked.

"*Ja*, I hear them sometimes. Schmidt was interested in Bernárd's formative years, and his education, and how he came to join the order."

"He was clever," Richter commented dryly. "Under the guise of friendship, he learned all there was to know about the man he'd been chosen to replace. By spending considerable time with him, he was able to learn his voice, mannerisms and history."

"He probably used a portable voice recorder to help with the voice."

After a quarter hour of further interrogation of the Abbott and the monk, Richter decided they'd probably learned all they could from the two men. Meyer agreed. They thanked the men for their cooperation and took leave of St.Thomas's with a copy of the documents provided by Brother Ignatius—and for each of them, a bottle of *Engelsflügel*.

# Chapter 28

## St. Emma's Revisited

Brother Gerontius walked towards the refectory and sighed a weary sigh as he watched two unmarked police cars pull up in the car park at the priory. Four officers exited the vehicles, including one new face; the others he recognised from previous visits.

"Back again, officers?" he asked rhetorically, as it was obvious that they were indeed back again.

"Brother Gerontius, I'm Detective Sergeant Church," Fenella Church spoke first as DCs Dodds and Curtis climbed from the second car. "I believe you know everyone else."

Sam Gable smiled inwardly at Church's authoritative forwardness. She'd clearly thrown the Prior a curve ball.

He hesitated slightly before replying. "Pleased to meet you DC Church. How can I help you officers today?"

"By making your people available for interviews, please. We still have matters that need clearing up if we're to solve the murders that have taken place."

"Er, yes, of course," the Prior replied. "Anything we can do to help."

"Good, thank you. Can you provide us with the necessary rooms to conduct our interviews?"

"Yes, of course. Please give me a few minutes to organise something appropriate for you."

"That will be perfect, thank you. Meanwhile, DC Gable can show me around. DCs Curtis and Dodds will wait here for you to organise things."

When Fenella turned to walk away, the Prior was taken aback by the scars on her face, and shock and pity were clear to see on his face.

"Not pretty, is it, Prior? Fire damage, I'm afraid. Nothing to be done, but life goes on, eh?"

"Wha—oh, yes. I'm so sorry. I didn't mean to stare."

"Don't apologise. You won't be the first and you certainly won't be the last. I'm used to it. Just concentrate on the *other* side of my face."

Without waiting for a reply, she walked away, with Sam Gable, and Brother Gerontius sighed with relief. Dodds and Curtis, having witnessed the exchange between Church and the Prior, allowed themselves slight smiles.

"Bit of a whirlwind, our new Sergeant, eh Prior?" Curtis asked.

"Yes … such a shame about her face."

"She was burned in a fire."

"Received a bravery award," Dodds added.

"Saved a child from a burning house," Curtis appended.

"A very brave lady, obviously," said the Prior.

"And a good investigator," declared Dodds.

"I'm sure she'll help us find the killer," Curtis went on.

"Now, perhaps you can go and set us up with the necessary interview space, Prior?" asked Dodds.

"Yes, yes, of course," Brother Gerontius replied, now a little less flustered for having had the brief interaction with the two detectives. He nodded and they returned to the car.

\* \* \*

Church and Gable had completed their brief tour of the priory, and were returning to where Dodds and Curtis stood waiting for Brother Gerontius to return.

Sam Gable took the opportunity for a last private word with Church before meeting up with their male colleagues. "You hit the Prior like a mini-whirlwind when we arrived, Sarge. I think the boys were well impressed."

"I did it deliberately, Sam. Sometimes, hitting hard and fast puts people on the back foot, and you'd be surprised what they let slip in situations like that."

"You don't think Brother Gerontius is the killer, do you, Sarge?"

"Probably not, but has anyone even considered him, so far?"

"Well no, but—"

"No buts, Sam. Everyone's fair game as far as I'm concerned. I agree he's an unlikely suspect, but it doesn't hurt to rattle a few cages, does it?"

"He's a friend of the Chief Constable," Sam said by way of a warning.

"So what? He's a suspect, no matter how unlikely, and the Chief Constable wants the case solved, does he not?"

"Yes, of course, but—"

"No buts, Sam. They're all equal in the eyes of the law. No free passes. Got it?"

"Got it … and, Sarge?"

"Yes?"

"I like your style," she grinned.

Fenella Church acknowledged Sam's grin with a wink and a knowing smile. "Let's go talk to some nuns. See if we can rattle a cage or two."

Before doing that, Church briefed DCs Curtis and Dodds. "We need to up our game on this case, guys," she spoke with authority. "DI Ross is under pressure, so *we're* under pressure, too. I know I've only just joined the team, and I don't want to rock anybody's boat, but my way may not be what you're used to."

"Just tell us what you want, Sarge, and we'll do it," said Curtis, and Dodds nodded his agreement.

"Good, now listen up. From reading all the previous statements obtained from these people at the priory, I've got a feeling we've been pussyfooting around with them a little bit. Nick, you were pretty forceful in your last round of interviews. We need to take that up a notch.

Just because they're nuns and monks doesn't mean they're totally squeaky clean."

"You think one of them might be bent, Sarge? I don't mean bent from a sexual viewpoint but…" Curtis began before the sergeant cut him off.

"I know what you mean, Tony," Church interrupted and then smiled, receiving one of his special 'cheeky' grins in return. She knew she'd got him on her side. "One thing we haven't done yet is look into the backgrounds and family connections of these monks and nuns. Who's to say one of them isn't tied to the group seeking vengeance on the Stasi for a crime committed against a relative or friend in the past?"

"You really think that's possible, Sarge?" Curtis asked with a furrowed brow.

"We won't know unless we do some digging, will we, Tony?"

"Whatever you say," he smiled and watched her stroll away. There was something about this new, no-nonsense approach of this new sergeant that he liked, and he lost no time in relaying his thoughts to Dodds as they waited for the first monk to report to them for interview.

"I heard she's a bit of a ball-breaker," Dodd stated after Curtis gave his opinion.

"Yeah, so did I," Curtis replied, "but only with anyone who doesn't pull their weight, and she won't find anyone slacking on this team, will she, mate?"

"That's true. We needed a fresh face on the team if you ask me. Might liven things up, and she's a real looker, isn't she?"

"Yeah, shame about the scar, though."

"See past the scar, Tony. I tell you, she's a bloody good-looking woman."

"Bloody hell, Nick, brains *and* good looks combined. That's one hell of a combination."

"Well, just don't let her know we've been talking about her like this."

"Are you joking, mate? I don't want to get on DS Church's bad side, that's for sure."

Brian L. Porter

\* \* \*

Fenella Church had decided they'd interview priory personnel in tandem, both officers questioning each interviewee together rather than one on one. She reasoned that the monks and nuns would be slightly more intimidated with this format, and more likely to let something slip if they had anything to hide. Although she and Gable would speak specifically with the nuns, she decided to begin with the Prior, leaving the rest of the monks to Curtis and Dodds.

"Brother Gerontius," she began firmly. "Can you tell us a little more about your background?"

"In what way?" the Prior, asked, looking mystified.

"Well, for example, let's start with your real name. You surely weren't born with the name Brother Gerontius, were you?"

"Oh, I see. I was born Bruno Holden. My father was a captain in the British Army and he met my mother while serving in West Berlin during the Cold War."

"So, your mother's German?" Church asked.

"Yes. Her name was Ingrid Haller. She died five years ago."

"I'm sorry for your loss, Brother. And where were you born?"

"West Berlin," the Prior replied almost reluctantly.

Church scanned his tense face. "Why have you never mentioned that during our investigation? One of your monks is killed, and he turns out to be an impostor, a former member of the East German Secret Police, you then have a second murder on the grounds, and you didn't think to mention your own German roots?"

"I'm sorry, but no, I didn't. Where I was born has nothing to do with what happened here."

"You don't think we might have thought it highly relevant?"

"No, Sergeant Church. Look, I don't like your inference … that you seem to think I could be implicated in the murders. I find it quite offensive, in fact."

"I'm sorry you feel like that, Brother. But surely you must realise that anyone with German connections might be of interest to us."

Brother Gerontius fell silent for a few seconds, his mind taking in all Church had said. When he replied to her last question, he sounded a little contrite. "I apologise. Yes, I can see how it must look to you, but I assure you I'm in no way connected with these terrible murders. I never thought to mention my background … because I didn't see it as being relevant, although I now see how it must look to you."

Gable had remained silent, observing Church's handling of the interview. Now, she took the plunge, joining in the questioning. "Brother Gerontius, how could you *not* think it relevant? You have a German background and the first victim was German, though I concede you believed him to be Swiss. You must see that we're bound to have doubts about you now we know the truth."

"DC Gable, you speak as if I've been lying to you. I haven't lied. Yes, I admit I was remiss in not telling you of my roots but I didn't think it was important. Perhaps my naivety stopped me from saying anything. I'm sorry."

Fenella Church wasn't about to let him off the hook so easily. "Again, Brother Gerontius, we only have your word that you didn't know he was German. You'd hardly admit to that if you were part of the group dedicated to tracking wanted members of the Stasi, would you?"

"But I'm not. How can I prove it to you?"

"We're going to have to look very closely at your past life," Church replied. "And the lives of every monk and nun at the priory."

"I see," he said softly. "Do you really think one of us had something to do with the murders?"

"We won't know until we carry out our in-depth check of all your people," Church emphasised.

"I presume you have no objections," Gable added.

"No, of course not," Brother Gerontius replied, clearly rattled by this turn in the investigation.

* * *

Meanwhile, Dodds and Curtis were applying similar tactics to the priory monks. First on their list was the former taxi driver, Brother Gareth, originally from Aberporth in Wales.

"You told DI Ross the last time he was here that you effectively spend your time either in prayer and meditation, or driving the priory's mini bus when required, is that right?" Curtis asked.

"Yes, as I told your gaffer, boyo. I suppose I'm a pretty boring old fart as far as you lot are concerned."

"Have you or any of your family ever travelled to Germany?" Dodds asked.

"Why on earth would we go to Germany?" The monk seemed genuinely mystified.

"Do you have a large family?" was Curtis's next question.

"No, boyo, just me and my parents, who are both retired teachers, and my sister, Bronwen, who's a nurse. Look you, boyo, why do you need to know about my family"

Ignoring the question, Dodds countered with, "Brother Gareth, what do you know about the Stasi?"

Gareth rewarded the question with a vacant look. "The whosie?"

"The Stasi. The East German secret police … until Germany was reunified," Dodds told him.

"Never heard of them, boyo. This has something to do with Brother Bernárd's death, does it? Brother Gerontius told us the brother was an impostor, not really Brother Bernárd at all."

"That's right," Dodds informed him. "So, you have no connection with any organisation dedicated to bringing former Stasi criminals to justice?"

The monk couldn't help himself and began laughing. "I already told you I've never heard of this Stasi. How on earth could I be involved in bringing them to justice?"

Dodds and Curtis decided they'd get no more from the Welshman, ended the interview, and began working their way through the other monks, meeting with similar responses from them all. Even the threat of having their families investigated didn't appear to faze any of them.

The former film stuntman, Brother Simon, which was his real name, added nothing to his previous statement, and both detectives were convinced he was being totally truthful. Brother Geoffrey, the ageing Cornishman, also used his real name, as did Brother Antonio, the Doncaster-born monk of Italian descent. When questioned on his family background, Antonio confessed that his grandfather—this according to his father, the restaurant owner—had been a member of the Fascist Party in Mussolini's Italy during World War Two, but had quickly switched allegiances when Italy surrendered, and eventually re-entered the war on the side of the allies.

"According to my father, Grandfather Guiseppe abandoned any allegiance he might have felt for the Fascists, faster than you could say *arrivederci*, and after cheerfully giving his backing to the ruling party just days before, denounced Mussolini and his cronies, and even took a job with the allies as a translator, due to him speaking perfect English." Brother Antonio took a quick breath and smiled. "My father said it was quite funny to most of the family, who regarded grandfather as something of a joke. But, as for him having any sympathy for the Communists who eventually took over in East Germany, his political leaning was always right of centre and he'd no more support the Communist regime than denounce the Pope as an atheist."

\* \* \*

Across the corridor, Church and Gable were facing a similar problem.

The Prioress, Sister Ariadne, was cooperative, but singularly unhelpful. "I explained before, I'm originally from Perth, Australia, and only came back to England with my parents when my grandmother became terminally ill. There are no German family connections in our family, as far as I know. Plenty of Schofields and Browns, but no Germans."

Things suddenly looked up a little when Ariadne, in all innocence said, "Mind you, I can't say the same for Sister Rebecca."

"Why do you say that, Sister?" Church asked nonchalantly, on the alert for any scrap of information at this point.

"I never thought of it before, but one evening after dinner, while I was clearing up in the refectory's washing-up room, I heard raised voices. Thinking that everyone had left, and not wanting to interrupt a private conversation, I peeked round the refectory door and saw Brother Bernárd and Sister Rebecca involved in what I could only call a heated discussion. Of course, I now know he was an impostor and maybe she knew that, and was taking him to task over it. You see, they were talking in German. I don't speak the language, but I do know German when I hear it. They were heading out the door, so I heard them for only a few seconds, not that it mattered, because I'd no idea what they were talking about.

"What I found odd, however, was that when I later asked Rebecca if everything was alright, she enquired why I was asking, so I told her what I'd overheard. She denied categorically having spoken German to Brother Bernárd, and I never got to speak with him again before he was killed." She sighed softly. "Rebecca said she had no knowledge of the German language and that I must have been hearing things. I apologised and agreed I must have been mistaken, but I know what I heard, Sergeant. I think Sister Rebecca doesn't want anyone to know she can speak German."

If Fenella Church had been fitted with an antenna, it would have been raised to its full height. As the Prioress left the room to summon Sister Rebecca, she turned to Sam Gable. "Well, well. Who says things don't sometimes fall into your lap when you're least expecting them to?"

"I remember Sister Rebecca," Sam replied. "A real Bible-thumping, holier-then-thou type. I seem to recall she deflected most of the questions she was asked by making reference to something Biblical. Funny, how Sister Ariadne suddenly remembered that slip of conversation, isn't it?"

"Not really," responded Church with a shrug. "It's quite normal to forget things that don't seem important when first questioned, and then remember them later. You must have come across such things, surely."

"Yes, of course. It just suddenly seems rather convenient, that's all."

"Convenient, but potentially useful," Church replied. "Let's see what comes of it, before we get too excited."

Their conversation was cut short by a firm knock on the door, announcing the arrival of Sister Rebecca.

# Chapter 29

### Wines of Distinction

Together with Klaus Richter and Emil Wägner, Sofie Meyer had been working hard at investigating the chief suspects' backgrounds. Joachim Weber and Jürgen Ackermann were, on the surface, nothing but two reasonably well-off businessmen with interests in various businesses, all of which appeared perfectly legitimate—at first glance.

Wägner had diligently looked into the financial advisor, Conrad Ritter and the trio met to compare notes and—at last, Sofie believed—they had something that might be the link they'd been looking for. As well as the core business, Ritter was listed as a director of a wine-merchants company, Wägner announced. *Falkenwinzer*, or Falcon Vintners, was a wine merchant with offices in Stuttgart and Berlin in Germany, Vienna and Salzburg in Austria, and Zurich and St. Gallen in Switzerland.

As soon as he'd provided this piece of news, Richter and Meyer stopped him from revealing anything else.

"What have I said?" Wägner asked, surprised at being stopped in his tracks.

"Emil," Richter said, excitement in his voice. "We've looked closely at the business interests of both Ackermann and Weber, and it appears we have a connection."

"We do?"

"Yes," Meyer added. "Ackermann and Weber are also directors of the same company. Falcon Vintners deal in fine wines and have a small but select client group across Europe."

"How did you find out who their clients were?" Wägner asked, curious.

"Simple," Sofie replied with a knowing smile. "We simplymerely looked at their website. They're a legitimate company and advertise through the website, where they list their major clients; obviously, they're endeavouring to acquire new clients. There will be other, smaller buyers, but *major* customers are their focus."

"What is also important," Richter added, "is that one of those major customers appears to be UK wine merchant Forbes & Ryan, based in Oxford, which is only just over 80 kilometres from London."

"Do you think the business is somehow connected to the Freedom Train?" Wägner asked eagerly.

"You catch on quickly, my friend," Richter nodded at his sergeant.

"It's perfect for them," Meyer went on. "A legitimate business, legitimate customers, all *perfectly* legal."

Wägner looked mystified. "But how is it connected to the Freedom Train?"

"As Sofie said, all perfectly legal on the surface," Richter replied solemnly. "However, she's already sent the information we'd found before you connected it to Ritter, to her colleagues in Liverpool. I'm sure they'll be looking into Forbes &Ryan, and we're going to ask our German counterparts if they have any information on Falcon Vintners. The answer to this question may lie not in the company itself, but in its employees."

"Just think, Emil. They have a wanted former Stasi officer who they need to get out of Germany, or maybe Austria or Switzerland, where perhaps they have them hidden in a network of safe houses, living under assumed identities. When they've decided on a new location for them, they'll give them a false identity, have them employed by Falcon as drivers, and they legitimately drive one of Falcon's fleet of container trucks across various borders—perhaps to England, or to France, Italy, or one of the other countries where they have customers."

"So, the *customers* are also involved?" was Wägner's next question.

"Not all of them," Meyer replied, "but Klaus and I believe that a few certainly are. All it needs is for the Freedom Train to have an agent employed—for example, as a Forbes & Ryan transport manager—and they have a fool-proof way to move their people from country to country."

"It's so simple, Emil, it's positively genius," Richter nodded sagely, in forced admiratiom.

"It is if it's true," Wägner agreed. "Presumably, once these drivers arrive in their destination country, they simply disappear?"

"We think so," Meyer replied. "It's possible they have a network of people, but not many, in various countries, who help escapees assume new identities, or arrange for their onward travel to another destination, South America perhaps."

"So, what's our next step?"

"We wait for Sofie to contact Detective Inspector Ross in England," Richter replied. "If what we think is true, after liaising with him, any further action must be taken by him; he's the senior investigating officer on the case."

\* \* \*

"Sofie, you're a bloody genius," Andy Ross exclaimed when she explained what she, Richter and Wägner had discovered in Feldkirch, and what they had subsequently hypothesised.

"Really, it was nothing, sir. Just a bit of digging and teamwork with our Austrian colleagues. It all seemed to fall into place. I just hope we're not barking up the wrong tree, as you say in England."

"I don't think you are," Ross replied, beckoning Izzie Drake into his office as she walked past the glass door. "Izzie's with me, now, and I'm switching to speaker phone."

"Right, sir. Hello, Izzie."

"Hi Sofie," Drake greeted her in return and took a seat in the visitor's chair in Ross's cramped office. "How're things in Austria?"

"I was just explaining to DI Ross that we may have a breakthrough at this end of the investigation."

"Just as well," Ross butted in. "It would explain why we haven't been able to make any progress here in Liverpool, *if* all the answers lie in Germany and Austria."

"It did appear strange that we made so little progress back in Liverpool," Meyer agreed. "Perhaps this link to the Vintners and their delivery network can open some doors for you and the team."

"I hope so, Sofie. I'll contact Thames Valley Police, who cover the Oxford area, and see what assistance they can offer. Any progress on this Retribution group?"

"I'm sorry, sir. We haven't yet made any further inquiries on *Die Strafe*, but I intend to pursue that line of inquiry at the first opportunity."

"I'm not trying to put you under pressure Sofie, but we're getting nowhere fast here. I've got our new DS leading a team at St. Emma's, carrying out follow-up interviews of the monks and nuns in the hope she might shake someone's tree."

"A new Detective Sergeant, sir? You have been keeping secrets from me?"

Ross felt a real fool and slapped himself on the forehead. "Oh shit. Sorry, Sofie. Detective Sergeant Fenella Church has joined us as part of the team expansion, as authorised by the Chief Constable."

"Ah, the detective from the Cold Case Squad? The one who was burned in a house fire? I spoke to her briefly when she brought you some case files. A nice lady, I thought."

"Yes, that's the one. And a bloody good detective she is. I'll tell you more when we have some time to talk. I need to get on to Thames Valley. Let me know if you get any more info on Ackermann and Weber, or if you find anything on *Die Strafe*."

"Of course, sir. Talk to you soon."

The line went dead and Ross turned to Drake. "That woman is going to be sadly missed when she goes back to Germany. She hasn't wasted any time over there. She's discovered more in three days than our whole team has discovered in two weeks."

"That's not quite fair, boss." Drake was firm in her rebuke. "We've been working flat out on this case, especially with the pressure from the Chief Constable's office. We were merely looking in all the wrong places, so it seems."

"I know, Izzie. It's just so bloody frustrating. Every time we've thought we were getting somewhere, it proved to be a bloody dead end." Ross sighed loudly. "I just hope Fenella gets lucky at the priory."

"That's a big ask, isn't it?"

"I agree, but she's good—maybe not as good as you, Izzie, but good nonetheless. Let's see what she comes up with, eh?"

She scanned his face and frowned. "Bloody cowardly worms, aren't they? Killing a monk who probably wouldn't have hurt the proverbial fly. It's as low as anyone could get."

"You'll get no arguments from me on that score. You know, Izzie?" Ross suddenly appeared pensive.

"What? I can tell when something's bugging you."

"Not bugging me, as such, but I'm going to miss Sofie Meyer when she goes back to the BKA."

"We all are," Drake concurred, speaking for the whole team. "The *Bundeskriminalamt's* gain will definitely be our loss, sir."

"Yes it will. Now, back to work, DS Drake. Phone Thames Valley, would you? See if you can find someone who can help us look into Forbes & Ryan."

"I'm on it," Drake replied, leaving Ross alone with his thoughts as she headed for her desk. On the way, she stopped off at Paul Ferris's desk, thinking he may know someone down south who could help her.

"Funny you should ask that," D.S. Ferris replied to her question, smiling blithely.

# Chapter 30

### Fenella Church Asserts Herself

Ross waited patiently for the phone to be answered. Ferris had given Drake the name of a friend of his at Thames Valley Police Headquarters who he'd liaised with in the past. Detective Sergeant Shannon Rice finally picked up the phone and was surprised to hear from a DI from Liverpool, until Ross mentioned Ferris.

"Ah, so you 're Paul's guvnor? He told me a lot about you when we worked together a couple of years ago."

"Yes, he told my sergeant all about you, and how he helped your people out with a drug smuggling case."

"That's right. How can I help the famous DI Ross?"

Ross laughed and went on to explain to Rice what he was interested in.

"Forbes & Ryan? Never heard of them, but I can do a little digging for you. I'm sure my guvnor won't mind when I tell him Paul Ferris is involved."

"I'd appreciate it," Ross replied, "and Shannon, if you don't mind me calling you that—"

"Why should I mind? That's my name and before you say anything, I know what you're going to say. You need this intel *yesterday*, right?"

"Right," he confirmed, finding himself liking this sergeant from Oxford„ who possessed a hint of an Irish accent.

Rice laughed and promised to get back to Ross as soon as possible.

"That sounded pretty amiable," said Drake, who'd been sitting in his office as he made the call.

"She sounded helpful. She's getting back to me. How are we doing here?"

"Waiting for Fenella and her team to get back to us. She's obviously being thorough at the priory. Derek's trying to get a handle on *Die Strafe,* checking HOLMES to see if the name's cropped up in any other forces' cases in the past."

"And Ginger?"

"He had one of his brainwaves. He's circulated an inquiry to INTER-POL to see if they have a record of any similar cases involving people being replaced by doppelgangers."

"Unless the people concerned were murdered, that's not going to get us very far, is it?"

"But if they were, and the bodies were found, and the impostors did a runner or better still, were apprehended, it *might* prove a connection. Just because they were caught doesn't mean they admitted belonging to the Freedom Train, does it?"

"You're right, Izzie. There could be a string of similar cases across Europe and nobody's put it together yet. Good thinking."

"Don't thank me, thank Ginger."

"I will, when I see him."

\* \* \*

Back at the Priory of St. Emma, Fenella Church was putting Sister Rebecca under increasing pressure. "You're being evasive, Sister, and I don't like people who are evasive with me."

The nun sat opposite Church and Gable with a stony look on her face. She didn't respond to Church's clipped words.

"The sergeant asked you a reasonable question, Sister. Why won't you answer it?" Gable added to the pressure that was building on the nun, who was refusing to reveal her family background and was denying being able to speak German.

"We can check your family connections with the order, unless you lied to them too when you became a nun," Church said. "We have a witness, who clearly overheard you speaking in German to Paul Schneider."

"But you won't tell me who that witness is," Sister Rebecca finally spoke.

"We're under no obligation to do so," Church responded firmly.

"You do realise, that your refusal to cooperate with us is giving us very bad vibes about you, Sister," Gable added. She'd quickly warmed to the direct and forceful interrogation methods employed by the newest team member.

Silence again.

"Okay, here's an easy one," Church changed tack. "How long have you been a nun?"

"Ten years," Rebecca replied unhesitatingly.

"And before that?"

"I visited various holiday destinations, assessing the accommodations and facilities. I worked for a large travel agency."

Gable thought there was significance in that reply, but wasn't yet sure exactly what it was.

Church, however, seemed to know exactly what she was doing. "And during that time, in your position as Accommodation and Facilities Inspector—yes, I know what your job title would have been—did you ever visit Germany?"

*You clever bugger,* Gable thought. *You set a trap and she just walked right into it. Get out of that one if you can, Sister holier-than-thou Rebecca.*

Sister Rebecca fell silent again.

"Well, did you or did you not have to visit Germany as part of your employment? Not too hard a question, surely?"

"Yes," the nun grudgingly replied.

"Yes, what? Yes, you visited Germany or yes, it's too hard a question?"

*Go girl,* Gable thought, swallowing a smirk. *You're tying her up in knots. She doesn't know what's hit her.*

Very quietly, Sister Rebecca replied, "Yes, I visited Germany."

"And you expect me to believe that an accommodation inspector for a travel company operating in Germany couldn't speak a word of German?"

*Gotcha!* Gable almost blurted it out loud.

Sister Rebecca grew mute once more, refusing to either confirm or deny Church's indirect accusation. After a lengthy pause, when it became obvious the nun wouldn't cooperate any further, DS Church made a decision, which DI Ross might see as controversial, but which she believed was the only way forward if they were going to achieve a resolution to the case.

"Sister Rebecca, I must ask you to accompany us to police headquarters, where you'll be questioned further regarding our investigation. You can come voluntarily to assist with our enquiries, or I can place you under arrest on a charge of obstructing a police inquiry. The choice is yours."

Gable's jaw almost hit the floor. She hadn't expected this outcome when they'd arrived at the priory.

Sister Rebecca looked visibly shocked, but rose from her seat, placed her hands together in prayer for a few seconds, then said, "I'll accompany you, Sergeant Church, but you're making a *big* mistake."

"We'll see about that, won't we, Sister? Perhaps you'll be good enough to go with Detective Constable Gable to the police car, while I inform Brother Gerontius of our intentions."

* * *

Brother Gerontius reacted with a mixture of shock, horror and surprise when Church knocked and entered his office, and gave him the news about Sister Rebecca.

"You can't be serious, surely? Sister Rebecca is probably the most pious person at St. Emma's."

"I'm deadly serious, Brother. She's definitely hiding something. Whether it's connected to the murders, I don't know at this stage, but unless she opens up and tells us the truth, we won't know."

"I can't believe she'd possibly have been involved in the murders, Sergeant. It's unthinkable."

"So are many things in life," she replied dryly.

"Yes, I'll admit that," the Prior agreed, appearing perturbed.

With that, Church left him standing behind his desk, open-mouthed, as she took her leave of him. Before returning to the car, she called into the room where Curtis and Dodds had been carrying out interviews, for a brief and unproductive update. She ordered them to wrap things up as soon as they felt able, and gave them the news about Sister Rebecca. She left them in much the same open-mouthed state as Brother Gerontius as she joined Sam Gable and began the journey to headquarters.

\* \* \*

After she'd left, the two detectives stared at each other for a full minute before Curtis broke the silence. "Is she real, or what? Five minutes on the team and she makes a breakthrough."

"She's a tough cookie, that's for sure," Dodds replied. "Looks like she don't take no shit from anyone."

"Yeah, I wonder what the boss'll say when she waltzes into headquarters with the ultra-religious sister in tow."

"Wish I could be a fly on the wall when that happens," Dodds said with a dark smile.

"Well find out soon enough, I suppose," Curtis shrugged. "Come on, Nick, let's get things wrapped up here and head back. Sooner we're there, sooner we'll find out."

Ross and Drake were definitely in for a surprise and, one way or another, Sister Rebecca could just be the key they'd been waiting for to unravel what Ross had called 'the nest of vipers' surrounding the murders at St. Emma's.

# Chapter 31

### Digging Deeper

"How deep does your boss in Liverpool want us to dig into the affairs of the wine merchants?" Klaus Richter addressed the question to Meyer. "The three of us aren't geared up to launch a full-scale investigation.

"Make that four, Richter," said *Oberstleutnant* Gruber, as he walked into the detectives bureau in Feldkirch police station. "I have decided to assist you in your investigation. I feel it's important to show our British colleagues how seriously we're taking this case. Don't worry, I'm not here to take over your investigation, merely to assist."

"Er, thank you sir, " Richter replied, unsure how to take the superintendent's offer of assistance. Having said that, he knew that the Chief of Detectives had a welter of experience behind him, after many years in the detective division.

"Now, please bring me up to date on where we stand," Gruber ordered.

Between them, Richter, Meyer and Wägner did just that. When they'd finished, Gruber sat on the corner of one of the office desks, lost in thought for a few seconds. When he spoke, it was with a smile on his face.

"I think I can be of help in dealing with Herr Ritter. I have friends in the Fraud Division. Let me get them to check into Ritter's business and see if they can give us something to use as leverage against him."

"That would be very useful, sir, thank you." Richter was impressed with his boss's enthusiasm for the job.

"Consider it done. I know what you think, Klaus, but I'm not ready to join the cows in the pasture yet, you know."

"Of course not, sir, I was only thinking—"

Gruber cut him off with a wave of his hand. "Tell me what you're doing to push the investigation forward."

Sofie Meyer looked at Richter, who nodded, and she took over the explanation. "Sir, we're satisfied that Ackermann is the senior man in the organisation in this area, and that Gustav and Helmut Schmidt could be his enforcers. I'd like to find out if either brother, or both brothers, left Austria in recent years. I suspect, if they aren't averse to the use of violence, one or both of them could have visited England and carried out the murder of the real Brother Bernárd."

"That's a big leap from being local muscle to international hitmen, don't you think?"

"Not really, sir. Think about it. They'd already know what the brother looked like, so would have no trouble recognising him when they got to England. They could have worked with Schneider while he was making friends with the monk here in Feldkirch, and worked directly under him upon arrival in England."

"The sloppy way the body was disposed of in England sounds like the kind of pathetic job one or both of the brothers would do, as well," Richter added.

"I see the possibility," Gruber agreed. "And how exactly did you come up with this theory, Sofie?"

"It was something Emil told me—that they were Ackermann's lap dogs and would do anything he told them. Who better to carry out a killing on his orders, and then keep their mouths shut?"

"If you find that they visited England around the time of the murder, how can we *prove* they did it?"

"I think we would have to leave that up to DI Ross and his team."

"He could be extradited to the UK under a European Extradition Warrant, so there would be no problem there," the superintendent stated.

"Then all we need is the evidence to back it up," said Meyer.

"Or a confession," murmured Wägner. He wore a look that invited the next question from the superintendent.

"Do you have something in mind, Sergeant?"

"Well sir, I wouldn't want to put you in a compromising situation, but…"

"But what, Emil? Come on, out with it man. What have you got cooking in that devious mind of yours" Gruber knew from experience that one of the reasons for Wägner's failure to achieve further advancement in rank over the years, was that he had a tendency to be rather unorthodox from time to time in his treatment of suspects. Complaints had been filed, but never substantiated. He was sure Wägner could extract confessions by devious means, though he had it on good authority that the sergeant was clever, and had never once used violence towards a suspect. That would have put Wägner in a situation identical to the Stasi, and that wouldn't have been acceptable.

"Well sir, let's say, hypothetically of course, that we pulled the Schmidt brothers in for questioning, and they were held overnight and kept in separate cells. Let's also say that, somehow, the light was accidentally left on all night in Helmut's cell and that during the night, a large number of spiders found their way into his cell."

"Spiders?" asked the chief, stunned.

"Yes sir, spiders, large ones. In fact, the larger the better. You see, I happen to know, from previous dealings with the brothers, that Helmut is absolutely terrified of spiders, and after a night of torment surrounded by the eight-legged little beasts, I think we could persuade Helmut to tell us what we want to know … unless of course, he wishes to spend all day and *another* night in his cell with his new cellmates."

""Emil, you're a genius—a pure evil genius." Richter laughed.

"Wouldn't that constitute torture or psychological pressure on a suspect?" Meyer sounded dubious, but Gruber hopped down from his perch on the corner of the desk with a broad smile and clapped with joy. "Let's do it! I'll personally sign the arrest warrant … on a conspiracy charge. Legally, it's nice and vague, and will have them guessing, and on the defensive. One question, Emil?

"Sir?"

"Where will you obtain the spiders?"

"Leave that to me," Wägner replied with an evil leer.

The four of them broke into spontaneous laughter and when Gruber left the room two minutes later, he still hadn't received an answer to the question.

"Come on, Emil, tell us how you know about Helmut's fear of spiders," Meyer urged.

"When that thug was last in the cells after a drunken brawl at the Black Boar Inn, Stefan Becker was the officer on cell duty. In the morning, Stefan sought me out and with a huge grin, told me what had happened during the night. Soon after midnight, when Stefan was dozing in a chair, he was startled by cries of "*Hilfe, hilfe, bitte hilf mir*"—help, help, please help me. When he responded, thinking the prisoner was maybe having a heart attack, he found Helmut perched on top of the bed, pointing to something on the floor." He chuckled. "Ordering him to stay where he was, Stefan entered the cell and looked to where the prisoner was pointing … and saw a tiny spider, no more than a centimetre across, in the middle of the floor. Being a soft-hearted soul, except with thugs like Helmut and his brother, Stefan caught the spider and put it outside. Helmut, as white as a sheet, sheepishly told Stefan that as a child, if he misbehaved, his father would lock him in the cellar of their home, which was infested with spiders. They'd crawl all over him, and he eventually developed a pathological fear of arachnids. I'm going to visit my sister who has a nice dark cellar and collect a small army of spiders, which should be enough to convince Helmut to talk to us."

Meyer and Richter laughed again, and a few minutes later, Richter and Wägner departed from the station, intending to arrest Helmut Schmidt. Meyer stayed behind, not wanting to reveal her presence in Feldkirch until she had to.

\* \* \*

Back in Liverpool, Andy Ross received the call he'd been waiting for from DS Rice at Thames Valley Police Headquarters.

"Thanks for getting back to me so soon. Do you have anything useful for me?"

"No problem, sir. I have something, though whether it's useful or pertinent to your investigation, I don't know. That's for you to decide."

"Okay, give me what you have."

"Forbes & Ryan are wine importers and wholesalers, which you knew, of course. I made a call to their offices and spoke to the sales director, Steve Hall, using that wine you mentioned, *Engelsflügel,* saying I might be interested in placing a sizeable order, for a chain of off-licences in the North of England. He told me they could handle orders of any size, and that all deliveries were handled by their distribution manager, Franz Ritter, who I could speak to if I wished."

"Did you say Franz *Ritter*?" Ross thought that this was one coincidence too many. Ritter was the name of one of Meyer's suspects in Austria.

"Yes, Ritter's the name, and I had a brief word with him. Sounded German. He said the *Engelsflügel* is shipped from the Austrian monastery where it's made, and that he only uses local drivers as it's a special wine and they don't trust contract drivers. Sounded a bit off to me, sir, but anyway, I said I'd speak to my boss and get back to him. That's all I could do, but I've got one of our DCs making background inquiries into the company, and if we come up with anything suspicious, we'll let you know."

"Thank you, DS Rice. You've been more helpful than you know and yes, please let me know if you dig up anything more on the company."

"Happy to help, sir. Say hello to Paul for me," Rice replied, referring to Ferris.

"Will do, 'bye." Ross ended the call and immediately called Drake into his office.

"It's coming together, Izzie," he said with a long overdue smile on his face. He told her the news from Thames Valley. "I'd better have a word with Sofie, if I can raise her on her mobile. If only we could get a handle on this Retribution set-up."

"That's my big worry on this case," she replied. "We're making progress on the cold case, the murder of the real Brother Bernárd, but we're no nearer solving the murder of Paul Schneider."

"I know, but maybe Fenella will come up with something at the priory."

Ross's words could have been prophetic, as no sooner were the words out of his mouth, than he and Drake heard a hubbub in the squad room. They went to see what was happening and were astounded to see Fenella Church and Sam Gable striding into the room with Sister Rebecca between them, being held by an elbow with the strong, guiding hand of his new Detective Sergeant.

"What the hell?" he exclaimed as he and Drake met the trio. "Fenella," he said, puzzled. "What's happening here?"

"What's happening, sir, is that Sister Rebecca has been telling lies, and I intend to find out why."

Quickly regaining his composure, Ross smiled inwardly, giving away nothing to confirm his satisfaction that the appointment of DS Church seemed to be producing results in double-quick time. "Well, don't let me hold you up," he replied. "I have a phone call to make."

Fenella Church nodded and turned to Gable. "Take the sister down to Interview Room One, please, Sam. I'll be with you in a minute."

"Right you are, Sarge." Gable led the reluctant nun out of the squad room.

Church scampered across the squad room, catching Ross before he had chance to make his call to Sofie Meyer. "Sir, a word please."

"Yes, Fenella, what is it?"

"I think the nun may be hiding something important, and I wondered if you'd like to sit in on the interview."

"Fenella, I have every confidence in your ability to do your job. If I didn't, you wouldn't be here. Sam Gable is an equally experienced detective. The two of you had better get on with it. If the nun is guilty of anything, find out what, and charge her."

"Yes sir." Church was pleased with Ross's response. Inwardly, she'd been thinking that maybe he didn't have complete confidence in her to conduct such an interview. After all, it had been a while since she'd done anything like this. She walked with renewed vigour across the squad room and made her way to the interview room where her interviewee—not quite a prisoner—was waiting for her.

Drake quietly closed the door. "That was good, sir," she said. "You knew she was hesitant about conducting the interview, didn't you?"

"I did, and it was very professional of her to seek my approval the way she did, offering me the opportunity to watch her at work. But that would have made her even more nervous than she already is. Anyway, Sam knows what she's doing, and if Fenella trips up a little, she'll put her right."

"Getting to be quite the psychologist, aren't you?" Drake smiled.

She and Ross were well known for having an empathic, some said telepathic connection. Some people even believed the pair could read each other's mind, something the duo would have strenuously denied.

Ross removed his mobile phone from a pocket and dialled, hoping that Sofie Meyer's phone would be in range of a cell tower, wherever she was.

* * *

Sofie Meyer was, as it happened, seated in the little coffee shop opposite the Police Station in Feldkirch. Richter and Wägner had gone to Ackermann's mansion-like home to bring in Helmut Schmidt for questioning. According to Wägner, the other positive to picking him up, without his brother also being taken into custody, was that Helmut was the weaker of the two brothers mentally; he'd be more likely to crack under pressure. Even though they'd be separated if both had been brought in, Helmut would have felt reassured by his brother's nearby presence. It was a slight edge, and they needed all the help they could muster if they were going to crack Helmut's composure.

For a few minutes though, in that coffee shop, with her coffee and a large slice of black forest gâteau in front of her, Meyer was able to relax a little. Then came the call from Andy Ross.

"It has to be a relative of our Ritter," she said, when Ross gave her the information about Forbes & Ryan's Distribution Manager. "It would also explain how they get their people into other countries. Who's going to suspect a lorry driver of being part of a clandestine organisation, helping criminals evade justice?"

"Or, perhaps in this case, commit murders," Ross suggested darkly. "They send a driver to England, or wherever, to eliminate the subjects due to be replaced by impostors, carry out the murders, and then disappear back to Feldkirch or whichever depot they came from, never to be heard of again in the country where the murder took place. It's ingenious, Sofie, and explains why it's so difficult to catch the bastards."

"I agree sir, and there's another thing I thought of."

"Go on," Ross urged.

"There must be a clinic or private hospital somewhere, where they perform the reconstructive surgery to turn the impostors into the victims' doubles. I can't believe they use various doctors to carry it out. I'll try and get my boss in Germany to make some inquiries."

"Maybe you should look in Austria, too," he suggested. "It could be the Freedom Train is based there instead of Germany. There'd be less suspicion on such a place there, whereas it might raise some questions in Germany."

"I see what you mean, sir. I'll see what I can do, and I'll let you know what I can find out about Ritter. Maybe the man in England is his son or some close relative."

"Okay, Sofie. Either way, it looks as if we're slowly putting the pieces together. But remember one thing, please."

"What's that?"

"Our job is to solve the murder of Paul Schneider and the gardener fellow, and if possible the murder of Brother Bernárd, which you look close to doing. It's not up to us to bring down this Freedom Train organisation. It's big and seems to have branches everywhere. From what you've told me there are police units already set up in Germany and in Austria, working with the Germans, involved in trying to bring them down. I don't want you and your Austrian friends putting yourselves in jeopardy, handling something that's too hot for you to handle, understand?"

"I do, sir, and I take your point. Don't worry. We'll concentrate on our case, and not try to derail the Freedom Train ... well, not too much, anyway."

Ross groaned. Whatever he might say, he knew Meyer would do whatever she thought necessary to solve the case. He just hoped she'd taken his warning on board, and didn't go too far. At least, he thought to himself, they were making significant progress. Now all he needed was for Fenella Church to squeeze some relevant information out of Sister Rebecca.

# Chapter 32

### Church Gets Tough

Sister Rebecca sat impassively opposite Fenella Church and Sam Gable in Interview Room One. If she was nervous about facing an interrogation by two police officers in the heart of police headquarters, her demeanour gave no clue of that fact.

"Sister Rebecca, you know why we've asked you to come here with us, don't you?" Church asked, watching her closely.

She nodded sedately, but said nothing.

"You're not under arrest or under caution, as yet, and are free to leave at any time, though I warn you now, if you do, we may be forced to place you under arrest. Is that clear?"

Again, she nodded.

"I strongly suggest you attempt to answer our questions, Sister. You're not helping anyone by your refusal to speak," Sam Gable added.

"I don't really know why I'm here," the nun finally said.

"You're here because we believe you know something about the death of Paul Schneider, the man who was masquerading as Brother Bernárd, and probably about the death of Daniel Parker, the man who came to cut the grass at the priory," Church explained.

"And because you refuse to reveal your true background before becoming a nun," Gable added. "We're having that checked as we speak. We do know how to find these things out, you know."

Sister Rebecca hesitated and Fenella Church had a sense of something, fear perhaps, in the nun's mask of stoicism. How could she break through that impenetrable mask? Suddenly, she had an idea. "I understand, you know. We need to rid the world of evil and, sometimes, God can lead us down quite unexpected paths in order to achieve His goals."

Sister Rebecca nodded gravely, as if she was agreeing with the sergeant's words, but still refused to say more.

"Surely, if you felt you were doing God's work, you have nothing to feel ashamed about?"

"I'm not ashamed of anything," the nun finally spoke.

"Then tell us your real name, before we have to involve the Benedictine authorities," Gable interjected. "At present, this is just a cosy chat. You're simply assisting with our enquiries."

"Very well. The Lord wouldn't want me to despoil myself or my order with lies and evasion. I was born Marie Nolan. My father was Sean Nolan, my mother Clara, neé Fowlds. As far as I'm aware, we have no German relatives in the family. It wasn't until Brother Bernárd arrived at the priory that I'd ever heard of the organisation known as the Stasi."

"Wait a moment," Church reluctantly interrupted. Those were the most words the woman had spoken since they began the interview back at St. Emma. "Are you now admitting to knowledge of the death of the man who was impersonating him?"

"Paul Schneider? Yes, though I only learned of his existence after he'd taken the place of Brother Bernárd."

"How did you learn this information?" Church wanted to get as much information as she could before the nun clammed up again.

"Oh, someone told me that Brother Bernárd was an impostor."

"And who was that person, Sister?" Church felt as if she were on the verge of a breakthrough.

"I don't like to say."

Church was astounded at the Sister's naivety. Did she really think she could choose whether or not to reveal her source? She grew frustrated. "Sister, you don't really have a choice."

"It was someone who'd suffered at the hands of the Stasi ... and that man in particular."

Church and Gable exchanged glances. Were they finally going to learn the identity of the murderer of Paul Schneider?

"Who told you the true identity of Schneider, Sister?" Church urged.

"I promised I'd never tell."

"*Who* did you promise, Sister?" Gable asked.

"I can't say."

Fenella Church had just about had enough of the intransigent nun. "In the name of God," she shouted, banging both her palms on the table that separated them, and Sister Rebecca visibly jumped in her seat. "I'm getting sick of this. You call yourself a nun. You profess to be a follower of Christ. You say you don't tell lies, and yet all you've done so far is evade our questions, lie about speaking German ... and now *more* evasion and lies. For God's sake Sister, tell us what you know."

"Are you a member of *Die Strafe*?" Gable added for good measure.

"What? *Die Strafe?* I know that means something to do with revenge or retribution, but what do you mean, am I a member? Of what, exactly? Is it supposed to mean something to me?"

"The organisation was set up to track down and seek retribution against wanted Stasi members. I suppose now you're going to tell us that you've never heard of it," Church challenged, nearing the end of her patience.

"I tell you truthfully, I've never heard of such an organisation," the nun replied, and for some reason, Church believed her.

Watching the end of the interview through the one-way mirror in the next room, Ross and Drake looked at each other questioningly. Supposing Sister Rebecca was telling the truth, could they have got things terribly wrong?

# Chapter 33

### The Camera Never Lies

Sofie Meyer received the phone call from Ross late that afternoon, shortly after Helmut Schmidt had been picked up for questioning. They had proof that Schmidt had travelled to the UK around the time of the murder of Brother Bernárd, when he'd served as a driver for Falcon Vintners. It was another link that connected Ackermann and Ritter to the movement of people across European borders.

Meyer, Richter and Wägner were now working on a couple of theories. Firstly, the transport of wines across Europe could be a clandestine means of transporting wanted men from country to country. Secondly, by using people like the Schmidt brothers as drivers, it was a means of moving hired killers across borders, under the guise of lorry drivers; they'd carry out their assignments and then innocently drive the trucks back to Germany or Austria, no-one being the wiser as to the real purpose.

Schmidt had been picked up at Ackermann's mansion, much to the chagrin of his brother, Gustav. Ackermann himself had protested vehemently at the arrest of his employee, despite Richter assuring him he wasn't under arrest, merely assisting the police with their inquiries. Ackermann had told Schmidt to say nothing to the police and that he'd have him released from custody in no time.

As soon as he was safely within the confines of the police station, however, Helmut Schmidt was arrested on suspicion of murder and unceremoniously dumped into a cell to await interrogation.

"That's really good news," Meyer said when Ross had brought her up to date with recent developments. "What's the next step?"

"Sister Rebecca hasn't requested a solicitor yet. She's not under arrest as we don't have enough evidence to charge her with anything. She's been given a break from questioning and DS Church is going back in there shortly. I think, given a little more pressure, she might tell us more."

"DS Church sounds like a very capable officer," said Meyer, who then gave Ross the news about Schmidt's arrest.

"Do they have any real evidence with which to charge him?" Ross asked.

"Not yet, sir, but they do things slightly different here. Anyway, once they put pressure on Schmidt, he might crack and tell us what we want to know," and she then told Ross about Helmut's arachnophobia, and Richter and Wägner's plan to force a confession from him.

"Very devious," Ross chuckled, thinking it was a simplistic but highly effective means of extracting information from the thug.

* * *

In common with many members of the criminal fraternity, Helmut Schmidt had an air of arrogance, believing that the police had nothing on him, and that this was, in effect, a 'fishing' expedition ... an attempt to find out, what, if anything, he knew. He was rather worried, however, because they hadn't told him who he was suspected of murdering.

He was sure they couldn't know that together, he and his brother had carried out a total of four killings in the last four years, on the orders of Jürgen Ackermann and/or Joachim Weber. He'd better be careful what he said, until Ackermann could arrange for his lawyer to spring him from jail. Schmidt knew his boss wouldn't abandon him; he knew too much for Ackermann to risk him talking to the police.

What he didn't know was that as he was being led into the police station, a squad of police officers, led by Wilhelm Gruber were descending upon the home of Jürgen Ackermann, armed with a search warrant enabling them to search his property and grounds for evidence connected with the illegal smuggling of wanted criminals across international borders. This coincided with similar raids, carefully coordinated, at properties owned by Ackermann, Weber and Ritter in Austria and Germany. The German police's action was being led by Sofie's boss, Boris Witt, and various teams of officers from the BKA, in the various cities where the properties were located.

Gruber, always thoroughly professional and able, had suggested that the raids be carried out simultaneously, to make sure that Ackermann, Weber and Ritter had other things on their minds than arranging a lawyer for Helmut Schmidt. In fact, the various task forces in both countries were happy to allow these actions to take place, as they'd deflect from their own clandestine investigations into the Freedom Train. What neither they, nor those involved in Gruber's well-organised raids could possibly know, was that they were much closer to the 'head of the snake', as Boris Witt described it, than they imagined.

"You are crazy people," Helmut Schmidt said to Richter as soon as he was seated in the tiny interview room. "I'll be out of here in no time. Herr Ackermann will see to it that I'm released very soon."

Richter smiled a knowing smile and Helmut felt the first pangs of doubt about his situation.

"We'll just wait and see about that, won't we, Emil?" Richter turned to Wägner, who smiled in return and leered maniacally at Schmidt.

"Oh yes, sir. We'll definitely wait and see. I hope you brought your toothbrush with you, Helmut. Oh, of course you didn't, but don't worry. I'm sure we can pick one up for you at the local pharmacy. We wouldn't want you to think we're neglecting your personal care while you're our guest."

"What are you talking about, copper?" Schmidt replied with a frown. "Why would I need a fucking toothbrush, you pair of morons? I won't be here long enough to need one of those."

"I don't think you'll be going home anytime tonight, Helmut," Richter told him, and another small percentage point of doubt entered Schmidt's mind.

Watching the exchanges between the men through the mirror in the next room, Meyer sipped a mug of iced coffee and smiled in approval. Feldkirch might not be as large as Hamburg or Liverpool, but there was nothing small-town about the way Richter and Wägner were conducting the interrogation of Schmidt. Ross would approve, she decided.

Schmidt remained confidently arrogant and self-assured until Richter asked, "And you continue to assert that you've never visited England?"

"I've told you already. No, never."

Richter nodded at Wägner, who turned on the monitor that was positioned on a corner of the table that separated them from Schmidt. As it flickered to life, Schmidt looked puzzled, as Richter said,

"Then maybe you can tell us who this is?"

The screen then clearly showed a lorry with the name *Falcon* visible on the cab and body of the truck, and was followed by a decent close-up of the man behind the wheel.

"Maybe you weren't aware of the fact that every vehicle that passes through the ferry terminal is recorded on video, and that includes the drivers. Or are you going to deny that's you? If we zoom in, we can even see the scar on your face."

Schmidt hesitated and then seemed to be thinking hard about how to respond.

Wägner gave him a verbal prod. "Come on, Helmut. We've got you and you know it."

"Oh yeah, I remember now," Schmidt blustered. "Herr Ritter's company was short of a driver and he asked Herr Ackermann if he could borrow me to take a shipment to England."

"So it was Herr Ritter who you worked for, was it?"

"Well no, I worked for Herr Ackermann, but the job was for Herr Ritter."

"Forget the little details for a minute, Helmut. Tell us what you did when you were in England."

"I made the delivery, stayed overnight in a small bed and breakfast hotel and then came back to Austria."

"You're a liar, Helmut," Wägner snapped.

"Says who?" Schmidt snapped back.

"Poor fool, Helmut," said Richter with a shake of the head. "Didn't they tell you about the CCTV at the Channel Ports? If you please, Emil?"

Wägner once again set the monitor to play and again, the Falcon vehicle was clearly shown, with Schmidt once again in the cab.

"That proves you're a liar," Richter gloated, pointing at the picture on screen,. "This was recorded five days later. What the fuck did you get up to in the time from your arrival until your departure, eh, Helmut?"

Schmidt was at a loss for words and looked at his watch, as though he was expecting Ackermann's lawyer to burst through the door at any moment and rescue him.

"Didn't we tell you? Herr Ackermann has other things on his mind, just in case you were expecting his lawyer to come to your rescue, Helmut. We have lots to talk about, but I think we'll leave it until the morning, unless you want to tell us everything now?"

"Fuck off copper," was Schmidt's crisp response. It was obvious he was considering what to do or say next.

"Take him to his cell, please, Emil," Richter instructed the sergeant, who dutifully led a bemused Helmut Schmidt down the corridor to the cells, where he deposited the hapless thug in the cell where they'd prepared a surprise for him.

"He's rattled," said Sofie Meyer, as she walked into the interview room after Wägner had led Schmidt away.

"He is," Richter agreed with a flat smile. "And he'll be even more rattled by the time morning comes around."

"I just hope Emil hasn't overestimated the effect our little eight-legged friends will have on him," she said, hoping that Wagner was correct with regards to Schmidt's likely response.

"Don't worry, Sofie. Helmut *never* over-estimates," was all Richter said in reply.

# Chapter 34

### Confession is Good for the Soul

After a break of just over an hour, Fenella Church and Sam Gable returned to continue their interrogation of Sister Rebecca. Before entering the interview room, Church was taken to one side for a quick update from Andy Ross.

"Just so you know, I'm impressed with your handling of Sister Rebecca so far, Fenella. We've received some news from Sofie in Austria, which might help to solve the murder of the real Brother Bernárd. If you can get the woman to shed some light on the murder of Paul Schneider and Daniel Parker, we might manage to turn this case around and give the Chief Constable something to smile about."

"I'll do my best, sir. I think she has something important and relevant to tell us, but she's very reluctant to come out with it."

"I feel the same," Ross agreed. "Do what you can, okay? Remember she's a nun, not a career criminal, so she shouldn't be too hard to crack."

"Trust me, I will," the sergeant replied, and she turned away to join Sam Gable, who was already seated in the room with Sister Rebecca.

The nun once again sat impassively, opposite the two detectives. What she didn't know was that during the break in her questioning, DC Derek McLennan had found out quite a bit about her background, after conferring with the Bishop's assistant. Expressing shock at the turn of events, the priest was able to obtain the Bishop's permission to reveal details about Sister Rebecca's background, which McLennan wasted no time in passing on to Fenella Church.

"We know quite a bit about you now, Sister. The diocesan office were happy to help us when we explained the situation. Seems you found God early in life, but didn't take Holy Orders until you'd spent some time working in the secular world, as you told us. You're now very devoted to your calling, some might say obsessively so, and if someone asks you for help, it's highly unlikely you'd turn them down. I believe someone asked you for your help in disposing of Paul Schneider and that you willingly assisted them in the act of murder. What I want to know is whether that person is one of your colleagues at the priory or an outsider, perhaps someone who visits St. Emma's frequently. So, which is it?" Church was taking a massive gamble. So far, they had no tangible evidence to implicate Sister Rebecca in Schneider's and Parker's deaths but, bearing in mind what Ross had said, she was prepared to take a risk and go for the jugular, so to speak.

Sister Rebecca gulped. It was plain to see the break between interviews had allowed her to assess her position, and she now realised that she was in a highly precarious place in the eyes of the police. Should she tell them the truth or continue her evasive tactics?

Sitting with Ross in the next room, observing the interview, Izzie Drake had been thinking. Now heavily pregnant, she was getting close to the time when she'd be starting her maternity leave, and wanted to clear this case before she temporarily departed the from squad.

"I've got an idea— well, more of a theory, really," she said quietly, not wanting to miss anything that transpired in the next room.

"Go on, Izzie, I'm listening." Ross perked up. Drake's theories were usually highly relevant, and he was already prepared to miss her input during her time on leave.

"The first time we interviewed the people at the priory, we were working in the belief that the victim was Brother Bernárd, a Benedictine Monk, right?"

"Right," he agreed, eyeing her keenly.

"We had no idea the man was an impostor and that the real monk had been killed and replaced. So, we spoke to everyone, working on the assumption the dead man was of Swiss birth. We didn't put much relevance in the place of birth of the monks and nuns at the time, since none of them were from Switzerland, and all professed not to know anything about him before he arrived at St. Emma's."

She paused for breath, and Ross suddenly had an idea where this might be leading, but he remained silent and waited for Drake to continue.

"When Fenella and Sam went with Nick and Tony to the priory to re-interview everyone, they were getting nowhere for a while … until Fenella and Sam got to Sister Rebecca. At that time, Fenella had to make a decision, which she did, and took the sensible step of bringing the sister in for questioning. But she and Sam didn't get to question the last couple of nuns, which included Sister Felicia, who just happens to be German."

"I can see where you're going with this, Izzie, but Germany's a big country. We've no guarantee that she knew anything about Schneider."

"That's true, sir, but we haven't asked her the question, have we? I looked at her statement and she was only asked if she knew Brother Bernárd before he came to St. Emma's and if she had much to do with him after his arrival. She replied in the negative on both counts, probably quite truthfully."

"But for your theory to hold water, she must somehow have found out that the monk they knew as Brother Bernárd had been replaced by a lookalike, who was in fact Paul Schneider. How do you reconcile that?"

"Damn, I hadn't thought of that. My bloody hormones are all over the place and I'm not thinking straight. Sorry about that."

"Just hold your horses for a minute. I'm not saying you're wrong. First we were on the trail of this Retribution group, but then we thought it might be a purely personal killing—but what if it was both? We know this vigilante group recruits the victims targets themselves or relatives of the Stasi's victims. What if this Sister Felicia is the relative of a victim of Paul Schneider and also happens to have been recruited by *De Strafe* after they learned about Schneider?"

"But how would they know about Schneider? With his face changed by surgery and his voice coached to sound like the real monk, the only ways they could have found out was…"

She paused and in the silence, Ross completed her sentence.

"If *Die Strafe* have someone on the inside of the Freedom Train," he said, completing her sentence when she paused. He watched her reaction closely.

"Shit, why didn't I think of that?" Drake demanded, angry with herself.

"Because none of us made a connection between her nationality and the monk. Get in touch with Derek and turn him round, back to the Diocese. I want to know everything there is to know about Sister Felicia. Drake rose and waddled out of the room, her hands on her back, which had begun to ache terribly.

\* \* \*

DC McLennan was halfway back to Liverpool when he got the call to turn around and head back to the diocesan office.

"What's going on, Izzie?" he asked Drake.

"The boss has got an idea that Sister Felicia might be the insider at the priory, and wants her checked out. Her original statement was accepted, but that was before we knew Schneider's true identity."

"How could we all have been so blind?" McLennan fumed. He didn't like to think he and the team had missed a vital link in the chain that led to the killer.

"Never mind that, Derek. Just get back there and find out where she came from and as much of her history as you can."

"Okay, I'm on my way," he replied over the hands-free, as he turned the car around.

\* \* \*

Meanwhile, Fenella Church was putting more pressure on Sister Rebecca.

"Sister, you haven't been very helpful at all and as we're investigating not one, but two murders, I have to take that to mean you're at the very least complicit in the killings, if not directly involved. I think, at this stage, it's only right that we caution you and put this interview on a more official level."

"What does that mean?" asked the nun, who must have been sweating profusely under her habit, Church having deliberately arranged for the heating to be turned up in the interview room while they'd taken a break.

"It means we'll be placing you under arrest and questioning you on a formal basis, if necessary with a solicitor present to represent you. Sam, if you please?"

It proved to be Church's master stroke of the day. Gable issued the official caution as she placed the nun under arrest on suspicion of being an accessory to murder, before and after the fact, and made sure she understood her rights. Sister Rebecca looked dumbstruck as the reality of her situation hit home to her. The woman dropped her head for a couple of moments, presumably in silent prayer.

When she looked up again, she spoke softly. "I will not be requiring a solicitor, thank you. My Lord will protect me. What I've done, I've done because there's too much evil in this world, and I saw it as my duty as a servant of the Lord … to eradicate those in the thrall of Satan, whom you know better as the Devil."

"What exactly do you mean by that statement, Sister Rebecca?" Church asked.

In the next room, Andy Ross held his breath, and Izzie Drake looked on in fascination. Both knew that Church had taken a big risk by formally cautioning the nun. If she clammed up and asked for a solicitor at this point, the interview would have to end and no more questions could be put to Sister Rebecca until she had a solicitor present.

Ross whispered a comment to Drake, even though he knew nobody in the next room could hear his words. "She's as nutty as a fruitcake."

Lightening the mood, Drake asked, "Who—the nun or Fenella ?" She too was aware of the risk Church had taken. Ross chuckled silently at her remark.

They fell silent again, hoping their new sergeant had correctly judged her suspect.

Sister Rebecca, after another moment of silence, finally replied to Church. "What I mean is that you and your vast machine of authority are the creation of man, but I answer to someone far higher than the petty laws of mankind. Only God will judge me on my actions."

"I see," Church responded quietly and calmly. "And just what were those actions, if you wouldn't mind telling me, Sister?"

Sister Rebecca seemed to stare into space, as if she could see, or perhaps feel, an ethereal presence. Church and Gable both saw that look. It was almost beatific, as if the nun had entered a blissful state. Church thought the woman looked rapturous, and she shivered involuntarily. Gable simply felt she was in the presence of madness.

The sister began to speak again. Her voice appeared to have changed, her manner of speech seemed different somehow, though if asked, neither officer could say how, or why. "I shall tell you all that happened, for I don't wish it to be said that I caused another to take the blame for my actions."

In the next room, Ross and Drake had noticed the unusual look and before the DI could say anything, Drake put their thoughts into words. "Bloody hell. If she wasn't a nun, I'd swear she was getting off on this."

"Just what I was thinking," Ross agreed. "She really believes that whatever she's done, it's because it was the work of God, and therefore absolves her of any guilt."

"Fucking hell, sir—and you know I hate using that word—she really is one bulb short of a candelabra."

Awed, they watched and listened as Sister Rebecca continued her story.

"One evening, some months ago, I was doing the washing-up after the evening meal in the refectory with help from Sister Felicia. She's a very nice person, as well as a dedicated nun, committed and devoted to her calling. Suddenly, I noticed a tear running down her face and out of a sense of compassion, I asked if anything was troubling her. She shook her head and tried to concentrate on drying the pots, but, after a minute, the tears were flowing freely and I knew something was seriously affecting her. I made her stop what she was doing and asked if she would like me to pray with her for help with whatever was troubling her. She replied and said that this was one occasion when prayer couldn't help her, and that shocked me. I pressed her to tell me what was wrong and eventually she opened up to me."

"And what did she tell you?" Church urged her to get to the point.

"She told me she was from a large extended family at home in Germany and that she regularly corresponded with many of her relatives. Apparently, two of her uncles had been trapped on the wrong side of the wall when it went up, imprisoning them in the GDR, as it was called, unable to return to the west. They'd been very young when the Berlin Wall was erected, but as they grew older, they both developed the urge to escape to the West and re-join their estranged family." She looked from Church to Gable and sighed softly. "Their escape plan, like so many at the time, was discovered by the Stasi. They'd been betrayed by a so-called friend, a Stasi informer. I was surprised to learn that almost everyone in East Germany was an informer, with neighbour spying on neighbour. The man who led the soldiers who captured them was a young lieutenant in the Border Control Guard. As her uncles made their bid for freedom, they were stopped and arrested. Even though they surrendered peacefully, with their hands up as instructed, the lieutenant callously took out his pistol and shot them down in cold blood. As they lay on the ground, still breathing, he walked up to them, screamed *Traitors* at them and took careful aim and shot both men in the head, making sure they were dead—"

"How did she get hold of such a detailed account of the incident?" Church demanded, interrupting her narrative.

"One of the border guards who witnessed the murders was apparently appalled at the lieutenant's actions against two unarmed men who were already technically in custody. When the Communist regime fell and the crimes of the Stasi became known to the public, the young border guard, by then a captain, gave evidence to the inquiry into the activities of the Stasi. He stated that the lieutenant leading the arresting squad that night, and the man who cold-bloodedly murdered the two brothers, was Paul Schneider. It was just one of the many crimes that led to Schneider being placed on the wanted list."

Fenella Church was thinking fast. She needed to know what happened to Schneider on the day of his death, and why the innocent gardener had to die. "But *who* told her all this, so long after the event and so long after Schneider evaded the authorities?"

"Sister Felicia has a cousin named Wolfgang. She gave no surname. He's employed by the German Visa and Immigration Service. He's also, secretly, a member of that group you mentioned—the vigilante organisation."

"You're talking about *Die Strafe*, I presume." Church felt another breakthrough was just around the corner.

"Yes, although I'm just presuming that to be the case, as Sister Felicia never named the group in her conversation with me."

"But how did this group know about Schneider's surgery to alter his appearance and replicate the face of Brother Bernárd?" Sam Gable asked, as that was one point that really confused her. "It's all very well telling us this, but whoever knew about the plan to kill Brother Bernárd and replace him with Schneider, had to have informed this cousin. Otherwise, how would the information have filtered down to Sister Felecia?"

"I asked this question myself," Sister Rebecca replied. "She told me that Wolfgang had sworn her to secrecy. Apparently, there was an informer, a mole she called it, inside the group who arranged the murder and replacement of poor Brother Bernárd."

"Did she tell you the name of this person?" Church asked.

"No, she told me she didn't know the name, but it was someone close to the top of the organisation set up to help the former Stasi people evade the authorities."

"And this all happened long after the substitution took place?"

"Yes, years after. I'd wondered why this person had suddenly turned against the evil organisation and concluded that whoever it was must have found God. The Lord Jesus gave him the strength and will to take action against the murderers and the killers."

"If he was so determined to help right the wrongs of this group, which by the way, Sister, is known as the Freedom Train, why not simply tell the police?"

"I don't know, and Sister Felicia had asked herself the same question, but the only person who could answer that is the informer himself."

"So, to conclude," Church said, hoping to finally get the truth out of the nun, "are you telling me that it was Sister Felicia who killed Paul Schneider, out of revenge for the murder of her uncles?"

Sister Rebecca's eyes widened. "What, oh no. What makes you think that? Sister Felicia wouldn't hurt a fly."

"Then who did kill him?"

Church almost expected the answer that now fell from the lips of the nun, as she sat placidly opposite her and Gable, still with that beatific look on her face.

"I did, of course, Sergeant Church. I killed Paul Schneider, not out of revenge, but out of a sense of divine retribution. It was the will of God … who answered my prayers as I slept … and told me *how* to do it."

"Fucking hell," Ross exclaimed in the next room. "I wasn't expecting that."

Drake was equally shocked. "Me, neither."

Meanwhile, Fenella Church wasn't finished. She was on a roll and had another murder to solve. Turning back to Sister Rebecca, she asked, "And Daniel Parker?"

The nun now did what Fenella Church considered her signature gesture: head down, hands together as if in silent prayer. "Daniel Parker was a sexual pervert, Sergeant Church, a deviant, I think you'd call him in your line of business."

Her explanation had been totally unanticipated and Church and Gable looked at each other, mystified.

"Could you explain that remark, please?" Church asked, stunned.

"There's a spare key to the garden shed that Parker had cut himself. He was clever with things like that. He kept it hidden under the water butt at the rear of the shed. I knew about it because he showed it to me soon after he'd made it. I suppose he thought it would impress me. He was always making little remarks, like how it was a shame I'd thrown my life away by becoming a nun, or how attractive I'd be without 'that horrible, ugly habit' as he called it. I ignored such comments. Once, I rebuffed him by saying he should pray for forgiveness for having such sinful thoughts. He just laughed and told me not to be silly, that he was only fooling around, but I knew he wasn't, and tended to keep my distance from him after that." She arched a shoulder and peered into the distance. Anyway, on the evening of Schneider's death, I had it all planned out. As you no doubt know, it's nigh on impossible to purchase potassium cyanide legally in this country, but it's sometimes used for medicinal purposes. I was trained as a nurse in my younger days, so I knew how difficult it would be to obtain. But I also knew that it was used in the jewellery trade and is manufactured for commercial sale quite widely in India. A few years ago, I was at a retreat in Chennai for a year and saw the tablets openly on sale in many places."

"It was a simple matter for me to obtain jewellery supplies in liquid form from a less than reputable supplier there, one who didn't ask too many questions. We have syringes in our medical supplies here and it was no problem to get hold of one. That evening, I only had to follow Schneider and wait for the right moment. I'd taken a spade from the shed in case the opportunity arose to incapacitate him with it. When he reached the furthest point from the kitchen garden, I came up behind him and just as he sensed my presence, I swung the spade with all the power I could muster. He hit the ground and I wasted no time in injecting him with the cyanide. I didn't wait to see the results, as I knew he wouldn't survive the injection. It was no trouble to dispose of the syringe in the pond at the far side of the grounds."

Church was grateful that the murder of Paul Schneider had now been explained. "But what has that got to do with Daniel Parker?"

"I'm coming to that," said the murderous nun. "What I didn't know was that Daniel Parker had seen me take the spare key to the shed the day before. He put two and two together and realised that I must have killed Schneider. A few days later. he approached me and tried to blackmail me in return for his silence."

"You're a nun," Gable said. "What could you possibly have possessed that Parker wanted?"

Sister Rebecca fell silent again, and, with her eyes turned away, as if afraid to look the detectives in the eye, replied, "My body. I told you he was a pervert. He wanted to have sex with a nun. Can you believe it?"

"You've got to be kidding us, right?" Gable gawped, incredulously at the nun.

"No, I'm not. That disgusting pervert said he'd keep quiet if I would 'partake', as he put it, in his favourite fantasy—to have sex with a nun while wearing her habit. There was no way in a million years I'd ever consider breaking my vows to buy his silence, but I needed time to think. I asked for twenty-four hours to think it over and he agreed. He told me to meet him in the barn the following day and had the temerity to tell me not to wear underwear, 'just in case' I agreed to his terms. I'm no fool, detectives. I knew that if I did agree to his perverted demands, he wouldn't be satisfied with doing it just once. I'd end up being his sex-slave for as long as he wanted me."

"But you met him at the barn the next day?" Church urged her to complete the story.

"Yes, I did. I'd decided there was only one way to silence Mr. Nosy Parker for good, so I got there first and found the pitchfork conveniently resting against the wall, as if it had been placed there specifically for me."

"A God-given gift of opportunity, Sister?" Church suggested.

"Perhaps, Sergeant Church. Who knows?"

"Even if Daniel Parker was what you say he was, I don't think God would have sanctioned his murder without a trial, do you?"

"Maybe not, but my mind was made up. I pulled on a pair of surgical gloves I'd taken from the medical chest, and waited. When he arrived, he had a leering, disgusting look of expectation on his ugly face. He sneered at me as he stood about ten to fifteen feet away and asked if I'd done what he asked. I knew he was referring to me not wearing any underwear, and at that point, I snapped. I grabbed the pitchfork which was leaning against the wall next to where I stood, and pointed it at him. I could see a laugh taking shape on his face and, without giving him a chance to dodge out of the way, I charged at him and stuck the pitchfork in his belly. He fell to his knees and looked up at me in surprise. He tried to say something, but only made a gurgling sound. I had to end his evil existence, and, despite the begging look on his face, I walked up to him, and pushed him with my foot so that he fell backwards, lying on his back, looking up at me.

"The expression on his face told me he realised he was about to meet his maker, where he'd be finally judged. I looked down at him. I remember saying something like, 'It's time to die, Mr. Parker, time to meet Satan, and burn for eternity' and I took careful aim … and drove the pitchfork into his chest. I pushed it as hard as I could until it hit something hard. I presume that was the floor of the barn. There was no need to check and see if he was dead. I left him with the pitchfork sticking up out of his chest." A smile tugged at the corners of her dry mouth. "Do you know, I felt good about what I'd done? I think you know the rest, Sergeant Church. Do you think I could please go to my cell now? I feel rather worn out and in need of some time in quiet contemplation and prayer."

In the next room, Izzie Drake could hardly believe the story she'd just heard. "What a cold, calculating bitch that woman is. She knew exactly what she was going to do when Daniel Parker walked into that room."

Ross blew air noisily from his mouth. He puffed his cheeks out in an exhalation of shock, mixed with relief that at they'd solved half the puzzle. "I agree with you. It must take a certain degree of resolve and hardheartedness to drive a pitchfork into a man's body, not once but twice."

"And the second time, with enough force to pin his body to the ground," Drake said with the shake of her head.

After a pause, Ross asked, "Well, what do you think of our new DS?"

"What? First day on the job, and she cracks a case we've been working on for so long? Either she's bloody brilliant or damn lucky ... or we're a bunch of incompetent fools."

"Don't be so hard on the team or yourself. Fenella came with a great track record, up until the fire that put her out of commission for a while. I gave her the file first thing in the morning and when she spoke to me about the case, I had a feeling that she might look at things a bit different to the rest of us. She wasn't confounded by the involvement of the Chief Constable or the Freedom Train, *Die Strafe*, and everything else that had got the rest of us tangled up in knots. She went at it like a battering ram, picked up the first hint of something not adding up in her mind, and ran with it, and hey presto! She hit pay dirt."

"Thank God she did," Drake responded. "I get the feeling you won't miss me quite as much as you were expecting to, with DS Church on the team while I'm on maternity leave."

"Don't you believe it," Ross reassured her. "There's only one Izzie Drake and I'm going to miss you like hell while you're away."

"That's nice to know. Now, what do we do next?"

They watched Sister Rebecca being led from Interview Room One by Fenella Church and Sam Gable. Ross wanted to speak to his new sergeant after she'd handed Sister Rebecca over to the Custody Sergeant. After that, he needed to speak to Sofie Meyer, still hard at work in Austria. Based on what Sister Rebecca had revealed to Church, there was still work to be done in determining how the information about Schneider was leaked to Sister Felicia, who would have to be spoken to as soon as Derek McLennan could bring her in for questioning. Brother Gerontius and the Chief Constable weren't going to be pleased at the events that had taken place at St. Emma's, and they still had more to discover.

For now, though, he smiled at Izzie Drake and said, "It was damn hard work, pleasurable too of course, but good to see how Fenella handled things in there. I think we're in need of a good strong coffee, DS Drake."

"Right you are, sir," she smiled at her boss, as he walked out of the viewing room. She closed the door and followed him down the corridor, and then back to the squad room. They had good news to report to the team!

# Chapter 35

### Itsy-Bitsy Spiders

Helmut Schmidt was as miserable as he could be, languishing in a cell in the relatively tiny Feldkirch police station. His mind was thinking of all kinds of scenarios to explain the non-appearance of Herr Gratz, Jürgen Ackermann's lawyer, who normally could be counted upon to attend if ever he or his brother were found in this type of situation.

That shite of a policeman, Richter, had merely told him that Herr Ackermann had more matters to worry about than his predicament, and that bastard sergeant of his, who'd made his and his brother's lives hell whenever he could over the years, had just grinned like a maniac. The only bright spot of the day had come when he was being taken to the cells and they'd passed a good-looking blonde in the corridor. There were things he could do with that one!

Now, it was night and the whole police station seemed to be deserted. There were no hustle and bustle sounds, typical of the place during the day. There was a solitary *Inspektor*, or constable, on night duty at the end of the corridor, and that appeared to be it.

What he wasn't aware of was that, in a nearby office, Klaus Richter, Emil Wägner, and the good-looking blonde, Sofie Meyer, were at that very moment watching his every move via a closed-circuit television feed. He hadn't noticed the tiny camera set high up into the wall of his cell, high up, and on the opposite wall to his bed, where he now sat disconsolately.

"Can't you at least turn the fucking light off, so I can get some fucking sleep?" he ranted for the tenth time, to no avail. The constable at the end of the corridor might as well have been a stuffed dummy for all the conversation he'd got from him. He tried another approach. "Hey, turd face!" It was equally non-productive.

There was one other thing that Helmut Schmidt was unaware of; under the bed, out of sight, was a ventilator grill, innocuous enough of itself, but which tonight would serve an entirely different purpose from allowing air into the cell.

The three detectives had been taking turns to watch Schmidt, one at a time, while the other two rested on camp beds, though nobody really got any sleep. As the clock ticked past three a.m, when traditionally the human spirit is at its lowest ebb, all three detectives were now alert. Another constable, *Inspektor* Franz Glassen, drafted by Richter for the job, had just released a box containing a hundred-plus spiders into the ventilation shaft that led to Schmidt's cell.

That afternoon, Wägner's sister, Greta, had been only too happy for the detectives to harvest a veritable colony of spiders from her cellar. She lived in one of the oldest houses in town and keeping it clear of the eight-legged beasties was an impossible task so anything that got rid of a few, was a blessing to her.

"Wait for it. Should be any time now," Wägner advised with a look of pure devilment on his face.

The camera feed wasn't of high enough quality to pick up one or two individual spiders, so they couldn't tell if their small arachnid army was already making inroads into the cell.

There could be no doubting their presence a minute later, however, when a shout that would have awakened the dead, demanded attention. Schmidt suddenly jumped up, and in a second, was standing on his bed, hopping from foot to foot.

"*Hilfe, hilfe!*" He screamed for help at the top of his lungs. "Somebody, please help me! They're everywhere. You've got to get me out of here!. Hey, you, *Inspektor* Numbskull, fucking get in here and help me for pity's sake!. There's at least a fucking thousand spiders crawling all over the place. Can't you hear me, you fucking moron copper? Fucking help me!"

"He's exaggerating a bit, don't you think?" Wägner laughed so much, he had to hold his belly with both hands.

"You're a closet sadist, I think, Emil," Richter laughed, too.

"Not so tough now, is he?" asked Meyer with a grin.

"Somebody get me out of here. I'll die in here! Oh shit, they're on the bed, on my legs! For God's sake, can't anyone hear me?"

"Now, sir?" Wägner asked after five minutes of Schmidt's begging, pleading and crying.

"I think so," Richter said, agreeing as previously arranged that five minutes should be long enough to break Helmut's resistance.

Meyer, however, had an idea. "Why not let me go in there? It should make him even more cooperative if a woman's the one to 'rescue' him."

"Yes, I like it." Richter chuckled.

Meyer took a moment to compose herself, clear the mirth from her face, which wasn't easy, as she'd laughed so much her cheek muscles were aching. She headed for the cells and collected *Inspektor* Glassen and the key on the way. Standing outside the cell, she could hear Schmidt crying from within.

Glassen unlocked the door and stood back to allow Meyer to enter the cell. The first thing she noticed was Schmidt's grey flannel trousers—or rather the dark patch around the groin. Helmut had wet himself in the midst of his panic and fear. He was still standing on the bed, doing his best to avoid the cavalcade of what were, in reality nothing more than small, common house or garden spiders, though judging by his reaction to their invasion of his cell, anyone would think he was under siege from an army of poisonous tarantulas.

Schmidt stared at Sofie as she casually walked in to his cell, his eyes round like saucers as he gazed agog at the invaders. He recognised her as the blonde he'd seen earlier, and felt immediate embarrassment at the obvious wet patch he knew must be visible. He tried to cover it with his hands, like a naked virgin trying to cover herself from the eyes of a voyeur.

"Whoever you are, please help me. I can't stand spiders," he pleaded.

"I can see that," Meyer said, trying, with some difficulty, to keep a straight face. "Aren't you a bit of a baby, a big man like you, afraid of a few spiders?"

"I don't care what you think. Just fucking get rid of them, you bitch."

"Now, now, that's not a very good way of getting me to help you, is it?"

"Okay, I'm sorry. Please get rid of them. Who are you?"

"I'm *Polizeikommissar* Sofie Meyer of the *Bundeskriminalamt*, Hamburg."

"Huh?" Schmidt looked puzzled, as well as afraid. The spiders were still crawling all over his bed. "What are you doing in Austria?"

"You answer the questions. I ask them," she replied casually. "Now, about the murder of the monk, Brother Bernárd, in Liverpool three years ago."

Schmidt suddenly screamed again. Another influx of spiders appeared, swarming across the floor, having been released by Wägner to coincide with that question from Meyer. "Get rid of them, please," he begged.

"When you answer the question, I'll consider it," she said, her face hard and implacable, leaving Schmidt in no doubt that until he complied, the spiders would be going nowhere. "Who killed Brother Bernárd, Helmut? I want the truth, or you can spend all night with your little guests, until Herr Richter arrives for duty in the morning."

Helmut Schmidt visibly paled at the prospect of a few more hours at the mercy of the eight-legged army; much to his great embarrassment, his body shuddered as his bladder voided itself once more. There was no way he could hide what was happening in front of the beautiful woman who stood, staring implacably, as the wetness spread once more. He tried, and failed, to cover his further embarrassment with his large, spade-like hands.

"Well?" asked Meyer and when he made no move to answer, she turned and moved as though to exit the cell. "Time's up, Helmut," she said. "See you in the morning."

That was all he could take. His fear now overcame all other emotions and senses. He knew there was only one way he was going to escape the threat of the spiders. "Okay, damn you, you bitch. It was me. I killed the fucking monk, alright?"

"Why?"

"Because Ackermann ordered me to. Now, get these fucking insects out of here, please!"

# Chapter 36

### The Leaving of Liverpool

Sister Felecia arrived at headquarters in the company of DC Derek McLennan, and as soon as she was seated in Ross's office, he was faced with the odious task of informing her of the results of her admissions to Sister Rebecca.

The German nun expressed her sorrow and grief in no uncertain terms. "Inspector Ross, although Paul Schneider was an evil man, one I fervently hoped would be brought to justice, in the courts so everyone would know the extent of his crimes, there is no way I would have wished him dead. Sister Rebecca must have a sickness of the brain to have carried out such terrible crimes. Daniel Parker too, that is almost unbelievable."

Her German accent was more pronounced than Ross had imagined.

"It would appear the murder of Daniel Parker was of a somewhat more personal nature, Sister. I can't go into details with you. I'm sure you understand."

"Yes, of course," she replied with a quick nod, her expression one of woe.

"I just have one thing to ask you," Ross said, hopeful of a positive reply.

"Please, ask anything you wish, Inspector."

"Have you any idea where the information came from—exposing Schneider to your informant?"

"No, Inspector. The only thing I can tell you is that I was told the source was highly placed in the Stasi's escape group. I didn't think much of it at the time. I didn't know it was such a large and wide-ranging organisation."

"Oh well, it was a bit too much to hope for, I suppose. I should tell you that, until DS Church managed to get the truth out of Sister Rebecca, we'd begun to suspect that you might have been the murderer."

"God forbid!" Felicia exclaimed in horror.

"Don't worry, Sister," Fenella Church said quietly. She'd been included in the interview as the arresting officer, along with Ross and Drake. "I had a feeling that Sister Rebecca was leading us down the garden path by letting us think you were involved. I admit I didn't see her as the murderer at first, but the more she told us—when she *finally* decided to talk—the more it was the only logical conclusion."

"It's so hard to believe that a nun, a member of our order, could have been responsible for such vicious and terrible crimes."

"I think we'll find, after she's been fully examined, that Sister Rebecca is suffering from some mental abnormality, though that's perhaps jumping the gun a little," Drake said, attempting to lessen the horror for the sister.

"Yes, I see," said Felicia. "Some kind of illness that tipped the balance of her mind? I could understand that."

Ross continued, "And I now have the odious task of informing the Prior of Sister Rebecca's arrest."

"That will not be easy," Felicia replied. "Brother Gerontius is a man who sees the good in *all* people. He will find it hard to accept that one of our flock has fallen so far."

After obtaining a statement from her, Sister Felicia was taken back to St. Emma's by Derek McLennan,

He said goodbye to her and was about to leave when he was hailed by Brother Gerontius.

"Please thank Detective Inspector Ross and the rest of your people for me," he said with a weary smile. "I know you all had an almost thankless task to do, but you all treated us with respect and tact, perhaps too much at times, bearing in mind you were looking for a murderer. But it's *very* much appreciated. Tell him that, will you?"

"Of course," McLennan replied. "I'm sure he'll appreciate hearing it."

"It was quite a shock when he called me shortly before you brought Sister Felicia back. But you know, just because we're monks and nuns at St. Emma's, doesn't take away the fact that under our habits we're all human, with all the human frailties and fallibilities as the rest of mankind."

"I'll remember that, Brother, and thanks for your understanding. Not everyone appreciates the job we do. It can be hard sometimes to do what we have to do, without upsetting people."

The Prior nodded and made the sign of the cross as he said goodbye to McLennan. As he drove away along the long gravel drive that snaked away from the Priory of St. Emma, the Prior gave a small wave, unseen by the detective, and said quietly, "Go with God, my son, and bless you."

\* \* \*

The eventual interrogation of Helmut Schmidt, carried out by Richter and Wägner, with Sofie Meyer in attendance, threw up some interesting facts. Striking while the iron was hot, they interviewed a very cowed Schmidt straight after breakfast, with his memories of his encounter with the spiders still raw in his mind. He was in no mood to be arrogant, clever, or argumentative.

They'd moved him to a different cell in the early hours of the morning, while the local insect controller cleared his original accommodation of the spiders. Such was his fear, that he'd babbled on about lots of things connected with Ackermann and, now, Richter wanted everything formalised.

He confirmed that Ackermann was a senior, if not the most senior member of the leadership of a group called the Freedom Train, dedicated to aiding former Stasi members, wanted for various crimes, evade justice. He confirmed that the murder of Brother Bernárd had been his first kill for Ackermann, the second being a French schoolteacher a year ago; he, too, had been replaced by a surgically altered ex-Stasi officer. He gave the name of the teacher and, equally importantly, the name of the ex-Stasi officer. Schmidt was low in the ranks of the organisation, but he'd given Richter enough to pass on to the German police and to the Austrian's own task force in Vienna.

At a nod from Klaus Richter, Sofie Meyer asked Schmidt the purpose of the recent visit of Joachim Weber to Ackermann's home.

"I don't know," he replied with a shrug. "I've seen Weber before, a few times, and I thought he must be an important person in the organisation … but not after the way Ackermann spoke to him the other day."

"What did Ackermann say to him?"

"Well, I guessed Weber must have crossed a line somewhere, because Ackermann told him that it didn't matter how much money he contributed to the cause, as he called it, but if he found, as he suspected, that Weber was leaking information about their activities to anyone on the outside, it wouldn't end well for him. Weber told him not to be stupid, but Ackermann took him to see Ritter, and Herr Weber looked very worried when they returned to the house later that day. Listen, if Herr Ackermann knows I've told you these things, my life won't be worth a euro. You have to protect me."

"And we will," Richter promised him.

It took another two hours for Helmut Schmidt to complete his statement, after which he was led away to a nice, clean cell.

Meyer got on the phone to Andy Ross in Liverpool.

"I was about to call you with the news from our end, Sofie but, please, you first."

"Okay, sir, we've wrapped up the murder of Brother Bernárd. As we expected, it was Helmut Schmidt, acting on orders from Ackermann.

And we managed to get another confession from Schmidt, which I think our friends in the Sûreté will be interested to hear."

"He's killed in France, too?"

"Yes, sir. Another insertion of a surgically altered substitute, this time it was a French schoolteacher. My own people in Germany will also be able to clear up another wanted case in regards to the ex-Stasi people. I'm going to let my boss in Hamburg know as soon as you and I finish talking."

"You've done a great job over there, Sofie, as well as our new friends from the Feldkirch Police Department.

"Thank you sir. Yes, I couldn't have achieved much without the help of Klaus Richter and Emil Wägner, and their superior *Oberstlieutnant* Gruber … and my boss in Hamburg, Boris Witt, played a part too."

"Just shows what we can do when we can call on cooperation from police forces around Europe."

"It does, sir. I agree. I can't see that there's much more I can do here. Richter and Wägner can handle whatever else is left to do and *Oberst* Gruber will be working with the other agencies in the investigation into the activities of Ackermann, Ritter and their people. Now, sir, what about your news?"

Ross spent several minutes updating Meyer on the events that had taken place in Liverpool and Oxford. It looked likely that the Thames Valley Police Force would be launching an inquiry into the underworld connections of Forbes & Ryan, the wine importers in Oxford. Though most of the company's business was entirely legitimate, there were certain people and activities connected with its activities that were decidedly outside the law. Ross's team would provide the Thames Valley investigators with whatever help they required as their investigation proceeded.

"That's great news," Meyer said as Ross completed his update. "So, I presume you'll be wanting me to return to Liverpool as soon as possible?"

"Yes, Sofie. We still have work to do in pulling all the details together to produce a case to go before the Crown Prosecution Service, and there's also the small matter of organising a leaving 'do' for Izzie, before she departs for her maternity leave."

"Of course," Meyer exclaimed. "I'd almost forgotten her leaving date was so close. I feel guilty at returning to Germany so soon after she goes on maternity leave."

"You've nothing to feel guilty about," Ross replied. "You've done some great work during your time here, Sofie, and we'll miss you too. It's a shame we couldn't get your attachment extended, but it wasn't to be, I'm afraid."

"I know, sir, and I'll miss you all too, but we shall still keep in touch, *ja*?"

"*Ja*, we will, for sure."

\* \* \*

Three weeks later, the whole team gathered in their favourite watering hole, the Pump House on Albert Dock, to bid a temporary goodbye to Izzie Drake as she prepared to depart on maternity leave.

In a surprise for Sofie Meyer, the team had turned it into a double leaving party; Ross had made sure she was included as one of the guests of honour. The team would be sad to see the two women leave, and there were laughs, reminiscences, and a few shed tears during the course of the evening.

Some old friends had turned up, as well. Former team member Detective Constable Keith Burton, shot and seriously injured during the case known as *The Mersey Mariner,* and now employed on desk duties, was there with his wife Dianne. Private investigator Arty Bryant, who'd also assisted the team on that case was in attendance, as was forensic pathologist Christine Bland; she'd travelled up to help see the two girls off, and of course, DCI Oscar Agostini was present, too.

Senior pathologist William Nugent was there, accompanied, as always, by his cadaverous-looking assistant, Francis Lees. Miles Booker, head of the Crime Scenes Investigation Team put in an appearance. The biggest surprise for Izzie and Sofie came halfway through the evening with the unexpected appearance of Detective Chief Super-intendent Sarah Hollingsworth. She not only came bearing gifts for Drake's expected baby, but a special presentation for Meyer: a wooden wall plaque bearing the crest of Merseyside Police, inscribed simply with the words, *To Sofie Meyer, with the gratitude of the Merseyside Police, Special Murder Investigation Team.*

Both women were touched and grateful for the immense feelings of warmth and affection afforded them, and it was left to DI Ross to have the final say on a memorable evening.

"Ladies and gents, I didn't want to have to make a formal speech this evening, but I've been told by DCI Agostini that it's expected of me. Thanks a lot Oscar." He winked. "Izzie, we've been together for years now, long enough to work together like a well-oiled machine. Well, a vital cog in that machine is leaving us, for a while at least, and I'm going to bloody well miss you, girl. I know everyone else will too, but you've been my strong right arm for so long, I already feel a part of me is missing. I'm delighted for you and Peter, of course, and hope the baby will be born fit and healthy, but can I just say, *hurry back?*"

Laughter exploded around the room.

"Bloody hell, Boss, give her a chance to have the nipper first," quipped Tony Curtis.

Taking a deep breath, Ross moved on to Sofie Meyer. "As you all know, we'll also very shortly be losing another team member. This time, I'm sad to say, permanently. Sofie Meyer arrived here from Germany on attachment, knowing very little about Liverpool, even less about its people. I think the highest compliment I can pay you, Sofie, is to say that as far as the people on the team are concerned, you'll be leaving us as an honorary Scouser."

That brought the biggest cheer of the evening and, for the first time that any of them could recall, Sofie Meyer actually had tears in her eyes.

Ross hadn't finished, however. "You all know of course, what a vital part Sofie played in solving our latest case, after we'd struggled and toiled trying to get a handle on it. I've heard today that the German

Federal police, the *Budeskriminalamt*, which happens to be Sofie's employer, has succeeded in shutting down the organisation we know as the Freedom Train—thanks to information received from a certain informer. He blew the lid on enough of its higher personnel to enable the police to take action in Germany and Austria, where they'd set up an effective satellite organisation. Sofie, you'll be pleased to hear that Herr Weber is now in protective custody and singing like the proverbial canary."

Sofie clapped and smiled at that piece of news.

Ross had one more surprise to spring on her, however. "Finally, as a thank you for the terrific work you did on the case in Austria, some more friends are here to join in this celebration of your time with us."

At that, Derek McLennan, who'd been standing next to the pub's double-entry doors, flung them open. In marched Klaus Richter and Emil Wägner, who'd flown over specially for the occasion. Wägner could hardly be seen as he was virtually hidden behind the massive bouquet of flowers he carried before him.

Sofie Meyer squealed with pleasure at seeing her two friends from Austria and hugged the pair of them, who both planted kisses on her cheeks, as everyone in the room applauded.

Ross still hadn't finished. "Finally, people, this is as good a time as any to mention that, in the absence of our esteemed DS … as of next week, Detective Constable Derek McLennan will henceforth be known as Acting Detective Sergeant. Congratulations, Derek."

Even more cheers resonated around the room and McLennan was subjected to much back slapping and kissing from the women, as well as receiving a special hug from Sam Gable.

"I thought you might be mad that I got the temporary appointment, Sam. I know you wanted it, too."

"Get away with you, you big girl's blouse," she quipped, "I wanted it, but you're the best person for the job by a mile. So congratulations, DS McLennan. Knock 'em dead, mate." She planted a sloppy kiss right on his lips, much to his embarrassment.

This brought another round of applause and typical ribald comments.

As the evening drew to a close, Drake pulled Ross to one side. "Don't go missing me too much, Andy. You've still got a great team there, you know, and Fenella Church looks like she'll be a terrific asset. When you get the other new team member, you'll be even stronger, and I'm sure Derek will make a great DS."

It was rare for her to call Ross by his first name, despite the years they'd worked together, and he knew every word she'd just said had come straight from the heart. "I'll miss you more than you'll ever know. We're not just colleagues, we're friends, and it's going to feel weird not seeing you around the office and the squad room every day—and having you tell me when I'm making an arse of myself, or making a bad judgement call."

"Use Fenella. I'm sure you made a fantastic judgement call when you recruited her to the squad and Derek will make a great DS. You're going to be even stronger when I'm gone. I know it."

Ross looked her right in the eyes and saw the beginnings of a tear forming. Not wanting there to be any sadness at the end of the night, he did the only thing his judgement told him to; he reached out, grabbed Izzie by the shoulders, pulled her as close to him as her baby bump would allow, and planted a firm kiss on her lips. "I'm the boss and if I say I'm going to miss you, I mean it, okay?"

The rest of the team cheered and Izzie's husband, in good humour, shouted, "Should I be jealous?" to which Izzie replied, "Terribly. I've waited years for him to do that," she winked and threw her head back in laughter.

Fenella Church turned to Ross's wife, Maria, who was sitting next to her, and said "Have I joined a team of madmen?"

With a knowing wink, Maria replied, "Most definitely, Fenella, most definitely."

Dear reader,

We hope you enjoyed reading *The Mersey Monastery Murders*. Please take a moment to leave a review in Amazon, even if it's a short one. Your opinion is important to us.

Discover more books by Brian L. Porter at https://www.nextchapter.pub/authors/brian-porter-mystery-author-liverpool-united-kingdom.

Want to know when one of our books is free or discounted for Kindle? Join the newsletter at http://eepurl.com/bqqB3H.

Best regards,
Brian L. Porter and the Next Chapter Team

# Acknowledgements

*The Mersey Monastery Murders* actually owes its existence to my publisher, Miika Hanilla at First Chapter Publishing (formerly known as Creativia), who, after publishing *A Mersey Killing,* said to me, "I like this. Do you think there's a series in it?"

Miika, with the completion of the seventh book in the series, the answer is a resounding "YES". So, thanks for the suggestion. As all the books in the series have topped the bestseller rankings at Amazon, I thank you sincerely for the original suggestion.

As always, I must say a big thank you to my chief researcher and proof-reader, Debbie Poole, who is often to be found in strange locations in and around Liverpool, even sometimes in, wait for it ... pubs ... all in the cause of researching subjects and locations for various parts of my books. Ah, hard work, but someone has to do it.

To my dear wife, Juliet, my undying thanks for the patience and extreme fortitude she has displayed during the long hours I've spent writing the book. How many times has she asked me to do something, only to be met with the reply, "Not now darling, I'm writing"?

Finally, as always, my thanks go to my growing legion of fans/readers who enjoy these books and have helped make the series the success it is today. I couldn't have done it without you.

# Bibliographical Note

*The Mersey Monastery Murders* is a work of fiction, though certain facts relating to the Stasi, the Secret Police force of the former German Democratic Republic, better known as East Germany, have been incorporated into the book. Where used, such facts have been referenced through the excellent book, *STASI, The Untold Story of the East German Secret Police* by John O. Koehler, published by Westview Press. All interactions between the characters in this book and real members of the Stasi are purely the results of the author's imagination.

# About the Author

Brian L Porter is an award-winning author, whose books have also regularly topped the Amazon Bestselling charts, eighteen of which have to date been Amazon bestsellers. Most recently, the third book in his Mersey Mystery series, *A Mersey Maiden*, was voted The Best Book We've Read All Year, 2018, by the organisers and readers of Readfree.ly.

*Last Train to Lime Street* was voted Top Crime novel in the Top 50 Best Indie Books, 2018. *A Mersey Mariner* was voted the Top Crime Novel in the Top 50 Best Indie Books, 2017 awards, while *Sheba: From Hell to Happiness* won the Best Nonfiction section and also won the Preditors & Editors Best Nonfiction Book Award, 2017. Writing as Brian, he has won a Best Author Award, a Poet of the Year Award, and his thrillers have picked up Best Thriller and Best Mystery Awards.

His short story collection *After Armageddon* is an international bestseller, and his moving collection of remembrance poetry, *Lest We Forget*, is also an Amazon bestseller.

### Three Rescue Dogs, Three Bestsellers!

In a recent departure from his usual thriller writing, Brian has written four successful books about three of the eleven rescued dogs who share his home, with more to follow.

*Sasha, A Very Special Dog Tale of a Very Special Epi-Dog* is now an international #1 bestseller and winner of the Preditors & Editors Best

Nonfiction Book, 2016, and was placed seventh in The Best Indie Books of 2016. *Sheba: From Hell to Happiness* is also now an international #1 bestseller, and award winner as detailed above. Released in 2018, *Cassie's Tale* instantly became the bestselling new release in its category on Amazon in the USA, and subsequently a #1 bestseller in the UK. Most recently, the fourth book in the series, *Penny The Railway Pup*, has topped the bestseller charts in the UK and USA. The fifth book in the series, *Remembering Dexter*, will be the next release in the series.

If you love dogs, you'll love these four offerings which will soon be followed by book five in the series *Remembering Dexter.*

Writing as Harry Porter, his children's books have achieved three bestselling rankings on Amazon in the USA and UK.

In addition, his third incarnation as romantic poet Juan Pablo Jalisco has brought international recognition with his collected works, *Of Aztecs and Conquistadors* topping the bestselling charts in the USA, UK and Canada.

Brian lives with his wife, children, and a wonderful pack of ten rescued dogs.

See Brian's website at http://www.brianlporter.co.uk/

His blog is at https://sashaandharry.blogspot.co.uk

## FROM INTERNATIONAL BESTSELLING AUTHOR BRIAN L PORTER

### The Mersey Mysteries

A Mersey Killing
All Saints, Murder on the Mersey
A Mersey Maiden
A Mersey Mariner
A Very Mersey Murder
Last Train to Lime Street
The Mersey Monastery Murders

## Thrillers by Brian L Porter

A Study in Red - The Secret Journal of Jack the Ripper
Legacy of the Ripper
Requiem for the Ripper
Pestilence
Purple Death
Behind Closed Doors
Avenue of the Dead
The Nemesis Cell
Kiss of Life

## Dog Rescue

Sasha
Sheba: From Hell to Happiness
Cassie's Tale
Penny the Railway Pup
Remembering Dexter (coming soon)

## Short Story Collection

After Armageddon

## Remembrance Poetry

Lest We Forget

## Children's Books as Harry Porter

Wolf
Alistair the Alligator (illustrated by Sharon Lewis)
Charlie the Caterpillar (illustrated by Bonnie Pelton)

*Brian L. Porter*

## As Juan Pablo Jalisco

Of Aztecs and Conquistadors

Many of Brian's books have also been released in Spanish, Italian and Portuguese editions.

You might also like:

Made A Killing by Zach Abrams

To read first chapter for free, head to:
https://www.nextchapter.pub/books/made-a-killing

CPSIA information can be obtained
at www.ICGtesting.com
Printed in the USA
LVHW032049081019
633405LV00002BA/511/P